For Harvey,

DIAMOND IN THE DESERT

A Hope Diamond Mystery

*Best wishes always
to my husband's
AF buddy —
Karen Gilleland*

By

Karen Gilleland

Library of Congress Cataloging-in-Publication Data
Gilleland, Karen 1939— Diamond in the desert / Karen
Gilleland

1. Diamond, Hope (Fictitious character)—Fiction.
2. Dennison, Matt (Fictitious character)—Fiction.
3. Our Lady of Sorrows Church, (NM)—Fiction.
4. Old School Confectioners—Fiction.
5. Icelandic Wind—Fiction.
6. Grand Med Pharmaceuticals—Fiction.
7. Global Shipbuilders—Fiction.
8. Diamond Security—Fiction.

Dedicated to

My husband, **G. Paul Gilleland**;

my daughter, **Anaïs Saint-Jude**; my granddaughter,

Madeleine McKenna Birchler;

my son, **Eric Gilleland**;

my daughter-in-law, **Miriam Sánchez Moreiras**;

my sister, **Valerie Van Meter and Family.**

In loving memory of my Mother, Father, and Brother.

ACKNOWLEDGMENTS

My deep gratitude to all those who were willing to help me with various aspects of this book and who took the time to read all or parts of the manuscript and make suggestions that greatly improved the story:

Janet Lawrence, author; Saytchyn Maddux-Creech, author; Paul Gilleland, Eric Gilleland, Miriam Sánchez Moreiras;

Betty Hester, Ann Capuano, and Debbie McClain.

Thanks to Anaïs Saint-Jude for listening patiently to my ramblings about the book every night.

Thanks to the team at Book Marketeers for seeing the book through production.

Special thanks to **Mary D. (Dickie) Socash** for creating the Hope Diamond artwork.

Most especially, thanks to **Margaret Coel,** *New York Times* bestselling author, who read the manuscript multiple times and provided invaluable editorial direction that moved the draft from an idea with promise to a polished manuscript.

"Be still and the earth will speak to you."

Navajo Proverb

CHAPTER 1

"What are you saying? A contract on the women I'm protecting?" Hope Diamond held the phone to her ear and paced back and forth, the stacked heels of her boots slapping the wooden floor.

"No, Babe. I'm just saying that the identities of the women and the name of the hotel popped up on the dark web. We don't know what it means, but it could mean trouble." Jake Sanders was FBI, and the two were in a long-distance relationship. He would not have called if he didn't consider the web hit a threat.

Diamond Security specialized in safeguarding high-profile clients like Janai Ross, who had arranged this meeting. Ross was a well-known, powerful woman who headed Icelandic Wind, a global cosmetics firm.

Hope ended the call and ran her fingers through her tousled blond hair. Diamond's reputation depended on keeping clients safe, no matter how dangerous the assignment. Four of the wealthiest women in the world were already streaking toward the resort aboard private jets. The call from Jake could mean their lives were in imminent danger.

Glancing around at the colorful Navajo tapestries, she took a deep breath and focused on the tranquility of the geometric designs to take the edge off the news.

Six months ago, when Janai had asked her to find a secure location for the week-long meetings, she had visited Secret Sands and was impressed by the intimate resort, which squatted low to the ground in the middle of a primordial landscape. The jagged hills—carved by waters that had vanished millions of years ago—appeared to be flung with abandon under the blue, blue sky. The hills perched on a vast carpet of silver, green, and gold sagebrush.

She rubbed her gold disc pendant between her fingers. The advantages of the isolated location in the middle of the Navajo Nation might now prove a danger. The rocks could conceal movement, and the sage could provide camouflage for a ground assault.

Frank Madison, her business partner, walked in. "Look at that gorgeous view!" he said, waving toward the window. "It's a beautiful day to welcome our guests." Muscled, mahogany-skinned and bald, Frank had just celebrated his fiftieth birthday. He shrugged out of his Wrangler jacket, hung it on the back of the chair, and sat down. "Heard from Janai?"

"I'm waiting for a text." Hope set her cell on the table. The meeting was shrouded in mystery. Janai would not reveal the purpose. Whatever it was, the woman was taking a risk by not informing her security team. What's more, Janai had persuaded her guests to use Diamond Security instead of bringing their own people, which quadrupled Hope's liability and put the future of her agency at risk if anything went wrong.

"Ask the team to come in."

"I'll round them up." Frank said, getting to his feet.

Lucy Martinez arrived and took the chair next to Frank's jacket. The sleeveless blue blouse and black slacks suited the slim figure and well-toned arms of the martial arts specialist. "The guys will be here in a minute. They're excited about being in the desert." In her twenties, Lucy always showed enthusiasm, whatever the task at hand.

Zach Cohen and Tony Manara jostled each other coming through the doorway, laughing at some joke. Zach caught Hope's eye and wriggled his fingers in greeting. The team's computer expert, he'd abandoned his corporate gear for the desert, and he looked much younger than his forty years in the Polo shirt and tan slacks. He plonked his computer bag on the floor and sat across from Lucy.

"Did you hear that screeching last night?" he asked. "Coyotes!" he added in mild amazement. He was strictly an urban animal.

"I heard them," Lucy said. "The manager says they sleep during the day. I sure hope he's right. Still, I reckon I could take on your average wild dog." She gave the others a mischievous smile.

Tony Manara, a former Interpol operative, had joined the team from Italy. He wore the Zegna deck-brown Sahara jacket the same way he wore a smile, full of confidence and style. "*Ciao*," he said and sat down next to Zach.

"Coffee's coming," Frank said, closing the door.

Hope put both hands on the back of her chair. "Jake Sanders called. Word about this meeting is on the dark web."

"No way!" Frank smacked the table with a fist. "We've been running closer to the ground than crabgrass. I didn't even give names to the hotel until we arrived."

"Which means one of the women slipped up," Hope said, dropping into the chair.

"Did Sanders give you any idea of the target?"

"No, it could be any or all of our clients. They're all billionaires. Besides Janai, we have the heads of a global candy company, shipbuilding empire, and a pharmaceutical firm." She folded her hands and looked around at her team. "You can imagine the damage to our reputation if anything goes wrong."

"Count on me to make sure everything goes right," Tony said. The others echoed his promise and bumped hands.

A young woman came through the doorway and rolled a cart over to the refreshment counter. She set out coffee and cinnamon rolls. The aroma of caramelized pecans drifted through the room. "Help yourself to anything in the fridge and let me know if you'd like something that isn't there," she said as she pulled the door closed behind her.

One by one, the team walked over and took coffee and rolls. When they were back at the table, Hope said, "Zach, try to find that web reference. The site may give us a clue to the target."

"It would help if we knew what the meeting was about," Frank said and took a bite of the roll.

"I agree, but Janai was absolutely tight-lipped about the purpose. I couldn't get her to budge."

"Since Janai called the meeting, could she be the target?" Zach asked.

"That's a possibility. Janai will be the most powerful woman here, but we can't overlook anyone else." A chilling thought was running through her head. Hope crossed and uncrossed her legs. She couldn't shake the idea that when the guests arrived, the enemy might be inside the hotel. A remote possibility, but in her business, even remote possibilities could not be swept away.

"We're in the middle of the Navajo Nation," Frank said. "The hotel won't be easy to breach. There's a reason this place is called 'Secret Sands.'"

Hope glanced out the window, then turned back to the table. "I'll ask the manager to have his people watch for outsiders. We'll concentrate on what we can control inside the hotel."

The cell phone buzzed. Hope touched the screen and read out the text. "Janai and her two aides will arrive at six."

"When are the others expected?" Zach asked. He lifted a napkin, carefully mopped his fingers, and pushed away the empty plate.

"Lydia Fallbrook should be here at noon," Hope said. "Gloria Gonzales, at two; Ellen McKenna at three. We'll have a lot of people to keep track of because they're each bringing one aide, including Ellen's last-minute guest." Hope drummed her fingers on the table. Fortunately, she had booked the entire property, but an unexpected desk was a danger trigger in a security operation.

Frank must have recognized her anxiety. "Having someone drop in on us is not ideal, but we'll handle it. I'll check over our plans and let everyone know what adjustments we need to make."

"Good of you to remind me that we're tops in our industry, Frank." She smiled and added, "As always, take a careful look around, inside and out. Make note of any places that could present a danger to our clients."

"Send me your notes," Zach said to the team. "I'll put everything into my probability model and assess the danger level of each area."

"How do you want to handle greeting the visitors?" Frank asked.

"I'll meet everyone in the lobby. You, Tony, and Lucy each visited one of the women. Join me in welcoming the lady you visited."

"Good plan," Frank said.

"You all understand how important this week is," Hope said. "Attend the champagne social and dinner and chat up someone you haven't visited. Fresh eyes on these people will be useful."

The team gathered up belongings and shuffled out of chairs. Hope put her hand on Frank's arm and waited while Tony poured a cup of coffee and carried it with him. He glanced back, she nodded, and he closed the door behind him. Hope rolled her chair closer to Frank's. "I'd like you to take a look in the guest rooms during the cocktail party."

Frank threw her a sidelong glance. "Illegal searches aren't normally our bag, Hope."

"In view of the web hit and the wealth of our clients, extraordinary actions will be our new norm this week. Fortunately, each room has two exits, a hallway door and a sliding glass door to the outside. As you said, this hotel is difficult to breach. The enemy could be one of the guests."

"I hate the idea, but you're right."

Pushing over a sheet of paper, she said, "Here's a floor plan with the guest names."

He looked over the sheet and slipped it into his jacket. "Consider it done."

When she was alone, Hope poured herself a glass of ice water and sat down at the table. This assignment should have been a routine protection job, with everyone secure in a hidden location for a week. She had doubled down on security by bringing extra agents, but the report about the dark web and the unexpected visitor upped the stakes.

She had put all her energy and a great deal of money into building up Diamond Security. Its success depended on flawless execution in keeping clients safe. A slip-up protecting four billionaires would be a fatal blow to her reputation and could sink the agency.

CHAPTER 2

At a little after noon, Hope and Frank stood in the lobby near a fountain surrounding a statue of an ebony horse rearing up on its hind legs. The floor-to-ceiling windows pulled in the red rocks and colorful wildflowers. Soft music played, and Mr. Desheenie, the hotel manager, smiled from behind the reception desk. The quiet interlude ended abruptly when the hotel van pulled up.

"We're on," Hope said.

Lydia Fallbrook stepped out of the van and came through the automatic glass doors. Her companion stayed outside talking to the porter and pointing to various cases. Hope smiled at their array of trunks. It appeared they'd packed an entire month's wardrobe, far more than she had found necessary, which was saying something.

Hope stepped forward. "Welcome to Secret Sands, Lydia. Frank and I will do everything we can to make your stay here enjoyable."

"Of course." Lydia said in her foghorn voice and adjusted a large silk scarf flaunting a modern design that she wore with style over a black tailored jacket. She sent a chilly gaze around the lobby. Hope had met Lydia once in Chicago. It was appropriate that the woman ran a pharmaceutical company. She was a hard pill to swallow.

"It's good to see you again, Lydia," Frank said. "I think you'll like this beautiful country." He extended his hand, and Lydia pulled Frank close and gave him a hug. Hope's teeth would have dropped on the floor had they been false. Lydia was not the hugging type.

"I doubt I'll see much of the scenery, not with Janai running the show," Lydia said. She looked around, leaned in. "She has an ambitious agenda. Did she tell you her plans?" They shook their heads. "It will be interesting if they pan out," she said with a touch of sarcasm.

Hope bit her lip to keep from asking about the agenda. She would respect Janai's privacy and talk to her about the purpose of the meeting at an opportune time.

The woman outside had apparently finished instructing the porter and came through the automatic door holding onto a computer case. She had a faded appearance, with short brown hair, protruding eyes, and thin lips, her only shot of color, a blouse in a shade of mustard over a long, printed skirt.

"Meet our senior chemist, Margo Knight," Lydia said. "Margo and I will be putting our heads together while we're here."

"The aerial view was spectacular," Margo said with an unexpected note of warmth. "I've never spent time on a reservation before. I believe they call it the Navajo Nation here."

Hope smiled, pleased with her reaction. "I encourage you to spend time out of doors among the wildflowers and amazing rock formations."

"Tons of science stuff to read," she said, shaking her head. "I'll probably hunker down in a dark corner with my computer."

"I insist you take time to relax, Margo. You've earned a break," Lydia said, an impatient note in her voice.

The woman shrugged, and Hope shot a glance at Frank. He stepped over to Lydia. "Let me take you to your room." Lydia took his arm, and the two walked down the hall. Margo's left eyebrow went up, but she smiled at Hope and followed them. The coolness between the two women contrasted sharply with the warmth of the desert.

# #

Later that afternoon, Hope sat at the lobby fountain with Lucy to greet Gloria Gonzales, the shipping magnate. The sun was playing on the rocks, and rays of light touched the horse, firing up the ebony. The van pulled in, and Gloria, a big-boned lady with plenty of sex appeal displayed in a clingy red dress, rushed in and threw out her arms.

"Lucy!" she cried, wrapping her arms around the young woman.

"Great seeing you again, Gloria," Lucy said, returning the hug. "This is Hope Diamond, the head of our company."

Gloria shook hands and introduced Dimitri Drako, vice president of Global Shipbuilders, who had followed her in. He bowed to Hope and Lucy. Both the name and the dark, handsome looks suggested his Greek descent, but Hope couldn't peg his age. His face and figure looked late forties, but his dark eyes held a calculating gleam that belonged to an older man.

Another van pulled into the drive. "Our Pittsburgh guests must be early," Hope said, hoping the afternoon wasn't going to slip from her control. She pulled out her phone and texted Tony.

A woman Hope took for Ellen McKenna, head of Old School Confectioners, stepped out of the van. She stood still, stopping her skirt from flapping in the breeze, her face as scrunched up as the skirt's material. She turned toward the huge boulders and the wide expanse of desert dotted with clumps of sagebrush. Hope drew a deep breath. Ellen acted as if she were going to turn around and step back into the van. After a moment, Ellen moved toward the automatic doors, another woman with her.

Gloria hurried over to the door. "I recognize you!" she said, throwing her arms out to Ellen. "We met on a Zoom call," she said over her shoulder to the others. She embraced Ellen enthusiastically. "It will be so nice getting to know all you girls. Isn't this place spectacular?"

Before Ellen answered, Gloria took hold of her arm and introduced Dimitri. He bowed in greeting. Ellen smiled and introduced Meghan Connors, the young woman with red hair and freckles trailing behind her. "Meghan is one of our admins."

Hope was about to step up and introduce herself, but Tony came hurrying in. He approached Ellen, who shifted her purse on her shoulder. Tony took her hands and greeted her, then nodded to the attractive young lady behind her.

"Allow me to introduce you both to Hope Diamond, the head of Diamond Security." Ellen held out a hand and shook hands with Hope.

"How was your flight?" Hope asked.

"Scary!" Meghan blurted out. "We flew through a thunderstorm! Lightning was flashing everywhere! The plane was rocking back and forth. I was scared we'd all be killed!" Her head swiveled toward Ellen, and she lowered her voice. "You were scared, too. Don't say you weren't. I saw you clutching your Rosary beads."

Ellen sighed. "We left early to beat the storm, but it caught up to us. We had a bumpy ride for about fifteen minutes. It was scary. Both of us are nervous flyers." Hope's shoulders tightened at the edge in the woman's voice.

"We had choppy weather out of New York," Gloria said in her bubbly way. "Fortunately, it doesn't bother me." She hesitated before tossing out what was apparently meant to be a compliment. "Dimitri is an old sea dog."

"I haven't flown very often, and this was Meghan's first flight." Ellen's voice was shaky, as if she were going to tear up.

At that moment, Meghan distracted everyone by saying in an insistent voice, "I have to use the bathroom. Where is it?" Hope handed Meghan the room key and sent her down the hall.

Mr. Desheenie came out from behind the desk and took over in a practiced manner, assuring the guests their luggage would follow.

As the lobby cleared out, Hope sat down by the fountain to reflect on the three clients. An oldies-but-goodies group came to mind, and she chuckled. These women could create their own band—Ice, Fire and Water. Lydia was ice, Gloria fire, and Ellen water. If they added Janai, they'd have earth.

Not so humorous, though, was the tension underlying the arrivals. The ladies seemed to have an odd relationship with the associates they had selected to accompany them. None appeared to be close friends or even comfortable business associates. Rather, their guests seemed to be antagonists. The possibility that any threat could come from an inside source was becoming more likely, and evil vibes shot through Hope like the hot desert wind.

# #

It was six o'clock when Frank texted that Janai and her entourage had arrived. Hope rushed out to the lobby. Janai was talking to Frank by the door. Her snow-white hair was swept up and away from her face, giving her a youthful look. She smiled and gestured toward the giant rocks. The tangy scent of her perfume wafted in the air. A man in a blue pullover sweater and a tall, thin woman stood beside her.

"This setting is right out of a Tony Hillerman novel!" Janai said. Hope and Frank exchanged a smile. Their client liked the surroundings.

Janai spread her hands out toward her associates. "You know Audrey Tremont and Robert Halloway."

"Welcome," Hope said. Audrey was Janai's assistant, and Robert was a finance officer who handled her foundation. She had had dealings with both Audrey and Robert at Icelandic Wind's headquarters in Los Angeles.

"I'm glad you're here," Hope said to Janai. "Everything is ready, and the other guests have arrived."

"I knew I could count on you. I'll dash to the room to dress for cocktails."

The porter was wheeling their luggage down the hall. Frank held out his hand. "I'll walk with you."

Janai smiled and nodded to Robert to follow.

"So nice to see you again, Audrey," Hope said.

"We're always rushing." Audrey shook her head, her graying hair tied back with a scrunchie. Oddly enough for a person in her position, Audrey never even wore lipstick. She had a beautiful complexion, so maybe she used Icelandic Wind's facial products. Audrey slipped off her pink, plastic-rimmed glasses, gave them a swipe with her cotton skirt and put them back on her nose.

"I won't be joining you for dinner. This trip has me way behind."

"I understand. Let me show you to your room."

"No need. Just give me a key." Hope handed her a small folder and stepped back. Audrey was already schlepping her bulky overnight bag toward the corridor.

Back in her room, Hope sat down at the desk. The suite had a fresh look with a whipped cream leather recliner and a king-sized bed topped with white bedding.

A vibrant, action-filled painting against the teal wall compelled her attention. Four Navajos on horseback were lassoing what she judged to be a demonic presence. Red distorted hills intensified the sense of malevolence. She shook her head to dispel the uneasiness stirred up by Jake's phone call that the FBI had noted a reference to the women on the dark web.

She opened her phone and looked at his picture. Visiting Jake in Washington was like stepping onto a magic carpet. He would whisk her to celebrity events and presidential balls. As much as she liked Jake, she kept their relationship private from her clients and staff.

Glancing at the clock, Hope gasped. Half-past six! *Stop dawdling.* A fashionista with a passion for designer clothes, she donned a Versace blue-and-green silk-chiffon dress that enhanced her dark blue eyes. She used just a touch of make-up, not the full regalia of products that Janai sold in salons around the world. She ran a brush through her hair and spritzed on perfume. Her lips curved up slightly, suggesting a permanent smile. That would be an advantage tonight when she wanted to conceal her jitters.

She put her gun into a black evening bag, especially chosen to hold the weapon without giving away its presence. The precautions they were taking were important, but no one could predict what an assailant would do at an opportune moment.

CHAPTER 3

The cozy atmosphere inside the Blue Sky room, the resort's gathering space, came from the blend of *latilla* ceiling, elegant chandeliers, and stucco walls offsetting the red tile floor, hand-crafted rugs, and saddle-leather sofas. Amid the reds and sands, Hope's blue-and-green dress stood out like an oasis in the desert.

She asked the elderly waiter behind the bar to set out the champagne. He positioned an ice-filled bucket with a magnum of Dom Pérignon on a tall table where red flower petals and crystal nuggets had been interspersed with hand-painted flutes.

Janai Ross swept into the room. "Hope, darling," she called, "I peeked into the Blue Sage room. Perfect for our meetings." The two women had just greeted when Ellen McKenna arrived, looking like a pink lollipop in a full-skirted dress cut just above the knees. Her brown hair haloed her face, and her smoke-gray eyes flashed around nervously, as if looking for someone she hoped wasn't there.

At thirty-six, Ellen was Hope's age and the youngest of the women clients. Hope thanked her for the box of candy and Janai for the Icelandic Wind gift set that had been delivered to the rooms.

"*Ciao!*" Tony greeted, joining them at the champagne table. "You ladies light up the room." Hope smiled. With his sunny Italian nature, Tony could always be counted on to warm up the atmosphere.

A whirlwind in a fiery silk dress swirled in. Gloria's dark, wavy hair bounced off her shoulders. "Janai!" She gave her a squeeze, then backed off. "Your pearls are dazzling! Thank you for inviting me to this amazing place!" She looked at Hope. "The view from my suite is spectacular!"

"I'm glad—" Hope began, but the woman threw out her arms toward Lydia Fallbrook, who was walking in with Dimitri.

"Lydia! Love the emeralds!"

Lydia's ice countered Gloria's fire. "Hello, Gloria. It's nice to see you ladies again."

"I'm sorry I couldn't meet you earlier," Janai said. "Now that we're all here, I'd like to propose a toast." Hope glanced at the waiter, and he hurried over. When he pulled the cork out of the champagne bottle, it popped, and Ellen jumped.

"Sorry," she said, her face flushed. She picked up the dipper by the punchbowl.

Tony took it from her hand. "Allow me," he said and filled the hand-painted cup with sparkling strawberry-pineapple punch. He poured himself a cup and saluted her.

Janai raised her champagne flute. "To all of you for accepting my invitation to join me at Secret Sands. And to the wonderful lady who arranged everything, Hope Diamond."

"Here, here!" the group chanted. Hope smiled and stepped back. The week was officially under way. Guests picked up drinks and drifted about the room. Fragments of conversation jabbed at her anxiety.

Lydia sounded irritated. "I see you have us meeting tomorrow, Janai. Saturday. You're not one to ever waste a minute."

"I can't afford to," Janai said with a smile. "There aren't enough minutes in the day."

Audrey put her hand on Janai's shoulder and whispered in her ear.

"All right, after dinner," Janai said. She faced Hope. "We have a space of time between dinner and the program, am I right?"

"About half-an-hour for people to change clothing for the campfire."

"See me then, Audrey," Janai said, her tone sharp. Hope's eyebrows went up. Janai was on edge, too.

Audrey nodded and ladled herself a glass of punch. Hope had nicknamed Audrey the "Shadow Lady." She worked behind the scenes keeping Janai on schedule, answering email, and running interference. She'd pop out unexpectedly, seemingly from the woodwork.

"Your dress is lovely, Audrey," Hope said. Audrey nodded and walked over to a sofa and sat down.

Gloria swung out her hand holding the champagne flute. "I'm loving the spiritual feel of the desert," she said. "It's timeless, like seeing the past and the future together. I can imagine the ancestors watching over the people who live here today."

"You're so whimsical, Gloria." Lydia said. "Somehow your romantic outlook doesn't fit with the shipping business."

"You're wrong there, Lydia. Sailors have a very romantic aura. Am I right, Dimitri?" She looked around.

Dimitri was standing by the bar holding what looked like a glass of whiskey. "Yes, it is true. Sailors very romantic." His accent was strong, his English halting.

"Secret Sands is beautiful and, I suppose, romantic, but I find the desert formidable," Ellen said. "It's so different from Pittsburgh." Hope flexed her shoulders. Perhaps homesickness was at the root of Ellen's nervousness. She'd probably relax once the meetings began.

"To me, this place is right out of the old western movies I watched in Italy," Tony said. "I keep waiting for the Man with No Name to ride in." He smiled at Meghan. "What do you think?"

"I like a place with a lot of trees, and I don't watch movies with no name." Meghan turned her back on him and walked to the drinks table.

Zach coughed into a handkerchief. A waiter offered Hope a smoked salmon and caviar canape, but she shook her head. Meghan's comment about those old "spaghetti westerns" wasn't absurd. The irony was that Tony probably didn't realize "The Good, the Bad, and the Ugly" was based on Civil War battles fought right here in New Mexico.

"Did you get everything settled in your room," Hope asked Meghan, who had picked up a glass of champagne.

"Yeah," Meghan said, then pointed her glass at Lucy. "That room is big enough for four people. Me 'n her could've shared easy."

Ah, the charm of youth. Hope turned her head away from Lucy's impish grin. It was evident that Meghan counted on her paycheck and knew the value of a dollar.

A blaze of color lit up the sky and reflected on the red tile floor. "Look outside, everyone," Hope said, gesturing to the windows. "The colors take your breath away." Every head turned. Reds, blues, and purples stretched out toward the horizon. A collective gasp sounded throughout the room, then stilled.

Lydia's foghorn voice dropped into the silence. "Does anybody mind if I smoke?"

Ellen cleared her throat. "I'm sorry, Lydia, but smoke really sets off my allergies."

Opening her Jimmy Choo glitter bag, Lydia said, "Margo, I forgot my cigarettes. Would you dash back to my room and bring me a few packs?" Lydia handed Margo her key. "Thank God the Navajos don't fuss about smoking."

Hope took a deep breath. "You bring up a good point, Lydia. Smoking is permitted anywhere here at the resort. However, since the pandemic, Navajo leaders have been outspoken about discouraging their people from smoking. It's probably a good idea that we smoke outside on the patio."

"Thank you for clarifying the rules," Lydia said, her voice dripping sarcasm.

Dimitri had pulled out a pack of *Karelias* that he must have brought from Greece. He appeared about to offer a cigarette to Lydia. After glancing at Hope, he put the pack back in his jacket pocket.

"I'm a smoker," Gloria said in her bubbly voice. "I'll join you on the patio, Lydia. Anyone else?" She looked around and spread out her arms.

Meghan glanced at Ellen, then said, "I'm in." She lifted her chin and walked outside.

Hope approached Ellen. "You might like to visit the gift shop one day," she suggested. "It has a nice collection of photo books and tee-shirts. Tony said you have a young son."

"Yes, Patrick will like pictures of the West." Ellen's eyes were watery. The woman was a bundle of nerves, which could signal that something other than homesickness was triggering her anxiety.

Margo Knight reappeared and handed Lydia several packs of Marlboros. "This pack was open on your nightstand," she said. "The others are from the carton on your desk."

"Thank you." Lydia put the cigarettes in her purse and snapped it shut. She looked around, then joined the others at a table on the patio.

Janai invited Ellen to sit with her on the sofa. Hope scanned the room for Frank. Not seeing him, she set down her glass and made her way over to the hall.

Robert, his black hair styled to touch his earlobes, came up to Hope. Swiveling his head around the room, he said, "I like the infinity windows and the way they allow the room to interact with the outdoors."

"You sound like an architect."

"I'm planning to remodel my place, so I've become an *Architectural Digest* junkie and pay much more attention to my surroundings. I have an old stucco cottage in the Hollywood Hills.

I'm talking 1920s. I like to think Clark Gable once sat on my veranda."

"I wouldn't be surprised if you were right."

Dimitri came in from the patio. He made a slight bow. "Sunset very beautiful. In Greece, sun drops into sea."

Hope flinched at the strong tobacco smell and edged back. "Have you been out West before, Mr. Drakos?"

"No, first time in this place. Nice."

Tony walked up with a broad smile. "*Ciao*," he said, straightening the shirt cuff under his tuxedo jacket.

They all chatted a few minutes, then Robert said, "I have to run back to the room."

Hope nudged Tony's arm. "Just where I was headed, *mio amico*," he said and put his arm around Robert's shoulder. The two disappeared around the corner.

Dimitri's lip twisted into a sideways smile, revealing the brown stain on his teeth. Tony had been quick to pick up her signal even though he didn't know what Frank was up to. Dimitri had obviously noticed. She spoke quickly to sidetrack his curiosity. "Is there anything in particular that you would like to see out here?"

"Indian casino?"

"Desert Luck is the closest casino. Ask the manager to make arrangements for you."

A soft gong announced dinner. Hope waited until Robert and Tony returned before going into the dining room.

Night had fallen, and stars twinkled across the black sky. Candles aglow on the long table created a sense of enchantment.

Hope counted place settings. Thirteen! She took a deep breath, fighting off the superstition. Audrey would have made fourteen.

Frank hurried into the room and nodded slightly. He hadn't been caught in the rooms. When everyone was seated, Hope took the empty place at the far end next to Meghan.

A woman in black top and turquoise skirt served them fry bread, corn-based soup, and Navajo tacos in colorful pottery. The smell was peppery and sweet.

"What's this stuff?" Meghan asked. Hope explained they were traditional Navajo dishes. The girl took a sip of soup and a bite of fry bread. She set down her silverware and folded her hands.

The serving woman came back to remove their plates. She looked at Meghan's dishes and sent a questioning look to Hope, who shrugged. A short time later, she brought salad and flame-grilled steak. Meghan ate a couple bites of the salad and pushed her plate away.

Hope leaned in and said, "I can ask the chef to make you something else."

"I had chicken salad for lunch. That's all I need. Don't want to put on weight." Her eyes slid toward Ellen, who was sitting across the table a few places down.

"Do you enjoy your job at the candy factory?" Hope asked.

"For now, it's okay," Meghan said, "I'm getting a promotion to the design center."

"Do you have a degree in design?" The woman's speech pattern didn't have the polish of a college graduate.

"I took a design class in college. When I landed this job, I dropped school. The thing is, Mr. McKenna says he can see I have talent."

From Hope's experience, corporations expected candidates to be more qualified than Meghan when handing out promotions. "I hope the new job works out for you."

"No worries. If it doesn't, I'll take a 'golden parachute,' as they say." Meghan kept her eyes on her food, although she didn't eat another bite. Across the table, Lucy sent Hope a commiserate look.

Dessert was warm Navajo style peach crisp and vanilla ice cream. Meghan took a spoonful and pulled a lipstick and compact mirror out of her beaded evening bag. She swiped a pale color across her full lips. When she finished, she smiled at Hope and smacked her lips.

"See you later," she said. She stood and walked away, a thin young woman in a blue dress. Hope looked at Ellen, whose eyes narrowed watching Meghan swagger out of the room.

After dinner, Hope returned to her suite and pulled on black slacks and a dark green fisherman's sweater. Even in June, the high desert nights were cold. She shivered, but not because of the chilly air. It was the cool atmosphere at the reception and dinner that bothered her.

All the guests, even Audrey, met in Blue Sky and walked the short distance up a curvy hill to the spot where the evening's entertainment would take place. Hope sat on the padded bench curved around a large open campfire.

Melodic singing, punctuated by the drumbeat of a tom-tom, filled the night air. Navajo dancers, in black velvet costumes and turquoise-and-silver jewelry, flashed in and out of the firelight. The rhythmic sway of their bodies radiated a sense of timelessness in the blackness. As the drumbeat faded, the performers melted away into a night lit only by the glow of embers and trillions of stars.

"Powerful," Frank said and took Hope's arm to move closer to the fire.

Guests passed them on their way back to the hotel. Meghan's face looked pale in the weak moonlight, like white icing dripping from a spoon. She squeezed by Lucy and walked with Lydia.

Nudging Ellen, Gloria said in her bubbly voice, "What did I tell you about timelessness?"

Ellen nodded, but brushed her arms, as if to push away any timeless spirits.

The guests carried flashlights and walked two abreast down the path. The line slowed as people skirted around Lydia and Meghan, who had stopped to light cigarettes. Meghan still wore her blue dress, but she had slipped into a long coat.

When Hope and Frank reached the patio, she glanced back and saw the glowing tips of the two cigarettes moving like phantom ships in a black ocean.

Inside Blue Sky, the handsome young Navajo flipping a cocktail shaker back and forth at the bar was the tom-tom drummer. Feeling edgy, Hope asked for a hot toddy.

"Mr. Desheenie said we must keep watch with the eyes of the eagle while you are here." The man spoke softly with a lilting cadence. "My name is George, but my Navajo name is *Apenimon*, which means 'worthy of trust.'"

"Thank you, *Apenimon*," Hope said. "I appreciate that." After finishing her drink, she stood near the hallway to bid the guests goodnight.

Lydia stopped and said unexpectedly, "No hard feelings over our little misunderstanding about smoking, I trust. Smoking is automatic with me. I'm sure you'll have to remind me again during the week."

Hope reached out and shook her hand.

Janai stopped also. "I'm glad you chose this location, Hope. I like having the opportunity to get to know the Navajo culture." She stood quiet a moment before saying, "The entertainment was very enjoyable, but you seem troubled."

Hope blinked at Janai's skill at reading people. She told her about the call from the FBI. "Nothing definite, but the fact that someone knew about the meeting makes me want to have eyes everywhere."

"I don't like the idea of people knowing I'm meeting with these women," Janai said, her forehead wrinkled. "I trust you will handle things efficiently." She walked away. As she vanished down the hallway, her gray dress fluttered out behind her like a veil of smoke.

Hope's anxiety increased. Whatever these heads of billion-dollar companies, whose stock traded on international exchanges, met secretly to discuss would likely have an impact on the world.

Hope sank down on the sofa, like a general after an intense campaign. A soft glow from a ceiling light and the stars outside kept complete blackness at bay.

Frank sat down beside her and said, "One day down and six to go. I don't believe I've ever seen you so nervous, Hope."

"My intuition is battering me like a desert haboob. That's a term Zach and Margo used. It means a violent sandstorm."

Frank chuckled. "Those two are on a wave link way above the rest of us. Seriously, Hope, I don't discount your second sight. What precautions can we take?"

"Let's double the guards during the women's meetings. One person can sit in the anteroom and another outside the sliding glass door. Even so, I'm not sure we can guard against the evil that I feel. It would be like trying to hush the coyotes." Just then, short barks and a high-pitched yowl sounded. Hope jerked, and Frank reached over and took her hand.

"Go to bed, Frank. I'll be fine."

"If that's what you want." He hesitated, looking into her eyes. She nodded, and he stood up and left.

Hope sank back and closed her eyes. They called second sight a "gift," but it could be terrifying. She was six years old, playing in her bedroom. Her skin prickled with goose bumps. She ran to the kitchen. Her mother was talking on the phone. She tugged at her dress. "Grandma's hurt," she said.

Her mother hung up and dialed 911. Half-an-hour later, they learned Hope's grandmother had collapsed. She survived thanks to the warning. Hope's mother had also had the gift when she was young. She told Hope her premonitions were taps on the shoulder from her Guardian Angel.

Over the years, Hope often experienced subtle premonitions. She'd surprise Jake by calling him just as he was about to call her. Or she'd get an urge to drive to a client's house in the middle of the night and find something amiss and call Frank. Once, she told Janai not to wear her purple outfit to a benefit luncheon. She changed to a pink print, and it turned out the guest of honor was wearing purple.

This premonition was different. It was a warning, and it was strong. She needed to take it seriously, but what steps should she take?

CHAPTER 4

At seven o'clock, the sun was warming the air. Hope sat at a patio table waiting for her pancakes, yogurt, and berries. She was gazing across at the giant rocks guarding the wilderness and jumped at the sound of Mr. Desheenie's voice.

"Miss Diamond, may I speak with you?" His cheeks were squeezed, and she had the feeling his words were going to have the bitter taste of a lemon.

"Of course, Mr. Desheenie."

He looked away from her, as if to pull comfort from the desert. He stood straight and took a deep breath. "I have very sad news to tell you."

He stopped speaking, and Hope folded her hands to squelch the impulse to shake him.

"What has happened?" she asked softly..

Mr. Desheenie stuttered, but finally words came out in a tired voice, as if they had traveled a great distance. "I am sorry to tell you. One of your guests died during the night."

Hope's heart raced. "Which guest?"

"It is the young lady with the red hair."

"Meghan Connors!" *Not Janai Ross.* Her body trembled with relief and then shame.

Mr. Desheenie flinched and bit his lip. "The lady left an order for breakfast," he said finally. "Alona went into the room and saw her sitting on the patio. When Alona could see her face, she knew her spirit had left her body. My people have a great fear of the dead. We never mention their name. A dead person's spirit, their chindi, can come back and bring harm."

Hope lowered her eyes. "Who are the authorities we must contact?"

"FBI field agent is Matt Dennison." After a moment, he added, "Tahoma Tso is our Bureau of Indian Affairs agent. I will call him." He turned and let out a deep sigh, as if dreading to make the call.

Frank joined Hope on the patio, and she told him about Meghan's death. "Agent Dennison will start out for Secret Sands as soon as word about Meghan reaches the FBI. I'd like to look over Meghan's suite before the room is taped off."

Matt Dennison left the FBI building in Albuquerque twenty minutes after the crime scene crew and medical examiner. He'd still beat them to Secret Sands. Matt was an old bronco buster, and he drove a car the way he rode a horse. Fast. The road was empty, and he tromped on the gas pedal. Even driving at top speed, it would take him a couple hours. He turned up the radio to tune out the roar of the wind and sang along with Waylon and Willie and Johnny Cash.

He stretched his legs. The Chevy Tahoe had plenty of room, but at six-foot-two, his legs cramped when he had to drive long distances. He was coming up on the medical examiner's van, which would be used to transport the body if an autopsy was required. He tooted and passed. A few minutes later he did the same to the van carrying the crime scene investigators.

The call from Tahoma Tso, the BIA agent, about a mysterious death at the posh resort surprised him. He wasn't given the name of the victim. Knowing native customs, he didn't expect a name; but when he asked about the cause of death, he was simply told it wasn't obvious. That meant it wasn't a gunshot, knifing or the ubiquitous blunt instrument.

The weather wasn't too warm, but he'd feel the heat later. Luckily, he'd worn his light blue suit that morning instead of his heavier black suit, like the rest of the team.

Spotting an old truck on a side road inching forward, he tapped the brake. He grew up in New Mexico and was used to farmers pulling out onto the highway. As he reached the intersection, the truck pulled out in front of the Tahoe. Matt swerved around it, tooted the horn, and waved.

He loved the wide-open desert, the blue sky, the red cliffs, the pink and purple, green and yellow shrubs and flowers. The only thing he didn't like here was the work. One day he'd find his way back to his old job in foreign counterespionage in Washington. He liked routing out spies more than policing the res.

Gripping the wheel tighter, he grimaced at the unpleasant task awaiting him. He had investigated murders in the Navajo Nation since he took up this assignment a year ago. All of them had been straight-forward crimes of passion, either between family members or as a result of drunkenness. He scratched his head about what he might find at Secret Sands.

# #

Hope assured Mr. Desheenie that her team would secure the scene until the authorities arrived. He seemed relieved that he didn't have to ask his own people to stay with the corpse. She took the key from him, and she and Frank entered Meghan's room.

"We can't touch anything," she told Frank when they stood inside the suite, "but see if anything strikes you as unusual."

The room had a lonely feel. Meghan hadn't brought many clothes, probably because of the last-minute invitation. Three blouses, two pairs of slacks, and two dresses hung in the closet. A romance novel was propped open on the nightstand. The painting on her wall was that of a Navajo father and son riding side by side in a field of blue sage. Peaceful. Hope closed her eyes. *May you rest in peace, dear child.*

The sliding glass door stood open, and she stepped out onto the patio. Meghan was leaning back in the chair. Her eyes were closed. She looked peaceful, as if she were sleeping. A glass half-filled with liquid sat on the table, along with an ashtray that held three cigarette butts. Hope's eyes filled with tears as she looked at the frail girl in her blue dress. Her coat hung off her shoulders. *Why was Meghan on the patio late at night?*

Frank joined Hope and nodded at the glass of liquid. "A couple soda cans were in the trash that weren't there during my visit. A used glass was on the bathroom sink. I'm guessing she had company. Some printouts that were on the nightstand are now wrinkled and on the desk. Nothing else."

32

Despite the calm expression on the woman's face, Hope ordered Frank to take photos. "Send them to Zach to add to the file. We need to work on a worst-case scenario."

Frank agreed and pulled out his cell phone.

"Please stay here until the authorities arrive. Call Tony to help. Just the two of you. Stay outside on the patio and block off the area with chairs." She explained the custom about not repeating Meghan's name, turned to go, then stopped. "One more thing, don't mention your search."

In her own room, Hope sat down on the desk chair. Her adrenalin was pumping. She took out her cell phone and touched a key. Jake answered, and she told him about Meghan Connors' death.

"That's terrible." After a moment he added, "But it could have been worse."

She closed her eyes. How callous they were to think that it was okay for an innocent young woman to die, but it would have been tragic had it been one of her clients. Her intuition had warned her trouble lay ahead. She should have prevented it.

"Can you come out and take charge?" Jake was a top investigator, and he'd know how to handle the women.

Several seconds passed before he replied. "I wish I could, Babe, but our new director has me digging into background information for a White House meeting. I'll try, but I can't promise."

"Can you smooth things with the local field agent?"

"Let me see who our agent is in that section. Hold on."

"It's Matt Dennison."

"Darn!"

"What's the problem?"

"No problem, exactly." He seemed to be hunting for the right words. Hope's fists tightened. Finally, he said, "Dennison is a good agent, but he's like a bull in a china shop. He thrashes around and doesn't care whose Ming vase he knocks over."

"Jake, I think Meghan may have been murdered."

She heard his sharp intake of breath. "Dennison isn't my favorite colleague, but he's a thorough investigator. If he smells foul play, he will follow the scent."

As she was about to hang up, Jake asked, "You've swept nothing under the carpet, am I right? Dennison will look for any excuse to get back to D.C."

"You know me, Jake, by the book," she said and cringed at Frank's illegal search.

She let the thought go. The next step was informing her clients about Meghan's death.

"Meghan Connors is dead!" Janai shrieked. Hope had closed the door before giving Janai the news. She'd caught her client prepping for the day. She was wearing a printed silk wraparound and hadn't yet applied her arsenal of beauty creams. She looked all of her fifty-five years. Her hair was bound in a silk turban. Sitting down by the desk, Janai folded her hands and looked at Hope.

"We're on a Federal Indian reservation. Major crimes here are investigated by the FBI," Hope said.

"Major crimes? Investigation?"

"Unless I miss my guess, the sudden death of a young woman will be labeled as a suspicious death. That means an autopsy and crime-scene investigation."

Janai tapped her long red nails together. "Do you know the FBI agent?"

"I haven't met him. His name is Matt Dennison." Hope shuffled her feet. Janai expected her to rattle off a complete bio on the agent.

Janai frowned, picked up the telephone, and punched in a number. She spoke as soon as the call was answered. "This is Janai Ross. What do you know about this FBI agent?"

A long silence. Then a low voice gurgled over the line. Janai hung up. "Apparently, Agent Dennison could be trouble. Mr. Desheenie said, 'If it's storming where you are, look out for the lightning.'" Hope mulled over the words. They reinforced what Jake had said.

Janai interrupted the thought and said, "I'll wait until the storm comes before I take action. What about reporters?"

"I'll ask everyone not to contact the outside world until we know the cause of death."

"That is essential. A slight breeze here in the desert could stir up a hurricane on Wall Street."

"I'd better talk to Ellen," Hope said and moved to the door.

Janai followed her. "I suppose it would be unseemly to go on with our meeting today."

Hope nodded.

"I'm counting on you to handle this matter quickly and discreetly," Janai said. The unspoken message was clear. *An investigation can ruin my purpose for being here.* What was the purpose for being here? She would have to confront Janai if the FBI ruled the death suspicious. The woman was resolved on keeping secrets, but Meghan's death might take that resolution out of her hands.

# #

"Oh, it's you, Hope." Ellen was dressed in a gray jogging suit. She held a pair of sunglasses in her hands.

"Are you going out?"

"Gloria and I are taking a walk before the meeting." Ellen sounded tired and glanced at the bed.

"Let's sit down. I have something to tell you." Ellen frowned, but Hope walked over to the chairs near the window. The desk held a tray with the remains of breakfast. The woman hadn't touched the food. Hope sat in a straight-backed chair and looked over at the painting of a Navajo woman holding her infant. A quiet scene, unlike the painting in her own room.

When Ellen was seated in the recliner across from her, Hope said, "I'm sorry to be the bearer of sad news, but Meghan Connors died during the night."

"No!" Ellen's face blanched, her eyes widened, and her body crumpled in the chair. Hope caught her breath at the woman's unexpected reaction.

"I can't believe it," Ellen said, her words coming between ragged breaths. "Did she have a heart attack? I know she took pills."

"We don't know yet. How do you know she took pills?"

"I picked her up to take her to the air terminal. She said she had packed in a hurry and forgot her pills. She ran back upstairs to get them." Ellen reached out for the phone. "I'll call my husband, Sean."

"We're asking everyone to refrain from calls until the authorities arrive."

"But we have to notify her family!" Ellen's breathing was becoming more ragged.

Hope stepped over to the credenza and picked up a brandy from the array of liqueurs. Ellen shook her head, and Hope set down the bottle.

"You will be able to talk to her family," Hope said. "But we have to wait until we know more. May I call Lucy to stay with you until you're feeling better?"

After a long moment, Ellen said, "No, you just caught me by surprise. I'll be fine."

Hope hesitated. The woman's face was pale, but her breathing was becoming steadier. "If you need anything, please call me." She wrote down her number on the desk pad and left Ellen sitting in the chair, eyes closed, chin resting on her hand.

In Lydia's room, Hope coughed at the stale cigarette smoke clinging to the air. She glanced at the blue sky and red rocks outside to keep from drawing a deep breath.

On hearing the news, Lydia said, "That's impossible. I was talking to that girl last night. We joked about how spooky the campfire program was."

When Hope told her what she knew and explained why no one was to contact the outside world, Lydia said, "No, no, we mustn't have reporters. That would be a disaster."

For Gloria, the news merely seemed puzzling. "Really, how odd. Why would Meghan just up and die?" Hope explained that the FBI would investigate the cause of death. She left Gloria standing in the middle of the room, looking like a woman waiting for a train but who didn't know how to read the signs to catch the right one.

Hope walked along the outside path and shuddered at the sight of Meghan's body, still sitting in the chair. The sun glared down like a spotlight on her red hair. Hope reached over to take the coat off her shoulders so she wouldn't feel the heat. Frank pulled her back. "Tony, take Hope to the bar and get her a stiff drink."

"No, I'm okay. Just a mental lapse." Frank let go of her arm, and she looked at Tony. "Ask Lucy to have Zach, Margo, Audrey, Robert and Dimitri go to the Blue Sky. Just say we have important news and want them all to hear it at the same time. Have a carafe of coffee put on the table. I'll be along shortly."

She turned to go but stopped. "Please make sure that one of you is here at all times until the FBI comes. We need to consider the area a crime scene."

"By the look on Meghan's face," Tony said, "I'd argue that she died from natural causes."

Hope glanced at the woman's body. She couldn't explain her intuitive feelings to Tony. He wouldn't understand. She spread out her hands. "Here's the way I see it, Tony. This very secret meeting shows up on the dark web. A young woman, whom we know nothing about, comes at the last minute. In the middle of the night, that woman dies for no reason that we can see. That's an elaborate coincidence. My intuition tells me that Meghan was murdered. And my concern is this. Is anyone else is in danger?"

After leaving Frank and Tony, Hope entered Blue Sky. She stood in front of the guests, who were still ignorant of the tragedy. She told them about Meghan's death and took in their reactions.

Dimitri pulled out his cigarettes, put one in his mouth, then took it out and put it back in the pack. "Sorry."

Margo Knight took out a facial tissue and blew her nose. "She was so young."

Robert picked up a handful of sugar cubes off the table and stuck them in his jacket pocket.

Audrey's pinched lips and narrowed eyelids lashed out in silent anger. She appeared to be blaming Hope because Meghan's death could throw off Janai's schedule.

Soon, questions started flowing. How did she die? What happens next? What should we do now?

"I suggest you go about your plans for the day," Hope said. "When the authorities arrive, they will have questions for all of us."

It was nearly ten o'clock when FBI Agent Dennison streaked into the parking lot of Secret Sands. The car kicked up gravel as it swung to a stop. Dennison jumped out, put on his cowboy hat, and strode through the automatic doors. A blond woman stood by the fountain. He glanced her way and went over to Tahoma Tso, who was talking to Mr. Desheenie at the registration desk. The blond woman moved in closer. Dennison frowned.

She cleared her throat, and Dennison turned around. "Is there something I can do for you, lady?"

"My name is Hope Diamond. I'm head of Diamond Security, the firm protecting the guests here."

"Howdy," he said, touching his hat. "The fact that I'm here suggests you haven't done a great job."

"That, of course, depends on," she looked at Mr. Desheenie and stopped, "the cause of death. I just wanted you to know that my two operatives have been guarding the patio and are awaiting your arrival."

"Much obliged," he said but clenched his jaw at the news of outsiders guarding a potential crime scene. She appeared to expect him to say more, so he added, "I plan to talk with everybody when I'm ready. So, you can go on with whatever you're doing for now." He'd have to talk to her. She might have useful information since she'd know all the guests, but he wanted it understood that he didn't want her meddling in his investigation.

Dennison turned back to the registration desk. "Do you have the information I asked for?" Mr. Desheenie handed him a manila folder. "Anywhere I can work in private?" He rolled his eyes toward the blond woman.

The manager nodded and led him to an office. It was a small space with a narrow window. Matt sat at the desk, opened the file, and looked over the names on the printout. He recognized one of the names and let out a low whistle. *Janai Ross!* She knew everyone who mattered in Washington, including the top brass at the FBI.

Picking up a yellow highlighter, he swiped across some names on the list. He excluded Diamond's team and the hotel staff, which Desheenie had put under separate headings. He also excluded Ross. He'd run his own background check on Ross if it turned out to be necessary.

He slipped the sheet into the copy machine on a cabinet behind the desk. When the copy came out, he tucked the original into his pocket and put the copy into the folder.

Matt opened the door and asked Tso to come in. He explained that the FBI would handle the investigation. He had a great deal of routine to initiate and reports to turn in, and he planned to learn as much as he could about the victim this afternoon.

By tomorrow, he'd know if the death was natural or a homicide. If it turned out to be murder, he would formally interview the guests and asked the BIA agent to be present. Tso agreed and left.

Matt heard a commotion, picked up the folder and went to the lobby. His team had arrived and were toting in equipment. He handed the file to a man rolling a large black case. "Background checks, Carl. Only on the names I've highlighted," he said, looking him in the eye.

Another van pulled into the parking lot, and the medical examiner walked in. He was a stocky Navajo and carried a large, strapped bag. "Dennison, did you put a Bugatti engine in that Tahoe? You must have your wall plastered in traffic tickets." The ME's name was Byue, which meant slow-moving stream of water.

Dennison laughed. "Come on, Pokey. Who drives sixty-five on that road? Let's get to work." He turned to the hotel manager. "Lead the way."

The team followed Desheenie through Blue Sky and out to the pathway, where he pointed toward Meghan's patio and left them.

Two men were standing at the edge of the patio. Diamond's team, he presumed. He clenched his jaw. She had probably gone through the room with a fine-tooth comb. He ran his eye over the men and motioned with his thumbs for them to move out of the area. He didn't want anyone else messing with the crime scene, if it was a crime scene. Somehow, Ross' name on that list made him pretty sure it was going to turn out that way.

The younger fellow left, but the bald man stepped up to him. "Frank Madison, Diamond Security," the man said and held out a hand. Matt shook his hand. "Tony and I will hang out two doors down until you're ready for us."

The medical examiner knelt by the body, and Matt watched over his shoulder. The woman looked very young, and she looked peaceful. *Maybe she simply died in her sleep.*

"What do you think, Doc?"

"I will not know until after the autopsy. Could be natural. Could be something else."

"If I offered you two to one, what would you say?"

"I would say, could be natural, could be something else." The ME grinned.

Dennison told his team to consider the area a crime scene. "Set up a tent. We've had enough onlookers pawing through here already."

While forensics were doing their job, he'd talk with the two Diamond operatives. He looked out toward the red rocks and bent over the ME. "Doc, when you're in the lab, check for *ja-e-na-i-o-kis'-ee.*"

The doctor looked over at the clump of poisonous cactus and back at the dead woman. "No way, Dennison. It would show on her face. That cactus twists the life out of your heart."

CHAPTER 5

George was setting a glass of ginger ale on a tray when Hope asked if he'd seen Ellen. "She has gone to the pool," he said. "I will deliver her order in a few minutes. Can I give her a message for you?"

"Thanks, George, I'll find her."

Hope strolled along the path to the Oasis. On entering the pool plaza, she stopped, awed by the sweeping view of the rock formations across the desert. The rocks had been sculpted by nature into exotic animals and ships and castles. They smoldered in tones of reddish brown under the eastern rays of the sun. She sniffed in the spicy fragrance of the sage and eyed the rich tapestry of colors. The beauty caught at her throat. *Awesome!*

The pool curled around a colossal boulder that took on the shape of a giant Gila Monster. The other edges of the pool were "L" shaped. Tables and chairs lined one edge, cushioned lounges the other.

Ellen was sitting at a table under an umbrella, wearing a hat, sunglasses and a coverup. Hope waved, but Ellen didn't respond.

Hope straightened her shoulders and walked over to her. "The FBI agent is here, Ellen. May I talk to you for a moment?"

Ellen shook her head. Her hands were trembling. "I don't feel like talking to anybody. I'm sorry."

Hope pulled up a chair and sat down. "Please, Ellen, why did you bring Meghan? Tony said it was a last-minute decision."

"Do you think the FBI will ask me questions like that?" Ellen took off her glasses. Her eyes were bright with tears, eyelids red and swollen.

Hope's shoulders tensed. "I do."

"Hello!" George was coming into the plaza, the man in the light blue suit following him.

"FBI." Hope nodded toward the man. Ellen grabbed her sunglasses and put them on. "You're not required to answer any questions until we know why Meghan died, and you're entitled to have an attorney present."

George stepped over to their table. He set down two glasses of ginger ale with ice. Hope smiled and looked around, expecting Dennison to join them. He was standing where she had stopped, looking at the rock formations. *He's pulled by the beauty of the desert, too.* Hope shivered at the clarity of her perception.

The man took off his hat, swiped his brow, put the hat on again and headed their way. He had sandy-colored hair, blue eyes, and craggy good looks. He was probably in his forties even though he had a youthful gait.

Dennison nudged George, and the man left. The agent swiveled his head between the two women; then his eyes settled on Ellen. "You must be Mrs. McKenna."

Hope stood up and faced him. "This gentleman is FBI Agent Dennison, Ellen."

Dennison edged past her and stood close to Ellen's chair. Hope bit her lip at his coolness. More ice in the desert.

"I understand Meghan Connors came to this *soirée* with you." He'd apparently talked with Frank and Tony.

Ellen nodded.

"Why?" he asked.

"Why?"

"Why did you bring her?" He sounded as though he were speaking through clenched teeth.

"To help."

"To help you do what?"

"Just to help."

"Expensive thing to do."

"Yes." Ellen gulped her drink, apparently close to the breaking point.

Hope stepped away, slipped out her cell and texted Tony. She could hear Dennison's question. "You just pulled her out of work at the last minute and dragged her here."

Ellen made no sound at all.

The man's manner wasn't so much aggressive as cold, his expression hard, as if he'd seen more than his share of sights that would make your skin crawl.

"Look, Agent Dennison, Mrs. McKenna has had a great shock. She is in no condition to answer questions."

Dennison shifted his back toward her. "Mrs. McKenna," he said, and Hope held her tongue. Making him angry wouldn't gain his cooperation. "Why did you wait until the last minute to invite Miss Connors to come to Secret Sands with you?"

Ellen took a sip of her drink and said nothing.

Tony was whistling as he came along the path. "Hey," he called. "I'm going for a dip. How about you, Ellen?" He walked around to the other side of the table, threw his towel on the chair, and held out his hand. She stood, moved away from Dennison, and dropped her coverup to the ground, revealing a one-piece, skirted bathing suit. She kept on her sunglasses and hat and held Tony's hand as she descended the steps into the water.

Dennison turned abruptly. "You get around. I suppose you texted Manara."

He was quick to reach that conclusion. She shrugged. "When will you have the results of the autopsy?"

Yanking a small notepad out of his shirt pocket, he wrote a few lines. "How well did you know Meghan Connors?"

"I met her yesterday afternoon."

"Did anyone else here know her?"

"I don't know."

He grinned. "What you're saying is that Mrs. McKenna is the only person here who knew Connors." He made another note.

Hope took a breath and held up her palms. "I'll be happy to answer your questions, Agent Dennison, *if* the autopsy turns up anything other than natural causes."

Dennison's eyes held a mocking look, and he turned away. This agent was nothing like Jake Sanders. She could forget about cooperation. It was impossible to deal with a man who treated you as if you weren't there. She started for the hotel. He stomped past, and Hope said, "Why won't you tell me if you're having an autopsy performed?"

He kept walking but muttered, "I suggest you look after your guests. You can't afford to lose another one."

Tempted to slam words back at him, Hope stopped before they came out of her mouth. If Meghan had been murdered, it meant Diamond Security had failed to protect one of the guests. The thought was as forceful as a blow to the windpipe, and she gulped for air.

She was breathing easier when she reached the Blue Sky. Janai and Lydia were drinking mojitos at a table by the window. Janai beckoned to her, and Hope joined them. The sun sent its glow over the rocks and created a panorama of pinks and golds across the table.

"Agent Dennison just talked to Ellen, but she wasn't up to answering his questions."

"You sound as if there's a chance that Meghan died of something other than natural causes," Janai said, arching an eyebrow.

Hope shook her head. "It's just my intuition stirring up my imagination."

"I set a lot of stock by your intuition, Hope. I'm going to call a friend at the FBI in Washington. You know him. He came out a couple years ago about my Van Gogh. Jake Sanders."

Hope controlled her expression. That was when she had met Jake.

"We may need him to come out here. I overheard that FBI agent talking, and I didn't like his tone. I'm not going to have my guests intimidated." She pushed her drink aside and left.

Lydia pulled a pack of cigarettes out of the Burberry tote on the chair beside her. "You don't mind, do you, Hope?"

"No," she said, wishing they were outside. "What did you talk about with Meghan last night, Lydia?"

Lydia took her time lighting the cigarette. "I've been thinking about that myself. I don't think she said anything that would lead me to believe she was about to commit suicide."

"Suicide!"

"What else could it be if it wasn't natural causes?" Lydia's eyes widened. She put both hands on the table. "You can't believe she was murdered?"

Hope blinked.

"You do think so! Come now, tell me the truth."

"Please, don't mention that word to anybody else. I don't want people to panic."

"All right, but I think Janai already has the idea. That's why she's phoning Washington."

"You may be right." *That was exactly why Janai was phoning Washington.*

"It's preposterous." Lydia took a drag of her cigarette and stuffed it out in the ashtray. "Ellen wouldn't harm a fly, and nobody else even knew Meghan."

"That's why I wondered what you talked about."

"Let me think." Lydia looked out at the red rocks, then turned back and shook her finger at Hope. "She was hoping for a promotion at work, but then, aren't all girls hoping for a promotion."

"Did she talk about her family?"

"Only that her mother had worked for Old School. She died last year, and the company offered Meghan a job. I pegged her as a girl with ambition who thought the sky was the limit. Nothing wrong with that in my book."

"That's good information, Lydia. You probably talked to her more than anyone else." Hope pressed her lips together. If she had spent more time with Meghan, she might have a clearer idea of why someone would want to murder her.

Janai came back to the table. Her forehead was wrinkled with a frown as she pulled out a chair and sat down. "Jake's tied up with some nonsense at the White House. I told him if we needed him, I would call the White House."

If she did, Jake Sanders would be on the next plane out to the Navajo Nation. Hope bit her lip to hold back a smile. Maybe Janai would pull rank and have Jake take over the investigation.

Tony and Ellen entered Blue Sky, and Hope said, "Let's not mention Washington."

"Agreed."

"How was your swim?" Hope asked when they stopped at the table.

"Refreshing," Tony said.

"I'd like to call Sean," Ellen said. "He should notify Meghan's family." She took off her sunglasses. Her eyes were still red.

"We need to wait until we know the cause of death," Hope said. "It would be worrying if you tell the family that she died, but you don't know what happened to her."

"You're right, I suppose." Ellen shuddered. "I need to lie down."

"I'll walk you to your room." Tony said and took her arm. After a few steps, he turned to Hope. "Ellen wants to go to Mass in the morning. I offered to take her."

Hope nodded, and they walked away.

"I hope the autopsy proves the girl died of a heart attack," Janai said. "The way Ellen is acting worries me. When will we know the results of the autopsy?"

"Agent Dennison hasn't shared that information," Hope said. "What do you ladies plan to do the rest of the day?"

"I will spend the day on the telephone," Janai said. "I'll also be meeting with Robert and Audrey."

"I'll do much the same. Margo and I have a lot to cover."

These women commanded giant corporations. Time was a precious commodity. She needed to get to the bottom of Meghan's death with or without Dennison's cooperation.

CHAPTER 6

A waitress was restocking the refrigerator in the Desert Rose when Hope entered. "I thought you worked later in the day, Cecelia."

"I am working extra today, maybe all week. Alona said chindi chased her when she saw the dead lady's body. She got scared and went home. Chindi holds everything that was bad about the person. If chindi catches you, you can get sick, even die. Alona's cousin says she is already feeling sick."

"I'm sorry."

"Others are scared, too, so they went home. Mr. Desheenie is training George to be manager, so he is covering for a lot of people and working extra shifts."

At a loss for words, Hope fiddled with her denim jacket.

"It was a blessing lady died outside. When a person dies inside, the house must be torn down." She turned and said, "I will bring coffee."

Hope gulped. The consequences of Meghan's death reached further than she had imagined. Traditional beliefs were nothing to scoff at. She had spent time with Meghan's body. The notion of chindi was disquieting, and she brushed her arms.

"Meghan's death has been a shock," Hope said to the team when they had gathered around the table. "At this point, we don't know how she died or what her death means in terms of the danger to our clients. Our role is to protect the women, so we will assume they are still in danger."

She ran her fingers through her hair. "Janai and Lydia are working in their suites. Ellen is lying down." She looked at Lucy.

"Gloria and Dimitri are working together in Gloria's suite."

"Let's talk about what we learned last night. We'll save Meghan until the end. I'd like to hear more about Ellen McKenna, Tony. She is the only one here who knew Meghan."

Tony opened the binder Hope had given all the guests. It contained the week's agenda and had blank pages for notes. He shuffled through pages. Then he sat back, not looking at his notes.

"Ellen owns Old School Confectioners, and she's as sweet as sugar," he said, aggressively. "The company is headquartered in Pittsburgh. Ellen lives near the original factory, and lots of family live close by. It's a tradition that women head the company." He rubbed his forehead, apparently reluctant to talk about Ellen.

Hope shifted her legs. His feelings could sideline the investigation. Frank's expression showed he was thinking the same thing.

"How did she become the candy goddess?" Lucy asked.

"Old School runs a cool tour in one of the factory buildings. Think Disneyland. You ride around in little railroad cars and see animated mock-ups of the company founders and the candy-making process. The one real thing is a giant vat of chocolate that's stirred automatically by large paddles. You can smell the chocolate outside around the neighborhood."

"I ate a couple pieces. It's delicious," Zach said.

"Who founded the company?" Hope asked.

Tony looked at his notes. "The founder was Ellen's Great Great Grandmother, Aoife (*ee-fa*). In Irish myth, Aoife is the greatest woman warrior in the world. By all accounts, Grandmother Aoife took after her namesake. She sailed to America in the late 1800s on her own at barely twenty years old. A male cousin and his wife in Pittsburgh sponsored her."

Lucy smiled and gave a thumbs-up.

"Aoife married a man named Bucher. He was from Switzerland, and he taught her how to make fudge. The Swiss were pioneers in chocolate. When he died, Aoife worked day and night making fudge in her kitchen. Her twin daughters sold it around the neighborhood." Tony looked back at his notes. "Ellen is president. She's a stay-at-home mom with a nine-year-old son."

"Who runs the company then?" Zach asked.

"Her husband, Sean McKenna. He's a big Irishman. Used to play football for the Pittsburgh Steelers. Ellen made him vice president after they married and he retired from football."

"Were Sean and Meghan having a fling?" Hope asked. "She expected a promotion."

Tony lowered his eyes. "Meghan sat at a desk near Sean's office. She stood out because she was young and attractive. Ellen walked past her without speaking, which was odd because she spoke to all the other women."

Hope crossed and uncrossed her legs. Facts seemed to be piling up against Ellen. It wouldn't help Janai's reputation or her own if Ellen turned out to be a murderer. *Slow down.* The girl may not have been murdered. When will Dennison have the autopsy report? She might have to call Jake.

"Does Ellen have any outside interests?" Lucy asked. "I'm wondering why she's here. All the other ladies are active in their companies."

"A transcontinental water pipeline," Tony said, looking again at his notes. "Ellen is backing a project to prevent rivers from flooding. Pittsburgh has three rivers, and her property has been flooded more than once. Her idea is to transport overflow water from the country's major rivers to draught-ridden areas in the West. She told me that coming here was a chance to gain support for the project."

"Impressive. I had no idea the lady did anything but make bonbons." Lucy smiled across at Tony. He turned his head away, and Hope frowned. She had enough to worry about with Meghan's death and Ellen's strange behavior. She couldn't afford conflict on her own team, not when lives were at stake.

Cecelia came in and pushed her cart to the refreshment counter. Along with the coffee, she set out six slices of peach crisp on brightly colored plates. The sweet aroma indicated the dessert had come right out of the oven. "You guys can fight over the last piece," she said and winked at Tony.

"*Grazie,*" He grinned and waved.

"A coffee break. Just what we need," Hope said, rising and walking to the counter. Everyone followed. They all drank coffee and ate the warm peach crisp. Frank and Zach split the last piece.

"Let's turn away from Ellen for the moment," Hope said, helping herself to another cup of coffee. "Tell us about Gloria, Lucy."

"Here's the tea." In Lucy's circle, "tea" meant gossip or hot news. "Gloria is Alexander Kosta's daughter. Think Greek shipping tycoon. The company is called Global Shipbuilders. Her mother died when she was ten, and she spent playtime at the office. Apparently, she refused to let her father out of her sight after her mother's death. Not much of a life for a young child, I don't imagine." Lucy lowered her eyes a moment. "At seventeen, Gloria was on the payroll. She's a true shipwright. She's forty years old, and Mr. Kosta made her the head of the company last year because of his health."

"What do you know about Dimitri?" Hope asked. The man had very acute antenna and a slightly sinister air.

Lucy turned a page in the binder. "He's fifty-four years old. He learned shipping from the ground up at Global and became vice president at thirty-five. He runs Global's day-to-day operations in Greece, and he's here because of a hush-hush deal." Lucy was rubbing her arms. "Can we turn the air conditioning down? I'm cold."

"I'll take care of it," Frank said, and he went over and fiddled with the settings.

"You sat next to Dimitri at dinner, Frank," Hope said. "Learn anything interesting?"

"Dimitri likes his whiskey. He thinks he should be president."

"Anything about the hush-hush deal?"

"Gloria has plans for expansion, but Dimitri didn't go into detail." Frank sat down at the table. "The only thing I gathered was that it had to do with cruise ships."

The room was quiet, and Tony said, "I tackled Robert on the charities he runs for Janai. Says he's just a rubberstamp that approves whatever the charities ask for." Tony shook his head. "Not this guy. Doesn't fit with his personality."

"I did a little checking on Robert," Zach said. "He worked for three financial consulting firms, all reputable. After he joined Icelandic Wind, he upgraded their old financial systems to the cloud."

"Sounds like you can't knock him as far as knowing finance," Frank said. "But his financial acumen validates what Tony alluded to. A guy who knows all the financial angles knows how to cover his tracks."

"Good point." Hope said and smiled at Frank. "You seemed to get along well with Lydia Fallbrook. Fill us in on her background."

Frank grinned. "I spent time with Lydia in Chicago. She's fifty-two years old. She and her brother Mark own Grand Med Pharmaceuticals. As you saw at the reception, she's a heavy smoker. She's also a formidable lady. Her brother criticized her, and she stormed back. I felt like a tennis referee."

"So, you'd say there's tension between Lydia and her brother?"

"I would."

"What's your take on Margo Knight?"

"She comes across as a sweetheart, but don't be fooled. Margo is a pit bull. Grand Med would be up the creek without her. She's up on all the lingo and is friendly with all the FDA people."

"I talked with Margo," Zach spoke up, and his face was flushed. "She loves the whole field of pharmaceuticals." His tone was defensive, and Hope closed her eyes. It could jeopardize the agency if both Tony and Zach became emotionally involved with the women in this case.

"Let's take a ten-minute break," Hope said. "Fresh air will help my brain absorb all this information."

Outside, the vastness of the desert lifted her spirits. She breathed in the fresh air and followed the curve of the rock formation off the trail. She sat on a ledge and ran her hands over the surface, slick from eons of battering winds and rain and sand.

Dennison wasn't going to be easy to work with, and the emotions evident in Tony's and Zach's comments could derail the case. Chindi was stirring up trouble. She leaned back against the rock, letting the spirituality of the place engulf her. A gospel hymn came into her head, and she sang softly. "Rock of ages, cleft for me, let me hide myself in thee." The rhythm and the words pushed chindi out of her head.

By the time she was back in Desert Rose, she was breathing easier. She explained about Frank's search and cautioned the team not to mention it.

Frank gave Tony a thumbs-up sign. "I ducked out of Robert's room when I heard you at the door. So, thanks, pal." He looked down at his notes. "Robert brought a couple paperback thrillers and a book on fundraising for political campaigns." He paused. "He also brought a hunting rifle. It was in a case stuck up against the wall in the closet."

"That reminds me," Lucy said, checking her watch. "I promised to go horseback riding with Robert, and I have to change clothes. Would you like me to cancel?"

"No, today's agenda is out the window," Hope said. "See if you can find out why Robert brought the gun. Be creative. He can't know we looked in his room."

"Okay. If that's the case, it's me and Diablo. That was the Cisco Kid's horse in case you didn't watch the Saturday morning reruns like Tony." He winked at her, and she left.

Frank continued with his report. "Audrey brought a cardboard filing cabinet. I didn't open it, but I hefted it slightly, and it weighs a ton. I expect she'll be working all week."

"I'm sure you're right," Hope said. "I don't think Audrey ever takes a vacation."

"Dimitri Drakos is a very rigid fellow. Everything was absolutely straight in his room, which made me wonder why his briefcase was sitting askew on the desk. It's possible somebody else went through his room before I did."

"Interesting. I'd assume it was Gloria if anyone went through the room. Sounds as if she may not trust him," Hope said.

"The one book on the nightstand had a picture of a poker hand on the cover. I don't know what it was about because it was in Greek. Apparently, he's a player."

"He did ask about the casino," Hope said. "What about Margo Knight?"

"Margo brought along her computer and a list of science articles. One odd thing. I found an envelope in her trashcan with the return address of International Biolabs, one of Grand Med's competitors. No telling what that might mean."

"Did you check any of the ladies' rooms?"

"Just Gloria's. Aside from lots of clothes, the lady had a computer. The box of candy that Ellen gave us was open, with many pieces missing. I ran out of time and couldn't search the other rooms."

"Thanks for handling that assignment, Frank. I'm sorry that things may get sticky."

"I'll handle it."

"Let's talk about Meghan Connors. She was a picky eater. I suspect she was anorexic. The girl was counting on a promotion. If she didn't get it, she mentioned a golden parachute. That makes me think she had some blackmail scheme in her head."

"If Ellen's husband was having an affair with Meghan, maybe he persuaded her to make sure Ellen didn't return to Pittsburgh, but the plan backfired." Frank said.

Hope paused and looked at Zach. "I know. Find out who inherits if Ellen dies."

"What did you find in the room, Frank?"

Tony put up his hand. "One quick thing. Cecelia said she did the turndown service in Meghan's room on Friday night. She noticed that the box of candy was open, and two pieces were missing, but she didn't find any candy wrappers in the waste can."

"I can't imagine Meghan eating candy. I suppose she could have given the candy to someone else. I'll mention it to Agent Dennison," Hope said. At least she'd try. It would mean he'd have to listen. "Did you notice the candy, Frank?"

"The lid on the box was closed, so I can't say whether any pieces were missing. She brought a romance novel. What I did find interesting was a collection of Internet ads for condos in downtown Pittsburgh. She had penciled in notes about why Sean, I presume, objected to each building. Her favorite condo was starred. 'This is it regardless of what S says.' Sounds like she was in a relationship with him."

"No way Sean could keep an affair secret," cut in Tony. "Pittsburgh's like my hometown of Messina. Small neighborhoods. Ellen's aunts, uncles and cousins are all in each other's pockets. Ellen would know about it."

"Maybe she did know," Hope said and wrote a note. "Ellen said Meghan took meds every day. Find anything?"

Frank nodded. "Medicine bottles in the bathroom cabinet. I couldn't read the labels without touching. After what's happened, I'm glad I didn't touch them. I assume Dennison is having all the bottles tested."

"That brings us to your meeting with Dennison."

"You mean 'Mister Cool,'" Tony said. "I have a few choice words for him in Italian." Tony went to the fridge and pulled out a Coke.

Frank smiled. "Dennison came over, sat down and asked if we had talked with Meghan. Neither one of us had said more than two words to her. When he learned Tony had visited Ellen in Pittsburgh, he fired off a lot of questions. Tony wasn't very helpful."

"Sorry, but he practically accused us of tampering with the scene," Tony said, sitting down. "He made a big deal about putting up a tent to keep us onlookers out of the way."

Tony was not a fan of Dennison's. Hope turned to Frank. "What was your impression? Do you think he's competent?"

"Under the ice shield, he knows what he's doing. He was targeting Tony and me with that remark, but the tent was a professional thing to do."

"He had a few cold words for me," Hope said.

"Like what?"

"Like I didn't do a great job of protecting my clients." She flinched at saying the words. "Meghan wasn't our client, but it still doesn't sit well with me that she died on our watch."

"Hold on," Frank said. "No agency can protect a person twenty-four hours a day if someone is intent on harming them. All we can do is make sure our clients are less attractive targets than somebody else. Meghan wasn't even on our radar. She came here out of the blue. You can't let Dennison do a head job on you."

"Thanks for reminding me, Frank. Isn't that the spiel I give to every new client? Has he ordered an autopsy?"

"He kept that information in the deep freeze, but he is having one done. We were in Tony's room and caught sight of his team taking away the body. Since everyone here leaves on Thursday, Dennison will likely push the ME for results. No idea, though, as to how soon he'll have them."

"Thanks, Frank." She turned to the others. "Send your reports to Zach as soon as you can. Include as much information as you can remember. It's important to keep current. The picture could change rapidly. Encrypt the file, Zach. I don't like the idea of somebody hacking into your system."

Hope went back to her room to compile her own report, but she stood looking at the painting of the horsemen. They seemed to be shouting at her, warning her to pay attention. She rubbed her eyes in frustration.

She sat down at the computer and typed up her notes. After sending the report to Zach, she pushed back in the recliner and thought about Meghan. The look she gave Ellen before going to the patio Friday night to smoke was arrogant. Ellen's expression when she watched her walk out of the dining room was angry. There had been a lot of tension between those two women. *Why did Ellen bring Meghan to Secret Sands?*

CHAPTER 7

At seven o'clock that evening, Hope stood by the tall table in Blue Sky. Fragrance from the large bouquet of fresh flowers drifted across the room. The night was designated as casual wear. In light of the tragedy, Hope wore a dark blue jacket and tied a muted, print scarf around her neck. To Janai, casual meant a jewel-embroidered bolero jacket and black velvet pants. Her hair was set off with a ruby hair clip.

"You look fabulous!" Hope greeted.

"It's not too much, under the circumstances, is it?"

"Not at all."

"We need Meghan's death cleared up, Hope. This unsettled state is putting a crimp in my plans. Have you found out why Ellen brought her?"

"Not yet."

"Results of the autopsy?"

Hope stood still. Janai expected answers. "The medical examiner is conducting an autopsy. If I don't hear anything by morning, I'll call the FBI agent in Washington."

"Do that." Janai walked over to the bar, her stiff bearing declaring her displeasure.

Hope was sipping a glass of ginger ale near the bar when the FBI man came into Blue Sky, still wearing his cowboy hat. She had seen him earlier with a small suitcase that he probably carried in the car for emergencies, along with a guitar case. He must be spending the night. He walked to the bar and hitched a thumb over his shoulder at George. The barman nodded and left.

Dennison passed Hope without speaking and went to the middle of the room. He rapped a glass with a spoon and stood silent until everyone was looking at him. *Oh, no! What was he planning to do?*

After identifying himself as FBI, Dennison said, "I know you've been antsy to hear the cause of Meghan Connors' death, but you won't like what I'm about to tell you." Dennison's eyes slanted toward Ellen on the sofa next to Tony and then over to Hope.

"Miss Connors' death was a result of heart failure." *Why wouldn't they like that news?* "The problem is the medical examiner can't figure out what caused the heart failure. He doesn't think it was natural. That means I'll be investigating the case as a suspicious death. I'll put it another way. I'll be investigating the case as a homicide."

When he stopped talking, voices buzzed around the room. Then the room quieted suddenly, as if words had been sucked up by a vacuum pump. Hope glanced at Ellen. Her eyelids closed, and her head slumped. Tony dipped his handkerchief into a glass of water and dabbed her face. She opened her eyes, but her face was chalky.

Hope headed to the man in the cowboy hat. The staccato clicks of her heels rapped out the rat-a-tat-tat sound of a machine gun. She stood in front of him and asked politely, "Would you join me outside for a quiet word?"

He raised his eyebrows and shrugged. "Why not?"

Janai and Lydia rose and followed. The three women surrounded Dennison. "Have you met Janai Ross and Lydia Fallbrook?" Hope asked, gesturing to each woman.

Dennison tipped his hat. "Pleasure."

Hope looked him in the eye. "Why did you purposely upset the guests?"

"I'm not concerned about upsetting anybody when it comes to murder, lady."

"Hold on. The medical examiner said she died of heart failure."

"It could have been suicide," Lydia said.

"That's possible." Dennison said, as if the thought were a new one. "But you are all visitors, and you plan to leave these parts in five days. If I don't start investigating this case now as a murder, you'll all be miles away by the time it's confirmed."

"What exactly did the medical examiner say?" Hope asked.

The man hesitated a moment, then said, "The only prescription drug in her system was for a thyroid condition. Despite the fact that she was a smoker, her heart was in perfect condition. It just stopped beating, and he finds that unusual."

"Heart failure sounds like natural causes to me," Janai said.

"When a medical examiner says something is unusual, I think a case needs dug into. I didn't know Miss Connors, but I know she was only twenty years old. If someone took away her life, I don't want that person to get away with murder."

Hope couldn't argue with his statement. "What are you planning to do?"

His expression said it was none of her business, but he heaved his shoulders and said, "It's a suspicious death. I plan to investigate it that way. That means questioning everyone on the property, from the hotel staff to the guests, including you ladies." He nodded to Janai and Lydia. "Just because you own half the planet don't get you no free ride."

So, he knew who the women were. He must have run background checks.

"We may or may not agree to talk to you without our lawyers present," Janai said.

"You'd better call 'em in then, because I am damn sure gonna talk to all of you."

"Then you'd better clean up your language," Hope said, and her eyes met his.

"I gotta lot'a wheels spinning, so excuse me if I cut out of our little gab session." He looked at Hope. "I plan to talk to Mrs. McKenna first thing in the morning."

"She's going to Mass in the morning. Your questions will have to wait."

"Ladies, you have an attitude like you're better'n the law. I got news. You ain't." Dennison turned and left.

66

The Blue Sky felt like the inside of a tomb when Hope returned. No one spoke, and every eye turned toward her. She looked over to the bar, but George hadn't returned. *Good.* She could mention Meghan's name. Maybe that was why Dennison sent him away. *Could the man be that considerate?*

"Here's what we know," she said when she reached the middle of the floor. "The medical examiner is puzzled as to what triggered Meghan's heart failure. Agent Dennison will be investigating the case as a suspicious death. He'll want to question all of us."

Dimitri spoke up, "I not know lady. Why should I answer questions?"

"Same here," Robert said. "What can we tell him?"

"It's a matter of understanding her state of mind. You all spoke to Meghan. Agent Dennison will want to know about her mood. Was she depressed? Had she broken up with a boyfriend? Small pieces of information can build a bigger picture. Even if you didn't know her well, you can add to that picture."

"Well put," Janai said. "We all want to put this sad event behind us, but it's important to clear the air."

The dinner gong rang, and meals were served on the patio. At nine o'clock, lights were lowered in Blue Sky, and the patio lights were turned off. The darkness outside was brightened only by a thin moon and the Milky Way.

Dan Nakai was a Navajo elder and storyteller. He had been asked to share tales of Navajo culture. He was Mr. Desheenie's uncle. Otherwise, he may not have come to a place where a recent death had occurred. Nakai had long, white hair tied back in a ponytail, a dark, wrinkled face, and an almost toothless smile. He wore a blue-and-white checked shirt and a black western hat

67

banded with circles of silver. He carried a rolled-up piece of fabric tied with a ribbon.

The elder sat up straight in the soft chair. His voice was low and gravelly, and his speech slow. He spoke with the same lilting phrasing as George. As he shared Navajo lore, Hope became lulled with the tales of the Navajo people, which, he said, were called *Diné*. He told how they passed through three different worlds until they emerged into this fourth world, known as the Glittering World.

Navajo, he told them, believed in Earth People and the Holy People, which they called *Yeis*. The *Yeis* had much power, and they could aid or harm the Earth People. The silence in the audience seemed to deepen, the listeners captured by the power of his narration. The *Yeis* taught the *Diné* to live in harmony with Mother Earth, Father Sky, and all living creatures. It was the *Yeis* that gave the Navajo the four sacred mountains that surrounded their land on the north, east, south, and west. "We honor the sacred mountains," he said and unrolled the flag he carried and held it up. "They are on our flag and our Great Seal."

Nakai told them tales about Coyote, a trickster who represented both good and evil. Hope bent in to listen more closely. "The world gets mad at Coyote because of his behavior," the elder said, "but we still need him for many things." Nakai stopped and took a sip of water. "One day, the people placed an animal hide in water. If it did not sink, no one would ever die. While their backs were turned, Coyote threw rocks on top of the hide. Naturally, it sank. Coyote explained his actions. If no one ever died, there would not be enough land for the people to live on."

The elder's voice continued to spellbind his audience, and the hour passed quickly.

Nakai leaned back in his chair and closed his eyes. Hope sat still, not wanting to disturb his thoughts. After a minute, he sat up straight and brushed the back of his hand over his eye. His words came slowly.

"I am happy to be here with you tonight. Great Spirit spared me from the sickness that took many lives across the world. It took many of us right here on the res. We are 574 nations in this country. Elders from every tribe suffered from the sickness and died. Apache, Blackfeet, Choctaw, Lakota, Mohawk, Muskogee." He stopped and took a breath. "When elders pass on, all their knowledge of Indian culture, our ceremonies, and our language is lost forever."

He paused, and his words slowed down. "It is my duty, and my honor, to pass on what I know to our young people, and to our visitors. We want everyone to appreciate the beauty, and the importance, of our heritage."

The room fell silent, and Nakai stood and said the Navajo Blessing Prayer. "Go forth in peace. Be still within yourself and know that the trail is beautiful. May the winds be gentle upon your face, and your direction be straight and true as the flight of the eagle. Walk in beauty and harmony with God and all people."

When he finished, Janai was the first one to walk up to him, say a few words, and shake his hand. As she turned away, she looked at Hope, closed her eyes and nodded. Obviously, she had been moved by his talk.

Hope, too, had been moved, and her eyes filled with tears at his words, as well as the thoughts of Meghan crowding her brain. She stood aside to regain her composure. After the others had all shaken Nakai's hand, she smiled and told him how grateful she was that he had come. She held his arm and walked with him across

69

the room. At the door, she handed him an envelope. He bid her good-by, saying his grandson was waiting for him.

Matt Dennison was outside talking to a young man. The FBI agent tipped his hat to the elder and held it in his hand while they spoke. Hope watched a moment, her eyebrows raised at his respectful gesture.

In Blue Sky, Dimitri rose and asked Hope if he could go back to Greece. "I am stranger in country. Not good for me to be mixed up with police."

"I understand how you must feel, but I don't think the FBI will allow you to leave. You don't have to answer questions without an attorney. I'm sure Gloria would arrange to fly one in."

"That good to know. I will stay. If FBI say I am guilty, I get attorney for sure."

"You can also ask for a Greek interpreter. Agent Dennison talks rough, but he will abide by the law and make sure he doesn't violate your rights."

Dimitri nodded. He took a pack of cigarettes out of his jacket, looked at Hope and put them back. "I go outside." His face held a worried look as he left.

Robert had been standing by. "Is it true we don't have to talk to the FBI agent without an attorney?"

"That's the law. Do you want Janai to arrange for an attorney to fly in tomorrow?"

"It's just that I didn't like Dennison's manner. He might trick us into saying something we don't mean, and then it's on the record."

Hope looked around for Janai. "Audrey, you're here." In her black dress, she was nearly invisible in the low lighting. "Do you think Janai will call an attorney?"

"I'm meeting her at ten-thirty. I'll ask." Audrey paused, then said. "No, she won't want an attorney." She turned to Robert. "Let me know before ten-thirty what you decide." She looked at her watch. "You have five minutes."

Robert shook his head. "I'll pass on the attorney. Good night. I want to do some reading before my midnight meeting with Janai."

"You're meeting with her tonight?" Hope asked.

"Janai doesn't believe in sleeping away a third of her life. She sleeps three hours a night. From three to six."

"That must be her secret for accomplishing so much." Hope's lips puckered at the idea of her client's late-night meetings.

Tony was still sitting with Ellen, and Hope asked, "What time will you leave for Mass?"

Ellen looked at Tony. "We'll leave here at eight."

"That early?"

"I'd better turn in," Ellen said, and Tony helped her to her feet. She looked on the verge of collapse. She held onto Tony's arm as they followed Frank and Lydia into the hallway.

Hope sat alone in Blue Sky, and it was quite dark. A sound made her jerk. No one was in sight, but she felt a presence. She stood and backed up to the wall near the bar.

Peering across the darkened room, she caught a movement. She pulled the gun out of her jacket pocket. She stood with her feet shoulder-width apart, right foot slightly behind the left, arms stiff. A cowboy hat seemed to sail through the air. Matt Dennison's body came into view. Hope let out a breath. "It's you," she said, still covering him with the gun. He walked over to her, both hands in the air. She relaxed her stance and put the gun in her pocket.

"Just checking to make sure we don't have any more dead bodies."

"What!"

He shook his head. "Go to bed, lady. You're wound up tighter than an eight-day clock."

"I am just fine, thank you. Goodnight." Her breath was coming in fast puffs. Dan Nakai's talk of coyote touched a nerve. Even though the medical examiner didn't officially rule Meghan's death a homicide, she had likely been killed.

She would have to discover which person at Secret Sands was coyote, and if another murder was on the agenda. She felt chilly, and her acute sixth sense was warning her that the trouble at Secret Sands wasn't over by a long shot.

CHAPTER 8

Tony greeted Ellen in the lobby at eight Sunday morning. She wore a yellow silk suit and held a straw sunhat in one hand. Although she seemed composed, her eyelids were red and puffy. Tony caught Hope's frown as she walked toward the dining room. She was as concerned about Ellen as he was.

Outside, the sky was a pale, watery blue. "Did you enjoy our storyteller," Tony asked, escorting Ellen to a white Toyota sedan.

She put on her sunglasses and waited while he opened the car door. "Yes, he was interesting," her voice trembled.

As Tony turned the key and stepped on the gas, he flexed the tight muscles in his neck. Ellen needed to pull herself together. Otherwise, she'd be shark-bait for Dennison.

It was forty miles to the church, and they passed scattered farms, house trailers, and what he had learned were *hogans*, traditional Navajo buildings with eight sides.

Tony's fingers tapped on the steering wheel. Finally, he asked, "Were your people able to reach Meghan's family?" With Dennison's announcement, they couldn't keep back the news of Meghan's death. Hope wasn't concerned about reporters since the medical examiner's report merely stated Meghan had died of heart failure.

"I talked to my husband," Ellen said and stopped. Tony glanced over. Tears were rolling down her cheek. She took off her sunglasses and dabbed at her eyes with a tissue. "Sean will talk to her aunt today."

"Did you know Meghan well?"

"No, I met her at the office Christmas party and saw her briefly whenever I dropped by to see Sean."

"I wondered why you invited her to come here with you."

She shuddered, but Tony kept his eyes on the road. After a long minute, she said, "I wanted to get to know her. Rumors were spreading about her and Sean. You know how it is. A lot of gossip. My Uncle Timothy told me last week that Sean planned to make the girl a manager. He said she wasn't qualified."

"You invited her to find out the truth?"

"Yes."

"Did you find out the truth?"

The silence lasted a long time before the word finally floated out. "Yes."

The wooden church sign fluttered in the breeze. Half the letters had been wiped out by the blowing dirt. "Here we are," he said, easing onto the driveway that led up to Our Lady of Sorrows, a low, timbered building with a peaked roof.

As they pulled up to the front of the church and stepped out of the car, a young man with black hair and mustache wearing a black cassock walked toward them. "I am Father Francisco Ramirez." He held out his hand.

"Antonio Manara, Father." Tony said and shook hands with the priest. "And this," he said, turning to take Ellen's hand, "is Mrs. Ellen McKenna."

"Welcome to Our Lady of Sorrows," Father Francisco said, and he opened the doors of the church.

Ellen touched the priest's arm. "Father, will you hear my confession?"

"Of course. This way." He led Ellen to a set of confessionals on the far side of the church.

Standing at a table, Tony leafed through flyers, prayer books, and pamphlets. He picked up a pamphlet and read descriptions as he walked around the church. He looked up at the traditional eight curved beams and sky hole of the *hogan*. There was also a hole in the center of the floor. The pamphlet stated, "Navajo people believe all forms of life came forth from a hole."

He admired the sculptures of Saint Kateri Tekakwitha, the first Native American saint, and Saint Katherine Drexel, niece of the founder of Drexel University. The pamphlet explained that she had devoted her life and fortune to helping American Indians and African Americans.

At the large bowl set on a rugged stump for baptisms, Tony stretched over the velvet rope and touched the satiny wood. The colorful etchings—a baby in cradle board, a young woman pounding a garment with a stone, an older woman weaving a rug, and an elderly man carving a piece of wood—represented the four stages of life.

As he neared the front of the church, Ellen and Father Francisco came out from the confessional. Ellen knelt down in one of the pews, and the priest walked over to Tony.

"You're from Italia?"

"*Sì*, Messina, by the sea in southern Italy."

"I've been there. I spent a year in Rome and had a chance to visit your cathedral. *Magnifico.* Did you attend Mass there?"

"I've been there, but that wasn't our *parrocchia.* It's been a long time since I've been to Mass, Father, if you're wondering. "

"I'm always looking for souls who have wandered onto a different path." He pointed a finger at Tony. "My guess is that you were an altar boy."

Tony grinned. "Good guess."

Ellen stood up and walked over to them. She was smiling, and Tony sent a questioning glance at Father Francisco. "I'll get ready for Mass," the priest said.

The service at Our Lady of Sorrows was defined in the pamphlet as inculturation, meaning a blend of Catholic doctrine and Navajo culture. The words of scripture that the priest read were quite different from those Tony was used to hearing.

Two elderly Navajo men walked down the aisle, stopping at each pew to pass the collection basket. Tony raised an eyebrow at Ellen's check for $5,000.

After Mass, Tony and Ellen waited until Father Francisco had greeted all the parishioners before stepping up to say good-by. The priest took Ellen's hand. "I'm glad you have found peace, my sister." She smiled and walked to the car.

He shook hands with Tony. "*Arrivederci, mio amico, Antonio.* Come back, and we'll talk about Italy and maybe even lost souls."

"*Ciao, Padre.*"

Today may have been Tony's first time at Mass in a while, but he knew the seal of confession was sacrosanct. Had Ellen confessed to Meghan's murder and been forgiven by Father Francisco? Was that the reason for her generous contribution?

Ellen turned toward him. "You're awfully quiet, Tony. Is something bothering you?"

"I was thinking about confession. Maybe I should have gone when Father Francisco offered. You seem a lot happier since you talked with him."

"Yes, I am. Meghan's death weighed on my conscience."

"Everything's okay now?"

"Well, not okay. I'll still have to talk to the FBI agent." She smiled. "You should have talked to Father. He has a gift of seeing straight to the heart of things."

"Next time I'm out this way I'll stop by." He looked off into the distance, miles of empty road leading to the future. Or away from the past? At the turn-off to Secret Sands, a roadrunner skittled in front of the car. Tony slammed on the brakes. The roadrunner twisted its long neck and bill toward the car. Tony bit back an angry remark. As the official state bird, roadrunners had the run of the road.

Tony helped Ellen out of the car and said, "I'd like to talk to you about the night Meghan died." Ellen shook her head. "It's important," he insisted. "I'd like to hear your story before you're grilled by Dennison."

She shrugged. "Let's eat on the patio outside my room in thirty minutes. I want to change into something cooler."

"Sounds good. *Ciao.*"

Tony took off his jacket with a sigh of relief. He had been sweltering at the church, but he hadn't dared remove his jacket because of the gun he carried. Goes with the territory. He was always on duty. He stripped and took a cool shower. Afterwards, he dressed, pulled on the tan jacket, put the gun in his pocket, and headed to Ellen's room.

The maid had cleaned, and everything was orderly. They requested a late breakfast and went out to the patio. "I'm afraid you've been worrying about me, but I assure you, I didn't kill Meghan."

Tony's face reddened. "I never thought you had anything to do with Meghan's death, but I'd like to know if you talked with her."

"Yes, I talked with her after the campfire program."

"Where was that?" Tony removed his jacket and hung it on the back of his chair.

"Meghan's room," Ellen said. "She caught up with me as I was heading to my room. She said we needed to have a heart-to-heart talk. She poured out ginger ales for both of us. We sat down on her couch, and she immediately pounced on me about a divorce. She said she and Sean had fallen in love and wanted to get married."

"Did Sean ever give you reason to think he wanted a divorce?"

"No."

"What did you say to Meghan?"

"I told her I was Catholic and didn't believe in divorce." Ellen shifted in her chair. She was clearly uncomfortable talking about Meghan.

"How did she react?"

"'Put that old-fashioned notion out of your head,' she told me and said that I should get into the Twenty-first Century. She was Catholic, too, but that didn't matter. She was going to marry Sean, and things would get ugly if I didn't agree to a quiet divorce." Ellen was breathing hard as she rattled off Meghan's words.

"Did you touch anything when you were in her room?"

Ellen opened her eyes wide. "Sure, I did. I drank some ginger ale. She showed me pictures of condos they were planning to buy. I spilled the glass of ginger ale and had to go into the bathroom to sponge off my outfit. I blush to admit it, but I looked into her medicine cabinet and saw the pills she was taking."

"Did you touch the bottles?"

"Yes."

"Why did you do that?"

"Meghan had made an excuse about forgetting her medicine. I wondered what medicines she was on."

"How long were you in Meghan's room?" Tony's skin felt itchy imagining what Dennison would do with the information.

"Not more than fifteen minutes. Do I need to tell all of this to the FBI?" Gradually Ellen's control had seemed to slip, and now she sounded genuinely worried.

Cecelia came along the walkway rolling a cart with coffee, bacon and eggs and toast. She greeted them and put the coffee and food on the table. "*Hágoónee*," she said. Tony was good at languages, and George was teaching him Navajo. He recognized the word for okay, all right then, or see you later.

He answered, *"Yá'át'ééh,"* which meant hello, among other things.

When Cecelia was out of earshot, Tony said, "You will have to tell Dennison you were in her room. He'll know because of the fingerprints. You don't have to tell him what you talked about. You can say it was a private matter. You should know, however, that he's probably already uncovered Meghan's relationship with your husband." He stopped, took a breath, and said, "You're entitled to have an attorney present."

"I understand," she said, but her voice was unsteady.

"The tricky part is the medicine bottles. Fingerprints there will be hard to explain." Tony cocked his head to the side. "You could say you were looking for aspirin."

"No, I won't lie." She gave him a pinched smile. "I don't want to go back to visit Father Francisco. Unless you want to go."

"No, I'm good. Well, since you won't lie, it's probably best to say nothing." Tony sipped his coffee and looked out at the rocks. Three squirrels were chasing one another up and down. He smiled at the fun they were having. It would be pleasant to chat about them with Ellen. Instead, he said, "What did Sean say when you told him Meghan had died?"

"He was shocked. He wanted to come out. I said it wasn't necessary."

"How old is your husband?"

"He's forty-one."

"Could be a mid-life crisis, and things went further than he had intended."

Someone pounded on the door. Tony walked into the room, opened the door and frowned.

"Where's Mrs. McKenna?" Dennison asked.

"She's eating breakfast on the patio."

Dennison grinned. "A *tête-è-tête*, eh? Well, don't let me interrupt. I'll expect her at one o'clock in the Gray Feather meeting room near the therapy pool."

Tony gritted his teeth at the man's sneer. He rushed back to the patio and told Ellen that Dennison wanted to see her in twenty minutes. "Hope plans to sit in on that meeting with you. I better go. I need to fill her in on our conversation. Don't worry."

"I'm not worried," she said, but her voice held fear. "Thanks, Tony, for taking me to Mass."

He pulled on his jacket and gave her a questioning look. "*Ciao.*"

A weight was pushing at his shoulders. He didn't think Ellen killed Meghan, but he was convinced she was holding something back, something that might convict her of murder. He needed to discover what it was before Dennison filed charges against her.

CHAPTER 9

Hope and Frank were eating blue corn tortillas and mutton soup in Desert Rose. She had dressed casually in jogging suit and tennis shoes, but in the desert, she felt as if she were in an office uniform ready for work.

The door opened, and Tony rushed in. "Anything I should know?" Hope asked.

"Ellen has to see Dennison at one o'clock."

"Can she pull herself together by then?"

Tony shrugged. "She talked with Meghan the night she died. They were in Meghan's suite." He paused. "She left fingerprints everywhere."

"That shouldn't be a problem if she admits she was in the room," Frank said.

"They'll find her fingerprints on the pill bottles in the medicine cabinet."

"Ouch! Why the pill bottles?"

"Here's what I know." Tony related the highlights of his conversation with Ellen, and Hope and Frank plied him with questions. "There's more to tell about our trip to the church."

Hope glanced at her watch. "I'd like to be with Ellen when she talks to Dennison, so let's save that report. Get with Zach. Have him input everything into the file. I need to fly."

She gathered up her purse and jogged down the hall to Ellen's door. It opened at once. "I was just leaving," Ellen said.

"I'll come with you. Dennison has been questioning the hotel staff. As far as I know, the ME still hasn't discovered how Meghan died."

"If he doesn't know how she died, why is he going to question me?"

"He says he has to start investigating now before everyone leaves, just in case it turns out to be murder."

"Sounds as if you agree with him." Ellen stopped and looked at Hope.

"To be honest, I do think Meghan's death is suspicious."

"And you think I had something to do with it."

Hope stammered that she didn't know what to think.

Dennison sat on one side of the table in the meeting room. Next to him was a uniformed officer. They didn't stand up. Dennison pointed to a vacant chair and looked at Ellen. "This is Tahoma Tso, Bureau of Indian Affairs. Have a seat, Mrs. McKenna." He looked up at Hope. "Why are you here, Diamond?"

"Mrs. McKenna is a client."

"You're not a lawyer. You can leave."

"No, I don't think so." Their eyes met; neither looked away.

Tso coughed and Dennison sighed. "All right, stay." Hope sat down. Without confirmation of murder, he was pushing the limits in questioning Ellen, a powerful woman who could have an attorney at her side in a flash, one who could accuse him of violating her rights. Not a good thing if he were trying to get back to Washington.

"Any news on how Meghan died?" Hope asked.

"I'll do the questioning," he said in his icy way. "And I'm talking to Mrs. McKenna." Tso started the tape recorder, and Dennison turned a page on a yellow, legal-sized tablet. "When did you last see Meghan Connors, Mrs. McKenna?"

"The evening she died."

Mr. Tso jerked up his head. "So, you admit it," Dennison said.

"Why shouldn't I? It's true."

"Where did you see her?"

"In her room."

Dennison and Tso shared a look. Obviously, they had expected her to lie or refuse to answer. "I'm glad you're being cooperative, Mrs. McKenna," Dennison said. He smiled, but his smile didn't touch his eyes.

"Why did you go to her room?"

"She invited me in, and I wanted to get to know her better. My uncle had told me that she was being considered for a management position. He wasn't totally convinced she was qualified and asked me for my opinion."

"Do you usually evaluate candidates?"

"Not usually, but I am president of Old School, and I'm free to evaluate candidates whenever I choose to do so."

Hope's eyes widened. This lady was not the same Ellen McKenna who had gone off to church with Tony a few hours ago. That woman would have been flustered and weeping barrels of tears by now. Hope settled back in the chair.

"Did you know your husband was carrying on an affair with Meghan Connors?" Dennison leaned across the table. His eyes drilled into Ellen's.

His look didn't appear to bother her. "I heard gossip, but you know what gossip is, a tale told by an idiot."

Hope bit back a grin at the sight of Dennison clenching his jaw. "You can take it from me that this gossip is true. Our agents questioned your husband last night. He admits he had been taking the girl out to dinner." If he expected a reaction, he was disappointed. Ellen waited without speaking.

"Did Miss Connors tell you they were buying a condo so the two of them could move in together?"

"Meghan said a lot of foolish things and showed me some pictures. I spilled my drink on them and had to use the bathroom."

Dennison hurried on. "When you were in Miss Connors' bathroom, did you go through her medicine cabinet?"

"I did."

"Why?"

"I wanted to see what medications she was on."

Dennison looked at Hope, and she shrugged her shoulders.

"Why were you interested in her medications?"

"I wondered if she was on medication for delusions."

Dennison not only clenched his jaw, which must be a habit, but he clenched his hands together as well.

"I'm not going to kid you, Mrs. McKenna. I think you're playing a game." He looked over at Hope. "And I think Manara spent four hours this morning coaching you." He looked back at Ellen. "I think you murdered that young lady, Mrs. McKenna. I don't know how, but I'm dang sure going to find out."

He was cleaning up his language. A minor victory. "Are we free to go?" Hope asked.

Dennison looked at Tso, who shrugged. He turned back to the ladies. "For the moment." He slammed the tablet on the table. "I'll talk to you later, Diamond."

Hope and Ellen sat down on a sofa in Blue Sky, and George came over from the bar. "Coffee," Hope said. Ellen asked for ginger ale. Hope waited until their drinks were on the table before opening the discussion.

"When I saw you leave this morning with Tony, I was afraid you might need a doctor on hand for your meeting with Dennison."

Ellen smiled. "I had nothing to do with Meghan's death."

"Frankly, I can't blame Dennison for considering you the prime suspect—in the event Meghan was murdered, I mean. You had motive and opportunity."

"I didn't think of it that way. Does Tony think I'm guilty?"

"I just saw him for a few minutes, but he's been in your corner from the start."

"I'm afraid he's changed his mind."

Hope leaned in. "You must tell me what happened at church."

"I can't."

A few seconds passed, and Hope looked her in the eyes. "Please, I have to know."

Ellen hung her head, took a deep breath, and then met Hope's eyes. "You were right to suspect me. I thought I was guilty. When Meghan told me about her affair with Sean, I was so angry that I wished with all my heart that she was dead. Can you imagine how I felt when I heard she had died during the night? I thought I was responsible." Tears sprang to her eyes, and she brushed them aside.

Hope looked away, giving Ellen a chance to recover.

"When Mr. Dennison looked at me last night, I almost confessed."

"What happened to change everything?"

A smile came into Ellen's eyes, and she said, "I went to confession. I told Father Francisco what I just told you. He was very kind. Of course, wishing Meghan harm was sinful, but he assured me that my thoughts did not cause her to die."

Hope remained silent, and Ellen straightened her shoulders. "I need to know how that girl died. I'm over the guilt, but I have a nagging sense that I could have prevented it. What if she did kill herself because I said I wouldn't divorce my husband? Will we ever know the truth?"

"We will do everything possible to discover the truth, and Agent Dennison will do the same thing."

"I feel better telling you," Ellen said. "Will you tell Tony? I don't want him to think I'm guilty."

"I have to tell my whole team. We all need to be working with the same information."

# #

In the Desert Rose, Hope sat down with Tony, Lucy, and Frank. "Get Zach," she said, and Lucy pulled out her cell.

Zach arrived and set his laptop on the table. "What's up?"

Just then Cecelia rolled a large carafe of coffee into the room and smiled at Tony. Frank went to the refreshment station and poured coffee into a large blue mug. "They know how to brew a good cup of coffee here," he said, holding the cup under his nose. "It smells heavenly."

Hope pulled out her notebook and set it in front of her. "Dennison questioned Ellen, and she handled herself like a pro. Dennison was floored. Then, again, I was floored myself." She shook her head and gave them an account of the conversation.

"I wish I could be certain she was innocent," Tony said, twisting his coffee cup back and forth between his hands.

Hope related the story of her confession. "With her background as a Catholic, I can understand why she'd be wracked with guilt."

"*Stupido!*" Tony put his head and hands down on the table. Then he looked up. "You won't believe my crazy thoughts. I thought she confessed the murder to Father Francisco and bribed him to grant her absolution."

"She tells a convincing story," Hope said, "but we can't write her off until we learn a lot more." She flexed her shoulders, stiff from tension.

"If Ellen is innocent, we're back beyond Square One. She, at least, was a logical suspect. She knew Meghan and wanted her dead. The question now is how do we unmask a killer we're being paid to protect when we have absolutely no motive or clue as to who that person might be?"

"I wish you hadn't phrased that question so logically," Frank said. "It sounds like an impossible task."

"We do have our work cut out for us. Any ideas?"

"What does Dennison think?" Tony asked.

"Dennison doesn't confide in me. I'm sure he will work hard at proving Ellen guilty. She had motive and opportunity. The missing piece is means. He'll put the full force of the FBI behind discovering how Meghan was killed."

"You can't fault him for that," Zach said, pulling a can of Coke out of the fridge. "To me, the facts point to Ellen."

"You're wrong, Zach," Tony said.

Hope lifted her hands, palms out. "Our tack will be different. We'll forget about how Meghan died and concentrate on finding the killer through those other two pieces, motive and opportunity. We can't overlook Ellen, but let's see who else comes to the surface."

The phone in the center of the table rang, and Lucy picked it up. "Yes, she's here." She handed the phone to Hope. "It's Mr. Desheenie."

Hope listened, then said, "Disturb her. She will want to know. You sent a car? Good. Thanks for checking."

Hope looked around the table. "Mr. McKenna just landed at Secret Sands' airstrip. Ellen had left 'do-not-disturb' instructions, so Mr. Desheenie called to ask what he should do."

Tony was shuffling out of his chair. "I'd better talk to Ellen. She told him not to come. She could be upset."

"Ask her if there's anything we can do, like arranging a separate suite for her husband," Hope said.

"Good idea." Tony put on his jacket and left.

Frank went back to the cart to top off his coffee. Hope toyed with the gold pendant on a chain around her neck. A scary idea was running through her brain. The more she thought about the idea, the more convinced she became that it was a valid concern.

When Frank sat down, she looked at him. "What if Meghan wasn't the intended target? Could Ellen be in danger?"

"How can we protect her when she's 'sleeping with the enemy,' you mean?" Frank lifted the coffee cup, held it a moment and set it back down. "There's another way to look at that idea."

"I know where you're headed," Hope said. "If Meghan wasn't the target, it doesn't necessarily mean Ellen was. It could be any one of the ladies."

"Right."

"I wonder if Dennison is considering that idea," Hope said.

"He should be if he's any good at his job, but a hint wouldn't hurt," Frank said.

"Zach, you said you had picked up a little information. Let's hear what you've found out."

"I checked on the charity foundation. The Janai Ross Foundation leadership team includes herself as chair and Robert as chief financial officer. He has a staff that handles requests and processes donations. He approves any amount over $10,000."

"Is everything on the up and up?" Hope twisted around in the chair and crossed her legs.

"There's no overarching federal control," Zach said. "In California, the Attorney General has oversight. I suppose Robert could, with his financial expertise, figure a way to stash away a few bucks."

"I'd like to know why Robert is here. What's charitable donations got to do with this conference?" Frank asked.

"Good question," Hope said. "The answer likely depends on the reason for the meeting," She walked over to the refreshment bar, lifted the carafe of coffee, set it back down. Her nerves were already jangled. She pulled out an apple juice. "Anything else, Zach?"

"You asked about Ellen's heirs. The company has passed down the female line. Ellen has no daughters. It looks as if the tradition will end, and her share will go to her son, Patrick. Sean will act as legal guardian until Patrick comes of age. Sean is in for a big chunk of change free and clear, about $100 million."

"Nice motive," Hope said. "Motives seem to be popping up all over. We need to sift through the sand and find the truth."

She shifted again in her chair. Chindi was poking at her thoughts, trying to confuse her. "One of these women is in great danger."

CHAPTER 10

"Do you know Agent Dennison's schedule?" Hope asked Mr. Desheenie, who was standing behind the reception desk.

"He gave me this list." He pointed to a lined, yellow sheet of paper. "I will take the women to the meeting room." He lowered his eyes, "Excuse me, please. I must see Ms. Fallbrook."

Hope glanced at the schedule of appointments. Lydia at two, Gloria at three, and Janai at four. She hurried to the Gray Feather room to catch Lydia before she met with Dennison.

"Would you mind if I sat in on your meeting, Lydia?" Hope asked.

"If you like." They walked into the room together.

Dennison looked up. "I suppose it's hopeless to get rid of you, Diamond."

Mr. Tso nodded at both women as they sat down across the table. Dennison introduced Lydia to Tso and said, "Ms. Fallbrook, you spent time with Meghan Connors the evening she died. I'd like to hear about your conversation."

"I've made some notes." Lydia opened her purse and pulled out sheets of small notepaper that matched the supply provided in the rooms. She looked over the pages.

"Before dinner, a group of us sat outside and had a drink and smoked."

"Who all was at the table?"

Lydia read off the names on one of the sheets. "Dimitri, Gloria, Margo, Meghan, and I."

Even though the tape recorder was whirling, Dennison wrote down the names. "Did Meghan seem despondent?"

"No, I wouldn't say despondent, just quiet. She was younger than the rest of us. I doubt she had much to say."

"Did any of the others seem interested in her?"

"Not that I noticed. I was talking to Dimitri, and Gloria was talking to Margo. Meghan didn't seem interested in any of us. She smoked a lot. I noticed that."

"Did you talk with her later?"

"We talked after the program at the campfire. I could tell the chanting and dancing made her nervous."

"Was anything else making her nervous?" Dennison smiled at Lydia, apparently pleased she was opening up with information that could prove helpful. He had a warm smile, and Lydia responded with a smile of her own.

"Here's my impression. Don't take it for gospel." Lydia coughed. She cleared her scratchy throat and leaned forward. "Meghan lived in a very small world. She was twenty years old, but this trip was the first time she had ever been outside the City of Pittsburgh, the first time she'd ever flown. She lived in the same apartment building all her life and knew all the neighbors. I think the people here, the desert, even the food unnerved her." Lydia stopped. "Do you mind if I smoke?"

Dennison shook his head and looked at Hope.

"It's fine with me, Lydia," Hope said.

She pulled a cigarette out of her purse and lit up. After a few deep drags, she said, "After the dancers left, we started down the hill. Meghan wanted a cigarette. I did too. She was out, so I gave her a pack with a few Marlboros."

Lydia took a deep breath and pinched her lips. "She made sure to tell me she'd pay me back as soon as she was able to buy cigarettes at the shop. 'Mrs. McKenna said I can put anything on the bill and not pay for it,' she told me." Lydia paused and blinked at tears. "I think she finally relaxed when she talked about her job at the candy factory."

"I'd be interested to hear what she told you about that job," Dennison said. His tone was more pleasant with Lydia than with Ellen or herself.

Hope frowned. Lydia had gotten Meghan to talk about herself much more than she had at dinner. Probably because Lydia was a smoker. Smokers seemed to enjoy a camaraderie.

"Meghan said she was being promoted to management. She said Mr. McKenna liked her and thought she was talented. I had a different opinion if you know what I mean." Lydia stopped talking and frowned.

"Anything else?" Dennison asked.

"At the hotel, she said she had to take care of something. She seemed nervous about whatever she intended to do."

"Did she give you any hints about what she intended to do?"

"No, she thanked me for the cigarettes and walked inside. I stayed on the patio and had a nightcap. That's all I can tell you."

"Thank you. You've been very helpful." He smiled again, then paused. "One more question." Dennison put his pen down on the yellow tablet and looked Lydia in the eyes.

"Why are you here? You run a big pharmaceutical firm. Why are you in the middle of the desert with three other ladies who should have stayed home?"

Lydia smiled. "I must say, Mr. Dennison, you have a direct manner. I will be equally direct. Why we're here is none of your business." Lydia stood up and walked out. Hope followed quickly.

"I'm going to change and go to the pool," Lydia said. "If you need anything, you can catch me there."

"I'll let Frank know where you'll be." Hope turned back to the meeting room to tell Dennison about Sean McKenna, but the door had closed.

Wearing swim trucks and the white terrycloth robe provided by the hotel, Frank found Lydia sitting at a table under an umbrella. The sun was high, and the red rocks shone like rubies.

Frank smiled a greeting. Lydia had an exotic look, with high cheekbones and deep-set eyes. Her hair hung loose on her shoulders, blowing in the slight breeze. The deep rusts and golds of her cover-up mirrored the color of her hair and eyes. Although Lydia was without her usual make-up and designer clothes, Frank had never found her so attractive as he did at that moment, looking natural and relaxed. She was smoking and drinking a mojito.

"Looks good," he said, pushing the button for service. "Mind if I join you?"

"I always enjoy the company of a handsome man," she said in her rumbly voice. "You don't smoke, do you?" When he shook his head, she moved the ashtray to the other side of the table.

"I wish I could say the same, but I've smoked since I was fifteen."

"I smoked for five years myself." He sat down on one of the green-and-yellow padded chairs.

"Why did you quit?"

Frank grinned. "I was going with a gal, and her pa told me I'd have to quit smoking if I wanted to come inside the house."

"Did you end up marrying the girl?"

"No, she dropped me for a fellow in the Navy."

"What did you do?"

"I joined the Army." Lydia chuckled and crushed out her cigarette.

"I'm curious, Lydia. How did your family come to own a company like Grand Med Pharmaceuticals?"

A surprised smile came to her eyes, but she answered. "Lucky timing. My Great Grandfather Melvin founded our company. He was an out-of-work chemist in Chicago during the Great Depression. A cousin got him a cleaning job at the university. The pay was free room and board."

She closed her eyes a moment. "The kicker was that it gave him access to the library. He read about the work of scientists who had discovered that viruses could be grown on the membrane of chicken eggs. As you probably know, their work eventually paved the way for vaccines."

She sipped her mojito. "By all accounts, Grandpa Melvin was a great talker. A professor friend introduced him to a banker. He talked his way into a small loan to start a company to produce a vaccine." She paused. "That is the over simplified story of Grand Med."

George came around the corner with a mojito, and Lydia gestured that he should give it to Frank and bring her another.

"Did you aspire to pharmaceuticals as a tiny tot?" Frank asked when George had gone.

"Hardly. I wanted to be a singer, but I didn't have a voice. Then I wanted to be a ballerina, but I didn't have strong ankles. Finally, I wanted to be a writer. No special physique required."

"You're a liberal arts person at heart."

"Yes, I love plays, concerts, ballet, and opera."

Frank smiled, picturing her in a box at the opera. He shook his head and asked, "Why didn't you pursue writing? How did you let your dreams slip away?"

"It's not polite to look into another person's soul, Frank."

He put up his hands. "I'm sorry. I didn't mean to pry. Please, forgive me."

After a long pause, she said, "My father was the patriarch of our family. He told me what I was going to do with my life. I rebelled at majoring in chemistry and compromised on business. I married a classmate right after I graduated. It was a disaster. Fortunately, Victor met someone else, and we divorced after a year.

That experience soured me on marriage, and I went to work for the company."

Frank reached over and took hold of her hand. "I'm sorry, Lydia. Your dreams didn't slip away; they were crushed."

Her eyelids blinked rapidly, and she said, "Tell me about yourself. Where did you grow up?" She sank back in her chair and smiled.

Happy and painful memories flooded Frank's mind. His voice took on a soft accent reminiscent of his childhood. "The 'Big Easy,'" he said, "but it wasn't easy for a lot of us."

He hesitated, and Lydia said there had to be more to the story.

"Pop worked pretty regular at Benson's Funeral Parlor. Can you imagine the stories the kids put into my head about Pop being a vampire and sucking blood?" Frank played with the rim of his glass. "Talk about nightmares."

Lydia lowered her eyes, and Frank went on. "But Pop played a mean trumpet, and all of us kids in the neighborhood idolized jazz musicians. He'd play at the local bars on a Saturday night, and I'd sneak in just to hear the music." Frank smiled at the memory.

"We didn't have much money, but every week, Pop, Mama and me'd be up front and center in our Sunday-go-to-meeting clothes at the Free Mission Baptist Church."

He stopped talking and took a deep breath. "My folks were two of the 1,833 people killed in New Orleans during Hurricane Katrina. Their roof just caved in on them."

"I'm sorry," Lydia said. George was back with the mojito, and he set it in front of Lydia. Frank smiled up at him and nodded.

After George left, Frank said, "I was out of the country. The owners of the place where Pop worked saw that my folks were buried proper. If you remember, graveyards flooded, and Katrina set coffins adrift. The only thing Mr. Benson could save for me was Pop's trumpet. It's all bent up out of shape, but I treasure it."

"Is that why you stayed in the service?"

"That was part of the reason. The other part was that I looked so dang good in the uniform."

Lydia laughed out loud, and her eyes sparkled.

"You should laugh more often. You look like a teenager."

"Not much to laugh about in my business," she said, and the smile vanished. She sipped the mojito.

"You said your company got its start with vaccines. I assume Grand Med was in the running for something similar during the pandemic."

She pulled out a cigarette and tapped it on the table. Frank picked up her lighter, walked around and lit the cigarette, catching the reflection of the flame in her eyes. She smiled and inhaled the smoke.

"You asked if we perfected a vaccine. We tried, but it didn't work out." She frowned and looked down at her drink.

He sat down, waiting, letting her take her time. "Like everyone else, we were scrambling to find a cure and a vaccine. Margo thought she had the answer, but I looked at the data and said it was too risky. I'm not a trained chemist, and Margo used her clout with Mark to ram the drug through testing. Unfortunately, the FDA bounced it because of possible side effects. That failure took a toll on our reputation and our resources."

She stuffed out her cigarette and got up. "Let's take a dip in the pool."

At three o'clock, Hope sat down with Gloria, Dennison, and Officer Tso in Gray Feather. Gloria's large, expressive eyes flashed at Dennison. She had not talked with Meghan alone. Her one observation was that Meghan did not seem the type of girl who would commit suicide. Hope had already let go of that theory, but Dennison looked interested. Gloria had formed that impression because of Meghan's body language.

"She seemed to be laughing at us, like she knew a secret that would blow us all away."

After going through his routine questions, Dennison looked Gloria in the eye and asked why the ladies had come to the desert. Gloria smiled and shrugged. "Janai called the meeting. You'll have to ask her."

Hope stayed seated when Gloria left the room. Dennison gave her a mocking look and said, "Yes?"

"Did you know that Sean McKenna arrived here a little while ago?"

"What! Have you talked to him?"

"No, but Tony has. He'll fill you in whenever you like."

Dennison clenched his teeth. "Thank you for telling me. Appreciate it."

"One other thing," she said. "We were discussing the possibility that maybe Meghan wasn't the intended target. If so, Ellen or any of the other women could be in danger. Especially with Sean here. Have you been working along those lines yourself?"

"The thought had crossed my mind," he said. "Anything else?"

"No." Hope waved and went out the door.

CHAPTER 11

Matt Dennison looked at Tso, shook his head, and took out his cell. He punched in a number. "I just learned that Sean McKenna arrived here at Secret Sands. I thought you bunch were keeping an eye on him."

He had put through a routine request asking the Bureau in Pittsburgh to let him know of any unusual activity that involved the McKennas. Heading out of his house with a suitcase in hand should have been recognized as unusual activity and triggered a call to New Mexico. There was a miscue, and Sean was able to fly out to the desert in the company jet without anybody knowing.

"What is his reason for coming, do you think?" Tso asked.

"That's one question I plan to ask the man. I would have gotten better answers if I'd caught him before he talked to his wife and Diamond's people. That's out the door now."

He looked at his watch. "Janai Ross is coming at four. Diamond will remind her that we don't know how Connors died, which pretty much hog-ties us. Ross knows the score. She'll call for her attorney if she doesn't want to answer questions. I'd like to know what secret stuff brought these women out here."

He looked at the tape recorder. "She won't want to be recorded, and she won't want to talk to two of us. You might as well go. Take the tape and email me the transcripts."

Tso nodded, took the tape out of the machine, and left.

"Dang!" He slammed his tablet on the table. How did Sean McKenna slip out here unnoticed? He hated being caught unawares, especially by an outsider, especially by anyone named Hope Diamond.

# #

The therapy pool was located just outside the Gray Feather. Janai had gone into the water while Dennison was talking with Gloria. Hope pushed open the outside door that led to the pool. She took off her tennis shoes and sat on the edge, dangling her feet in the water. A little hot, but it was the perfect place to talk. No one else was around.

"The ladies have all met with Dennison," Hope told Janai.

"How did Ellen do?"

"Fine. Ellen was poised and answered all of his questions."

"That takes a weight off my shoulders."

"Ellen's husband, Sean, just arrived." Janai raised an eyebrow but didn't comment.

"Dennison asked Lydia about the purpose of your meeting. She told him it was none of his business."

"What has our meeting got to do with Meghan?"

Hope patted the surface of the water with her fingers. "Dennison could be thinking the reason why you're all here is the motive for the murder, if indeed it was murder," she said, keeping her eyes on the water. "Which is not a bad assumption."

"You'd like to know why we're here, too, wouldn't you?"

Hope looked at Janai. "Very much so. Trying to keep you all safe without knowing the reason you're here puts me at a handicap."

"All right, listen. I suppose you'll tell your team." Hope nodded. "I am here to lay the groundwork for running for president of the United States on the Republican ticket." She raised an eyebrow, as if expecting a reaction.

"Why did you invite these specific women?" Janai's answer fired up Hope's safety concerns.

"Financial support is critical, of course, but I'll expect the women to hold events where I can meet influential figures."

"I see. They have friends among the powers that be in different states."

"We also share similar values. I'm Pro-life, as is Ellen. My cosmetics company is working at becoming more environmentally friendly, and so is Lydia's. Gloria is from Greece and her husband is from Venezuela. They're sensitive to racial equity issues, with which I agree. Not all my views are in line with historic Republican values, but change is happening."

She sighed and shook her head. "Of course, if any one of us proves to be a murderer, my hopes will fly in the wind just like sand in the desert."

"I'm just speculating, but if Meghan wasn't the intended target, you could be in danger."

Janai crouched down until the water came over her shoulders, then she stood up straight. "All right. I'll think about giving Agent Dennison a few hints, but I won't tell him I'm planning to run for office myself. I don't want that idea floating around Washington just yet."

Hope's shoulders jerked when she turned and saw the Shadow Lady standing behind her with a large, striped towel and a hostile expression. She blamed Hope for allowing Meghan to die at Janai's conference.

"Time to get ready for the FBI," Audrey said.

"I'll sit in on your interview with Dennison if you don't mind," Hope said.

Janai stepped out of the pool, and Audrey slipped the towel around her shoulders. Janai laughed. "All right," she said to Hope. "Keep me honest."

Pushing up her joggers, Hope splashed the warm water on her legs. Janai running for president lifted the lid to other motives. Jealousy, for example, could arouse strong passions. Nobody was jealous when a name in the headlines became president. But if the president were a friend, feelings could heat up. Lydia had mentioned Janai's ambitious agenda. *Was she jealous enough to make sure Janai didn't get elected?*

Hope glanced at the window of the Gray Feather. The sun glared off the glass, and she couldn't see inside. Ever since she saw Meghan's body, chindi had been haunting her whenever she was alone.

She had pulled her gun on Dennison, for heaven's sakes. At least he hadn't mentioned the incident during the sessions with the other women. Navajo myths had no business in the middle of a murder investigation. The problem was it wasn't a Navajo myth. It was her own intuition prodding her to do something. Someone had murder in mind, and her clients were in danger.

"Where's Ross?" Dennison asked as Hope entered the meeting room. He was wearing his hat, but Tso was absent.

"She's coming. Have you reached any conclusions?"

"You're one pushy lady, Diamond. What makes you think I'd tell you what I've learned?" The ice had cracked. The remark was rude, but there was a smile in his voice, if not on his face.

"We all want to find out what happened to Meghan Connors. These people will be going home on Thursday. Believe me, you won't be able to keep them here if they want to leave. Their attorneys will see to that. It would be nice to have the matter wrapped up before people scatter. Wouldn't you agree?"

"So?"

"You learned from the maid about the missing pieces of candy in Meghan's room, right?"

"How did you find that out?"

"No matter. Did you have the candy analyzed?" She stepped over to a table, poured herself a glass of water from the iced pitcher, and took a drink.

He was silent until she was back at the table. "Tell you what," he said, his head tilted at an angle. He pointed a finger at her. "I'll tell you the lab results when I get the report if you tell me the reason for this confab in the desert."

"Hello," Janai said, coming into the room.

"You're late," Dennison said. "Sit down, and let's get started."

Hope cringed and stood up. "Mr. Dennison and I have agreed to exchange a little information, Janai. It may help us to find the truth sooner."

"All right," Janai said and sat down. "What can I do for you, Mr. Dennison?"

"Did you have any conversations with Meghan Connors?" He turned over a sheet on his tablet. Instead of switching on the recorder, he picked up his pen. Janai Ross was the most powerful woman at Secret Sands and would not want to be recorded. Dennison was savvy when it came to high-profile suspects.

"I had a brief conversation with Meghan about the Icelandic Wind gift sets I gave to the guests." Janai had probably left a set in Dennison's room, but he didn't comment. "Meghan was appreciative and said, and I quote, 'It smells good. Not like that stinky stuff I bought at the drugstore down the corner.'"

Dennison's lips twitched. The girl had had a curious way of expressing herself. "That's all?" he asked.

"Yes, I met Meghan here for the first time, so I'm afraid I can't tell you anything about her death."

Dennison put down his pen. "Here's something you can tell me. Why did you bring these ladies out to the reservation for a secret powwow?"

Janai folded her hands in front of her, elbows on the table. "We came to discuss the next presidential election, with an eye toward supporting a candidate."

Dennison sat silent, twisting the FBI ring on the pinkie finger of his left hand. Then he leaned back, head on his hand, and looked at her for a long moment. "Would I be way off the mark if I suggested that you were that candidate?"

Hope's sip of water went down the wrong way. She choked and looked at Dennison. His eyes didn't move away from Janai. After several seconds, Janai gave him a gracious smile. "Not way off," she said. "That is my private business, and I'd appreciate your keeping it in this room."

He nodded. "That opens a whole different discussion." Instead of speaking, he sat there looking at her, head on hand, eyebrows raised.

"You're thinking I could be the victim of an assassination plot because I want to become president. I'm not even in the running yet. My decision depends on the meetings here at Secret Sands, which, because of Miss Connors' unfortunate death, haven't yet begun. If I can't gain endorsement from these ladies, I'll drop the idea."

He straightened up. "Did Meghan Connors or Ellen McKenna know anything about you that Audrey Tremont or Robert Halloway might think she'd be better off not knowing?"

"Audrey or Robert? You must be joking."

"I'm not. As I'm sure you know, most murders are committed by family or close associates." Hope's thoughts were moving in the same direction.

Dennison took his time before saying, "Maybe someone tried to get at you, and Connors helped you dodge a bullet."

A hostile silence resonated in the air. Janai said, "I would be horrified to think that were true." She stood up and left.

Hope followed her out and closed the door. "We have to take Dennison's warning seriously," she said as they walked along the hallway.

When they reached Janai's door, the lady said, "Hope, I am not going to change my plans because of what Agent Dennison thinks. I am confident you and your team will make sure nothing more happens at this conference." She inserted her key and opened the door. "I will see you at the social."

That missing candy became more important. How long would it be before Dennison had the lab results? *If the candy showed evidence of poison, the killer might be planning the next attack.*

CHAPTER 12

"This trouble is all your fault, Hope Diamond!" Audrey came rushing down the corridor. "Janai could have been murdered!"

"What makes you think someone is trying to kill Janai?"

The woman was panting. "I can put two and two together same as anybody else. Who'd want to kill Meghan Connors? Nobody, that's who. Somebody is trying to kill Janai. You're responsible for bringing us to this wilderness, Hope Diamond."

Audrey was shaking. "I'm going to insist that we all leave here today." She knocked at Janai's door, opened it with a key, and entered.

Hope went back to the Desert Rose. She pulled a Coke out of the fridge for a quick hit of caffeine. Frank walked in. When he got close to her, he asked, "Everything all right?"

Hope drew a deep breath and let the words rush out about her encounter with Audrey.

"I've only met Audrey a few times," he said. "I wouldn't have classified her as an hysterical woman."

Hope swung around to the window, allowing the red rocks and blue sky to calm her emotions. When she turned back to Frank, she felt grounded. "She has a lot of influence over Janai. It won't surprise me if we all have to pack up and leave."

Frank rubbed a finger across his chin. "This meeting is too important to Janai to allow her secretary to dictate terms." Frank's calm manner helped ease the stiffness in her shoulders.

The team arrived together and helped themselves to drinks. "I'll wait for coffee," Frank said, taking a bag of pretzels to the table.

Hope sat down across from Tony. "We're all interested in what happened when Sean McKenna arrived."

Tony looked around the table. "The van pulled up, and Ellen walked outside. I sat by the fountain where I could see what was happening. Sean rushed up to give her a hug, but she pushed back. They stood outside and talked for a long time. I figured I'd stay until they came inside and take my cue from her."

"What were your impressions of Sean?" Hope asked.

"I saw his face when she pushed him away, and he seemed crushed. I don't know if he was hurt or surprised that she didn't fall into his arms when he'd flown out to her rescue."

"What does he look like?"

"He's a very big guy. Muscle, not fat. He has dark, wavy hair and blue eyes. He had on a black Brioni suit, probably out of respect for Meghan." Tony was as much a fashionista as Hope was herself and recognized all the designers.

"He must have been sweltering out in the sun without a hat," Tony said. "He talks with a strong Pittsburgh accent, like Ellen, and his hands never stop. He could've been Italian." The others laughed, and Tony clasped his hands in front of him.

"Where is he staying?"

"Ellen asked Mr. Desheenie to have his suitcase taken to her room." Hope knit her brows. You couldn't prevent clients from doing what they wanted to do.

"Ellen introduced us and invited me to join them for a drink. Sean ordered an *Ahrn City* beer, as they say in Pittsburgh, meaning Iron City. George brought a Coors. Sean drank it and relaxed, but he was wondering why I was hanging around."

Tony stopped talking as Cecelia rolled in the coffee cart. "Perfect timing," Frank said. He poured coffee into a blue mug that seemed to be his favorite. Cecelia shot Tony a smile and pushed the cart out the door.

Frank piled blueberry muffins on a large plate. "Enjoy," he said, passing the plate to the others.

"Did Sean say anything about Meghan?" Hope asked. She took a muffin off the plate and peeled off the paper liner.

"I could tell he didn't like talking about her with me there, but he answered Ellen's questions. Meghan called Sean that night and told him what she had said to his wife. He was shocked. He believes Meghan committed suicide because he told her he had no intention of marrying her."

"The story adds weight to the suicide theory," Hope said. "I can imagine that after Meghan talked to Sean, she went out to the patio to have a drink and smoke. The question is if she committed suicide, how did she do it?"

"Sean admits he was flattered by Meghan's attentions," Tony said. "He took her out for dinner a time or two. He swears that's all that happened. He doesn't know why she thought he was going to divorce his wife and marry her."

"Dennison will talk to Sean. I will try to be there." She locked eyes with Tony. "Dennison may ask you about Sean. Please tell him everything you've told us."

Tony grimaced but said, "Okay."

Frank turned to Hope and asked, "Did you learn anything from Dennison's interviews?"

Hope gave them the gist of what she had learned from Ellen, Lydia, and Gloria. "I'll save the more interesting bits from Janai until after your reports."

She pushed away the Coke and poured a cup of coffee. "Frank, you spent time with Lydia. Anything we should know?"

"There is friction between Lydia and Margo." He explained that Margo had influenced Mark to push through a Covid drug, and it backfired."

"So, Lydia has a motive if Meghan was not the intended target," Hope said.

"Margo could have one, too," Tony said.

Zach cleared his throat. "Theoretically, I don't think Margo would have as strong a motive for killing Lydia as Ellen would have for killing Meghan. My reason is that Margo just works at the company, whereas Ellen was worried about losing her husband."

"I disagree, Zach," Tony said. "Margo—and all of the other people here—could have as strong a motive as Ellen, even if it wasn't personal."

"You're just blinded by Ellen's personality," Zach put in. "Lots of sweet ladies have been murderers throughout history. Look at the facts. Dennison has the right notion."

"I'm not blinded by anything, Zach! You've just got the hots for Margo."

"I don't have the hots for anybody, Tony!" Fury came through in his voice.

"Hold it," Hope said. "Let's put that kind of talk away. We've got to find a murderer, and we don't have much time. We can't be fighting among ourselves."

Tony's face flamed a bright red. He stood up and went to the refrigerator and pulled out a bottle of root beer. Hope looked at Frank, and he nodded. He would handle it.

Hope said, "Lucy, have you had any luck with Gloria?"

"No, I haven't talked with her today."

"Okay, then—"

"Wait, I have a little information," Tony said. His voice was quiet, and he held the bottle in both hands. "I overheard an argument Gloria and Dimitri were having in Greek on her patio. The words were coming fast, but I caught the gist. Gloria wants to bid on a contract to build a cruise ship. Dimitri doesn't approve, and he said her father doesn't either."

"Can she sign without their approval?" Frank asked.

"Yes, that's the issue. She says the deal would open up a new market for Global, but Dimitri claims they don't have the expertise to pull it off."

"What did Gloria say?" Hope asked.

"Global must expand to survive. The Chinese have already moved in on cargo shipbuilding and in 2020 cut steel for their first cruise ship."

"It's a motive for both of them," Frank said, looking at Tony and Zach. "Gloria wants Dimitri out of the way to expand the business, and Dimitri wants her out of the way to have a shot at running the company. Both are very passionate people, which makes both of them dangerous."

"It adds to our catalog of motives," Hope said.

She looked at Lucy. "Did you learn why Robert brought the rifle?"

"I brought up cowboy movies and shooting and asked if he ever went hunting. He said he goes deer hunting in Canada. George is taking him to a shooting range for a little target practice."

"I hope that's all he has in mind," Hope said.

She looked around the table. "I found out the reason why Janai invited these women to the meeting."

"Great," Zach said. "We can finally line up our ducks in the right row."

"Janai wants the women to back her run for president on the Republican ticket."

Comments buzzed around the table. Lucy gave the men a big smile. "Good for her!"

Hope described the interview between Dennison and Janai. "He's sharper than I thought. Janai told him the meetings were to support a candidate for president. He pegged her right off as the candidate. He warned Janai to beware of Audrey and Robert. Most homicides are committed by family members or close associates.

We need to heed that warning, especially now that Sean McKenna is at Secret Sands."

"What was Janai's reaction?" Frank asked.

"Janai is going ahead with her plans. She expects us to protect all the women. Zach, you're the best person to learn more about Robert since his area is finance. Lucy, add Audrey to your special interest people."

"I'll try. She stays pretty invisible in her room. I wonder if Janai will hire another executive assistant and split up the work between company business and her run for office."

Hope looked at Frank, who was nodding his head. Lucy had a knack for putting her finger on a point they had overlooked. "Good observation," Hope said. "Audrey is very possessive of her relationship with Janai. She might not like sharing her position of trust with someone else."

"Could Janai have a second person in the room whenever she's meeting with Robert or Audrey?" Frank asked.

Hope rocked back in the chair. You didn't issue orders to Janai. "I'll try to find a tactful way to suggest it. You asked why Robert was here. He must be helping with the financial end of the campaign."

"He did bring that campaign fundraising book."

"We've heard strong motives against lots of people," Tony said, looking over at Zach. "How do we narrow down the list?"

"Zach, create a list of all the motives we've discussed," Hope said. "To answer your question, Tony, we'll focus on opportunity and tactics. You all looked around the property. Where are the best opportunities to commit a crime here at the hotel?"

"I ran the information through my probability model," Zach said. He clicked keys on the computer. "The top threat area is the pool because it's isolated. The therapy pool came in second. It's not quite so dangerous because it's close to occupied parts of the building. The sauna was third because it's elevated, which makes it difficult to sneak up on a person."

He explained that the trails and campground were a mixed bag. Low risk because it's unlikely guests would go there alone. High risk if they did decide to stroll into those areas alone. Similarly, the rooms were low risk because not everyone had expertise in getting through locked doors. On the other hand, if the villain knocked at the door and were admitted, the risk would be high.

"Thanks, Zach." Hope said. "Let's make a point to be with the women at both pools. What other steps can we take?"

"We should ask for their plans each day," Frank said. "That way, we can make sure we're on the spot."

"Make it casual," Hope said. "We don't want to create a panic."

"What's the program this evening," Lucy asked.

"The seven o'clock cocktail hour, as usual. Dinner is in the dining room," Hope said. "After dinner, Zach will entertain with his own special brand of comedy."

Everyone clapped and hooted, "Zach! Zach! Zach!"

"I haven't had time to write much new material. Don't be disappointed if you hear the same old jokes."

"We'll laugh anyway," Lucy said. "I love your routine, old or new."

Hope always had the sensation that Zach entered a phone booth as a computer geek and emerged as a stand-up comic. She was lucky to have him on the team. She needed a tech-savvy employee. Zach had worked in the IT industry for fifteen years. When his company was acquired, he walked away with an attractive package. A friend told her about his computer moxie. She took in his comedy act at Joke Spinners and spent several hours over margaritas persuading him to visit Diamond Security.

# #

Zach opened the middle drawer of the credenza, pulled out a thick folder and set it on the desk. As he leafed through the pages, he put a hand on his forehead because of his flare-up with Tony over Margo. He pushed the folder aside. Truth be told, he found her attractive. She was ten years older than he was, but that didn't matter when they were together. She was bright and interesting, and he liked talking to her.

Locking his computer in the safe, Zach shuffled his brain cells over to the humorous side of life. His Uncle Ezra had inspired his love of comedy. Uncle Ezra was a Biblical scholar, and he encouraged Zach to study ancient Jewish humor.

It was from the past 100 years, however, that Zach pulled his material, especially the old Catskill jokes. "Patient: 'I have a ringing in my ears.' Doctor: 'Don't answer!'" He'd update jokes like that to, "Patient: 'I have a ringing in my ears.' Doctor: 'Let the machine get it.'" What made people laugh were his body language and cadence. He'd practice for hours in front of a mirror.

He looked at himself in the long mirror by the closet. Like his ancestors, humor helped Zach cope with life. At forty, he was still looking for that special love. He wasn't handsome like Tony, nor did he have Frank's *je ne sais quoi* that made him attractive to women. Thanks to Frank and Diamond Security's fitness requirements, though, he was now buff. He grinned and raised his fists over his shoulders, like the Charles Atlas ads in the old comic books he collected. His appearance had a funny uniqueness, and he drew on it for his routine. He was five-feet-nine-inches tall, had a high forehead, dark hair, and heavy-lidded eyes, the kind people called "bedroom eyes."

He stopped. A line popped into his head. *That's good!* He rushed over to his joke folder and added: *I have bedroom eyes. Too bad my eyes haven't seen many bedrooms.* Another line came to him, and he wrote it down. *I'm a member of Mensa International. I wish brains had the sex appeal of a Lamborghini.*

He smiled. He was on a roll!

CHAPTER 13

"*Vestito bello!*" Tony said, taking in Hope's one-shoulder black jumpsuit. He cocked his head. "Simple, audacious. Not Italian. French." He kissed her on both cheeks.

"You're right." Tony had a great sense of style, and she smiled at his approval. She had fallen in love with the outfit at a fashion show in Paris. She preferred the vivid colors of Pucci and Versace, but black seemed appropriate for this evening.

"I'm looking forward to meeting Sean McKenna. Do you think he and Ellen will join us?"

"They said they were coming." Tony glanced about. "Here comes Margo."

Margo wore a satiny, pumpkin-colored dress that swished as she walked. "Good evening. I see George is ready for us," she said and headed to the bar.

"Are things square between you and Zach?"

"I talked to Frank. I'm sorry I lost my cool. I'll apologize."

Hope nodded toward the hall. Sean and Ellen were coming in. Although a tall woman, Ellen looked tiny beside Sean's massive frame. Ellen seemed skittish as she introduced her husband. "It's nice to meet you, Mr. McKenna," Hope said, shaking hands. He had a strong grip. His left arm stayed around Ellen's shoulders. *Was he being protective or preventing her from leaving?*

"Same here." He nodded at Tony, who said hello and walked over to Gloria. "Ellen's told me how helpful you've been. She's never had to deal with the police before."

"It's hard on everybody, but we all have to put up with being questioned."

Robert Halloway joined them, and they sat down on the chairs and sofa near the bar. Robert and Sean fell into easy conversation about football. Ellen didn't say much, but she appeared interested in the discussion.

"I played left tackle," Sean said. "I screwed up my leg and ended up retiring."

"Tough break," Robert said.

"It was a tough break." Sean laughed. "The docs put in a lot of hardware. I can tell when it's about to rain. In Pittsburgh, it rains a lot. My leg feels great out here in the desert."

George brought over drinks for everyone. Hope thanked him for the ginger ale. He always remembered what each person drank.

"I'm curious how you handle charitable donations," Robert said to Sean. "I run the foundation for Icelandic Wind, and I'm always on the look-out for ideas."

Sean smiled at Ellen and took a swig of his beer. "We're in the candy business, so we invest a lot in child welfare, childhood diseases, and K-through-12 literacy." He pointed his thumb at Ellen. "My wife earmarks her own special interests, like Catholic

Charities, churches and schools. How do you handle things at your show?"

"I'm streamlining the process to make more efficient use of our funding," Robert said. "Like you, maybe dedicate our resources to a specific area where we could really make a difference. Perhaps charities that deal in disfigurements or teenage issues, like pregnancy. Teenage girls are a target audience, so we like to invest in them."

Hope fingered her glass. Robert hadn't confided to Tony about his ideas. They seemed sound. Even so, the huge amounts of money he controlled troubled her. *Could money be the motive for what had happened here?*

Matt Dennison, wearing his cowboy hat, strolled into Blue Sky and stopped by Sean. "You're new here," he said, addressing Ellen's husband.

"Yes, I'm Sean McKenna." He got to his feet. He was about two inches taller than Dennison and much broader, at least 300 pounds. "I arrived this afternoon. And you are?"

"You're paired up with this lady," Dennison said, pointing to Ellen.

"Sean, this is Agent Dennison, of the FBI," Hope said. "He's here because of Meghan." Dennison sent her his mocking look.

"I see." Sean did not extend a hand. "Have you learned how Meghan died?"

"Look, pal, that isn't the way things work. I question you. Not the other way around."

Sean puffed out every ounce of his 300 pounds. "I don't think my question was out of line, Agent Dennison, so I suggest you watch your tone."

Every head turned toward Dennison. "No offense intended, pal, but in a murder investigation, you don't answer questions from suspects. You ask 'em."

"Suspects? I just got here."

"Let's save it for the morning, unless you don't care whether everyone hears what you have to say."

Janai Ross arrived and joined the group surrounding Sean. The flowery fragrance of her perfume filled the space. "Good evening," she said.

"Janai, this is my husband, Sean." Janai extended her hand.

"Very nice to meet you," Sean said. "Won't you join us?"

"Thank you, I'd like that. First, I was hoping to snatch Hope away for a few moments." She turned to the FBI agent. "Mr. Dennison, you're not too busy for a quick word, are you?"

As Hope moved away with Janai, Dennison said, "I'll see you in the morning, McKenna."

The three of them went out to the patio. Hope sent a questioning glance to Janai. She hadn't talked with her since the exchange with Audrey. Janai shook her head and smiled. They weren't going to bolt.

"What's on your mind?" Dennison asked. He was much taller than Janai, and she looked up at him.

"I've thought about what you said, Mr. Dennison. I'm not deliberately ignoring your warning, but it's important that I go ahead with the meetings. The ladies and I will meet at ten tomorrow. Does that fit in with your plans?"

He shrugged. Obviously, he'd had experience dealing with wealthy people in Washington and knew he wasn't going to change her mind. "I'll be questioning Sean McKenna. He thought it necessary to jump on a plane and come out here, and I'd like to know why. I've talked to most everyone else. After that, I'll pack up and call it a day."

When he turned to Hope, his stare lingered a long moment, almost as if he were seeing her for the first time. She sent him a questioning glance. He shook his head and said, "Unless you know more than you're telling, Diamond. We haven't had a real sit-down, and your people have been chatting with the suspects."

"Suspects?" Janai said.

"In my book, everyone here is a suspect, including you. Nevertheless, I'll be leaving tomorrow. Mind you, I think there's a murderer loose in this hotel, but without support from the medical examiner, there's nothing more I can do. I'd caution you to be careful because you could be in danger."

"I understand," Janai said. "Hope, let's talk after the program." She walked away.

"You agree the women are in danger, yet you plan to leave tomorrow," Hope said.

"I'm paid to investigate homicides. As of now, the medical examiner cannot confirm that this case is a homicide." He stopped, then added, "People start calling in lawyers when you question them without cause." He raised an eyebrow at Hope, apparently letting her know he understood why she sat in during his interrogations.

He turned and started to move away. Hope caught his arm.

"Did you get the lab results on the candy?" He looked at his arm, and she let go. "We had an agreement."

"Yes, we did." He bit his lip. "Can't see no reason not to tell you. The lab tested every piece of candy left in the box. Nada. We haven't traced the missing pieces, so that's a wild card, but it's not enough to keep me here."

Hope put a hand on her forehead. "I'd like to hear what Sean McKenna has to say when Ellen's not around. The fact is, he's the only one here who really knew Meghan."

"I haven't missed that point, thank you. I don't think you'd add any value to my discussion with McKenna. Keep your calendar open. I do plan to talk to you before I leave."

He swiveled away but stopped and cocked his head toward her. His look, a cross between surprise and admiration, caught her unawares, and heat crept up her face. She kept her eyes on his and smiled. He blinked and walked off.

After dinner, guests settled into chairs arranged in a semicircle. Hope stood in front and said, "We have a special treat tonight. Our own Zach Cohen is a professional comedian. He's agreed to favor us with a taste of his act."

She extended her hand toward the patio. Zach, in a suit, tie, and black fedora, strutted in and sat down on a tall stool. The audience gave him a warm welcome.

He did his repertoire of jokes underpinned with traditional Jewish humor. When he finished, he received rousing applause. Margo stepped over and told Zach how much she enjoyed his performance. He stammered thanks, and she smiled.

"I loved your new lines, Zach," Lucy said. "You do have bedroom eyes!"

"You're my Number One fan, Lucy. I can't believe you remember all my jokes." He picked up a Coke at the bar and saluted her.

"You did a great job, as always, Zach," Hope said. She slipped an envelope into his pocket. He shook his head, but she put up a finger, and he shrugged. Just because he worked for the agency didn't mean he shouldn't be paid for his comedy gigs for their clients.

Tony toasted with his drink. "*Excellente,* buddy!"

"I better start saving for a Lamborghini," Frank said, raising his glass.

Hope smiled at the camaraderie and prayed it would carry through until the case was solved.

Janai was sitting at a table apart from the others, and Hope joined her. "I didn't like Mr. Dennison's suggestion about Audrey and Robert," Janai said, "but I'd like your opinion, Hope."

"Dennison is right about the possible threat. It would be prudent to not meet with Audrey or Robert alone, especially late at night."

"That would be difficult."

"Could you have them in with you together? Or have a member of my team with you?"

"I'll ask Audrey to join my meetings with Robert when she can." She paused for several seconds. "I'll have to live with the risk from Audrey. If you have any other ideas, let me know." She rose and waved as she walked away.

Ellen was sitting by the window, and Hope took a seat next to her. "Was your husband able to talk with Meghan's next of kin?"

"Sean spoke to her aunt. He assured her the company would pay all funeral expenses. They wanted to know when her body will be flown back to Pittsburgh."

"It will depend on the medical examiner," Hope said.

Ellen sighed, as if the topic had an unreal sense about it. "I'm sure her family would like to have the funeral."

Ellen appeared to be holding back a yawn. "Sorry, it's been an emotionally draining day." She stood and moved toward Sean at the bar. "I'm going back to the room."

"I'm bushed, myself." He looked at his watch. "Nearly one o'clock Pittsburgh time." He set his beer on the counter and nodded at George.

He put an arm around Ellen, but she twisted her shoulders. "This mess is all your fault, Sean." He lowered his arm to his side, and they walked away. Hope heard her waspish remark and closed her eyes.

Matt Dennison took his guitar out of the closet and strummed "Pretty Woman." The song had been running through his head ever since he noticed Diamond in that black outfit. She was really something special. He closed his eyes. Her smile haunted him. That smile was a challenge, and it had put him in his place.

Being back in the country where he grew up must be making him nostalgic. *Get a handle on your emotions, cowboy. That gal is out of your league.* He walked over to the credenza and pulled a beer out of the small refrigerator. Just as well that he'd be leaving tomorrow.

He didn't like taking off with the case unfinished. He wished the ME could prove it was a homicide. Mrs. Mac seemed like a nice lady, but all the facts pointed to her as the killer.

She was the only one at Secret Sands at the time who knew Connors. Her husband was having an affair with the lady. It was a simple case, like other cases he'd handled in the Navajo Nation. Wife learns her husband is carrying on and takes revenge, usually on the husband, but sometimes on the other woman.

Maybe he'd learn something in the morning from Mr. McKenna. That was as likely as waking up to a foot of snow. He took a swallow of beer.

Maybe it was just as well that Byue was stumped. Digging up enough evidence to take the case to court might take a long time, and these people were leaving in five days.

CHAPTER 14

"Dennison's calling off the investigation," Hope told the team in the Desert Rose.

"Really," Zach said. "He's leaving everything up in the air?"

"There's not much more he can do. The medical examiner can't explain why Meghan's heart stopped functioning. Dennison will interview Sean and wrap it up."

"What are we going to do?" Tony asked.

"We have to protect our clients. We'll assume the murderer is close at hand. Janai and the women are meeting at ten. I think—"

The night manager hurried into the room. "Miss Diamond, Mr. McKenna is very ill."

"In his room?"

"Yes. I called a doctor, but it will take him twenty minutes to get here."

"Let's go!" Hope said. She led the way down the corridor.

Frank pounded on the door. Ellen was crying when she opened it. She pointed to Sean lying on his back and vomiting on the bathroom floor. Frank rushed over. "He's swallowing the vomit. He'll choke to death. Let's get him into a sitting position."

Sean was such a large man that Frank and Tony each had to take one arm to pull him up to a sitting position. "Deep breaths, Sean," Frank said. "Deep breaths." Sean kept vomiting.

Frank looked over at the manager. "Bring a basin!" Frank applied pressure on Sean's forearm to help quiet the nausea. "Let's try some water."

"Lucy, open a bottle of water," Hope said.

Frank put the bottle to Sean's lips. The man took a sip but spit it up immediately.

"Zach, get Dennison," Hope said.

Hope took a washcloth off the rack, ran cold water on it, and gave it to Frank. He applied it to Sean's face. "Deep breaths," Frank kept repeating, but the man continued to vomit.

"What's going on?" Dennison asked, coming in with Zach.

"We don't know," Hope said as the FBI agent knelt down beside Sean. "It looks like poison."

Ellen, who was standing in the doorway, gasped. "Poison!" She slipped toward the floor, and Tony grabbed her.

"Take Ellen into the other room so she can sit down," Hope said. "Lucy, get her some water."

"Is a doctor coming?" Dennison took the wet washcloth and patted Sean's face.

"Yes," Hope said.

Frank held the water bottle up to Sean's lips, and he took a swallow. He was breathing easier, and the vomiting had slowed. He took another sip. "I think he's coming out of it," Frank said.

The manager came in and set a basin down near the men. Dennison looked around at the mess on the floor. "I have to collect samples." He grabbed his case, put on latex gloves, and pulled out several small bottles. "What's he eaten?"

"Lucy, ask Ellen what Sean ate or drank since dinner."

Ellen returned to the doorway. "He had a couple beers in the Blue Sky room and a few pieces of candy when we got back here."

"Candy!" Hope and Dennison exclaimed in unison.

"Just a couple pieces, not enough to upset his stomach."

"Let me see the patient," said a man in sweats coming through the door. "I'm Doctor Valdez."

Frank stood up, and he and Dennison hovered over Sean as the doctor took over. The others stood outside the bathroom with Ellen. Sean was taking deep, regular breaths. The doctor asked if Sean had a history of heart ailments or allergies.

"No," Ellen said.

After his examination, the doctor pulled a syringe out of his bag and drew blood."

"Doc, FBI Agent Matthew Dennison." He pulled out his identification card. "I'll take that blood sample and have it analyzed."

He reached out, but Doctor Valdez looked around, as if puzzled why the FBI would be there. Hope nodded, and he gave the vial to Dennison. "Someone should help him clean up," the doctor said. "I'll come by in the morning. He should drink plenty of liquids. If he relapses tonight, call me immediately." He handed Frank a card.

Ellen went to the closet and brought out a pair of pajamas and handed them to Tony. He went into the bathroom, and Frank closed the door.

Dennison asked Ellen, "Where's the box of candy?" She pointed to it. He picked up the box and slipped it into a plastic bag. He wrote on the bag and put it into his case.

"Did you eat any of the candy?" Dennison asked.

"No."

"Why not?"

"I didn't want any."

"Were you in this room alone any time after your husband arrived?

"Yes."

"When was that?"

"About six o'clock. I was dressing for the evening, and Sean went to the gift shop."

"Do you mind if I search your room?" Dennison asked.

"I suppose not." She looked questioningly at Hope, who nodded.

"Sit down, Ellen," Hope said, guiding her to a chair near Zach and Lucy. Hope leaned against the credenza. Dennison walked around the room, looking into every nook and cranny. He spent time leafing through a large binder and papers on the desk. *The man knows how to search.*

"Would you open the safe?" he asked Ellen, and she opened it for him. Hope saw half-a-dozen jewelry cases. Dennison opened and closed every case. Then he closed the safe. As he finished, Frank and Tony emerged from the bathroom and helped Sean onto the bed.

"What would you like to drink?" Frank asked. "Water or soda?"

"Ginger ale," Sean said, so softly Hope could barely hear.

"Ellen, would you like Tony or Frank to stay here with your husband?" Hope asked. "The manager will give you another room."

Sean said, "I'm all right. Just tired." He set down the drink, yawned, and lay back against the pillow.

Dennison went into the bathroom. Hope watched from the partially opened door. He looked into the medicine cabinet and pulled out drawers. Ten minutes later, he passed her but didn't give her any sign.

Sean had fallen asleep, and Ellen took both of Frank's hands. "I don't know what would have happened without you, Mr. Madison."

"I'm glad I could help," Frank said and handed her the doctor's card. "You get some sleep."

Tony said, "Ellen, I'm right next door. Here's my extension." He wrote it on a desk pad. "If you need anything, call me. Never mind the time."

"I have to run this stuff to the lab," Dennison told Hope, "but I'll be back in the morning. Give me a shout if you need me. Anytime." He reached into his wallet, pulled out a card, and handed it to her. A maid came in with a bucket, and the others walked out.

"Tony, let's step into your room," Hope said. "This poisoning puts a new light on Meghan's death. Dennison won't be bailing out after all."

"What was all that talk about candy?" Lucy asked.

"Dennison suspects Sean was poisoned, and unless I miss my guess, he thinks Ellen just tried to kill her husband," Hope said.

"Frankly," Zach said. "It looks that way to me also."

Tony sighed and turned away. Hope looked at Frank. The animosity was back. She didn't like conflict among the team, especially when the future of her agency was on the line.

CHAPTER 15

The air was crisp when Lucy met Gloria at seven Monday morning. Lucy laughed at their blue jogging gear, hiking boots, and sunglasses. "We're twins!" she said. They set off along the path that wound up into the rocks, and the red dirt powdered their shoes. The sun peeked over the hills in the eastern sky and deepened the burnt orange and red cliffs into chocolate.

"It's so fresh and beautiful," Gloria said, spreading out her hands. "Big problems are really just blips in the universe."

Lucy breathed in the fragrance of the sage. She hated to interrupt the moment, but her job was to gather information. "I'd love to hear more about your business. You and Dimitri are always wrapped up in meetings."

Gloria lifted her hand. "Look. There's an eagle!" The bird soared toward them, dipping, and then banking sharply. The sun sent shimmers of gold off its feathers.

"He checked to see if we'd make a tasty breakfast," Lucy said, watching the eagle burn a hole in the blue sky.

"You asked about shipbuilding." Gloria shrugged her shoulders, as if used to the fact that business took priority over beauty. "First, you have to appreciate our heritage. Archeologists trace shipbuilding back to the Stone Age when some hearty souls sailed from Asia to Borneo in what amounted to hollowed-out trees."

Lucy visualized men flopping around in the ocean atop logs. "That doesn't seem possible."

"I can't imagine how they did it, but, somehow, they made it, and the heritage of shipbuilding was born. With heritage comes pride. Shipwrights specialize, and people don't like change."

"Why would they have to change?"

"Our company builds cargo ships. I want to enter into a relationship with a cruise line. Dimitri tells me that our workers wouldn't be happy. He's been in the trade a long time, so he may be right."

The eagle was circling again, and Lucy stopped to watch it. From the spot where she was standing, the desert floor stretched out flat and far. Clumps of sagebrush made the ground look like a bumpy blanket. "Must be a bunny around," she said.

Suddenly, the eagle shot like a homing missile into the curvy hills. Gloria shaded her eyes. "You could be right."

Lucy trudged ahead. "Could a competitor be trying to undermine your company?" she asked, her mind swinging toward a conspiracy theory.

"Dimitri on somebody else's payroll? It's possible, but my father is against the idea, too. You can imagine the pushback he had to deal with when he put a woman in charge of the firm. Now, he's threatening to replace me with Dimitri."

Lucy's eyes opened wider. "If that's the case, maybe Dimitri isn't interested in supporting your plan."

Gloria shrugged.

"Is shipbuilding all that you do?"

"No, we operate a cargo business as well. It brings in a major portion of our revenue."

Just then, Lucy saw a flash of movement in the distance. She was facing the sun, so the image was distorted. "Did you see something up ahead?"

"Yes, I think it was a deer."

They continued walking, and the image grew clearer. "Why it's Margo!" Gloria said. As they came closer, they waved to each other. "You're up bright and early, Margo." Gloria's spirits seemed to bounce back.

"Hi," Margo gave a little wave. She was wearing jogging pants and a hooded sweatshirt. "Isn't it beautiful here?" She jogged in place.

"Did you fall," Lucy asked, noticing the red dirt on her pant legs.

"A rabbit ran across the path right in front of me. Caught me by surprise. I think that eagle got him."

"We've been out for half-an-hour." Gloria said, glancing at her watch. "We'd better turn around."

"Since you two are walking, would you mind if I pass?" Margo asked.

"Not at all," Lucy said. Margo jogged ahead and was soon out of sight on the curvy trail.

Lucy turned to Gloria. "When I was at your place, you were about to tell me how you met your husband, but we were interrupted."

Gloria laughed. "It's a crazy story but scary because my father nearly died." Lucy's eyes opened wide. "We were in New York on business, and he started having chest pains at eleven o'clock at night. I called 911, and the paramedics got to the hotel in minutes. I was in pajamas and my face was smeared with green cream, but no way was I letting my father go off alone. I grabbed the hotel bathrobe and slippers, and I dashed out with the paramedics."

She stopped talking a moment. "They took him into surgery, and I sat there crying hysterically. Ramon was just going off duty. He sat down and talked to me all night. In the morning, we found out my father had survived a four-way bypass."

"I'm so glad," Lucy said, her eyes glistening. She had lost her own parents.

"When we heard the good news, Ramon and I hugged, and he asked me to marry him. What could I say? Love hit me over the head. That was ten years ago. He's fifty now, still handsome and romantic."

Lucy sighed. "Love at first sight. I'm glad it can happen. You're always so cheerful. You must have a good relationship."

"We do sail along great together." Gloria laughed. "Lucy, you've given me a good reminder. Dimitri and I both have hot tempers, but I know we can work things out."

Hope was standing in the lobby when Dennison's Chevy Tahoe sped into the parking lot, gravel flying. She shook her head. *The man must be a terror on the highway.* He stepped out of the car and came inside wearing his hat and carrying a large suitcase. He stopped in front of her, his eyes bloodshot, his face scruffy.

"Did you get the lab report back on Sean McKenna?" she asked.

He lowered his head and closed his eyes. Then he lifted his head. "Good morning to you, too, lady."

Hope covered her face with her hands. "Sorry. Guess you didn't get much sleep."

"Let's say it's a good thing McKenna is such a big man and that he vomited so much."

Hope drew a deep breath. "What are you planning to do?"

"Do you mind if I put my gear away and grab some grub?" He started down the hallway.

She followed. "I was just going for breakfast myself. Mind if I join you?"

He stopped and turned. His mouth opened and closed. Finally, he sighed. "Meet you in the dining room."

Fifteen minutes later, his face had a freshly shaven look. He sat down and put his hat on the chair beside him. Hope smiled at the polite gesture. Cecelia brought coffee and took their order.

"Any idea who poisoned Sean?" Hope asked after the girl left. Her anxiety was eating at her. She had been so afraid the man would die.

Dennison saluted Hope with his cup and drank the hot liquid before speaking. "I don't suppose I'm letting out any secrets. They're just my own thoughts. I think Mrs. Mac planned to kill Connors before she ever left Pittsburgh. When her husband came out here, she poisoned him with arsenic."

"Where did she find arsenic?"

He looked around the room, and Hope followed his glance. Robert and Margo were at the far table, and they stood up.

When they had gone, Dennison said, "Let's talk about that arsenic. Between you and me and the Silent Knight, I know Frank Madison was a busy beaver in Meghan's room. We found his fingerprint on the printouts about the condos. Just one, because Mrs. McKenna dumped her drink on the pages. Nevertheless, one is as good as a dozen."

Hope stiffened. Jake had warned that Dennison was looking for any excuse to get back to D.C. The agent must have picked up on her alarm. He squinted and said, "I figured he'd have some explanation, like she showed them to him. What I want to know is did he find anything in her room that could have contained arsenic?"

"I wouldn't know about that. We stay away from bending the law."

"Sure you do." His tone was frosty. "If Madison remembers anything useful, send me an anonymous note."

"What else did you discover?" she asked.

Dennison shook his head. "Diamond, you don't tell me a dang thing, but you expect me to dump out everything I know."

"Not much I can say to that."

"Here's what I'd like you to tell me," Dennison said. "What have you and your team learned from your talks with the guests."

So, he had been paying attention to what they were doing. "We've picked up a bit of tea, as Lucy would say, but we haven't strung together any clues that explain what happened to Meghan."

"Come on, spill the tea." He apparently was up on millennial speak. "Gossip that means nothing to you may mean a great deal to me."

"Let me think that over," Hope said, playing with her napkin.

"Don't take too long. The murderer may strike again before you come down off that high horse and feel like sharing."

His eyes held that mocking look. She looked out beyond the rocks at the spread of desert. If the information they'd collected could help him solve the murder, she had to turn it over.

When she turned back, he had his head on his hand and was smiling. The smile lit up his eyes, and his whole appearance changed. "I'm curious how a gal like you became a big shot in the security game."

Hope sat back and laughed. "Nothing subtle about you, Dennison."

"I don't see much sense beating around the bush. Waste of time. What's your story?"

Hope looked at him for a very long time without speaking, but he kept silent. She took a breath. "I grew up in Hollywood. My dad's a police chief, and my mom's an actress. She does commercials, but occasionally she has a part in a series. I majored in criminal justice at college, hired on as a police recruit in San Diego, and went through the academy."

"You were a cop?" Dennison held up a hand. "I never would have guessed."

"Sworn officer, if you please."

"Yeah, right. What made you leave that cush job?"

"That cush job put me in plenty of danger." Her eyes narrowed. Cecelia arrived with their breakfast burritos, and they ate in silence.

A scene at the San Diego Airport played out in Hope's mind. The sun had just risen, so the airport sidewalks were nearly empty. A man and woman were rolling their luggage. The man, who turned out to be an oil executive, had an infant in his arms. The woman had a small girl beside her rolling a miniature suitcase.

A large man in a dark suit came up behind them and grabbed the child. Hope had just come on duty and witnessed the kidnapping.

The man was running toward her. She pulled her gun, shouted at him to stop. The child had her hands against his eyes and was struggling. He let the child fall, and her father, who'd been running after them, picked her up and ran inside the terminal.

The kidnapper was ten feet away. Hope warned him to stop. He pulled out a gun and was stretching his arm toward her. Hope fired, and the man fell. It was the first and only time she had had to use deadly force. She drew a deep breath to slow her heartbeat at the memory.

Cecelia came back, refilled their coffee mugs, and took the plates. Hope looked up to see Dennison watching her with a somber expression, as if he knew what she'd been thinking.

"You know I was just torching you about the cush job," he said, holding his cup to his lips and looking at her over the rim. "I was out of line, and I'm sorry."

She closed her eyes and nodded. "Apology accepted," she said and smiled.

After a long moment, she said, "Here's how a gal like me became a big shot in the security game. I met an oil executive who needed protection for himself and his family. We hit it off, and he offered me the job. I quit the Force, opened an office, and moved back in with my folks to save money."

"No kidding! I would'a thought you'd be rooming with a significant other."

"You're skating on thin ice, Dennison. Do you want to hear the story or not?"

"I do. Go on."

"My mother introduced me to friends in show business who needed security. One thing led to another—" She hunched her shoulder and put her palms up.

Dennison was twisting his FBI ring, a nervous gesture he'd displayed when he interviewed Janai. "How did you land an ace operative like Madison?"

Hope opened her mouth, and he glanced out the window. He must have run a background check on Frank when he found his fingerprint. He was probably running checks on all of them right now.

She pushed aside the veil of vulnerability and looked him in the eyes. "I met Frank at a security conference in Toronto. He had just retired from Special Forces and was looking to take on something new. He came to L.A. and checked out my operation. I offered him a partnership in Diamond Security, and he accepted."

Dennison was nodding, and she went on. "It was a beautiful break for me because he had loads of experience protecting high-level officials. He helped me land the Icelandic Wind account, our largest client." She picked up her coffee cup, letting him know that was all she planned to share.

"I'm impressed. I thought you were just another pretty face, especially in that get-up last night."

Hope let the remark pass. "What about you? How did you land on the reservation?"

His raised eyebrow revealed he wasn't used to answering questions, but after several seconds, he leaned back in the chair and said, "I got an ROTC scholarship and spent a decade on active duty, mostly in military intelligence in Iraq, Syria, and Afghanistan. I came back to the States and finished out my third tour at the Pentagon. Then I hooked up with the FBI." He grinned. "I've been a G-man going on three years."

Hope added up the numbers in her mind. "You are only thirty-six years old!" She blurted out and had the grace to blush.

He laughed. "Now who's being subtle? Thirty-seven. How old are you?"

She laughed, too. "Women never answer that question." I'm sorry, you weren't finished when I interrupted. Why are you here?"

"My boss and I had a difference of opinion. I'm spending time in the penalty box."

Hope took a sip from her coffee mug. "Couldn't you get help from friends up the chain?"

"Friends disappear when dirt flies. I can't complain. You see how beautiful it is here." He pointed out the window. "I'd like it better if I was Navajo. It gets under your skin when people don't trust you." He gave her that mocking look.

"I have no idea who murdered Meghan Connors. And, yes, I agree with you that she was murdered. I've learned to trust my instincts. I can't quite buy into your notion that Ellen is behind everything."

"You're wrong. Despite what I learned about Ross, nobody else had any reason to harm Connors."

"Let's agree to disagree," Hope set her cup down and polished a spoon with her napkin. He sat there, quiet. He seemed to understand she needed time to reflect. After a full minute, she looked up and said, "I'll have Frank talk to you about his quick glance through the rooms. Nothing struck us as significant, but you may spot something we missed. I'll also ask Zach to give you a copy of the team's reports."

Dennison let out a low whistle. "You're a classy dame, Diamond. I was going to warn you about the consequences of obstructing justice." She looked into his eyes, those older eyes of a man who'd spent a decade in combat zones. He meant what he said.

"I owe you a favor."

He cocked his head and frowned. "How's that?"

"The other night in Blue Sky when I pulled a gun on you. I appreciate your not embarrassing me by mentioning it in front of others."

"Embarrass you? You did exactly the right thing. You were alone in a dark room with a murderer at large. I was impressed at your correct Fighting Stance. My training should have told me right then you'd been on the Force." He cocked his thumb and finger at her. "That's one up to you."

She smiled. "One other thing." Her Guardian Angel was tapping her shoulder. She let out a breath. "We're going on a hayride tonight. Can you come along to keep an eye on the women?"

He clenched his teeth. The idea of getting too friendly with the suspects probably troubled him, but after a few seconds, he nodded. "Count me in."

"I'm worried about Janai," she said. Milling around in the dark with a murderer afoot wasn't part of any protection game plan, but calling off the event would put the guests at loose ends. After Audrey's hysteria, she wanted to keep everyone busy.

Cecelia came back and asked if they needed anything else. They both shook their heads. "I think Sean should be awake by now." Dennison said and put on his hat.

"Can I come along?"

"How can I say no?" He put his hands on his hips. "You hornswoggled me, Diamond! That's why you invited me to breakfast, so that you could finagle me into agreeing about McKenna."

Hope grinned. "Would I do a thing like that?"

CHAPTER 16

Sean McKenna invited them to have coffee on the patio. The sun was beating down, and Hope took off her jacket and slung her purse on the back of the chair. Sean's face looked pale and his eyes worried.

"How are you feeling, Mr. McKenna?" Hope asked. He'd had a close call. *How did his poisoning relate to Meghan?*

"Like I've been run over by a Mack truck. The doc says I'll live, so I'll take his word for it."

"I'd like you to tell me what happened from the time you left the Blue Sky room until you got ill," Dennison said.

Sean sighed. "I was tired. You know, the time difference between here and Pittsburgh. I left the party and came back to the room with Ellen. I saw the candy and popped a couple of my favorites. Half-an-hour later, I was on the floor. Thank you, by the way, in case I didn't say it last night. I was knocking at the Pearly Gates."

"You say you ate a couple of your favorite pieces of candy," Dennison said. "Who would know they were your favorites?"

"My wife, I suppose. But I have a lot of favorites. It wasn't like the two pieces I ate were my only favorites."

"Can you think of anyone who would want to harm you or your wife?" Dennison asked.

"Honestly, no, I cannot. We don't really know the people here. Why would they want to kill us?"

"That's the question we've been asking ourselves," Hope said.

"You seem to be saying that the candy was poisoned. Was it?"

Dennison nodded. "You were lucky. No way your wife would have survived."

Sean blinked, and the cup in his hand shook. "Should we leave and go home right now?"

"No, I'm afraid you can't do that," Dennison told him. "I'm investigating a suspicious death in Meghan's case and attempted murder in your case."

"What should we do?"

"Tony will keep an eye on you," Hope said. "Please let him know your plans. We're dedicated to keeping you and your wife safe." The sun was in her eyes, but she caught the grim expression on the man's face.

"I plan to keep an eye on you, also," Dennison said. "Why did you fly out here yesterday? Did your wife ask you to come?"

"No, she didn't. I could tell there was trouble in the wind. She's my wife. Of course, I came."

"If you feel that way about your wife, how is it that you got hooked up with Meghan Connors?"

Sean blinked. "Meghan? We weren't really hooked up. I took her to dinner a few times. That's all."

"It must have been more than a few dinners to make your wife invite her on this trip. She admits she heard rumors about you and Meghan," Dennison said.

"I don't know why Ellen invited her to come."

"Here's what I think," Dennison said. He rocked his hands back and forth on the table, pointing a finger at Sean. "Either your wife murdered Meghan on her own, or you convinced her to do it."

"That's crazy! Ellen and me, we would never do such a thing!"

"Maybe you convinced Meghan to murder your wife, but something went wrong."

Sean stiffened. "I'm not answering any more questions without an attorney, Mr. Dennison." Hope sighed. Sean was no dummy. He didn't need to be told his rights.

"Hey," Tony called. "Sean, you're up. How are you feeling? We brought you tea and toast." Tony set the tray down on the table, and Ellen walked around and put a hand on Sean's shoulder.

The flash of suspicion Sean shot at his wife and Tony alarmed Hope. She looked at Dennison. He stood up and said he'd be moving along. Hope picked up her jacket and purse, and they walked along the path together.

"You didn't pull any punches," she said.

"Not my style."

"We've got to figure out who poisoned him. If we don't, they'll never trust one another again."

"I saw his look," Dennison said. "I'm not sure it's going to be that easy. Mrs. McKenna is a very bright gal, and I think she's found a fool-proof way of getting herself out of a murder rap. If I can find the arsenic, I might be able to pull her in for the attempted murder of her husband."

His words were making an impression. Did Ellen poison her husband? She had told Sean this mess was all his fault. Maybe she hadn't killed Meghan, but poisoning Sean was a very different matter.

"You agree she's the best suspect we have for the poisoning, don't you?" Dennison said.

Hope took a deep breath. "I need to handle a few things. I'll leave you here."

He grinned, and she walked away, cringing at his mocking smile following her down the path. What bothered her more was that Dennison could be right in suspecting Ellen of poisoning Sean and perhaps being mixed up in Meghan's death.

# #

Hope was pouring out a glass of milk when Frank came into the anteroom of the Blue Sage area where the women would be meeting. She settled her glass on the coffee table and sat down. Frank poured himself a coffee, took a piece of coffee cake that smelled liked browned apples, and joined her on the sofa.

"Too much caffeine already this morning?" he asked, looking at the glass of milk.

"I had breakfast with Dennison. He found your fingerprint on Meghan's papers, and I told him about your search." She watched Frank and took a breath when he smiled. "He'd like to talk to you about what you found."

"Sure. With the exception of Ellen, we're nowhere close to identifying anyone that looks good for poisoning Sean or killing Meghan."

"I didn't like mentioning your search to Dennison without talking to you first, but cooperating with him gives us a better chance of closing the case. Anything we can do to help Dennison will help us."

Frank nodded. "I'm with you all the way."

Janai and Audrey passed by heading to the conference room. Janai wore a gray suit with a silver broach, a statement that she meant to get down to business. "We've lost two days," Janai said without stopping.

Hope stood and followed the women into the conference room. "Good luck with your meetings, Janai. Everything is set as far as drinks, snacks and meals are concerned. You can conduct all your business without leaving the room. My team will be at both doors if you need anything."

"We'll have to take breaks, I'm afraid. Lydia and Gloria won't make it through the day without smoking."

Clean ashtrays had been set out on a table along the wall. Even shorthanded, the staff could be counted on to handle arrangements properly.

"Frankly, I'm glad Ellen spoke up about her allergies," Janai said. "Smoke irritates my contacts, especially in this dry climate."

Ellen, Lydia, and Gloria arrived together punctually at ten o'clock. *These women knew the value of time.* They exchanged greetings, and Hope went into the anteroom and closed the door. She looked at Frank. "Finally."

Tony and Zach walked in, joking as they often did. Zach must try out his one-liners on Tony. Lucy arrived, wearing shorts and a halter top, carrying a large tote bag. Her outfit raised cat calls from Tony and Zach.

"I plan to take an outside shift or two," she said and took a cotton sunhat out of her bag.

"Sit down, everyone," Hope said. "I had a conversation with Agent Dennison." Tony and Zach pulled chairs in closer. Lucy sat at the end of the sofa.

"Dennison confirmed that Sean was poisoned. It gives him an excuse to stay on at Secret Sands. I agreed to share our intel because we need to discover the truth before the women leave on Thursday."

"Exactly how much do you want to share?" Zach asked. "The encrypted report that details everything we know?"

Hope nodded. "Print out everything except the notes about Frank's searches. Dennison found his fingerprint in Meghan's room, but that fact doesn't need to appear on paper."

"I don't want to rock the boat," Tony said, "but are you sure we can trust this guy? He is relentless about pinning everything on Ellen. He cornered me yesterday about Sean. It was clear he believes Ellen is guilty."

"When you stack up the facts, she is a suspect," Hope said. "As far as we know, she was the only one with access to poison the candy last night."

Frank spoke up. "Look at it this way, Tony. If we work together, we have a better chance of solving the case and clearing everyone who's innocent."

Lucy and Zach shrugged and said, "Agree" at the same time.

"Okay, you can count on me."

"Thanks, Tony. We need all hands on deck because our culprit has been ahead of us so far. Spend time with Sean today. He's lucky to be alive. Dennison said he was given a hefty dose of arsenic."

No one said anything, and Frank got up and poured coffee into his cup.

"Anything more about Dennison?" Zach asked.

"A couple things. I invited him to come along on the hayride. An extra pair of eyes in the dark will be useful. I'm also going to invite him to our meeting tonight."

Tony grimaced but didn't object.

"Zach, give me two copies of the report. I want to go over the entire document myself before I hand it over to Dennison." She'd make sure no incriminating material had seeped in unknowingly.

CHAPTER 17

Before settling down to the dossier, Hope put the documents in the safe and changed into a black racing swimsuit and a coverup. A few laps in the pool would refresh her mind. The case was moving at warp speed. Saturday a murder. Sunday a poisoning. The warning from the painting shot through her. The evil was real. Her security was tight. *But was it tight enough if the murderer decided to act again?*

Carrying a large, striped beach bag, she headed to the pool. It was nearly eleven. She stopped at her favorite spot, smiled, and scanned the spectacular rock formations beyond the property. She picked out a large shape that looked like an elephant, christened it Nero Wolfe, and took a photo. She chuckled at the whimsical thought, but a voice jerked her back to the moment.

"Hi," Robert Halloway called from the shadow of the rock wall at the other side of the pool. She hadn't seen him and frowned at her inattention. Missteps were dangerous in her business, especially with a murderer haunting the resort. She waved and took off her coverup, stuffed her cell and sunglasses into her bag, and set down her gear at the edge of the pool.

"You look like you're set for laps," he said.

"Just a quick break," she said, walking down the steps.

"We haven't had a chance to talk privately," Robert said. "I've noticed you talking with everyone else, including the FBI guy."

Hope smiled. "Just happenstance, like meeting up with you here at the pool." *This man keeps track of what everyone's up to.* He swam over to her and stood up. His arms were covered in tattoos.

"Great tatts," she said, eyeing the designs. One arm featured a large tiger's head. "Any special meanings?"

"No, just whatever I fancied in the artist's catalog. Can you tell me what's going on? Janai said the FBI would be leaving today, but Dennison's still hanging around."

"I don't know Mr. Dennison's plans, but the women are meeting."

"I know because Janai was all smiles. She's been like a tiger on the prowl." He ducked down in the pool and came up squeezing water out of his hair and slicking it back. "Are you familiar with the reason for the meeting?"

"Yes, Janai confided in me about her plans," Hope said, moving her arms about in the water.

"Good, then I don't have to pussyfoot around that issue."

"Will you be part of her campaign?"

"She's counting on me to run the finances. That's why I'm here. I'm mapping out a financial strategy."

"What if she wins. Do you see yourself as part of the cabinet?" Hope leaned back in the water and floated on her back. She closed her eyes against the sun.

"I think I'd do a good job as Secretary of the Treasury, but Janai hasn't made any promises. She may need someone else's support and plans to dangle that carrot in front of him or her."

"What do you think of her chances?" Hope flipped over and swam to the other end of the pool and treaded water.

"Long shot," Robert said, coming up alongside her. "One, she's a woman. More than that, she hasn't held public office. The Constitution doesn't require it, but only six presidents have ever been elected without holding political office."

Hope squinted. "I can think of three—Donald Trump and the two generals, Dwight Eisenhower and Ulysses Grant."

"Very good. You've hit fifty percent. The others are William Taft, Herbert Hoover, and Zachary Taylor, who was also a general."

He dipped down under the water and came back up. "The main things Janai has going for her are her charisma and her deep understanding of global politics. A major part of Icelandic Wind's success comes from her alliances with businesses and governments abroad. She's very savvy when it comes to the world's powerbrokers."

Janai had charisma and political savvy in spades. Hope had been to Europe with her during Fashion Week. They'd gone to parties and ceremonies attended by prime ministers and kings. When Janai entered a room, electricity crackled in her wake, and she always managed to secure private meetings with influential figures.

"She is also an excellent leader," Robert said. "She built this company from a small cosmetics business into one of the largest skin care firms in the world. I'd say she's more than qualified to be President, but it will be an uphill battle."

"Let me ask you a question," Hope said. "Can you think of anyone who would like Janai out of the way before she could run for president?"

He was treading water, coming close to her, then moving back. "What you're asking is can I think of anyone here who would be happier if she had died instead of Meghan?" He kept circling.

Hope floated to the middle of the pool. He splashed down under water, came up by her, and said, "No, I can't think of anyone at the hotel who has a grudge against Janai. I'm the closest thing to a would-be suspect, and I have nothing to gain and everything to lose."

Controlling millions of dollars earmarked for charity was a temptation for anyone. He was a close associate of Janai's, and Dennison warned about killers being close associates. "I can think of one reason."

"Is that right?"

Uh oh, she'd put him on the defensive. His expression darkened. Treading water didn't put her in a great position to fend off an attack. She leaned back in the water, flipping her feet, moving, but the steps were a long way away. He swam toward her. His face was on a level with hers, his body threatening. "Tell me the reason you said you could think of."

He was right in front of her, and she pushed his shoulders. He fell back into the water, and Hope swam toward her bag, which held her gun. Before she reached it, he came up out of the water and grabbed her arm. "It sounds like you're accusing me of something," he said, his face red with anger.

157

"Let go!" she yelled and twisted out of his grip.

"Tell me what you meant."

She reached the steps and walked up, her body releasing the tension. On firm ground, she could handle herself. "I was thinking that you handle a great deal of money. Money is always tempting."

"I wouldn't go around saying things like that if I were you," he called to her from the pool.

Back in her room, the heaviness of his threat weighed on her shoulders. He posed a danger to Janai, and she met with him at midnight every night. Janai promised to have Audrey at all the meetings, but what if she neglected do so?

Hope showered and slipped into a hotel bathrobe. She pulled a bottle of juice out of the refrigerator and sank down in the recliner to read the material from Zach. It was a thick file. She had asked the team to include as much information as they could remember, even comments only loosely connected to the case.

Along with the chronological reports, Zach had pulled out all the information about each guest and put that data together in a separate section. He also compiled a list of motives. Her attention was so focused that she jumped when the room telephone rang.

Wondering what the next crisis would be, she took a deep breath. "Hello."

"You sound nervous, Babe. What's up?"

"It's nothing, or rather everything, Jake. The medical examiner can't come up with a definite cause of death. Last night, someone poisoned Ellen McKenna's husband, Sean. Fortunately, he's okay."

"That's why I'm calling. I just read the report about McKenna. What does Dennison think?"

"He thinks Ellen is guilty, but he doesn't have any evidence. I don't agree with him completely."

"How does he get along with Janai Ross? She wields a lot of influence here in Washington." The nervous note in Jake's voice came through the line. Janai must have threatened to go over his head.

"I think Janai is warming up to him."

"That doesn't surprise me. That cowboy has some undercurrent of charm that I don't understand. I've seen A-list women in Washington come on to him."

Hope ran her fingers through her hair. Dennison's appeal came from the smile in his eyes. If women were coming on to him, he was smiling at them.

"What do you think of Dennison?"

Her opinion of the man was changing. His cold shoulder had irritated her, but he was persistent in his belief that Meghan had been murdered, and he wasn't intimidated by the wealth of the suspects.

"As you said, he's a bull in a china shop, but he's thorough. I watched him search Ellen's room last night. If anything had been hidden, he would have found it."

"I agree. He is thorough. What's your own strategy?"

She looked at the painting and cringed at the evil vibes it set off in her body. "We want to find the killer before the women leave on Thursday, so I've taken Matt into our confidence. He's coming to the cookout with us tonight. He'll keep an eye on Janai."

"Matt, eh?"

"We're all one big happy team."

"I miss you, you know, Babe," Jake said.

The telephone slipped out of her hand, and she grabbed it. "Jake, that's unfair. We live in two different worlds, and they don't often collide." She took a breath. "For what it's worth, I have no interest in Agent Dennison."

"Right." His voice was cold, like Dennison's. "Let me know if anything breaks." He disconnected.

She slammed down the phone. Jake was the one who appreciated their arrangement. Two ships passing in the night, he'd say. She picked up her cell and looked at his photograph. Annoyed that he was manipulating her feelings, she set it down. She lifted Zach's dossier, sat in the recliner, and began reading. *Concentrate on one mystery at a time. Murder and poisoning take priority over what was bugging Jake Sanders.*

CHAPTER 18

Outside the Blue Sage, Lucy was spreading lotion on her arms. Margo Knight stopped and said, "Your shoulders are getting red."

Lucy rubbed more lotion on her shoulders. "I don't often have a chance to sit in the sun," she said.

"Mind if I sit with you? I'm taking a break." Margo set her laptop down on the table.

"Not at all." It was a good time to learn more about the lady Zach seemed so fond of.

Margo pulled up a chair close to Lucy. She was wearing a long-sleeved blouse, long skirt, and a broad-brimmed floppy hat. "I stay out of the sun. It's being in the health business; I see the statistics on skin cancer."

"Lydia doesn't seem to have the same concerns. She's a pretty heavy smoker."

"Lydia does what she pleases," Margo said.

"Do you always travel with her?"

"No, it's just that we're in the middle of a major project. So far, mostly what I've done is fetch and carry," a bitter note crept in her voice.

"What are you working on?" Lucy asked.

"I can't talk about that project because it's secretive."

"I understand. Our business is the same, not something we can talk about."

"You seem wrapped up in your work. Anyone special in your life?" Margo leaned back with her arms on the armrests.

"No special crush at the moment. How about you?"

"I fly solo myself. Work eats up my time, but rain or shine, I run ten miles a day. It keeps me sane."

Lucy shifted in her lounge chair and put on her sunhat and sunglasses. "What's it like working for Lydia? She seems a bit uptight."

"She expects a lot of you, but she pays what you're worth. How about Hope? I admire her breaking into a predominantly male field."

"Hope is a great boss, and she has good instincts. When I disagree with her opinion, it turns out she's always right."

"Do you think you'll stay in the protection field?"

Lucy was quiet a moment. She wasn't doing a good job of gaining information from Margo. It appeared the other way around.

"Right now, I'm learning the business, and I enjoy the variety. Something different every day. I don't sit at a desk, and I don't get bored. Is your work boring?"

"Not at all. I feel like a detective most of the time, learning about new drugs, tracing their history, looking at their performance, and publishing in medical journals. I'm getting ready to publish a paper about our experiments with enzymes." Margo explained what the outcomes of successful testing would mean, such as the prevention of heart attacks.

"You make your work sound interesting," Lucy said, surprised at the thought of pharmaceuticals being like the detective business.

"It's a fascinating field. My great grandparents came from Ludwigsburg, Germany, which is the birthplace of Charles Pfizer."

"Is that right?"

"Did you know it was the Swiss who discovered how to make antiseptics from dyes?"

"No!" She smiled at Margo, encouraging her to go on with the story.

"In the mid-1800s, Switzerland was a lively trade center for silk weaving and dyeing. Merchants shipped goods all along the Rhine from Basel, a city that's been around for 2,000 years. Some bright entrepreneurs discovered that dyestuffs had antiseptic properties. Next thing you knew, the world had the new industry of pharmaceuticals."

"I had no idea."

Margo shook her head. "Sorry. I could talk on the subject for hours."

"It's interesting," Lucy said. "Who would have thought the drug industry was based on fabric."

"The history, and even the future, isn't all rosy. I don't want to sound like a documentary, but researchers claim that of the

3,000 plants active against cancer, seventy percent come from rainforests. The forests are disappearing. An article in *Time* magazine stated that twenty-seven percent of the Amazon will be gone by 2030."

"Yikes, what will you do?"

"We're working hard to figure it out." Margo stood and picked up her computer. "I'd better get back to work." She turned and waved. "Don't stay out too long in the sun."

Hope answered the knock on her door. "Matt!" She was still wearing the hotel bathrobe and held the door open a few inches.

"Zach said he gave you a report for me. I thought I'd pick it up."

"It's in the safe," she said, not wanting to invite him into the room. "I'm going for lunch in a few minutes. Have you eaten?"

"I was planning on skipping lunch, but why not."

"I'll dress and meet you there." A fashionista even in casual wear, Hope slipped into a soft blue pant suit. Dennison was at the far table near the window, the same one where they had sat during breakfast. She passed Robert at a table with Dimitri, caught his look, and returned his scowl.

"What's wrong? You look like you got nipped by a rattlesnake," Dennison said.

"I did," she said, then shook off the comment with her hands.

"Tell me."

"It's not important."

"Tell me."

He wasn't going to let go of the subject, so she explained what had happened at the pool. Matt glanced at Robert. "You think he may have his fingers in the cookie jar. I'll check with a guy I know in D.C." He pulled a small notebook out of his shirt pocket and made a note.

"There's something else," she said. "Robert's arms are covered in tattoos. The centerpiece on one arm was a tiger's head."

Matt nodded. "Power and strength."

"The tiger tatt also signifies vengeance and punishment. I saw a lot of those tatts when I was a cop."

"If Janai is a target, Halloway is in a prime position to do her harm." Hope shivered and rubbed her arms. "Maybe he just likes tigers," Dennison said quickly, apparently not wanting to add to her alarm. He wrote another note and slipped the book into his shirt pocket.

Cecelia took their order for chicken fajitas, and Hope asked, "What have you picked up in your investigation?"

He smiled. "The FBI doesn't give out information during an active investigation. I've told you more than I should have already."

"I wouldn't expect you to tell me anything under normal conditions, but we're on a timeclock. Tell you what, come to our intel meeting after everybody's tucked in for the night. We share all our secrets." She smiled at him, "And, of course, we'd expect you to share yours."

"I generally abide by FBI protocol."

"Is that a fact?" She leaned back in the chair and watched him fiddle with his ring. *The mention of FBI protocol was making him uncomfortable.*

After a short silence, he put his hands on the table and smiled. "What do you do when you're not protecting dogs and cats and goldfish?"

Hope laughed. "Nobody's as rude as you are without practicing."

"The only thing I practice is what Will Rogers said. "'The best way out of a difficulty is through it.' You have to be blunt in this business if you want to find out things people don't want to tell you."

Cecelia arrived with their chicken fajitas. When she left, he took a bite. "Hot!" he grabbed a glass of water.

"Thanks for the warning." Hope took a tiny bite. "What do I do when I'm not protecting goldfish, you asked. In an ideal world, Lucy and I do martial arts training three times a week, and I swim laps four times a week. My world is not ideal. Client needs change from day to day, often minute to minute. I skip training and laps more often than I make them. The only habit I fight hard to keep is going to Europe or New York during Fashion Week. I love seeing the new designs, colors, and fabrics. For me, that trip makes working worthwhile."

He shrugged and nibbled at the fry bread. "You've never been in love?"

Hope's conversation with Jake Sanders flashed in her mind. *You know I miss you.* "I can't say that, but nothing of the forever-after type." Her voice held a sharp edge. "Furthermore, my love life is none of your business."

Matt smiled and put up a hand like a traffic cop. "Pump the brakes, lady. I'm not hitting on you. I just like to know the lay of the land."

"Well, know this." She leaned in, her face close to his. "I am not the lay of the land."

Matt laughed so hard, he wiped tears from his eyes. When he recovered, he said, "Diamond, you win." His laugh was so infectious that Hope put her fingers on her mouth to keep from laughing herself.

"One more thing before we end this cozy chat. Why did your folks give you a 45.52-carat-diamond name?"

Hope stared. *Why did he throw her off-balance? An FBI tactic.* "You know how many carats are in the Hope Diamond?"

"Of course. I had to guard it once. If you put the Hope Diamond under an ultraviolet light in a dark room, it phosphoresces. I saw it glow orange for about a minute. It's impossible to counterfeit."

"You take the cake, Dennison. After that tidbit, I have to tell you why my mother gave me the name of a 45.52-carat diamond."

"Really? That was a 100-to-one shot."

"You just hit the trifecta." She fiddled with her napkin. "I told you my mother was an actress. When I was born, her fantasy was to make me the brightest star in the universe. With a last name like 'Diamond,' how could she not give me the name of the most famous diamond in the world."

"I gotta meet your mother. She sounds like my kind of lady. From what I know of you, you take after your dad, the cop."

"Just so."

He tapped his fingers, then folded his hands. After a few seconds, he said, "I'll be at your intel meeting tonight. I may have a few bits to share." Hope smiled and said she was happy that they could work together. He shrugged. It was better to have his grudging cooperation than nothing at all.

Cecelia came to the table and asked about dessert. "Nothing for me," Hope said, and Matt told her he'd pass also. As they stood up, Hope said, "Come back to the room, and I'll give you that report."

"You're full of surprises, Diamond. I thought you'd give me some dope story about it being gone with the wind."

She took him inside her room, went to the safe and pulled out the papers. She turned around. He was holding her copy of Walt Whitman's poems, *Leaves of Grass*, written in 1855.

"Here's the dossier," she said.

He didn't answer. She waited several moments and then coughed. "Here's the file."

He looked up. "You read Walt Whitman?"

"I find him compelling," she said and tilted her head. "Any problem?"

"No, no problem." He set down the book. "Coincidence, that's all. I have the same volume in my room."

The file folder slipped out of her fingers. Papers scattered on the floor. "Clumsy," she said.

Matt stooped down, picked them up and shuffled the papers into a neat stack. "Looks like I'm going to spend a little time reading." He grinned. "Too bad."

Hope pointed at the door."

He laughed and left. She walked over and picked up the book. *That cowboy carries around Walt Whitman!*

CHAPTER 19

"Looking good, Tony," George called from the bar. Tony was wearing jeans, plaid shirt, leather vest, western hat and boots.

"I'm taking a trail ride with Sean," Tony told him. "Any tips? Something easy because Sean had a rough night."

"I heard. I am happy he is better. Ride our Appaloosas. They are beautiful and easy riding." George was drying glasses. He set one on the shelf and turned back to Tony. "We have 40,000 horses running wild in the Nation."

"No kidding! I didn't know there were that many wild horses left in the country."

"We love the horses," George said, "but this land is hard. Farmers get mad because horses rob food from the sheep and cattle. Navajo Nation pays people to round up the horses. They are sold or killed. Still, the herds grow."

"Ch'įįdiish nizhóníyee'! I hope that's right," Tony said. "I was trying to say, 'amazing.'"

"Close enough," George said.

Although Tony picked up languages easily, he'd been struggling with learning even a few phrases of Navajo. "Yours is the most difficult language I've ever come across."

"You are right, Tony. Do you know about our Navajo Code Talkers in World War II?"

"No. They sound interesting," Tony said, resting an elbow on the bar.

George closed his eyes a moment. "My Grandfather was just a kid, but he remembers the stories. A man named Philip Johnston grew up here. He convinced some major out in California that Navajo was the perfect language for war codes. At the time, it had never been written down. It did not have an alphabet, and it did not use symbols. Only Navajo people right here on the res could speak it."

Setting down the cloth, George leaned on the counter across from Tony. "The military agreed and began recruiting our people. The first twenty-nine Navajo warriors were assigned to the U.S. Marines. They could translate three lines of English to code in twenty seconds."

"No kidding!" Tony had studied cryptology. What George was telling him was unheard of. A code-breaking machine would take thirty minutes.

"Our Code Talkers helped the Marines win the battles in the Pacific, especially at Iwo Jima," George said. "Six Code Talkers transmitted more than 800 messages during that battle, and they did not make a single error."

"Phenomenal!" Tony said. "I'm surprised I haven't heard of them."

"Their work was classified for decades, but in 2001 the first twenty-nine warriors received the Congressional Gold Medal. Another 250 received the Silver Medal."

Tony reached over and shook George's hand. Just then Sean came into the room. "Sorry to keep you waiting," he said.

"No problem," Tony said and waved to George as the men moved toward the door.

Sean adjusted his dark brown Stetson. "Mighty proud of this headpiece, Tony. The shop steams up the brim just how you like it."

"You look like Walt Longmire. I'll have to call you 'The Sheriff.'"

"Can't do that," Sean laughed. "'The Sheriff' is Peyton Manning's handle, one of the greats in football."

They reached the corral and leaned over the fence, watching the horses swishing their tails. Sean took off his hat and brushed at the flies.

Two leathery Navajos walked over. "You thinking of riding?" asked the taller, bowlegged man. "I'm Sani, and this here is Ray."

"George said to try the Appaloosas," Tony said and introduced himself and Sean.

"Tahoe and Cash are good horses," Sani said. "Wait here." The men walked back to the stables and were gone quite a spell before returning with two light-colored, spotted horses saddled and ready to go.

"*Bellisimo!* They found one big enough for you, Sean," Tony said, pointing at the gigantic horse.

"He's magnificent!"

"This is Cash," Sani said, holding the big horse. "That one is Tahoe."

Ray gave Tony a leg up onto Tahoe. Sean was big enough to hoist himself onto Cash. The wranglers adjusted the stirrups. "Hold the reins like this," Sani said, demonstrating. "Rest your legs on the sides and squeeze gentle-like to slow down."

"Water is in the canteen," Ray said, tapping the container hanging from the saddle horn, "and this here is a bit of grub." He pointed to the mesh bag. "If you get lost," he said to Tony, "say, 'Home, Tahoe,' and Tahoe will bring you back."

Before they started off, Sean pulled out his cell phone and asked Sani to take pictures. Then he and Tony rode off at an easy gait.

"I'll send my boy, Patrick, the picture of me and Cash," Sean said with a grin. "I'd like to bring him out here. He'd feel like a real cowboy."

"My folks will laugh. I've never ridden a horse before," Tony said.

As they rode along, the landscape opened in front of them. Sean pulled back on the reins. "I have to take a picture of this amazing scenery."

Tony stopped with him, and the two sat quiet, gazing at the landscape, patches of color stretching flat for miles, then bumping up against jagged rock formations.

"You come from Italy, right, Tony?" Sean asked, putting the camera in his shirt pocket.

"I lived near the ocean. It's hard to imagine that we're sitting in the middle of an ancient body of water."

Sean shook his head, peering around at the dirt and sagebrush and rocks. "It must be nice to live near the ocean. I took Ellen to Atlantic City for our honeymoon."

Tony squinted his eyes. "Why not somewhere more exotic, like the Caribbean?"

"Ellen doesn't like to travel. Atlantic City was the first time she had ever been out of the state. When she told me she was coming thousands of miles out west, you could've knocked me over with a feather." Sean clicked at the horse and patted its rear. Cash started moving, and Tahoe followed.

"Do you think you'll ever find out what happened to Meghan?" Sean asked as they rode side by side.

"We're trying."

"That FBI agent questioned me today. He acts like Ellen and me had something to do with Meghan's murder, or as he put it, 'suspicious death.' He even thinks Ellen tried to poison me."

Tony's face flushed. "Ellen had nothing to do with Meghan's death or with poisoning you!"

"You seem very sure of Ellen." Sean frowned at Tony.

"Come on, man. You, of all people, should have faith in her. Can you honestly imagine Ellen poisoning you?"

The man's doubt was sending warning sparks through Tony. *Was Zach right?* Could his personal feelings be affecting his professional judgment?

"I don't know what's gotten into me," Sean said. "Must be the phantoms of the desert."

"Can you tell me anything about Meghan that would make anyone want to kill her?"

"I think Meghan had mental issues," Sean said after a moment. "Maybe she said or did something that hit the wrong person the wrong way."

Tony considered that idea as he rode along. The camaraderie of the desert inspired him to ask a personal question. "Sean, how is it that you became involved with Meghan?" It was hard to imagine this worldly executive involved with the unsophisticated Meghan.

Sean apparently sensed that confidences were natural for two fellows on horseback. "It was a lot of things. Pressure at work. Ellen tied up in Patrick's world." He stopped talking, as if trying to figure out, himself, how things had started.

"Meghan worked near my office at the factory. She'd stay late and say, 'I missed my bus. Can we grab a cup of coffee? I don't like waiting another hour all by myself.'"

Sean looked over at Tony. "What would you do?"

Tony shrugged.

Sean heaved a deep sigh. "Truth to tell, I was flattered. Meghan was a young, attractive girl, and I found her amusing. She had a different point of view from most of the people I hang out with. We never went anywhere fancy. That wasn't her style. She always picked a two-bit diner in the neighborhood. She'd bring along a coupon and make me use it." He laughed. "I made up for it with the tip."

Sean rode in silence for several minutes, then looked over at Tony. "One night, Meghan asked me to drive her home. I pulled up in front of her building, and she snuggled up and started kissing me. I was a jerk not to nip things in the bud right then and there."

"What happened?"

"Things didn't go as far as you might be thinking, more flirting than anything else, but I was no angel. Mind you, I never went up to her apartment." He blew out a breath, as if realizing he had come close to a cliff and had stepped back.

"We went out to dinner a few more times, but I began to get nervous. She had a way of twisting what you said. Like once she asked if I thought she'd be good in the design center. I remarked that she might be good at that, just making conversation, you know. Next thing, she was telling people I promised her a promotion. Can you imagine how I felt when Ellen told me she was bringing Meghan on this trip?"

Tony chuckled. "Sorry, man, it's not funny, but I'm surprised your hair didn't turn white."

Sean laughed. "It very nearly did."

"How did you feel when Ellen told you Meghan had died?"

"I'm ashamed to admit it, but I felt relieved. Now, of course, with the FBI trying to hang a murder rap on Ellen and me, we're living in a nightmare. Ellen blames me, and she's right. I don't think we'll ever be the same until we know the truth."

Sean reined in Cash. "How about we have a drink and some grub?"

"Good idea," Tony said. They took the caps off the canteens, drank the water, and ate the apples and peanut butter crackers packed inside the mesh sacks.

"The salt in these crackers hits the spot," Sean said. "I could feel the sun taking a toll. Used to feel that way after a workout on the field in August." He took off his hat and wiped his brow.

When they finished their snack, they sat on the horses, enjoying the panorama. Fluttering red dust, clusters of sagebrush, pale yellow wildflowers, snow-capped mountain peaks off in the distance.

Sean looked over at Tony. "You know a lot about me, Tony. What about you? Are you married?"

"No, but I have a steady girl. Maria's her name."

"Steady girl? Not your partner or significant other?"

"I'm out of fashion, but that's how I think of her. She has her own place, and I have mine." He pulled out his phone and showed Sean a picture.

"She's gorgeous! Is she a model?"

"She's a spokesperson for Janai's company."

"From what I see, she'd be perfect for that job."

"Maria is good at what she does. She travels a lot. Right now, she's in Spain, and I'm here."

The sadness gnawing at his stomach made him put his hand on his chest. Maria was hurt because he didn't go to Spain to meet her family. He'd explained about the job, but they both knew it was his fear of commitment that made him stay home. Her family would expect him to propose marriage.

He had talked with Frank about Maria. Frank said he was thirty years old and had dated Maria for two years. He couldn't keep a girl like that waiting forever. He may have waited too long. He called every day, but she never answered. He sighed, took a last look at her picture, and put the phone in his pocket.

His eyes wandered over the landscape. "*Mama Mia!* Look over there!" Tony shouted and pointed toward the east. Horses were kicking up a red dust storm. A golden palomino was leading the herd. Dozens of horses of all colors were following. And they were all racing furiously right at Tony and Sean.

"Unbelievable!" Sean yelled. "I'll never see anything like this again in my life!" He grabbed his cell and took pictures. Cash was shuffling its feet as the horses thundered nearer.

"Grab the reins!" Tony yelled. "We need to get out of here!"

Sean's big horse whinnied and lowered its head. Sean stuck the camera in his pocket and pulled back on Cash's reins. The horse reared up on its hind legs. "Whoa, boy! Whoa boy!"

Tahoe was shifting its feet, and Tony held tight to the reins. He started sweating watching Sean atop the furious horse. He shouted a prayer. *"Santo Dio, aiutare!"*

Sean was slipping off the saddle. Cash lowered its head, and Sean righted himself just before the horse threw back its head and reared up again. Sean bounced up and down, shouting, "Whoa, boy!"

Tony watched in horror, his heart pounding. He turned back to the herd. The horses were galloping toward them at high speed. If they continued straight, he and Sean would be killed. He couldn't leave Sean alone, and Sean couldn't control Cash enough to get out of the path of the wild horses.

A scene from an old western flashed vivid detail of a hero shooting his rifle up in the air to turn a herd of buffalo. That trick might not work with horses, but Tony pulled the gun out of his shoulder holster and raised his arm. When the horses were fairly close, he shot straight up in the air. A blast of wind and a dust storm hit the men as the herd swerved. Dozens of horses raced by. Tony closed his eyes against the dirt, then looked over at Sean.

"Man!" Sean yelled, breathing hard, but Cash had stopped bucking. Sean touched the horse's side. "His heart is pounding faster than mine."

"Mine is pounding, too! I can't believe you stayed in the saddle. I'm sorry, man, but there was nothing I could do to help."

"What do you mean, Tony? You saved our lives!

"Do me a favor, Sean. Don't mention that shot, okay?"

"Sure, Tony." The men looked at each other. "Tony, you and me. We're life buddies. You don't share an adventure like this and ever forget."

Tony stretched out his arm, and they fist bumped. "Are you okay to go on?"

"Yeah, my heart is slowing down."

Tony and Sean rode quietly for another twenty minutes before deciding to go back. Tony's eyes opened wide as he surveyed the landscape. "Sean! Which way did we come?"

"I dunno. Ask Tahoe."

"Right!" Tony whispered into the horse's ear, "Home, Tahoe." Sure enough, Tahoe turned a ninety-degree angle, picked up the pace and headed home.

As he rode along, Tony thought about Sean. The man had been genuinely frightened, but at the same time, he loved the excitement. Sean didn't shy away from danger.

CHAPTER 20

Matt Dennison was drinking a root beer at the bar when Frank walked in. Dennison lifted his glass mug. "Join me?" He was interested to hear about Frank's search. That elusive arsenic worried him. No telling when it would turn up again. The next person might not be as lucky as McKenna.

Frank nodded at George and said he'd have the same. George slid a mug and a bowl of pretzels down the counter.

Dennison hooked a thumb over to the corner, and the two men sat down on the leather chairs. "Madison, tell me what you found in Conners' room when you had that look-see."

"Nothing much," Frank said. "I saw the printouts about condos in Pittsburgh. She was obviously under the impression that Mr. McKenna was going to divorce his wife and marry her."

"That's what I think, too. It gives Mrs. Mac a good reason to want her out of the way."

"I won't argue the point. Tony has a different opinion."

"I know Manara's view. That don't matter much to me because the McKenna-Connors connection is the only one that makes sense."

"One thing about those printouts," Frank said, "according to Meghan's notes, Mr. McKenna was pushing back, and she was frustrated. To me, that says he'd never leave his wife to move in with her, let alone marry her."

Matt finished his drink and toyed with a pretzel. "Another motive for the McKennas to want her out of the way. Plus, you can't get around the fact that Mrs. Mac always turns up in the middle of the scene. Look what happened to her husband, and she was the only person in the room."

"The only person we know about," Frank said.

"Have it your way." Dennison lifted his hands toward the ceiling. "As Buddha said, 'Three things cannot long be hidden: The sun, the moon, and the truth.'"

Frank said he hoped the truth would come out before many more moons.

Matt chuckled. "Did anything catch your attention in any of the other rooms?" If only he could find the arsenic, he might have the evidence to build a case against Mrs. Mac.

"In Margo's room, I found an envelope in the trashcan with an International Biolabs return address. Most mail goes over the internet, so I wondered if it was an employment offer."

"Any reason she'd want to cut loose from Grand Med?"

"I don't know of any reason. Maybe Biolabs was trying to recruit her."

"Something to keep in mind. It might tee off Lydia Fallbrook. Anything else?"

"Robert Halloway brought along a rifle. He told Lucy he was going target shooting with George."

"Can't see George using a rifle. I've gone deer hunting with him. We used bows and arrows."

"You're a man of hidden talents," Frank said with a grin.

Just then, George appeared and refilled their glasses. Matt looked up and held out a finger. "Did you go target shooting with Robert Halloway?"

"I did. I took my bow. Robert uses a Remington bolt action."

"Is he a good shot?"

"Good enough to hit a deer standing in front of him." George turned and left.

Matt grinned and took a sip of root beer. "Guess we don't have to worry about that rifle."

He set down the mug and leaned on one elbow, his hand under his chin. "Can you think why anybody here would have murder in mind?" He'd read Madison's backgrounder. The man had served in the same dangerous parts of the world as he had himself, but years earlier.

"I knew this was a high-stakes assignment, but I truly didn't expect to find us in the middle of a murder investigation." He pointed a finger at Matt. "It was your friend who wound things up the minute we arrived."

"My friend?" Matt furrowed his brow.

"Well, Jake Sanders, the FBI guy in Washington. He called to say the ladies' names and Secret Sands had been found on the dark web."

"That's news. I know Jake, and I know he's looking at the reports. He apparently didn't think it necessary to mention the web hit." Matt grumbled under his breath. "Nice to stumble around in the dark and then learn your own people could shed a little light on things."

Frank smiled. "Just the joys of working for the government."

Still annoyed, Matt shoved his drink aside. "Diamond invited me to your intel party tonight. I'll be there. Sounds like I might learn a bit."

"She mentioned you might come."

"These ladies are hard for me to figure out," Dennison said, letting go of his anger. "All of them are worth a bundle. Yet they still work eighteen hours a day, except McKenna. Why don't they find some nice guy, marry him, and enjoy life? McKenna has the right idea."

Frank laughed. "You're behind the times, Dennison. Where did you grow up?"

"Clovis, right here in New Mexico. Straight over from here to the Texas border." He pointed out the direction. "I grew up a bronc rider. We had a lot of gals who could stay in the saddle, but they enjoyed themselves, too. Not all this nose-to-the-grindstone stuff like these ladies. Diamond's the same way from what I can tell."

"She is in a league with these ladies as far as work ethic goes. She's often out in the middle of the night checking client houses. I know because I get called when something's amiss."

"Maybe that's why she hasn't found herself a fellow. She never locks the office door."

"I haven't known Hope to be in a serious relationship, but then she keeps her private life private. Why the interest?"

"Nothing special. You don't run into many ladies in her field, so I'm curious." He ate a pretzel and watched a bunny hopping among the rocks.

"Will you be out here long?"

"No telling," he said, turning back to Frank. "If I can break this case, maybe the folks that stuck me out here will find me another spot. Not that I'm unhappy. Problem is, I prefer foreign counterespionage, and that work goes on in Washington."

"Is that what you were doing before you came here?"

"It is. If we wrap up this case, maybe we can sit down and talk over a couple of real drinks." He pulled back his root beer and finished it.

"One nice thing about Diamond, she seems to have a sense of humor."

Frank chuckled. "You're right. Stop by the office in L.A. when you get out our way and look at a clipping framed on her wall."

"It may be a while before I get out to your part of the world. Tell me about it."

"You agree Hope's a beautiful woman, right?"

Dennison nodded.

"Picture this," Frank said, and he held up his two hands depicting a picture frame. "A gossip columnist didn't like it when Hope refused his advances. He published what he thought was a rude description. 'Don't be fooled by this Diamond. Her topaz eyes, ruby lips, and pearly teeth are cut glass from the five-and-dime.'"

"What! Did one of you punch that joker's lights out?"

"No need. Hope marched up to his office and asked him to sign the clipping to hang in her office. He never tangled with her again."

Dennison slapped his knee. "I gotta see that clipping."

"Are you coming on the hayride tonight?"

"Diamond asked me to come along to keep an eye on folks. It's fine with me." He shook his head. "If something happens to these ladies while I'm on the case, I'll never get back to Washington."

# #

The sun was slowly sinking, and Lucy, wearing a blue-and-white-striped swimsuit with a terrycloth robe draped over her shoulders, walked down the path to the Oasis. She kept looking around. The pool area was quiet and pleasant. Flowers bloomed in pottery decorated in Navajo designs. The giant rock provided a formidable wall of privacy, but Zach had warned that the location was the most dangerous at the hotel.

She dove into the pool and swam laps. The water felt fresh after sitting outside. When she came up out of the water after her final lap, her body stiffened. Dimitri was standing at the edge of the pool watching her. He had a glass of whiskey in his hand.

"Nice," he said and moved toward the tables topped with umbrellas.

Lucy put her hands on the edge of the pool and jumped out. *How long had he been standing there?* She took off her swim cap, shook out her hair, and dried off with the hotel's striped beach towel. Then she slipped into a white terrycloth robe and sat down at a table.

"May I join you?" Dimitri asked, gesturing to the chair.

"Of course. What have you been up to today?"

"Work. I come here for coffee. Would you like?"

"No, thanks." Lucy opened her bag and pulled out a bottle of water.

"May I smoke?" He finished his whiskey and set down the glass.

"Not a problem out here in this breeze," Lucy said, the air current rippling her hair.

Cecelia arrived with Dimitri's order. She set a bright red coffee pot on the table, along with two yellow mugs. Then she placed a basket of tea cakes next to the coffee. "I saw you come this way, so I brought enough for both of you," she said to Lucy. "Where is your friend?"

"Tony? I haven't seen him this afternoon."

"I hope he is not lost," Cecelia said as she walked away.

Lucy opened her water and took a long swallow. She was beginning to feel cool in the breeze and in the shade of the umbrella. "The coffee smells good," she said. "I'll join you after all."

Dimitri was drinking his coffee and watching her. "You bring beauty to place."

It was an unexpected remark. "It's a very beautiful place," Lucy said, shifting in the chair. "I'm sorry our time here has been spoiled by Meghan's death."

"I think same," Dimitri said. "She very young."

"Did you talk with her?"

Dimitri studied his coffee, and he was quiet for a time before answering. "Yes, here." He gestured to where Lucy was sitting. "We have coffee."

"Friday, the day you arrived?"

He nodded. "Can you tell me what you talked about? It might be important in understanding her mood."

Dimitri sat back and sighed. "I not tell FBI man. Not like to talk to police. Friday, Mrs. Gonzalez and me argue. I come here. Meghan come, and she ask why I am upset. I foolish. Say too much." He stopped talking and poured coffee into the cup.

"I get the picture," Lucy said. "She hinted that she'd be speaking with Gloria."

"Yes." He stubbed out his cigarette in the ashtray. "I shocked. Think girl try to blackmail me!"

"She was an opportunist," Lucy said and brushed off the eerie feeling of the isolated area. She was a black belt in judo. She'd had encounters with men who thought she was an easy target, and she'd put them on their backs.

She smiled at Dimitri. "When I think of shipping, I think of pirates. Guess I've seen too many movies."

"I tell you this. Pirates and smugglers make our business dangerous." He sat up straight, frowning at his coffee cup. "In

186

2019, everybody celebrate. Pirates no bother us. Best record in twenty-five years. In 2020, pandemic. Pirates stir up trouble again."

"How do they attack the ships? Like in the movie, 'Pirates of the Caribbean'"?

"I not see movie." He shook his head. "Pirates find you on high seas. They toss up ropes and climb on board. Sometimes they have handguns, sometimes assault rifles. They steal what they can. Gangs know everything—crew, cargo, and where ships are sailing."

"Sounds as if they have inside information."

Leaning back, Dimitri narrowed his eyes, a hint of a threat coming across the table.

"I haven't seen many smuggling movies. Gloria said you operate cargo ships. Do you worry about smugglers?"

"Yes. Our cargo ships are big. Carry hundreds of containers. Containers are big, like railroad box cars. Smugglers hide stuff inside containers. They seal up containers at dock and sail to another country. They open containers and take loot. Easy."

"What do they smuggle?"

"Drugs, weapons, people, anything that pays. U.S. Customs make big bust on ship in Philadelphia. Found 20 tons of cocaine, over a billion dollars U.S."

"Incredible!" Lucy took a piece of banana bread out of the basket. Dimitri would be very useful in a smuggling operation. "Have you been approached by smugglers?" He could have a strong reason for wanting Gloria out of the way.

His dark expression sent over a wave of menace. "You ask many questions."

"I find what you're telling me interesting, but I'd better get ready for the hayride."

He stood up with her and said something in Greek that Lucy took for good-by. She pulled the robe tighter as she walked away.

# #

The vivid painting against the teal wall in Hope's room reached out and held her attention as she was about to get ready for the hayride. The horsemen were sending her a message, but she couldn't figure it out, just like the reports she'd been reading. The information was there, but the message was hidden. She ran her fingers through her hair and put the dossier in the safe.

She showered and tried to sort out her feelings about Matt Dennison. She'd met him three days ago, and his coldness chilled her to the bone. Today, Monday, he was stirring up feelings in ways no one but Jake Sanders had done for a very long time.

She liked the way he showed respect to the Navajo elder, and she was astounded that he carried around *Leaves of Grass,* but it was the look in his eyes when she was wearing her black outfit that aroused her feelings.

She slathered on Icelandic Wind moisturizer. The desert air was drying out her skin. After she dressed, she frowned at her image in the mirror. She was wearing denim wide-legged pants, a long-sleeve checked shirt, and brown leather vest, an outfit she'd ordered on the Internet specifically for the hayride. *Too rustic.*

She pulled off the checkered shirt and slipped on a blue satin blouse with four-inch cuffs. She ditched the vest and finished the ensemble with a pair of shiny black boots. She swiped on a rich, red lipstick and spritzed on the perfume Janai had given her.

She grinned at her jazzed-up downhome look. The outfit was closer to Carrie Underwood than Calamity Jane.

With that thought, she switched off the lights and turned to the door. She stopped. She took the Smith & Wesson out of her purse, put it in the deep pocket of the wide-legged pants, and threw the purse on the counter. Handling the gun brought her mind back to the seriousness of the moment. One of the guests was a murderer, and she needed her full attention on her clients.

Chapter 21

"You look like a movie star!" Hope had been in Blue Sky five minutes when Matt Dennison strode in wearing a black pointed-collared shirt with silver studs and a white embroidered design, black jeans, and a black Stetson. He took off his hat and bowed to her.

Hope was shaking her head.

"Guess Mark Twain was right when he said, 'Clothes make the man.'" Matt laughed and put on his hat.

"Where did you get that amazing outfit?"

"This ole thing? Had a messenger service bring it over from my place this afternoon."

"Why, if it isn't Roy Rogers and Dale Evans," Frank, outfitted in a black velvet shirt like the Navajo dancers, hugged Hope and shook hands with Matt.

It was eight o'clock, and guests began arriving. Janai wore a bright red blouse and full skirt with crinoline peeking out an inch below the hem. She sidled up to the Fed. "Hi Tex. I claim you as my date for the evening."

Matt took off his hat and bowed. "My pleasure, ma'am."

Lucy moved close to Hope and said in an undertone, "Who'da thought that guy was such a hunk." Hope blinked. The girl had plucked the thought right out of her head.

"I gotta get me one of those shirts," Sean McKenna said to Dennison. He was holding onto Ellen's arm. Hope smiled and told Ellen how festive she looked in the pink-and-white checked top and full skirt.

"Another handsome cowboy!" Gloria called out when Tony came in wearing a white leather jacket, bolo tie, and pin-tucked tuxedo shirt. She bounced over and took his arm. "Janai claimed the FBI guy, so I'm claiming you." Her beaded blouse sparkled in the light from the chandeliers.

Tony glanced at Hope as if to ask, *what's going on?* but he said, "Happy to oblige."

Swishing her multi-tiered skirt back and forth with both hands, Lydia curtsied to Frank and asked him to be her escort.

Hope smiled. The woman's grim look apparently wasn't frozen. Dimitri and Robert took Lucy by each arm and headed up the hill. The fashion parade was fun to watch.

Hope and Zach waited for Margo. She came in wearing jeans and a frilly blouse. She latched onto Zach, and he gave her a wide smile.

As she was about to start up the trail, Audrey rose from the couch. Hope had overlooked the Shadow Lady. Audrey was rigged out in apparel like the clothing Hope had left in the room. "Nice outfit, Audrey," Hope said. "You and I are the last to leave."

Two wagons, each drawn by two horses, were standing by the corral. Hope introduced herself to the driver, whose name was Sani. He set up steps, and Matt stood to the side and helped passengers into the wagon. Lydia and Janai stepped up first. The wagons had straw on the floor bed, but the sides were lined with benches and cushions.

The wagon was drawn by black mustangs that Sani called Paco and Icer. When half the guests had boarded the wagon and settled in, Sani snapped a whip and yelled, "Giddy up," and the horses marched along at a slow pace. The other group would follow in five minutes to avoid dirt kicked up by the lead horses.

Janai and Matt were sitting close to the driver across from Lydia and Frank. The sight of Janai and Matt chatting with their heads together brought a frown to Hope's face. She was at the other end of the wagon with Margo, Zach and Audrey.

Lydia pulled out a cigarette and asked if anyone minded if she smoked. No one spoke, and Frank held her lighter for her.

"I can't believe what a hit that FBI agent is," Audrey said quietly. "You'd think he'd be on the job investigating instead of partying."

"Well, we're all here, so you could say he is investigating," Hope said tartly.

About half-an-hour later, Sani reined in the horses near a small corral, past several parked vehicles.

"Are we here already?" Janai smiled at Matt. "I enjoyed our conversation, Tex."

"Same here," he said and hopped off the wagon. The driver set steps, and Matt helped each of the ladies down. Miffed at his gallantry, Hope gritted her teeth when he took her arm.

"Have I done something to offend you?" He held onto her arm.

"No." She looked him in the eye and smiled. "I'm glad you're here." She wanted Matt to look after Janai. That was the reason she'd invited him. The closer the two stuck together, the better. *Lighten up, girl.*

Janai walked beside her the short distance to the campground. Hope smiled and nodded when Janai confided, "I didn't realize Tex was so handsome and charming."

Not to mention rude and insulting. Aloud she said, "He's a nice guy when he's relaxed."

The night had turned black and twinkled with stars. Matt stepped over and whispered, "Look up, Diamond. The heavens are full of jewels, lots of diamonds."

She brushed her hair out of her eyes and stared up at the stars. Janai took Matt's arm and guided him to a seat at the table. The other wagon pulled in, and Hope walked back up the path to greet the passengers. Sani was tying the horses to a fence on the other side of the wooden comfort station.

The guests stepped off the second wagon, and Dimitri walked over to Hope. "You look beautiful, Miss Diamond."

"Thank you." She smiled when he offered his arm. They followed Sean and Ellen down the path. A row of pine trees stretched along the pathway down past the tables. A large firepit crackled, and smoke from pine wood logs mingled with the aroma of the steaks. The scent drifted across the fresh night air.

Looking back toward Hope, Sean said, "Grub smells delish." Ellen was walking beside him. She missed a step and tripped. Sean caught her before her knee hit the ground. He pulled her close and held her in his arms for a long moment. Ellen held onto his arm the rest of the way down to the tables. They appeared to be a happy couple, *but how safe was she with Sean?*

Red-and-white-checkered tablecloths, white flowers and flickering candles looked festive on the two long tables under the stars. George was setting out napkins, and he pulled out a cushioned chair for Hope. Dimitri sat next to her, across from Frank and Lydia. Sean and Ellen, Zach and Margo sat at the same table.

"Tony and I had quite an adventure today on the horses." Sean said.

"Tell us about it," Zach said.

"It was an experience that will make me quiver for years to come. Mind you," he pointed at Zach, "a herd of wild horses was thundering right at us. Dozens at first. Then hundreds. Those horses stretched out a mile behind a golden Palomino that appeared to be flying. All four feet sprang in the air at the same time. Here he came. Ears back. Hooves high. Mane a-flying. Galloping, galloping, galloping." Sean clapped three times as he pronounced the words.

Looking at each person, Sean paused, then spoke faster and a bit louder. "Red dirt was a-spinning high in the sky like a Texas tornado! All we could hear was the sound of those horses as their feet pounded the ground. Here they came. Pounding. Pounding. Pounding." His hands thumped the table with each word.

"Here was I atop a giant horse rearing up on his hind legs. What a ride! I felt like king of the rodeo! I shouted and waved my hat at that golden Palomino!"

Sean leaned in toward Zach and his voice quieted. "We were nose to nose now. My mind raced. Should I jump onto that magnificent beast and ride with the herd?"

He stopped, pointed a finger on both hands at Zach. "What would you have done?"

Sean stopped talking, and everyone clapped. He had the Irish gift of storytelling and spun that tale out like a cowboy lassoing cattle. Zach reached over and shook his hand. "I bow to the master, my friend." The others raised a glass in salute.

Ellen slapped at Sean's arm. "You could have been killed!"

"Nah, I make it sound scarier than it was." He put his arm around his wife and kissed her cheek.

Frank turned to Tony, who was sitting behind him at the other table. "And where was friend Tony during this madness?"

Tony looked over his shoulder. "I lassoed Sean and dragged him back to the ranch."

Although Hope laughed along with the others, she rubbed her hands at how dangerous the situation may have been. Matt winked at her, and she smiled. *What was it about that cowboy that was jumpstarting her adrenalin?*

After the meal, the sounds of lively country music drew the guests to a large plank floor. Flames flickered in old fashioned lanterns strung up on poles at the corners of the dance floor.

"It's square-dancing time!" shouted a big man with a white mustache and beard. Big Jim introduced himself and waved his black hat at another man dressed in western gear. Sawyer Redstone ran his bow over the strings of his fiddle. Sani and the other driver sat next to the fiddler with spoons and clackers.

Janai and Matt lined up together, and Dimitri took Hope's arm. The other pairs joined in, and George asked Audrey to be his partner.

The dancers made two squares of eight people each. Big Jim started the dancers off with a handful of steps, like Circle Left, Allemande Left, Do-si-do, and Promenade. Then, the fiddler played "Jim's Guitar Rag," and two squares of dancers swirled around the floor as Big Jim sang out the calls.

Dimitri told Hope that square dancing was like *sirtaki*, Greek folk dancing. She easily followed his lead and enjoyed the energy of the music.

At intervals, Big Jim called for people to switch partners. Hope danced with Tony, Frank, and Sean. He was a big man but very agile on his feet. He said he'd never been square dancing before and was having a great time. When the music stopped, he said, "I like this dancing, but it plum wears you out. I have to sit a spell." Sean left the floor and walked over to the tables.

Throughout the evening, most guests took a break, leaving only one square of dancers on the floor. The others sat at the tables or walked up to the restrooms. Matt stuck close to Janai.

After two hours, Big Jim said, "Time for our last dance, which will be a round dance." He asked people to change partners, and the fiddler played "Goodnight Irene."

Hope's hand was taken unexpectedly from behind, and she swung around. Matt said, "That Janai's quite a gal." Hope's shoulders tensed, and Matt pulled her close. His cheek, raspy with whiskers you couldn't see, brushed hers, and she felt a surge of electricity.

"Thanks for letting me crash this shindig," he said. "I haven't had this much fun in donkey's years."

"I'm glad you came. I didn't have to worry about Janai." She looked around. Janai was dancing with Robert.

Matt laughed. "Struck me you worried about her a little too much." Hope jerked, and his grip tightened. "Come on, now, what's a little joshing between friends." The smile in his eyes was so warm that she rested her head on his shoulder and closed her eyes as they danced.

The music ended, and the guests applauded the fiddler and caller. The McKennas were near Hope and Matt. Sean told Ellen that they should host a square dance as a school fund raiser.

"That's a great idea." Ellen said and promised to plan one for September. She'd likely do it, too, if Dennison didn't arrest her for murder. He closed his eyes and lowered his head.

Dimitri waited for Hope at the table, where coffee and cake had been set out. "Great party. Like in Greece. Dancing and music." She smiled and said he had been a great partner. He lifted her hand and kissed it. "You make America special."

"You're very gracious. Thank you."

When she turned her head, Matt was watching, and his eyes held a surprised, hurt look, odd for a cowboy who had spent a career on the other side of the world in places where he must have learned to guard his facial expressions.

Her heart raced a little, but she turned away and checked on each of her clients.

Checking her watch, Hope saw it was time to "mosey back to the corral," as they say in the old westerns. Guests moved up the trail toward the corral.

One driver had finished hitching a wagon. Audrey said she wanted to get back, so she boarded the wagon that was ready to leave, not the one she came in.

Sani was having trouble settling down Paco. Matt walked over and stroked the horse's forehead. Hope asked if she could do anything, but he shook his head. When Sani had the wagon hitched, the group boarded. The night air was crisp, and blankets had been placed on the seats. The horses trotted at a gentle pace along the trail.

"Hope, this cookout was a great success," Janai said. "Everyone relaxed and had a good time."

"I agree," put in Lydia. "It's been a very special evening." She smiled and held onto Frank's arm.

Just then, Sani yelled, "Whoa Paco!" Hope looked around. She was sitting behind the driver, next to Lydia and across from Matt. The horse was pumping its head up and down. As the wagon started down a slope, Paco bolted, and Acer raced alongside but couldn't keep the same pace. The wagon bumped along precariously.

Matt stood up and grabbed the railing. He stepped up onto the bench and swung himself over onto the driver's seat. Hope's stomach lurched, and she clenched the edge of the bench.

Leaping onto Paco's back, Matt reached for the horse's collar, but the two horses careened toward one another, and Matt was catapulted down between the two horses. He pushed at Icer and finally caught hold of Paco's collar. Then he grabbed the horse's mane with his other hand. Hope's heart pounded as he hoisted himself up onto the horse's back.

Paco twisted its head back and forth, swinging Matt from side to side. Somehow, Matt held on. Suddenly, Paco reared up on its hind legs. The wagon tilted. Hope flung out her arm over Lydia, but her eyes stayed riveted on Matt.

"Whoa Paco. Easy boy. Good boy." Matt hollered, but the frantic horse kept twisting and jerking. Matt stuck to the horse. At last, Paco stopped bucking and came to a shuddering standstill. Matt wrapped his hands around the horse's neck and bounced down to the ground. He kept hold of the horse's mane and talked calmly to the agitated animal. "Good boy. Good Paco."

Hope's heart was beating fast. She tried to stand up, but her knees buckled, and she sank back. She took a deep breath and hopped over to Janai. The two women hugged each other.

"Close call," Janai said, and Hope felt her tremble. "Good thing Tex knew what he was doing."

Frank wrapped his arms around Lydia. Margo seemed dazed, and Zach arranged a blanket around her shoulders. "Stay seated everyone," Hope said. "Everything seems to be under control." She touched Zach's shoulder and nodded to Janai. He picked up a blanket, moved over and put it over her lap. He nodded, a signal that he would stay by her side.

Hope sprang down from the wagon, nearly fell but caught herself. She ran over to Matt, who was examining the leather straps on the horse. She wanted to throw her arms around him and tell him how scared she'd been that he'd be killed, but her eyes met the icy glare of the FBI.

"Seems we were having too much fun," he said. "We missed someone tampering with this horse. What they did, I don't know."

She wrapped her arms around herself. "Deliberate sabotage?"

"That's my guess based on what's happened here."

"Is it safe to continue, or should Zach walk on ahead and have the hotel send cars?"

The horse was standing still, and Matt rubbed its side. "He's still breathing hard. Let's give him a chance to calm down." He called up to the driver. "Any apples or carrots?"

The man looked at Matt, eyes bulging, but he didn't move. Matt called out again for something to give the horses. Sani shook himself, reached down onto the floor, and tossed a sack to Matt. "Give Paco those carrots. I would feed Acer, but I better stay here in case they get frightened."

"I'll give Acer carrots," Hope said. She walked over and stroked the horse's forehead. Sani threw down another bag. "Here you are, Acer, good boy," she murmured.

After a while, Matt said, "I think we can move on. I'll walk alongside Paco." The driver nodded. Matt helped Hope back into the wagon. "Be careful," he whispered.

When they arrived back at the corral, two wranglers hurried over and talked in undertones to the driver, who nodded, pointed to Matt, and kept shaking his head.

Hope jumped down. Tony was standing by the corral. "What happened?" he asked quietly. "I was about to start out to find you."

"I'll explain later," Hope said. "Go back to the hotel and make sure everyone is okay." He nodded and left.

Matt set up steps for the guests. Hope stood close by. "I'm sorry about our unexpected adventure," she told Margo, who was the first one down. Margo shook her head, and Zach jumped down and walked with her to the hotel.

Lydia's face was white. "Keep that blanket around you till you're in the hotel," Matt said. "Then have a very large brandy." She smiled, and Frank took her arm.

"I don't know how you stayed on that horse, Dennison," Frank said.

Matt grinned. "Truth is, I'm not sure, either."

"There was nothing I could do. I'm sorry."

Matt held out his hand and shook Frank's. "There wasn't anything you or anybody else could have done." Frank patted Matt's shoulder and walked Lydia down the trail.

When Janai reached the bottom step, Matt held out his arms, and she put her hands on his shoulders. "When you want that transfer back to Washington, Tex, let me know."

"That's a nice thought, but I doubt my boss wants me back in Washington." He smiled at Janai, the smile that lit up his eyes.

"I wasn't making a comment. I was making a promise."

Matt looked at Janai a long moment. "I know you mean it. But if I can't get back to the Big Top on my own, it's best I stay here."

Janai nodded, took his arm, and the two walked down the path.

Taking a deep breath, Hope waited a few minutes to recover from the excitement of the ride and from what she had just heard. Jake had said Dennison was looking for any excuse to get back to Washington. Not many people would have passed on that offer. Janai delivered on her promises.

George was working behind the bar. He frowned when Hope asked for a shot of whiskey, something she'd never ordered before. "You are late getting back," he said, handing her the drink.

"Paco had a fright and bolted."

George squinted. "Not like Paco. He is a good horse, calm horse."

"Maybe he saw a rattlesnake."

"A snake would scare him."

"Matt saved the day. He jumped on Paco and brought him under control. Everyone is safe. That's the main thing."

"Dennison is old hand with horses," George said, surprising Hope.

She handed him her empty glass, and he said in a grave voice, "We never have trouble here at Secret Sands. Dead lady's chindi is angry."

George walked out from behind the bar and took Hope's hands. He recited the Navajo Blessing Prayer in his soft, measured cadence.

"Thank you, George," she said when he had finished, and she kissed his cheek. She felt calmer, but the vision of Matt falling between the horses flashed across her eyes.

Chindi was seeking revenge. Who would be the next victim?

CHAPTER 21

It was nearly midnight. Hope was in the Desert Rose gazing out at the stars splashed across the desert sky, pulling in their serenity. When the team gathered, she stood behind her chair, rolling it back and forth.

"We're into Tuesday, and the women will be leaving in two days," she said. "Our killer is getting desperate." She took a deep breath and shot a look at Frank.

He said in the quiet way he had of calming her nerves, "It was a pretty terrifying adventure. Fortunately, we all came out of it okay."

Lucy poured herself a glass of ice water. "What happened? No one on your wagon stuck around to talk."

Hope smiled. "We had an adventure right out of those old westerns Tony talked about. One of the horses, Paco, bolted and nearly capsized the wagon. If it weren't for Matt, we could have been killed."

"How's that?" Tony asked.

"Paco started running like the possessed. Icer, the other horse, couldn't keep up. The wagon was tilting helter-skelter, and the driver was no match for the demon horses."

Her heart began pounding, and she stopped a moment to gain control. "Matt jumped down onto Paco, and the horse tried to throw him off. I don't know how he hung on."

As if on cue, the door opened, and Matt Dennison strode into the room. He had changed into dark slacks and a pullover sweater and wasn't wearing his cowboy hat. Hope's eyebrows lifted. He looked too ordinary to be the heroic cowboy who had been bouncing up and down on the bucking horse.

Frank started clapping, and the others joined in. Matt stopped, looked over at Hope.

"I was telling the team about our adventures. You were a regular matinée hero."

Before he could respond, the door opened again, and Cecelia pushed a coffee cart over to the counter. "Coffee." Tony said. "Just what I need to stay awake." Cecelia poured a cup, smiled, and handed it to him. Lucy rolled her eyes at the personal service.

Matt took a beer out of the fridge and sat down next to Tony.

"Do you have any idea what caused the horses to bolt?" Frank asked.

"My guess is Paco was tampered with," Matt said. He uncapped the beer and took a long swallow.

"Was the person trying to kill everyone or just one of the people in the wagon?" Lucy asked.

"We don't know," Hope said. "Janai and Lydia were in the wagon." She was tiring, obviously a reaction from the scare. She ran her fingers through her hair.

"Are you okay?" Matt asked. "We can do this in the morning."

"Let's go on. Frank can take over if I wear down."

The room was silent for several seconds, then Lucy asked in a hushed voice, "Do you think the person who tampered with the horses was in our wagon?"

Hope nodded to Zach, and he opened his computer. "Frank, call off the names of the riders in each wagon, so Zach can enter them in the dossier."

Frank set down his coffee. "Wagon one: Janai, Lydia, Margo, Audrey, Hope, Matt, Zach, and Frank. Wagon two: Gloria, Ellen, Lucy, Robert, Dimitri, Tony, and Sean."

"Wait," Hope said. "Audrey was in our cart on the way to the cookout, but she switched wagons on the way back."

Matt pulled a notebook and pencil stub out of his back pocket. "Interesting," he murmured and made a note.

"Could it have been an accident?" Tony asked.

"Trained horses don't go loco without reason," Matt said. "It's possible an animal flashed by, or Paco sensed a snake. If something like that happened, there'll be evidence. I'll take a look in the morning."

"Mind if I come along?" Hope asked, anxious to know if they could rule out attempted murder.

"Please yourself."

"Can we eliminate anybody as a suspect?" Lucy asked. Zach read off the names again.

"It's like tossing a dart at the board," Frank said. "We don't have reason to suspect one over the other."

"What pops up," Zach said, "is the fact that Sean and Ellen were in the other wagon."

"It's pointless to discuss until we know for sure it wasn't an accident." Hope said and asked Matt if he had discovered any clues in the reports that they had missed.

"You gave me facts that I hadn't turned up myself. So, thank you." He tapped his fingers on the table and then said, "I have one suggestion."

"What's that?" Zach asked.

"Include impressions in your reports. When people have a different impression of a person, it can lead you down a different path. For example, my impression of Sean and Ellen ain't anywhere near like Tony's. Diamond hedges on Sean, too."

Tony started to interrupt, but Matt put a hand on his arm. "Let me finish. I suspect the McKennas. But two people I respect have a different impression. I'll set aside my impression and see if the facts take me down a different path. If not, I'll go back and follow my own road. Most of the time, my impression is on target."

Tony cocked his head. "Fair enough."

"That's a slant I hadn't considered." Hope looked around. "Let's include our impressions of whether a person is a villain or a victim whenever we can. Lucy, tell us about your day."

"I had three conversations of interest. Gloria early this morning. Later, Margo came by, and we sat outside while I was on guard duty. Then I went to the pool. Dimitri has coffee there in the afternoons.

"Start with Gloria," Hope said.

"Gloria and I went on a hike. We met Margo on the trail. She runs ten miles every day. We chatted briefly, then she ran on by." Lucy hesitated, bit her lip. "Gloria's father has threatened to replace her with Dimitri."

The statement dropped like a bomb and set off an explosion of comments. "That gives Dimitri one huge motive," Frank said, first out of the box.

"It gives Gloria the same motive," Hope said. After others commented, she asked, "What did you learn from Dimitri?"

"He thinks Meghan was trying to blackmail him."

It was as if another bomb had exploded. "Tell us about the blackmailing," Frank said.

Lucy shrugged. "Dimitri was upset over an argument with Gloria. Meghan wheedled the story out of him and implied she was going to tell Gloria. I don't think she really wanted anything from him, but what if Meghan tried to blackmail someone else?"

"Good point," Frank said.

"Did Dimitri talk about the business?" Hope asked.

"We discussed pirates and smugglers. Both use informers. Dimitri became upset when I asked him if he had been contacted himself by anyone wanting inside information."

"That's new information," Dennison said, making a note. "He wouldn't tell me much because he doesn't like talking to anybody who smells like police, or *Ellinikí Astynomía,* as they say in Greece."

"What about Margo?" Hope asked.

"I learned a lot about pharmaceuticals. You get antiseptics from dyes. Who knew? She threw some shade on Lydia because she's been treating her like a go-fer."

The third bomb exploded, and Dennison said, "Honey, you've just given me motives that I didn't have when I came in here."

"Well, sweetie, I'm happy that little ole me could help out a smart dude like yourself."

Matt laughed. "Okay, you made your point. The honey jar's empty."

"Thank you," Lucy said. "Back to business. I think Margo's too smart to be a victim. She would smell treachery a mile way."

"The crisis in pharmaceuticals is counterfeit medicines," Matt said, flipping pages in his notebook. "For crooks, profits are twenty-five times higher than, say, heroin trafficking. No connection has been established with Grand Med, but it leaves the door open for question when it comes to Janai's bid for the presidency. Would she pose a threat to Lydia?"

"You mean because she could launch a federal investigation, if, in fact, Grand Med was somehow involved?" Frank asked.

Dennison nodded.

Frank frowned. The possibility was real. It could be a motive for Lydia.

"Have you run checks on the other companies?" Hope asked.

Matt let out a breath and fiddled with his ring. "I'm not comfortable tossing out confidential information on multi-billion-dollar companies. If we can keep what I say in this room, I will share a few facts that you could dig up yourself if you spent a little time digging."

Hope looked at the team. "Does everyone agree to those terms?"

"Sure. Fine. Okay. I guess," were the responses.

"I will speak for the team, Matt. Yes, we will abide by your conditions."

He flicked over a few pages. "Grand Med's quarterly results are down the worst of any drug company of comparable size. Is Lydia worried that a competitor has an inside source? Does she suspect that source is Margo?"

Frank and Zach looked at each other and shrugged.

Matt continued. "Icelandic Wind is fighting a takeover bid from Living Green Cosmetics. Is Janai worried that Robert Halloway or Audrey Tremont might be offering LGC inside help?"

"Is that a recent development?" Hope asked. "Why would Janai pursue the presidency if she's in a fight for control of her company?"

Ruffling through the pages of his notebook, Matt said, "The facts came to our notice two months ago. You were looking at Secret Sands six months ago. Janai must have made up her mind about running for president well before the takeover fight started."

Hope's eyes opened wide. "How do you know when I visited Secret Sands?"

Matt shrugged. "Routine background check."

The man obviously knew a good deal about her. "I just promised not to mention what you told us outside this room, but is there any way I can mention the takeover business to Janai? It could represent a motive that puts her in danger?"

Matt put his face in his hands, then he turned to Zach. "See if you can find a reference on the web."

Zach punched in keys and scanned the screen. "Yes," he said, "and I'd guess Janai has a good deal of clout with the papers. Here's a very small paragraph in the business section, titled, 'Cosmetic companies engage over environment.'"

"Good enough," Matt said and turned to Hope. "Reference that article when you talk to Janai."

"Thanks, Matt. What about Old School?"

"Sweet business. Sean is the mastermind behind its recent success."

"Why do you say mastermind?" Tony asked.

Matt set aside his notebook. Apparently, he was up to speed on the McKennas and didn't need any refresher. "McKenna graduated at the top of his class at Penn State despite playing football. Old School was doing fine before he came along, but he put the company into the global branding game, which has sent profits into the billions."

"Impressive," Hope said.

"Sean works at the factory a good deal because it's close to home, but he has a plush office in the company's skyscraper in Pittsburgh's so-called Golden Triangle. Marketing is in that building, which includes the design center. You remember Connors expected a promotion and was looking at condos downtown."

"So, if he told Meghan she was going to be promoted, it would happen," Frank said.

"Right. That's why the McKenna-Connors connection is hard to overlook," Dennison said and looked at Tony.

"Let me put in a word," Tony said. "Sean said all that talk of a promotion to the design center was a figment of Meghan's imagination. He made a casual remark, and she turned it into an expectation."

Dennison shook his head. "I'll grant you that Connors interpreted conversations from her own point of view. That doesn't change the fact that the McKennas have the best motives for wanting rid of her."

Tony pushed his coffee cup aside, went to the fridge and took out two beers. He sat down and handed a beer to Matt. "What you say is interesting, but it doesn't make Sean a killer."

"No, it doesn't." Dennison said, opening the bottle. "Thanks."

"I heard Sean's version of your horseback ride, Tony," Hope said. "Was he exaggerating?"

"It was scary." Tony took a deep breath. "Sean was on a gigantic horse, and it was rearing up out of control. He could have been stomped to death if he'd been thrown off. Not to mention the herd. That was true. Those horses were coming straight at us like a freight train. I asked him not to mention it, but I had to draw my gun. I shot in the air to try to turn the horses. Fortunately, it worked."

"Good thinking," Dennison said. "Stampedes will run through anything in their path."

"I'll tell you what else he said about Meghan," Tony said. "Sean thinks the girl had mental issues. He suggested that she said something to someone that hit a nerve. Just like the blackmail hints. I'm wondering if he isn't right." He turned to Matt. "My impression is that Sean is a victim, not a villain."

Lucy asked, "What does the FBI say about Global Shipbuilders?"

"Gloria's company is registered and operates out of Greece. It is true that the Chinese have entered the cruise ship business, but that industry was dealt a severe blow during the pandemic. It's hard to understand why Gloria wants to jump into that arena now. Could she be mixed up in something under the covers that Dimitri wants to prevent?"

"I suppose it's possible," Lucy said, but she didn't sound convinced.

"Do you know anything about her husband?" Hope asked Dennison.

He checked his notebook. "I will share facts you could read in the paper if you spoke Spanish," and he looked at Tony. His background check must have turned up the fact that Tony was a linguist.

"Ramon was a highly respected M.D. in Venezuela and vocal about politics. His home was bombed, and his parents and sister were killed."

Lucy gasped. Hope patted the girl's arm. Matt gave her a curious look, but Lucy said, "It's okay. Go on with what you were saying."

"Ramon got help from friends and emigrated to the United States. Because of the difference in medical credentials, he's not licensed here to practice as an M.D."

Matt sat back, as if finished, but straightened up and said, "Dimitri keeps popping up on my own radar as a person of interest. A friend with Interpol did some checking. Dimitri is a frequent visitor to Monte Carlo, where he plays high-stakes poker. He's in debt at the moment for roughly $20,000. It could be an incentive for wanting a promotion sooner rather than later." He sat back and closed his notebook.

"Thanks, Matt," Hope said. "You've called our attention to possibilities we hadn't considered. Frank, did you talk to anyone?"

"Just Matt. He's too slick to be a victim, so I'll classify him as a villain."

Matt laughed. "Be careful, Madison, I still have that fingerprint." He swiveled around in his seat. "If we've covered everything, I'm going to hit the hay."

He stood up and turned to Tony. "I talked to Sean this morning. He didn't open up about Meghan. It's something to think about."

After Matt had left, Hope asked, "What was it you and Matt talked about, Frank?"

"I can tell you why he was able to handle that horse. He grew up in New Mexico and learned bronc riding as a kid. He likes it here, but his specialty is foreign counterespionage. If he solves this case, he'll have a shot at going back to Washington."

"Okay, let's wrap it up for tonight," Hope said. "The ladies will meet tomorrow, so we'll follow our normal routine."

Hope stayed at the table after the others left. Her mind was spinning facts like a kaleidoscope: Janai fighting a takeover bid, Audrey switching carts, Dimitri in debt, illicit drug makers, the McKennas riding in the other cart. When her mind settled on Matt turning down Janai's offer to return to Washington, she pushed her coffee cup aside, picked up her bag, and walked out of the room.

The hallway was dimly lit, and chindi began taunting her. Her foot stepped on something, and she tripped. Frank must have heard the commotion. He opened his door. She lay sprawled out on the floor. "What happened?"

"I wasn't paying attention and tripped." She was holding her arm, and he helped her up.

"Come in. I'll check your arm." After examining it, he said, "It's not broken, but you'll have a nasty bruise. Sit here a minute." He went into the hallway and came back holding a metal sphere. "This pellet could have been dropped by anyone at any time, so I'm not saying it was deliberate. It does seem an odd object to be rolling around randomly on the floor."

Hope smiled. "I'm fine."

She got up to leave, and Frank said, "I'll walk you to your room."

The fall wasn't an accident. Hope's sense of chindi was her own intuition prodding her to pay attention. Someone was being deliberately wicked. Even a minor accident might put her out of commission, and she couldn't afford time away from solving the case.

CHAPTER 22

At eight Tuesday morning, Hope and Matt met up to inspect the trail. The sky was pale blue and the air crisp. Matt parked the Chevy Tahoe in the sagebrush at the spot where he had gained control of Paco. The two walked slowly, their eyes on the ground. Matt pointed out signs of the agitated horses along the trail. They finally reached the place where the melee started.

Hope pulled her cell out of her jean jacket and squatted down and snapped pictures on both sides of the road.

"No animal scared those horses," Matt said.

"Not even a snake?"

"No. If a snake was here, we'd find his dead hide because Paco would have stomped it. If he made it by Paco, we'd find slither marks. There's nothing like that here."

"Where does that leave us?"

"Let's go back and examine Paco."

At the stables, Hope followed Matt inside the building. The smell of hay and horse was pungent, and she held her scarf over her nose. Matt walked into a tiny, glassed-in office. Sani sat at the desk, and two ranch hands were hovering over his shoulder looking at papers.

Hope wandered along the row of stalls. She recognized Paco and stopped. When she reached out her hand, the horse snorted and stretched its neck back and forth. She put her hands on the barnwood half-door and spoke softly.

Matt's voice behind her made her jump. "Sorry," he said. "We're going to take a good look at Paco in the sunshine. Sani examined him last night and didn't see signs of a needle."

Sani took a bridle off a hook on the wall. He opened the half-door and talked to the horse, then put the bridle over the animal's head. The horse moved about in an agitated manner, but Sani calmed Paco down and led the animal to the corral.

Hope took a deep breath of the fresh outdoor air. She leaned against the fence and watched Matt and Sani run hands over the horse's body. Matt opened Paco's mouth and looked at its gums. The men picked up each hoof and examined it by sight and with their fingers. After they finished, they traded sides and went through the routine again.

Matt patted the horse and came over to Hope. "No signs of a puncture. Sani will call the vet and have him do a blood draw. I'll have a deputy take the sample to the lab."

He stepped away and took out his phone. Hope looked at Paco. Her vibes were telling her the horse had been drugged.

Lucy was sitting outside the Blue Sage. "Got enough sun, I see," Hope said, taking in the girl's bright red caftan.

"Margo's words are ringing in my ears. Too much sun can cause skin cancer."

"Did the women mention how long they'd be meeting?" Hope glanced into the Blue Sage and sat down at the table.

"No, but Lydia said she'd like to go home." Lucy gestured toward the sliding glass door.

Janai stepped out, and Hope joined her at the edge of the patio. "What did you learn about last night?"

"Mr. Dennison and I examined the trail and couldn't find any reason for the horses to bolt. The vet is taking a blood sample. We should have the results later today."

"We have been discussing our options," Janai said. "Lydia and Gloria are anxious to go home. It's Ellen who insists on staying. She's afraid if we leave, people will think she was involved in Meghan's death. I see her point. For now, I'm siding with her, but I won't be able to keep the ladies here if they decide to leave." Janai looked around at the red rocks. "Our reservation is up in two days."

"Janai, may I ask a sensitive question?"

"Of course."

"Zach noticed an article on the web that mentioned you're fighting a takeover bid from Living Green Cosmetics. It raises the question of whether Robert or Audrey might be offering inside information. Would it make things easier for LGC if you were out of the picture?"

"The case is in the hands of my attorneys. I can't rule out the possibility of Robert or Audrey or anyone else, for that matter, conniving with the company, but I cannot be sidetracked by that business. The ladies are spooked, and I'm disappointed by all these distractions. I'm going to focus on the reason I'm here, not on what my employees may or may not be up to." She turned abruptly and went back into the room.

Hope ran her fingers through her hair. Janai had expected a peaceful venue for a week of meetings. Instead, Diamond Security had delivered utter chaos. A girl was murdered. A man was poisoned. Janai, herself, was nearly killed by runaway horses.

She went inside the anteroom and asked Zach for a copy of the dossier. She took it back to her room, read through the accounts slowly, and then re-read them. The second time, she made notations in the margins. When she finished, she lay down on the bed, closed her eyes and let the information flood her mind.

An hour later, she found Matt outside the lobby talking with a man in a dark suit, probably a deputy. The man hopped into a white Chevy Tahoe, and Matt came inside. "Have you had lunch?" he asked.

"No. I'd like to." Something in what she'd just read was an important clue, but she couldn't isolate it. Chindi was clouding her thinking. She needed a distraction to relax her mind.

They sat down at a table by the window, and Matt set his hat on a chair. Hope picked up a menu and decided on chicken salad. He said he'd have the same. "What have you been up to?" Matt asked after they'd ordered.

She told him what Janai said about the ladies' wanting to leave. "Our reservation runs out on Thursday. This place will be happy to see us leave. We've caused a lot of trouble."

"You're lucky the whole place didn't shut down."

Hope shuddered. "Just so you know, I did broach Janai on the takeover issue. I referred to the news article as you suggested. It didn't faze her. She doesn't intend to let anything distract her attention from the meetings at hand."

"I expected as much."

"When will you have the lab results?"

"In a few hours."

Cecelia returned with their chicken salads and fry bread. Hope munched on her salad, twisting around to look out at the rocks. The desert was mocking her, vast and silent, keeping secrets. Her intuition nagged at her, but the message kept edging away. She needed to let go of her troubling thoughts.

She looked at Matt and smiled. "Last time we had lunch you asked me some personal questions. My turn to ask you."

"Fair's fair." He looked out the window, as if to see what had changed her mood.

"Where did you go to school?"

"The University of Colorado at Boulder. Pretty town, about 500 miles straight north." He pointed out the direction.

"What was your major?" She didn't care. She just needed him to keep talking to force chindi out of her head.

"Political science, and a minor in drama."

"Drama! I have a hard time visualizing you as an actor."

"I never intended to be an actor. I figured acting would be a valuable skill for an undercover agent." He ran his tongue over his top teeth.

She ignored the undercurrent that he was playing a part with her. "Were you ever in a stage production?"

His quizzical look was a statement, like why was she asking these dumb questions. Nevertheless, he answered. "I played the lead in 'Richard III.'" He put his hand over his heart and his other hand out toward her. "'Now is the winter of our discontent. Made glorious summer by this sun of York.'"

"Richard was a great villain. The part must have been perfect for you."

He gave her that warm smile she found so attractive, but he was clearly puzzled. He didn't speak.

Her stomach was in knots, and she pushed her plate away. Chindi's presence was growing stronger. "When you were doing rodeos, did you have any really frightening moments? Last night didn't seem to bother you much."

He nibbled on a piece of fry bread. "It wasn't at a rodeo, but yes." His eyes closed for a moment, as if a part of him that had been buried in the past had been jerked unwillingly into the present.

She sipped from the glass of water, watching his eyes. It was a moment of trust between them, and it was important to her. He shifted his body in the chair, then picked up his hat and put it on. She opened her eyes wider, afraid he was leaving.

"Never told nobody," he said and locked eyes with her. That look issued a challenge to respect his confidence, and she nodded.

Twisting the napkin, he finally pushed it away and said, "I was a cocky ten-year-old, and my friends dared me to go into a pasture with the most ferocious bull in Curry County. I jumped down from the fence and sashayed over to that critter. The kids started throwing stones. Bulls don't like that much."

He smiled, but he was reliving the moment. "I backpedaled and tripped, then froze. That bull weighed 2,000 pounds. He snorted and pawed the ground. His face was inches above my nose. I smelled his breath, but all I saw were those sharp horns."

The sense of danger was as real as the events of last night, and she took a deep breath to let go of the tension. "What happened?"

"I promised God if He saved me, I'd do something great in this world. That beast nudged me, turned me over and walked away. He was making a statement. Don't mess with danger. I should have paid attention."

"That's a scary story."

A grin crossed his face. "I'm still figuring out the something great I should be doing in this world."

"Last night should count."

He took his hat off and set it back on the chair. "Are you going to tell me why you squirmed around all during lunch? My Aunt Mildred would say you had ants in your pants."

Her shoulders moved up and down, but she returned his trust by saying, "I read the entire dossier twice. Then I lay down on the bed and let my impressions wash over me."

"Any conclusions?"

"A tingling sensation that there is an important clue in the report, but I missed it."

He tented his hands under his chin. "You found something, but you're not telling. Dagnabbit, lady, I'm going to read that report a hundred times if I have to until I figure out what you're hiding."

"I'm not hiding anything, I promise. Something I read is tantalizing me. I keep reaching, but I can't catch hold."

"Best thing is to go for a swim. It'll come to you."

Hope nodded, stood up, crossed her arms over her heart, and recited: "The quality of mercy is not strained; it droppeth as the gentle rain from heaven.'"

Matt laughed. "I'll never get the better of you, Portia."

# #

No one was in the pool, and Hope began swimming laps. Swimming was great therapy. Her mind cleared as she stroked lap after lap, forgetting about everything else. She finished her swim, towel-dried her hair, and slipped on her coverup.

Robert Halloway came into the area. He stopped and turned. Then he turned back. She picked up her bag and held it tight against her.

"I want to apologize about yesterday," Robert said. "I hope you'll forgive me."

Hope set her bag on the table. "Of course. Everyone is edgy since Meghan's death." She held out her hand, and he took it. "Would you care to join me for a cup of tea?"

"I'd love to," he said.

George arrived and set down a tea service for two. He must have noticed Robert walking toward the Oasis.

"I heard about the excitement last night," Robert said. "Do you know what caused the horses to go crazy?"

"It's a mystery. The vet took blood samples, and it will probably turn out it was just an accident. Did you notice anybody fooling around with the horses?"

"Let's see," he leaned back in the chair and marked directions in the air. "The restroom shed was this side of the horse corral. I did notice people walking back and forth along the path. I used the facilities myself."

His words gave Hope an idea. She'd drive over to the cookout grounds and look around at the footprints.

"The main person I noticed, of course, was Janai," Robert said. "I normally keep an eye on her when traveling. I didn't need to bother. That FBI fellow stuck close to her all night except during the last dance when he danced with you."

She nodded, thinking again of Robert's acute sense of awareness. "Anyone else?"

"Just about everybody went to the restroom. You know, sometimes they only had one square going on the dance floor, which meant a lot of people were free to wander. The first person I noticed was Lucy. She's hard not to notice. After that, things get blurred."

In Blue Sky, Zach was sitting with Margo looking out at the rock formations. The moment felt special, and Zach had an impulse to reach over and take Margo's hand. His arms stayed rigid at his sides. "Did you notice anybody walking up the path toward the horses last night?" he asked.

"Practically everybody, but I didn't notice anyone in particular looking at the animals."

"What does Lydia think about all the trouble we've had?"

"She's nervous because she's smoking more than ever. She wants to leave." Margo had several bracelets on her arm and slid them up and down.

"That's understandable. How about you? Are you ready to head back to Chicago?"

Margo smiled, apparently pleased by Zach's friendliness. "Mark called, and he wants us to come back. Lydia said she'd like nothing better, but she's committed to staying until the other women leave."

"What about Mark? Does Lydia want him to come out? After all, he is her brother."

"Mark volunteered to come, but Lydia says we can't all be away with FDA inspectors popping in and out."

Zach enjoyed talking with Margo. Her enthusiasm about pharmaceuticals was infectious, but he hated asking prying questions. He toyed with his pen and stiffened his shoulders. "Margo, have Grand Med's products been counterfeited?"

Margo slid her bracelets up and down on her arm. "You've struck at the heart of a global crisis. Counterfeit medicines are killing people all over the world. I can't talk about our company because the steps we're taking are confidential." Her lips tightened.

"How do bogus pharmacies get away with the counterfeiting?"

"The Internet. Upwards of ninety percent of online pharmacies sell counterfeit drugs in packages that look like the real thing. The crooks purchase pill presses and manufacture copycat pills. We're talking an illegal industry that's raking in hundreds of billions of dollars. And these criminals are draining away our profits." She stood up and said she had work to do.

Zach sighed in frustration at the enormity of the counterfeiting. Money on that scale could certainly be a motive for murder. He'd put their conversation into the dossier. He'd like to keep in touch with Margo after they left Secret Sands, but he probably wouldn't, just as he didn't reach out and touch her hand. There had to be a funny line in there for his act, but he couldn't think of it at the moment.

CHAPTER 23

Hope borrowed a car from Mr. Desheenie, adjusted the seat and pulled on the safety belt. It was the hottest time of day, and she cranked up the air conditioner. The sun dazzled her eyes, and she lowered the visor.

On the ridge where Paco had bolted, she looked across the floor of the ancient sea and imagined water creatures among the rocks. She pulled her mind back to her mission. She planned to take photos of footprints at the cookout site.

She parked twenty feet above the horse corral. The air was still, the trees silent. In the brooding quiet, her heartbeat sounded in her ears. She was foolish to come here alone with a killer on the loose. She had called Matt from her room phone in case he wanted to come with her, but he didn't answer, and she didn't leave a message.

She pulled the cell phone out of her jacket pocket. A sound made her jerk, and the cell dropped to the ground. Nobody was around. She picked up the cell and blew away the powdery dirt. The camera worked. *Get a grip, Diamond.*

She took some general staging photos of the area first and then snapped shots of the deep bootheel marks of the women and the broad marks of the men around the corral.

Farther down the path, the tables brought back memories of the evening, and she smiled watching the images flash across her mind. Janai laughing with Matt. Margo dancing with Zach. Frank lighting Lydia's cigarette. Audrey walking to the restroom. Sean entertaining them with the story of his horseback ride. Matt whispering to her to look up at the jewels in the night sky. She looked up at the blue sky, and a flash of danger jolted her. *Get out of here.*

A fly buzzed by her head. She ducked and swatted as if it were a colony of wasps. Then she stood still, took deep breaths, closed her eyes. Matt winked at her. Her hands steadied, and she took photos of footprints around the tables.

At the dance area, the dirt around the plank floor had plenty of footprints. Something flitted against her arm. She yelped and brushed her arm. She stepped up onto the dance floor. Matt held her close, and she touched her face, feeling his face against her cheek. She stepped down and took photos.

She opened the antique icebox near the chuckwagon. It held a block of ice, as well as bottles of water and soda. She shut the door. *Get out of here.*

Stuffing the cell in her pocket, she headed to the car. Something fluttered underneath a table. She shoved a padded chair out of the way and crouched down on her knees. She stretched out to pick up the small square paper.

The sound of a motor revving came through the stillness. Then a scrape sounded behind her. She started to turn. A blow crashed down on her head. *Matt, why did you let chindi catch me?* Fireworks, then blackness dropped like a hood over her eyes.

# #

"Are you ladies finished with your meeting?" Matt asked Ellen, who was sitting with Tony in Blue Sky.

"Yes, we were exhausted and told Janai we had had enough meetings for the day."

"Good you stood up to that lady. If I know Ross, she'd have you in meetings twenty hours a day."

Matt asked Tony about the team meeting. "The others are probably in Desert Rose," he said. Tony's eyes slid toward Ellen.

Just then, Sean arrived carrying a helmet. He'd been dirt biking. They chatted a few minutes, and Matt started to the conference room. Tony rose and followed.

Everyone was in Desert Rose except Diamond. Cecelia wheeled in a drink tray. Matt poured himself a cup of coffee and sat down. "Where's our fearless leader?"

"I'll call her room." Frank picked up the phone on the table. He shook his head. "No answer. I'll try Desheenie." After talking a minute, he said, "Hope borrowed a car to go to the cookout area a while ago. She said she'd be back soon." He dialed her cell. "No answer."

Matt slammed down his coffee, splashing hot liquid onto the table. "I'm going up there to check."

The others wanted to go, but Matt said, "Zach, stay here in case she comes back. Take these sheets. I did a timeline of people's whereabouts. Thought you might add them to the dossier." Zach nodded and put the sheets into his briefcase.

"Lucy, go to Blue Sky and make a list of everyone who's there," Matt said. "Ask George who's been there over the past couple hours. Probably nothing's wrong, but we should cover the bases. Give your notes to Zach. Then make sure the women are safe. Ellen is with Sean."

"But I— Okay." Lucy's voice sounded disappointed. "If you need me, Tony has my cell number."

Matt, Frank, and Tony raced to the black Chevy Tahoe. Matt's foot hit the gas pedal, and the car spewed gravel, screeched past the stables, and shot up the trail, red dirt flying out behind. Matt's anxiety hit tilt because he had been remiss in not examining the area himself. He would never forgive himself if something happened to Diamond because of his carelessness.

"She's here!" Frank yelled at the sight of the white Toyota.

The car skidded to a stop next to the sedan. As Frank and Tony opened the doors, Matt shouted. "Stop! Don't mess up any footprints!" Matt led them down along the edge of the path.

He spotted Hope's body and started running. "Tony, call an ambulance!"

Matt reached Hope and slid to the ground. He felt her pulse and yelled over his shoulder. "She's alive!" His hand trembled, and he whispered, "Barely."

Frank pushed him aside. "Let me. I'm a medic." Matt shook his head but stood up and Frank took his place beside Hope. "She's got a good bump. Concussion, for sure. Help me turn her over." Matt knelt and held her head steady between his hands as Frank rolled Hope onto her back. Then Matt settled her head onto his lap.

"Tony, go back to the hotel and get some brandy," Frank said. "Tell Desheenie to alert Valdez."

"On my way!"

"Frank, see if there's water in that ice chest," Matt said, his head clearing and his instincts kicking in. Frank brought back a bottle, opened it, and handed it to Matt.

He pulled a clean handkerchief out of his Levi field jacket and poured water on it. Then he brushed the water onto Hope's lips. She blinked and licked at the moisture. He put the bottle against her lips. "Try some more," he coaxed.

"Do you have first-aid gear in your van?" Frank asked.

"In the back."

Frank went up the path and returned in a minute. "Hope, this may sting. I'm going to clean the wound and brush on antiseptic. Raise her head a little, Matt."

"Ow," she moaned.

"You're going to be fine," Matt said when Frank finished. She blinked, and he brushed her lips with the handkerchief. "Why did you do such a dang fool thing as come out here on your own?" She closed her eyes, and her head fell back against his chest.

Frank put his hand on Matt's back. "She needs to stay awake. The ambulance guys will want to ask questions before they treat her."

Putting his lips close to Hope's ear, Matt whispered stories from his time as a bronc rider. Her lips parted occasionally, and he touched them with the moistened handkerchief.

He kept talking. "The Navajos say, 'Certain things catch your eye but pursue only those that capture your heart.'" She opened her eyes briefly. Hope had captured his heart in that black outfit. It was the way she carried it off. Her confidence and femininity. Her smile.

That haunting smile. He touched her lips and silently repeated a phrase from Shakespeare. *"When I saw you, I fell in love, and you smiled because you knew."*

Tony came back with the brandy. "I got glasses for all of us. I know I can use a drink."

He handed a glass to Matt, who dipped the hanky in the brandy and brushed it against Hope's lips. She licked her tongue against the moist handkerchief.

"That's the way, Diamond. You'll be jiggling your spurs faster than a cowboy hightailing it from a bull moose." Matt repositioned her head, and she moaned. The white, waxy look on her face when he found her was gaining a blush of color.

"What happened?" she asked, the words slurred.

"Someone tried to bash your brains in, Diamond, but you're just too dang hard-headed." He looked over at the ragged rocks in the hedges and closed his eyes. She was lucky to be alive.

"Your face is as pale as Hope's," Frank said "Drink this. Doctor's orders. I don't want two patients on my hands." He handed Matt a glass of brandy. He swallowed it in one gulp and choked.

"That's better," Frank said. "Let's see if we can get Hope on her feet." The two men put their arms around her back and hoisted her up. She groaned.

"You're fine," Frank said. "We want to keep you awake and moving." He and Matt took a couple steps, and her legs moved a little. "That's it. You're doing great."

"Here's the ambulance," Tony said. "I'll take your side, Frank, and you can talk to them." Tony slid his arm around Hope. Frank eased out and headed toward the ambulance. It skidded down the path in front of him.

"There go the footprints." Matt said and clenched his jaw.

The paramedics jumped out of the vehicle. Both were Navajo. One was an older man; the other was a young woman. Frank talked to them, and the woman said they would take the patient to the hospital.

"Frank!" Hope squeaked, and he put his ears close to her lips. "No hospital."

"You could have a skull fracture." Frank looked at Matt.

"She has to get checked out," Matt said, his voice hard.

"No hospital," Hope said in a firm voice. She was hanging between Matt and Tony, and she stepped forward. "Ouch."

"Bring her to the ambulance, and we will check a few things," the woman told Frank in the same lilting accent as George. When the paramedics completed their exam, they stepped aside and spoke to each other. After a short discussion, the man turned and addressed Hope.

"That wound on your head is ugly and should be scanned, but your vital signs are good. If you can see a doctor this afternoon, we will not take you to the hospital. You need to ride in the ambulance to the hotel."

"Fine," Hope murmured. "Dr. Valdez is an old friend."

Matt chuckled. "Glad you haven't lost that keen sense of humor, Diamond."

The paramedics helped Hope onto the stretcher and slid it into the ambulance. The woman attendant jumped into the driver's seat, and the man got into the back with Hope.

Matt caught Frank's arm and handed him his keys. "Drive my car back. I'll ride with Diamond and see she doesn't give this feller any trouble." He hopped up onto the ambulance. The attendant raised his eyes from his chart but didn't say anything.

Hope was strapped onto the stretcher, her eyes closed. Rubbing his fingers gently over the back of her hand, Matt prayed. *Please, God, let her be all right.*

His eyes were bleary. Diamond was bringing back feelings of tenderness that had been long gone. He lived in the dark world of criminals, spies, and traitors. The quotes he carried in his head, strumming the guitar, and the faith of his youth kept him from drowning in that sordid underworld.

Even the beautiful, sophisticated women he'd met in Washington hadn't softened his heart. He let out a deep breath. *How did he find a diamond in the middle of the desert?*

He bent over Hope, and she opened her eyes. He gave her a smile filled with love. "You scared me, Diamond. Don't do it again."

CHAPTER 24

It was after five when the ambulance arrived at the hotel, and the attendants wheeled the stretcher into the lobby. "Dr. Valdez is on his way," Desheenie told Matt.

Janai came around the corner. She stopped short at the sight of Hope on the stretcher, and she clasped her fingers around Matt's arm. "What's happened? Is she going to be all right? I can have a plane here within the hour to fly her back to Los Angeles."

Matt rubbed a hand across his brow. He didn't really know how serious the injury was, and Janai's anxiety unsettled him. His voice cracked, and he cleared his throat. "If Dr. Valdez advises her to go to a hospital, I'll call you. Trust me."

She nodded and nudged past Sean and Ellen and Lydia, who were crowding around the stretcher. Matt whispered to Frank, "Tell the guests Hope had an accident, that she fell. Stick close to Janai and Lydia."

Matt hovered as the attendants helped Hope into the recliner in her room. She leaned back with her eyes closed. "Stay awake until the doctor sees you." The female paramedic put her hands on her hips. "If you take a turn for the worse, call 911."

"I'll see she follows your instructions," Matt said, and the attendants left.

A tapping sounded on the glass door, and he glanced over. "Lucy and Zach are outside, Diamond. Okay to let them in?"

She nodded, and Matt opened the door. Lucy and Zach rushed over to Hope. "Tony said you were hurt pretty bad," Zach said, pulling a chair close. Lucy was crying and cradled her head on Hope's knee.

"Lucy," Hope said and brushed at the tears on the girl's face. "I'm fine. Just a little bump."

"Lucy, help Hope get cleaned up and out of those dirty clothes," Matt said sharply. The girl's crying was fraying his nerves.

Lucy sniffed and stood up. "Bring her into the bathroom. I'll take over from there." She swiped her hands across her eyes.

When Hope returned with her face washed and wearing a white nightgown, she looked so much better that Matt rested his shaky hand against the desk. She even smiled. He helped her into the recliner and tucked a cotton throw around her.

A knock sounded at the door, and Zach opened it. Dr. Valdez said, "You people are keeping me busier than my wife on wash day."

"Always nice to see you, too, Doc." Matt said.

Zach and Lucy went out to the patio. Dr. Valdez examined Hope's head wound. "How did this happen? I heard you fell. This bump wasn't caused by a fall."

"Somebody hit me over the head," Hope said. Matt's heart pumped harder hearing her describe the attack.

Valdez straightened up and looked at Matt. "Yes, someone deliberately tried to kill you." Hope closed her eyes, and Matt's forehead started sweating. He should have gone up to the cookout himself.

"Does your head hurt?" the doctor asked.

"When I move."

The doctor checked her eyes, reflexes, breathing. "You're very lucky. You have what I'd consider a moderate concussion. It's best to have a scan, but I understand you won't go to the hospital."

"No."

"Well, when you get home, go for a scan at your local medical facility." Dr. Valdez took out his prescription pad and scribbled a few lines. "Give this note to the doctor. Promise me you'll go."

"I promise."

"I'll see that she goes," Matt said. That's a promise he intended to keep.

"With a concussion, it's best to rest, drink fluids, and eat plenty of protein. I brought a couple pain pills in case you need them." He reached into his bag and pulled out a tiny white packet and handed it to Matt, who put it on the end table.

"Call me if you need me," the doctor said. "I'm sure you have my number on speed dial."

Hope chuckled, but it must have hurt her head, and she squeezed her eyes. As Dr. Valdez opened the door, Frank and Tony arrived. "The ladies are in their rooms," Frank said.

Matt waved to Zach and Lucy, and they came back into the room. Hope reached out to Matt, and he took her hand. "Lab results?"

He smiled. She was getting better. "The lab says Paco was given a large dose of LSD."

"LSD!" Lucy said. "How?"

"My guess is the person used the old LSD sugar cube trick," Matt said. "Must have given Paco a handful of sugar cubes."

"We now know for sure the hayride was attempted murder," Tony said.

"Frank," Hope said, closing her eyes again. "I'm drifting off. Can you take over?"

"Let's get you to bed." He lifted her up and carried her over to the bed, set her down, and pulled the covers over her. "You need to rest," he said and kissed her cheek.

Zach whispered to Matt. "I'm developing an algorithm for those timesheets. We'll be able to play around with the numbers and see where people were at different times."

"I like that idea," Matt said. "Let me know when you have it running." He looked over at Hope. "Before we break up in here, you should take shifts staying with Diamond through the night. The murderer could try again. Frank, would you line up your team?" The man nodded and reached for the notepaper on the desk.

"I've got to file reports and catch up on things," Matt said. "Call me if anything happens here." He looked Frank in the eye. "Any time, day or night."

Matt plodded down the hallway. His stomach was churning, and his feet were slogging through molasses. In his room, he sat on a straight-backed chair and did deep-breathing exercises. Then he filed a report on the day's events. Jake Sanders was reading the reports. Matt slammed down the lid on his computer, letting off steam that the man hadn't told him about the dark web. He hung his head. It wasn't Jake. It was himself he was upset with. His simple oversight could have gotten Diamond killed. He was too skilled an agent to have let that happen.

He opened his guitar case and pulled out the guitar. Strumming usually took the edge off his anxiety. His fingers began picking "Goodnight Irene."

Memories of Hope rushed through him: holding her close, swaying to the music, inhaling the scent from her hair. The stirrings in his soul sent up a sharp warning, and he stopped playing the song.

He was an FBI agent. His work was his life, and it was dangerous work. He'd kept clear of love tangles. He never wanted a wife who might become a widow. Diamond had softened his resolve. *Reset, cowboy, and get back to your priorities.*

Diamond had asked him if he'd ever been scared. That time with the bull had been long forgotten, yet the scene had come back in vivid color. The terror was real, yet innocent.

Not like when he'd been scared overseas. When he'd had to kill men up close and personal. Always in self-defense. But what did that mean? They were dead because of him. Statistics in his file in Washington. Matt set aside the guitar and did more deep breathing exercises to free himself of the memory and the guilt and the faces.

A different face came into his mind, and he squeezed his eyes against the sight of Diamond on the ground. He was too emotionally involved. If she hadn't been rattling his brain, he would have, for sure, checked out the campground that morning, and she would not have gone there alone. *Rein in your feelings, cowboy.*

He picked up the guitar and strummed Willie Nelson's "On the Road Again." The music lifted his spirits and took away thoughts of Diamond that shouldn't have been there in the first place.

When he set down his guitar, he felt calmer. He fixed himself a cup of coffee and let his mind roam over the suspects. Looking beyond the McKennas, he thought about the other ladies and their staffs: Margo Knight, Audrey Tremont, Robert Halloway, and Dimitri Drakos. Where were they at the time of the attack? Zach might pull up something with the timing algorithm. Diamond had herself a champ computer jock.

Picking up the dossier, Matt pushed back in the recliner and began reading. He paid a lot of attention to Dimitri. He'd ask Lucy to find out a few things. Having Diamond's team at his disposal was useful, but he shouldn't be depending on them. That wasn't FBI protocol.

What a crock. He'd told Diamond he followed FBI protocol. If that were true, he wouldn't be playing sheriff in the Navajo Nation. He'd uncovered a breach of security. He should have followed protocol. Not likely. That would have taken time and cost the agent his life. Going it alone had only cost him his job in Washington.

He stretched out his arm and lifted Diamond's binder off the desk. The silver diamond etched on the front was classy, like Diamond herself. Her face came into his mind, and he rotated his shoulders back and forth.

He skimmed the evening events. A social at seven, dinner on the patio, followed by a pianist. He would attend everything and observe the players without Diamond to distract him. He would stay close to Janai. He liked the lady and admired her spirit, but her life could be in danger.

Nothing illegal had been noted by the FBI as far as Robert and the charities were concerned. The L.A. office was locating the parlor that had inked Robert's tiger tatt. They'd find out if the tattoo was selected randomly or whether Robert chose it because it represented vengeance and punishment.

# #

Tony found Sean and Ellen at the Oasis pool. He surveyed the landscape. *What a setting.* He'd buy a postcard to show Maria. Maybe he'd bring her here one day. If she ever talked to him again. He waved at Sean and Ellen in the pool and sat down on a chaise lounge.

The truth would have to come out before the two of them would move past their distrust of one another. *What was the truth?* He leaned back, eyes on the clear water. The truth was that Meghan was either naïve, streetwise or had mental issues. She wasn't naïve. What mattered was that she acted as if she and Sean were in a relationship. Ellen found out and was jealous.

Why did Ellen invite Meghan to come to a luxury resort with her, miles away from her home? That was the hard question. It was more than what she had told him. She had some action planned, but was it murder?

The couple were splashing about in the pool. Suddenly, Sean grabbed Ellen, held her tight, and kissed her passionately. Tony turned away and pulled his hat over his face.

The image of Hope's white face haunted him. He wanted her safe, but he wanted to be the one to protect her, not some stranger like Matt Dennison. The man irritated him. Maybe because he had picked up on vibes between Dennison and Hope. Maybe because the man suspected the McKennas. A little of both probably.

A stiff breeze came up and blew off his hat. He jumped up and caught it before it hit the water.

He sat down, and his lips curved in a smile at his first encounter with Hope. He'd been on his way to L.A to interview with an oil company that needed someone who spoke Arabic. He was in the first-class section, and Hope sat beside him. She looked fabulous in an Emilio Pucci creation. He complimented her, and they struck up a conversation. He blushed to recall how much he had told her about his life and his goals.

In Los Angeles, Hope asked him to visit Diamond Security. The oil company made him a generous offer, but he turned it down. He never regretted that decision.

He pulled out his phone and dialed Maria. It would be the middle of the night in Spain, but she might be back in Los Angeles. The message recorder came on, and he hung up. His eyes flickered, but he smiled when Sean called out to him.

"Hey, Tony, like a drink? I'll order us something," Sean and Ellen stepped out of the pool. Ellen slipped into a coverup, and Sean put on the hotel robe.

"Sure. A Coke is good."

"How is Hope?" Ellen asked. "We were so scared for her."

Tony took a breath and grinned, "She's good. The indestructible maiden."

"Do you think that fall was really an accident?" Sean asked.

"Why? Do you think it wasn't?" Tony walked over to the table. Cecelia arrived with Cokes, beers, water, and ginger ale, along with hamburger sliders and the fixings.

"You're amazing, Cecelia," Tony said. "How did you know we were planning to order a snack?"

"I seen you guys headed this way. I would not be working here if I did not know by now what you like." She flashed her eyes at Tony and left.

"You have an admirer," Ellen said, smiling at Tony.

"Nah, she just likes to flirt. George is her man." He turned to Sean. "What were you saying about Hope's accident?"

"People have been talking. The word is that all these accidents tie back to Meghan's death."

"Who have you been talking to?" Tony put a slider on a bun, doctored it up with catsup, pickle and tomato, and took a bite.

"Robert, mostly. His theory is that Meghan was murdered, and the killer has been covering their tracks." Sean fixed himself a plate with a slider and potato chips.

The idea rolled around in Tony's mind. "How would poisoning you help the killer cover their tracks?"

"Heck, I don't know, but it makes sense when Robert tells it."

Ellen was looking at Sean, as if wondering if the poison were meant for her.

"Aren't you having a slider?" Tony asked Ellen.

"I'm not hungry," she said and sipped a little ginger ale.

Tony sighed. The team still had no clue as to why Sean was poisoned or who had poisoned him.

"Robert's theory is as good as any other," Tony and left. "But look at it this way. If he's right, the killer thinks you know something that could be dangerous. What could the killer think you saw or heard that would help the FBI?"

Sean's eyes widened, and he pushed aside the empty plate. "Nothing. I've told everything I know, which doesn't amount to an inch of peppermint patties." He helped himself to another slider and drank his beer.

"Did either of you see anybody coming back into the hotel late this afternoon?" Sean and Ellen made the same gesture of putting an elbow on the arm of the chair and covering their mouths with their hands.

"Let's see," Sean said. "I went dirt biking. You and Ellen were in Blue Sky when I came back. After you left, I spent a little time in the gift shop. I bought Patrick a black sweatshirt with the Navajo seal. Bought a blue one for his friend, Neal."

He fixed another slider. "I noticed Margo walking outside. She had on a big hat. Her face was a little red."

"What time was that?

"I don't know. After four."

"What was Margo wearing?"

"A long skirt, and she carried a big, floppy bag. She had on those high-heel sandals. I was afraid she'd do a face plant on the cement."

"That information could be helpful." Tony said. He'd send Zach an email.

Sean stood up, and Ellen said she needed to buy souvenirs for people back home. They gathered up their things, and Tony walked back to the hotel with the couple.

He would try to convince Dennison that the McKennas were innocent. Hope wasn't sold on Sean, so he'd have to do more thinking about him. He liked the man, but that wasn't a guarantee that he wasn't a killer.

Sean had one of the traits the murderer would have to have. He had nerves of steel. Sean didn't shy away from danger. From what Dennison said, Sean was a mastermind at business. Maybe he was also a mastermind at murder.

CHAPTER 25

Frank fussed with the grass-and-feather flower arrangement on the tall table in Blue Sky. His hand trembled when he thought of Hope. He had stayed in her room to take the first shift, and he hated to leave. Someone had tried to kill her and would likely try again. He should be at her side, not smiling and playing host for the murderer.

Glancing around the room, he noticed Dennison leaning against the bar and holding a can of Coke. He looked relaxed, but he was watching each person the way Frank used to watch people in a crowded room in Afghanistan when he was seeking someone who didn't want to be found—alert, muscles taut, angry.

Dennison came off as a loner, but his reaction at finding Hope unconscious revealed more than casual interest.

Janai arrived and asked how Hope was doing. "She's going to be all right," Frank said, pushing away thoughts of how close she had come to being killed.

"I'm relieved to hear that news. Audrey is at me to go home."

"I know Audrey is nervous, but I hope you'll stay." Frank said. "We're working with Agent Dennison to find out who's behind these attacks."

"That's why I'm hanging in. I have a lot of faith in you and Hope. I have confidence in Agent Dennison, as well."

"Has Robert ever mentioned why he sports a tiger tattoo?" Frank asked.

"Tiger tattoo? I never noticed he had one." Janai patted her necklace. "I like adornments that you can put on and take off."

"Your necklace is beautiful."

"It's turquoise and was created by a local artist."

Lydia joined them, and Frank complimented her on her turquoise necklace. "We went to the shop together," she said. "This bracelet is made of Sonoran gold turquoise stones. I've got the saleslady's spiel down pat."

Frank reached over and lifted her wrist. "Very nice." He held her hand for a few moments enjoying the smile in her eyes. "What time were you ladies in the gift shop?"

"Between three and four, right, Janai?"

"Sounds about right."

Sean and Ellen joined the party. Ellen was wearing a turquoise necklace. "I almost bought that piece myself," Janai said. "That's a natural Royston turquoise stone. See, Lydia, I paid attention to the saleslady, too."

"I bought it as a surprise for Ellen," Sean said, pride showing on his face.

"I wonder if Gloria bought something." Lydia looked around. "Yes, here she comes, and she's wearing the beaded necklace. It's perfect for that dress."

Frank was clicking off times as the ladies commented on the jewelry. Sean and Gloria must have visited the shop after Lydia and Janai. Zach should be able to confirm times with the shop.

Lydia said, "I'm going to have a Scotch and a smoke on the patio before dinner. You'll come out, won't you, Gloria?"

"Right behind you."

After dinner, Mr. Desheenie brought a tall, lanky, young man with hands the size of a baseball glove over to meet Frank. The gleaming Steinway had been rolled to the middle of Blue Sky. "This is Paul Johns. He plays the piano and says Miss Diamond hired him."

Johns had a long, smooth face and brown eyes. A short fringe of bangs circled his brow, and his brown hair touched his shoulders. He wore a white shirt and dark pants held up by suspenders.

Where did Hope find this character? Frank didn't know the man's credits, so he introduced him simply as Paul Johns and said he would play the piano. The guests applauded limply. Matt sat down on the sofa next to Janai and clapped heartier than the others.

Johns walked over to the piano, bowed his head, and sat down on the bench. Music bellowed out of the Steinway. Powerful, then fluttery like a baby's cooing, then rocketing. He brought to life Duke Ellington and Scott Joplin, then Chopin and Tchaikovsky. He ended with one of Frank's own favorite pieces, "Slaughter on Tenth Avenue."

When Johns dropped his head over the keys, the guests sat in silence. Frank jumped up and clapped. The others joined him and kept up the applause for several minutes. Johns sat down again and played a little boogie-woogie, his hands soaring over the keys. He finished, and the guests stood again and applauded.

"Great job, son," Frank said. "You blew us away!"

"Thank you. This Steinway is as smooth as peanut butter." Frank handed Johns an envelope.

Janai walked up and shook his hand. "A wonderful performance, young man. I'd love to have you play at another event sometime."

"Sure," Johns said. "The Diamond lady has my number." He loped off across the room.

"Where did you find that piano rock star?" Matt asked Frank. "He must channel Van Cliburn."

"Hope found Johns, and his playing was sensational."

"Of course, as Bach said, 'All one has to do is hit the right keys at the right time, and the instrument plays itself.'" Frank laughed. He was getting used to Matt's repertoire of quotes.

"How is she doing?" Matt asked.

"Lucy said Hope slept the whole time she was on watch. Zach is with her now."

"Good to hear." He would have stayed with Hope himself, but that wouldn't have been proper for an FBI agent when her own team was available. "I'll see that Janai gets to her room safely," he said and joined the lady at the bar.

Matt entered his own room and hung his hat on a hook. The red light on his room phone was flashing. He listened to Jake

Sanders' voice. "Call me when you get this message, no matter how late." The clock said it was ten-thirty, twelve-thirty in Washington.

He had worked for Jake when he first joined the agency. Even though their personalities jarred, it was Jake who had stuck up for him last year and persuaded the brass to send him to the reservation rather than kick him out of the agency. Matt sat on the edge of the bed and tapped his cell phone.

Jake started speaking without any greeting. "Dennison, what were you thinking letting Hope go off on her own? It's lucky she wasn't killed. You need to get your act in gear and take better care of her and everyone else out there."

Matt fired back. "Whoa, cowboy. If you think you could've done any better, you should have come out here yourself!"

"You're right. I should have taken charge when Hope called me."

The unexpected words stung. "Hope called *you*. Why?"

"Because I'm in love with her." Apparently, the words flew out before he could stop them.

The words sucked the air out of Matt's lungs. After a moment, he said, "Well, good thing you stayed home, cowboy. We don't need anybody who's emotionally involved muddying the waters." He closed his eyes at the irony of his words.

"And you're not emotionally involved, I suppose."

Matt's eyes opened wide. "Man, what have you been drinking?" Why would Jake Sanders think he was emotionally involved with Diamond? He was dang sure he hadn't let that notion slip into his reports.

Jake's deep breathing came over the phone. "Sorry, Matt. I shouldn't have jumped down your throat. I just feel frustrated that I'm not out there helping. I'm prepping our new director for a White House meeting, and he refuses to let me leave. He said you could handle things."

"My compliments to the chief." Matt swallowed hard. "How long have you and Diamond been an item?" The words sounded casual in his head, but his heart was pounding.

"A while. I love her, and I think she loves me, but our lives are miles apart."

"Why not get reassigned to Los Angeles?"

"I like my job. I like Washington. You know how it is."

"I know how it is," said the agent-in-exile. *Why didn't the man figure out something if he was so much in love?* "Look, man, she's doing fine. Just a concussion, like I said in the report. I probably made more out of it than I should have. I'll let you know if anything changes. Gotta run."

They disconnected, and a herd of buffalo stomped on Matt'st chest. He walked over to the long cabinet against the wall, opened one of the tiny whiskey bottles and threw it back.

True, he mouthed, tipping the bottle at his reflection in the mirror, you swore you were reining in your feelings. Why should you care if Diamond and Jake Sanders are in love?

He turned away from the mirror and pulled in a deep breath. Jake's words cut deep. Not only that. Jake was right. She could have been killed. He did need to get his head in gear and stop acting like a star-crossed lover.

Diamond and Jake Sanders, of all people. His old boss. He slumped in the chair and put his head in his hands.

#

Frank hadn't slept at all when he knocked on Hope's door at one in the morning. Tony answered and whispered that Hope was still sleeping. Frank stepped inside. The drapes were closed, and the room was nearly pitch black. Only a soft glow from the night light in the bathroom filtered into the room.

Although Frank wanted coffee, rather than turn on the light, he took a Coke out of the small refrigerator. He set it on the table by the recliner and went over to the bed. Hope was breathing regularly.

Sitting down in the recliner, he thought about the case. The guests all seemed too reputable to be up to this kind of skullduggery. He couldn't put his finger on any one of them whom he considered likely to have attacked Hope. He thought about Sean and Robert and Dimitri, but even they were long shots.

His eyes started to close, and he shook himself and took a sip of Coke. Suddenly, in the black stillness, a rustling sound, as soft as a caterpillar creeping on a blade of grass, made his scalp tingle. He sat up stiff, listening, but the only sound was Hope's soft breathing.

He had spent too many nights in tents in Syria not to recognize danger close at hand. He slid out of the chair, drew his gun, and edged along the wall toward the sliding glass doors.

Silent and smooth, Frank maneuvered in military fashion, controlling his breathing. He reached the patio door, and his fingertips touched the linen drapes. He reached for the cords. He took a deep breath and jerked hard, but the drapes stuttered before opening, warning the intruder.

"Damn!" He peered through the glass but caught only a glimpse of black on black, the merest suggestion of substance before blackness swallowed the shadow. Frank fumbled with the lock. He pushed the door aside and stepped out on the patio, but the phantom had vanished. He put the gun in the holster and pounded his fist in his hand. If he'd been quicker, he might have caught the killer.

Frank locked the door and pulled the drapes closed. He went into the bathroom, closed the door, and dialed Matt's room. The man meant it when he insisted Frank call him day or night if something happened. Matt answered immediately. Frank told him about the attempted break-in. He said he'd be right over and dust for prints.

In what seemed like a minute, Frank heard a rustling outside the glass door. He pulled the drapes open a few inches and watched Matt dust for prints by the light of a small lantern. He must not have gone to bed because he was fully dressed. When he finished and stood up, Frank unlocked the door, and Matt came inside. "No prints," he mouthed, shaking his head.

Frank needed a strong dose of caffeine. "Would you stay with Hope while I rustle up some coffee? Our villain knows she has protection so I don't think they'll be back, but she shouldn't be left alone for a moment."

He heard Matt inhale. Both of them cared a great deal for Hope. They couldn't slip up. The killer was intent on harming her. "I'll be right back," Frank said and left.

Matt sat down at the desk and heard Hope fidgeting. He rushed over to the bed. She was pulling at the covers.

"What do you need?"

"Matt? You're here?" The words were groggy.

"Frank went for coffee. He'll be back in a minute."

"Why did you leave me with chindi?" He had a hard time making out her words.

"Leave you with chindi? When?"

"Cookout."

Matt's heart thumped. It was all his fault. He should have been there. "I'm sorry."

"You came back, fooled chindi." She smiled. "Head hurts."

Matt's hand shook. He found the packet of pills on the table. "Doc left a couple pain pills," he said, picking up the packet.

"Too strong." She pointed to the bathroom. "Just one."

Matt found pills in the medicine cabinet and poured a glass of water. "Here you go." She struggled to sit up, and he set the pill and water down and put his arm under her to help her into a sitting position.

Hope's hand rested on his arm. Matt shivered and yanked his arm away, but he clenched his jaw against the hurt that flashed across her eyes. "Are you hungry? There's berries and other stuff in the fridge."

"No. Don't need to stay. I'm fine."

"You're not fine, and Frank will be right back."

She swallowed the pill, and he set the water glass on the nightstand. "Ginger ale," she said.

"Good idea. Doc said you should drink a lot, but I guess he didn't mean whiskey." She chuckled, and the sound lightened his heart.

"I'll be up in the morning," she said. Her voice sounded stronger, and the words came more clearly.

"You shouldn't rush it."

"Concussion's nothing. Fellow hit me over the head with a forty-five. That hurt."

"Diamond, you're incorrigible."

"Them's big words from a poor cowhand who talks like he ain't got no schoolin'."

Matt smiled. "You've got my number, Diamond." *Social distance yourself, cowboy.*

She wriggled a finger at him to come closer. When he bent down, she kissed his cheek. "Thanks for saving my hard head, Dennison."

He bent over to embrace her, but a knock on the door stopped him. "Frank's here." His face brushed against Hope's lips as he pulled away. Saved by the bell, but his heart was racing.

Frank walked in with a carafe of coffee and asked softly, "How's our patient?"

"Ornery. She just took a pill and drank some ginger ale. I expect she'll sleep now." He opened the door to leave.

"Get better, Diamond," he called.

CHAPTER 26

On Wednesday morning, Hope opened her eyes at eight-twenty. She pushed back the covers and gently swung over the side of the bed. Lucy rushed over to her. "How are you feeling?" she asked in a breathless voice.

"Hungry."

Lucy drew open the drapes and smiled. "I'll order tea and toast."

Hope blinked against the sunlight. "Add scrambled eggs and orange juice."

"You mean it? You're that much better?"

"I'll get dressed. We'll eat out on the patio." Her head gave a lurch, and she almost fell. She steadied herself and walked into the bathroom. In the shower, she let the water massage her neck and shoulders. She felt stronger, and the pain in her head wasn't so sharp. She dressed in jeans, put her gun in the pocket of the jacket, and went out to the patio. The sunlight sent wavy lines in front of her eyes, and she asked Lucy to bring out her sunglasses.

Lucy was fluttering around, and her nervousness put Hope on edge. "How was the concert?" she asked.

Lucy sat down at the table. "The pianist was amazing."

"I knew he'd be a hit." Hope had heard Johns play and was astounded by his talent. He had asked for $200, but the check Frank gave him was for $2,000.

"Any updates?" she asked.

Lucy hesitated, but Hope took off her sunglasses and gave her a stern look. "Everybody's looking at the timing stuff."

"What timing stuff?"

"The FBI makes timelines of people's movements. Zach created an algorithm to check where people were yesterday."

"That's interesting. Where are they working?"

"They're in Desert Rose now. The ladies will meet at ten in Blue Spruce."

After breakfast, Hope made her way slowly to the Desert Rose. Frank, Tony, and Matt were hovered around Zach. The men looked up, and Frank and Tony rushed over and hugged her. "You look much better," Tony said. "You scared us plenty."

She smiled and walked over to Zach. "Sit here," Tony said, indicating his own chair, and she sat down. Matt's eyes were focused on the screen, and he didn't greet her. His coolness bothered her, but she had a murder to solve.

Zach pointed to the white board where he was projecting some squiggly lines. She looked at the board, but the images were blurry. She rubbed her eyes. Still blurry. She looked at Zach's computer screen and was able to read the text a little better.

"The idea," Zach said, "is to find out where people were at any particular time. Of course, the information must be in the database. That's what we're doing now. I've entered all of Matt's information, and Frank and Tony are filling in blanks."

Lucy walked in, and Zach asked her to fill in times on Gloria and Dimitri.

Frank spoke up. "Zach, check with the sales staff in the gift shop. They can tell you when the guests were buying turquoise."

Zach wrote on a slip of paper. He looked at Hope. "I'll give you a demonstration. Say you want to know where Robert was at eleven o'clock." Zach tapped the keys. Words and numbers flashed.

Hope blinked, but she couldn't read the screen.

"You can see everybody's whereabouts in a single list," Zach said. Information flickered around. More blurry images taunted her.

"I don't think we can all stay here with our clients roaming about," Hope said. "The ladies plan to meet at ten."

"I'll email you my times, Zach," Frank said.

"Me, too," Tony said, and he and Frank left. Lucy waved to Zach and followed.

"I'll leave you two to your work," Hope said to Zach and Matt. She stood up, but her legs gave way, and she grabbed onto the chair.

Matt jumped up and grasped her arm. "You should lie down," he said. The words were the first he had spoken to her since she entered the room.

"I forget my head doesn't like sudden movements, that's all." Matt removed his hand from her arm and sat down.

Hope waved to George and sat on a couch in front of the window in Blue Sky. Janai approached. "How are you?" she asked and sat down on the sofa next to her.

"I'm fine." Hope squared her shoulders. "Have you made any progress in your meetings?"

Janai looked around. No one else was nearby. "I will tell you in confidence that the ladies have agreed to support my candidacy for president."

"Congratulations! I may be talking with the next president." Although she smiled at Janai's good news, she clenched her hands because the statement boosted the woman's risk from a relentless killer.

"Do Robert and Audrey know?"

"They are my staff, Hope. I either trust them, or I get rid of them. Right now, I've decided to trust them."

"I understand." There was no arguing with Janai. "If things are settled, why are you ladies meeting today?"

"We have to deal with a lot of unsettled business." She sighed as if she expected everyone to simply agree with her plans and let her handle everything in her own way.

"All the women have multiple agendas," she said. "Take Ellen, for example. She wants me to support a transcontinental water pipeline."

"I heard Ellen has done some groundwork."

"Yes, she has. One nephew is designing a pipeline from the East Coast to Colorado. A niece is studying environmental impacts. A nephew is looking into how the homeless could be employed. That's only the half of what she's done."

"Impressive," Hope said, although Janai's words were fading in and out, making it difficult to follow the conversation.

"If her plans are workable, we'll be miles ahead." Janai put up a hand. "But that's not all she wants. Ellen and I agree on the ethics around abortion, but we need to find a middle ground on funding. The government pumps billions into agencies that perform abortions. Ellen wants me to stop all that funding, but those clinics also perform other health services."

Hope squinted, unable to understand many of the words. It was like listening to a symphony and hearing only the drums.

"Gloria wants a comprehensive healthcare plan," Janai went on. "I agreed to appoint her husband to any committee that studies the issue. He also wants sweeping reforms to improve relationships with our neighbors down south."

"What about Lydia?" Hope concentrated but still could make out only the drum beats.

"She insists on FDA reforms to speed drugs through clinical trials, but think about the thalidomide tragedy. That drug left thousands of children without limbs. It was the FDA's Frances Kelsey who blocked it here." Janai smiled. "Kelsey worked for the FDA until she was ninety years old, and she died at 101."

"Amazing!" Hope said, responding to Janai's enthusiasm. The words were blurring, and she couldn't keep her thoughts straight.

"There's more. Lydia wants us to crack down on illegal online pharmacies. I could go on and on."

"Janai, why on earth do you want to be president?"

She chuckled. "I think a woman can make a difference in the job and in the world, and I'd like to be that woman." Janai stood up. "I must go. Don't overdo things today, Hope. You look peaked."

"I'll take care." Janai would make an efficient president. She was always two steps ahead. If she were the murderer, nobody would ever catch her.

Hope's headache was getting sharper. She pulled a small pill bottle out of her purse; but before she could uncap it, Dimitri stopped at the sofa.

"You gave us a scare," he said, and she invited him to sit down. He took out a pack of cigarettes, then stuck the pack back in his pocket, a gesture he'd made on other occasions. "Why you go to campground?"

Hope took a deep breath. Her mind was murky, and her words were starting to slur. "Lost earring. Went to find it."

Frowning, he tilted his head slightly. "Did you find it?" She touched her earlobe. *He knew she hadn't worn earrings.*

"Under a table."

"You bump head? I heard you fall."

Stuck in a quagmire of lies, Hope said, "I'm not sure. I blacked out. Memory is spotty." That much was true.

"Pianist very good," Dimitri said, and Hope smiled.

He stood up and moved toward the door. "Enjoy the day. No more accidents."

George came over and set a tray containing two carafes, one with water and one with coffee, along with cups and glasses on the table. "How did you know?" Hope asked.

He just smiled. "If you need anything else, just wave. I will be watching."

"Thank you, *Apenimon.*" His reassurance was as welcome as a pair of cozy slippers. Chindi had been close ever since she woke up.

Outside, wildflowers danced crazily in the breeze. She shifted her eyes back and forth watching, trying to restore her vision. A whisper startled her. "How are you?" The Shadow Lady moved around to the couch and sat down.

"I'm okay."

"We were worried. I nearly convinced Janai to take us all home. This place is getting on everyone's nerves. Even Robert agreed we should leave. Nobody believes you had an accident. Someone tried to kill you."

"Where were you yesterday, Audrey?"

The woman gasped. "Do you think I tried to kill you?"

"No. Did you notice anyone? Need to eliminate as many people—" Her voice trailed off.

"I see," Audrey said. "I was in my room. Can you imagine how much my work has increased since Janai had this foolhardy notion to run for president?" Apparently, Audrey was so caught up in her own thoughts that she didn't recognize Hope's fatigue.

"You don't think it's a good idea?" Hope asked, still missing words.

"A crazy idea, in my humble opinion. I don't know how we'll manage now that she has the ladies on board. She says she's hiring another assistant." She slid off the couch and left.

Even though Hope's mind was muggy, she sat up straight. *Had Audrey tried to ensure that the women wouldn't back Janai's bid for the presidency, perhaps by trying to make Meghan ill, but, somehow, the girl died?* Audrey had the ability to slip in and out of rooms without anyone noticing. A good habit for a murderer.

Hope was resting her eyes. She felt the presence of someone nearby and forced her eyes open. Zach sat down. "Thought you'd want to hear what Matt and I learned."

"Yes."

"Between two and five, Margo strolled up to the horses. Dimitri was at the corral and then drove to the casino. Sean went bike riding. Audrey worked in her room." The words were coming too fast. She couldn't understand what he was saying.

"I'm sorry, Zach. Information is muddled in my head. Let's talk later."

"Sure."

"What is Dennison up to?" Although piqued at his attitude, she was interested to know his plans.

Zach leaned in and spoke slowly, enunciating every syllable. "Matt borrowed my computer to poke around with the numbers by himself. Do you need anything?"

"No, you go along."

Zach got up but stopped. "Maybe I should stay with you. Whoever bonked you may try again."

"Absolutely not! Just having trouble understanding meanings." All this concern was spooking her. "Go!"

Zach looked around. "George is at the bar," he told her. "I'll ask him to keep watch."

Hope reached for the coffee carafe. The sugar cubes reminded her of someone, but her head was too groggy to think straight. She closed her eyes. A scene flashed before her eyes. She was telling about Meghan's death, and Robert stuck a handful of sugar cubes in his pocket. She'd mention it to Matt.

At that moment, Matt headed her way. Their eyes met, and he detoured toward the lobby. She tried to get up, but the giant ball bouncing inside her head caused her to stumble.

Matt rushed over and put his arm around her. "What is wrong with you, Diamond? You trying to kill yourself?"

Hope pushed him away. She gathered the words in her mind before speaking. "I don't need your help, but I'll ask you the same question. What is wrong with you, Matt? You act like I've been sprayed by a skunk."

He laughed. "Diamond, I must be rubbing off on you."

His laugh softened her anger. "Seriously, Matt, what's wrong? Can we have lunch and talk?"

He stood looking at her, and it was a full minute before he rubbed his forehead with both hands. He clasped them in front of him. "You need to know that last night while Frank was on guard, our killer tried to get into your room through the glass door. I checked for fingerprints, but nothing. You're in danger, and you need to let your team protect you."

His words were clear, and he was right. Chindi had been battering her all morning. "Thank you for telling me."

Matt was twisting the ring on his pinkie finger. He took a deep breath, and she waited. His words hit her like a blast from a shotgun.

"Diamond, here's the thing. You're in the protection racket, and I'm on the other side of the fence. I get involved after the protection breaks down. I admit your team has been helpful, but you shouldn't even be involved in the investigation. Your guys could get hurt. You *did* get hurt."

She stood still, her face flushed. He didn't seem to notice her distress and kept speaking.

"I'd like you to go on doing your job, protecting the ladies that are still standing. But leave me alone to do *my* job, and that's investigating a murder and bringing the person to justice."

She locked eyes with him. His eyes held the same icy coldness as on the day they'd met. She turned and walked away.

# #

Settled in her recliner, Hope rehashed Matt's words. His arguments were valid. Their responsibilities *were* totally different. She was being paid a handsome salary to protect these women. So far, she hadn't done a great job.

Chindi was setting off goosebumps on her arm, and she looked at the painting. The man in the blue shirt and tan cowboy hat reminded her of Matt. It should have been comforting, but an ice curtain had cooled all the heat between them. She was at a loss to understand why or why she cared so much.

Hope called Frank and asked him to come to the suite. His presence brought the warmth of friendship into the room. She recounted her conversation with Dennison.

When she finished, he asked, "What do you want to do?"

Her head was clearing, and she put her thoughts into words. "We need to focus on protecting the women. You, Tony, Lucy, and Zach have been sticking to our clients like glue. I'm the one that veered off center, playing detective. I guess my old cop instincts kicked in."

She tilted her head and was silent a moment. "Truthfully, at first, I didn't think Dennison would solve the case."

"Have you changed your mind?"

"In some ways, yes. In other ways, I'm not sure."

"Explain."

"Dennison knows the routine to follow. He's the one who came up with the timeline stuff. He had the background information on the women's companies. He's got a large organization at his disposal that can do much more than we can, like analyze blood samples, run background checks, and provide instant support in many other ways."

Frank was nodding. "All good points."

"On the other hand." Hope massaged her temple. "If he keeps after Ellen and she's innocent, he may let the real murderer escape."

"What do you want our team to do?"

"Cooperate with Dennison but push him to look at suspects other than Ellen."

"Tony is on that train," Frank said.

"True." Hope smiled. "Tony has become very fond of Ellen and Sean. Keep an eye out to make sure Tony's not being blindsided. I'm pretty sure of Ellen, but I have a very open mind about Sean."

She crossed her legs. "Zach should keep working with Dennison on the timelines. They can pinpoint our most likely suspects."

Frank took the notepad off the desk and began writing.

"We need to share our intel," Hope went on. "Along with the timelines, Zach's dossier is critical to solving the case."

"I agree." Frank made another note.

"Furthermore, we must respond to anything Dennison asks us to do. No holding back." Frank frowned but kept writing. "Dennison won't ask for help unless it's vital."

"Finally, I don't want the team to know about my conversation with Dennison." Frank started to object, but she held up a hand. "Hear me out. Tony isn't Dennison's biggest fan. Hostile feelings can slip through and become a roadblock. If we don't cooperate fully, we won't get the job done before the women fly off into the sunset tomorrow. Do you agree?"

"Yes. Nobody wants to go home with an unsolved homicide hanging over our heads. Are you going to talk to Dennison?"

"That's where you come in, Frank. Let him know we'll continue doing what we have been doing, but he doesn't have to worry about me going rogue."

Frank straightened up in the chair. "I'll talk to him, but I'm not throwing you under the bus. You had a lead, and you followed it. Turns out you were right. As luck would have it, our culprit got there ahead of you."

Tears came to Hope's eyes, and she blinked. Frank respected her judgment, and she needed that reassurance.

"One more thing. I'd like you to lead our team meetings. My head isn't all back together. I can't concentrate on different pieces when they come at me too fast."

"I'll do everything you've asked, but tell me the truth about what you personally plan to do. I know you too well to believe you'll step aside totally."

"Fair enough," she said. "I plan to read the dossier over and over until I nail the clue that is free-floating in my mind. I'm close, Frank, but the answer is eluding me."

She shook her head in frustration, and the sharp pain made her wince. "I also plan to spin the timesheet information around until I'm dizzy. What I won't do is go off on my own looking for clues. Are you good with this plan?"

"I'm all in," Frank said and got up to leave, but he turned at the door. "I don't know how you feel about Dennison, but I can see he's hurt you, and I don't like it. That's between you and him. I'm proud of you for doing what you believe is right."

When he left, Hope leaned back in the recliner. She tried to get a handle on her emotions. How *did* she feel about Dennison? She didn't really know him. Why should his indifference bother her? She ran the back of her fingers lightly across her cheek and felt again that spark when his face touched hers. An odd moment that meant nothing; yet, somehow, it meant everything.

She struggled out of the recliner, went to the safe and pulled out Zach's dossier. She saw the words clearly and smiled. *You're back in the game, Diamond.*

CHAPTER 27

Frank ran into Tony in Blue Sky. "Have you seen Dennison?"

"He was going into the fitness center."

Catching Dennison in the fitness center was as good a place as any. Frank hurried to his room and changed into workout clothes. Frank admired Dennison, but he resented having his hands slapped for stepping on his toes when the team was providing the FBI assistance.

Frank pulled open the glass door at the gym. The room was set up with treadmills and bikes in front of large windows. Punching bags and the bench press area were arranged along one end of the room.

Matt was wearing boxing gloves and punching a long, leather bag. Sweat poured down his face and soaked his T-shirt. As he watched, Frank gripped the towel around his neck and let his annoyance slip away. This man was in pain.

Moving over to the weights, Frank began a workout. He would catch Matt another time. He went through his routine, no longer paying attention to the boxer. He had just stretched out on the bench press equipment when a voice asked, "Need a spot?"

He looked up at Matt. "Sure, that would be great." When he finished bench pressing, he offered to spot Matt.

"Nah, I've had enough for the day."

"Can we catch a cup of coffee?" Frank asked, standing beside him.

Matt wiped his face with his towel. "Half-an-hour in Blue Sky."

The room was empty when Frank and Matt sat down on chairs around a coffee table, but Cecelia came over quickly. They ordered and waited in silence for her to come back.

Matt's coolness was different from the easy companionship they had shared in the gym. Frank puzzled over what had caused his change of attitude toward Hope and himself. Cecelia arrived with the coffee, and he smiled at the interruption.

"All right, Madison, spill it. You've been hedging around about something for ten minutes."

Frank took a breath. "I heard about your talk with Hope."

Matt's jaw clenched. Frank added a little milk to his coffee and stirred. Hope's name changed the dynamics. The man had been cool, remote. Now he was hot under the collar. Frank shoved the cup to the side, folded his hands, and leaned over the table. "Here's how we propose to work with you, even if you're too bullheaded to want our help."

Matt's grip tightened on the coffee cup, but Frank ignored his embarrassment. He delivered Hope's instructions. The team would provide any help Matt asked for. They would share their notes.

269

Zach would put his computer skills at Matt's disposal. Matt was welcome at their meetings. They would work with him just as though nothing had changed.

"In fact, there's no reason to mention this conversation to anyone else."

Matt nodded. He apparently understood what Frank meant.

"We'll go on with our own protection services. Any clues we discover, we'll turn over to you. We want to be helpful because we want the ladies to leave knowing the killer is in custody."

"That's more than fair." Matt drank his coffee, set down the cup. "I just don't want anybody else getting hurt."

"Neither do we." Frank gave Matt a hard stare. "It doesn't always take a crack on the head to hurt a person. Words hurt, and they take longer to heal."

Matt looked down at his coffee cup, and Frank let the moment linger. "Well, it's my turn for guard duty." He pushed his chair back, stood up, and stepped closer to Matt. "If you need Zach, he's outside Blue Spruce."

Matt caught Frank's arm as he moved away. "Tell Diamond Robert knew a tiger's head tattoo meant vengeance and punishment."

# #

The sun was high, and Tony revved up the engine on the dirt bike. He was wearing sunglasses and a helmet, but he squinted against the shimmering glare from the desert floor. Sean was taking him in a different direction from their horseback ride. The ground stretched out flat with sagebrush and wildflowers.

Tony glimpsed the hills off in the distance. They were nothing like the hills in his hometown of Messina. The hills there were stacked with apartment buildings and alive with people. The only open space was out on the ocean.

He never minded the closeness. He liked people around him. Yet he saw the hand of God in this primitive, empty world with stretches of land that hadn't been totally disfigured by humans. He grinned. The Great American Desert had snuck into his psyche and touched his spirituality. Maybe he would visit Father Ramirez.

After half-an-hour, the riders reached clumps of low, twisting, rocky hills. Sean gave Tony pointers on how to handle the bike on the cliffs. It wasn't long before the men were swooshing around the curves and jumping off ledges. "How long have you been doing this stuff?" Tony shouted when they met up at the bottom of a cliff.

"A friend put me onto dirt biking after I had to quit football," Sean said. He was breathing hard. "Pittsburgh's full of hills, not open land like here. We bike through the trees."

Tony took off his helmet. "Sean, can I ask you a personal question?"

Sean took off his helmet, too. "Sure, Tony."

"You love danger. Like this dirt biking. I don't have the impression that Ellen shares that love. What do you two have in common?"

Sean laughed out loud. "Football, man! Ellen loves football!"

"No kidding?"

"Man, Ellen's passionate about the game. Be warned, Tony, don't mess with Ellen during the NFL draft. She takes no prisoners if you disagree with her picks."

"I'm surprised. She's never mentioned football to me."

Sean tilted his head and smiled. Maybe the comment reassured him that there was nothing between Ellen and him. Tony looked off into the distance.

"That's how I met Ellen," Sean said. "Old School was sponsoring a charity event. Hundreds of kids came into the stadium for a day of fun and a chance to meet some of us players. Ellen comes up to me and asks for an autograph. Can you beat that? She had my rookie card and my pro player's card. I took one look into those smoldering gray eyes, and I was hooked."

Sean shook his head. "Ellen has a lot of money, Tony, but I wasn't looking for money. I was a first-round draft pick in the NFL. I made plenty. Had plenty of girls, too. Meghan was a mistake, one I will never make again."

"I'm glad for you, Sean. I think Ellen's special, too." Tony had grown fond of Ellen, but Maria was in his heart. He took a deep breath. She still wasn't answering his calls. Tony pulled out his water bottle, took a long drink, and put on his helmet.

Sean pointed to a range of low, rocky hills about half-a-mile away. "Let's go over to those hills. I didn't ride there yesterday."

Other cyclists had left marks all over the cliffs. Tony followed Sean through twisting canyons and unexpected overhangs where he flew ten feet off the ground.

At times he hung on for dear life, but he was loving the thrill of flying. *"Fantastico!"* he shouted as he shot through the rocks.

Riding back to the hotel, Tony thought that it would take a person with Sean's edge to pull off the stunts that had happened at Secret Sands.

Had he slipped something into Meghan's pill bottles before she left Pittsburgh? He said he hadn't been up to her apartment, but was he telling the truth? When they drew near to the hotel property, Tony saw bike tracks leading to the cookout area. He stopped his bike, and Sean drew up beside him.

"Were you over that way yesterday?" Tony asked and pointed to the trees.

"Made a quick pit stop. Just at the edge of the trees."

"Did you notice anybody in the area?"

"No, I was only there for a minute," Sean said, revving the engine.

Tony's heart sank. It would have been around the time of Hope's attack. Maybe Dennison was right on insisting Sean was behind Meghan's murder.

Zach asked George for a Coke and sat down on a sofa. The Blue Sky was empty, but Zach enjoyed taking his breaks in the room. The patterns on the Navajo rugs appealed to his mathematical bent. Symmetrical diamonds and squares in beautiful reds and tans and turquoise that echoed the red rocks, tan desert, and turquoise sky.

Robert Halloway came in and stopped at the bar. Zach enjoyed talking to Robert because of his computer acumen, and he invited him to sit down. "I was wondering if you had noticed anything odd yesterday afternoon."

Robert squinted. "I was at the pool. Hope was there. Later I was here in Blue Sky. Then I went up to the corral."

"Was anyone else at the corral when you were there?"

"Several people were milling around. The only person I remember is Janai. Any special reason for asking?"

"Just wondering."

"I suppose you have to play your cards close to your vest. Hope didn't have any accident, did she? Somebody attacked her."

"Any thoughts on who that may have been?"

"No. Frankly, I wish we could leave, but Janai won't hear of it."

"What are you reading?" Zach asked, noticing the "blackhat" trademark on the brochure Robert was holding.

"Do you attend Black Hat?" Robert asked.

"I wouldn't miss it. In this job, you have to understand what hackers are up to."

"Same in my job."

"It's funny to think that a web platform our government created to protect naval intelligence is the root of the dark web," Zach said. "'The Onion Ring.' Great name, isn't it? What were they thinking when they open-sourced TOR and invited all the illegal traffickers in the world to dive in?"

Robert moved closer to Zach and lowered his voice. "Did you know this meeting hit the dark web."

"Where did you hear that?"

"A friend who plays around under the surface."

"Does he know anything about the site where it surfaced?"

"Impossible. He said he wouldn't even try to identify it."

"Chances are good that your friend is the webmaster of that site.

"No way!"

"Nobody knew the women were coming here. That leak came from someone with inside information."

Robert looked down at his beer. "You could be right. Steve watches my place when I'm out of town, and he wanted to know where I'd be in case of an emergency. I guess I shared more information than I should have."

"It's good to know how the cat got out of the bag," Zach said. "I'll need to tell our team."

"Janai doesn't need to know, does she?"

"That's up to Hope."

# #

Hope's head was pounding, but she didn't want to take any more pills. She leaned back in the recliner and closed her eyes. She visualized drifting on the warm, gentle water in the therapy pool. The scene was so appealing that she rose, donned a bikini and coverup, and started for the pool. She breathed in the fragrance of the potted flowers as she crossed the courtyard. A short distance from the pool she saw a body floating face down in the water.

"Sean!" She raced to the pool, sprang down the steps and lunged at the body. Sean's "dead body" came roaring up out of the water and barely stopped swinging in time to miss her face. "Matt!"

His hands gripped her shoulders, and she let out a squeal. "What are you doing!" he shouted. "You could have been killed!" Matt closed his eyes, his hands still on her shoulders. She felt his heart pounding along with hers.

"I thought you were Sean. I thought you were dead!" They looked at each other without moving.

Finally, he dropped his hands from her shoulders. "I came to loosen up sore muscles from when I foolishly thought I could relive my bronc-busting days. I was doing a Navy SEAL exercise holding my breath. I was up to three minutes before your attack."

"Attack! I was saving your life!" Her coverup floated around her, but her flipflops drifted across the pool. She held her hands over her pounding heart, moved over to the steps and sat down, waiting for the inside of her head to stop rocking. She spoke in a soft voice. "I didn't mean to disturb your training. I'm sorry."

Matt paddled over to the steps. "I was about finished. I'm sorry I swung at you. It was a reflex."

Looking at him standing in the water, hair matted to his face, she wanted to reach out and push it back, tell him how she felt. She opened her mouth, but the words stuck in her throat. He waited, his eyes on hers, as if wanting to hear the words. When she didn't speak, his eyes frosted over.

"Robert stuck a handful of sugar cubes in his pocket on Saturday," she said quickly. "I don't know if it's a habit, and I don't know if it has anything to do with Paco, but I thought you should know when you look at Robert's timeline."

He reached up to his chest as if to pull out his notebook, an automatic gesture, and she chuckled. His lips crinkled up, too. "I'll make a note," he said and started toward the steps.

"Please, don't leave. I'll go." She stood up and turned so quickly that she lost her balance and fell backwards toward the water.

Matt caught her. "Seems like I'm always falling into your arms," she said.

He took his arms away. "You stay. I have things to do. By the way, I talked to Frank. Thanks."

The coldness in his voice felt like a slap. He fished her flipflops out of the water. "You'll need these. The pavement's hot," he said, handing them to her.

He walked up the steps but turned back. "Mind you don't go falling into anyone else's arms."

CHAPTER 28

Staring out the sliding glass door of his room, Matt longed to take a horse and ride as fast as he could across that endless landscape. Maybe that's what he'd do when Diamond left. Take a horse and ride. Dumb thought. No way could he out-ride the pain in his heart. This must be what that poison cactus, twisted heart, feels like.

He curled his hands into fists, ashamed of the way he acted, but the Code of the West meant not making moves on a sidekick's gal. Trouble was the hurt in Diamond's eyes made him want to take her in his arms and hold her tight. Then he'd say something foolish that hurt her more.

He pulled the drapes closed, swung around, put on his hat. *Get a move on, cowboy. You've got a killer to catch, and time is a-wasting.*

Lucy was sitting outside the Blue Spruce. "May I join you?" Dennison asked.

"Sure, sit down. I'll get us some water," she said and went into the anteroom.

He could see the ladies around the table. What a shame to come to a beautiful place like Secret Sands and bury yourself in meetings.

He turned and looked at the setting behind him. He'd been to the resort once before officially, although not on a murder case, and a few times unofficially. He and George had taken horses and camped out overnight. His job was high stress, and riding a horse, breathing in the scents of the desert, singing and strumming around a campfire, just being out in nature restored his spirit.

Lucy came back with two glasses of ice water and sat down at the table.

"Any luck finding out where Dimitri was yesterday?" Matt asked.

"Up at the corral, but none of the hands saw him. Around four, he said he was at the Desert Luck Casino. Zach is taking a photo over. He figures the poker dealers would remember him."

"What made Dimitri go up to the corral?" Matt took a long swallow of the cold water.

"He wanted to look at Paco. He said the horse must have been doped."

"That's all we need, another investigator mucking around in the mud." Lucy's expression warned him that he'd said the wrong thing. "No offense, but amateurs can get hurt messing around with things that don't concern them."

"Hope is no amateur!" Lucy crossed her arms over her chest.

He held up his hands, palms outward. "You're right. I'm just exasperated thinking what might have happened to her." *Diamond was right. He had a bad habit of making offensive remarks.*

"I know how you feel," Lucy said. "Hope isn't only my boss; she's my friend."

"From what I can tell, all of you think of her as more than a boss."

"That's the great thing about the company. We're family really. We care about each other."

"How did you happen to get this job?" She seemed very young to be in the protection business. She flinched, and he put up his hands again. "That's okay. I just wondered." *Come on, Dennison, be careful what you say to this girl.*

She smiled. "I was taking a class at UCLA, and my parents were killed in a car crash. My professor knew Hope, and she recommended me. Hope met me at school, and we talked outside on a bench. I thought she'd send me an application, but she said, 'I'd love having you work with me at Diamond Security.' She sent me for training, and I passed everything." The girl's beautiful brown eyes lit up.

Matt swallowed the lump in his throat. Diamond had a depth in her soul that touched people. *Why did she have to touch him when she was in a relationship with Jake Sanders?* He exhaled. "Diamond says you two do martial arts training together."

"She's a black belt in karate. I'm yellow. But I have a black belt in judo."

"Remind me to watch my mouth around you two gals. I wouldn't want to be on the wrong end of a *krav maga.*"

"You're trained?"

"Spent time in Israel. They wean their kids on that move."

"I bet you've traveled all over the world," she said, with a touch of awe.

To this girl, I must seem as old as Methuselah. "I've spent time in most of the world's hot spots. Haven't taken the time to visit many pleasure spots."

"Why don't you take the time now that you're here?"

The question was a good one. "I guess staying in the same place feels like a vacation, especially surrounded by all this beauty."

"The desert is beautiful, but I miss the big city," she said.

"Where do you go on vacation?"

"At Christmas, Frank, Zach and I stayed at Hope's place on Maui. Hawaii is more beautiful than I ever imagined." Her eyes opened wider, and her voice became excited as she talked about the islands and learning to surf and hula and parasail.

"And the food," she said, "well, I could go on," and she did, giving Matt details about the unusual foods she had tasted. He listened patiently, amused by the girl's naiveté.

"How come Diamond didn't go to Hawaii?"

"She visited a friend in Washington."

Matt stood up and said he needed to get back to work.

# #

Hope found Zach in Blue Sage with his laptop open. "Anything new?" she asked.

"I spoke with Robert and learned about that web hit."

Hope's blue eyes lit up, and she parroted Matt's phrase. "Tell me."

Zach explained about Robert's sharing information with his friend. "He's worried you'll tell Janai."

"It's good to have one mystery solved, but I will talk to him about security." *Was it a simple mistake, or did Robert have some sinister reason for leaking the information?* "Let Dennison know what you learned."

She sat down next to Zach and asked, "Can we look at the timing information you came up with?" Her eyes were clear, and the timing piece could help solve the mystery.

"I'm looking at some data myself. I'll show you." She moved close so that she could see the screen.

Zach tapped the keys. "Here's a look at one time frame. The spread shows what everybody was doing at three o'clock yesterday. The red squares indicate alibies that haven't been verified. Green squares mean we've checked out their stories."

"I see that Margo was near the stables. Dimitri and Robert also mention the stables. Can they corroborate each other?"

"Lucy checked with Dimitri, but he didn't see Margo. Robert only remembers seeing Janai."

"What else can you do?"

"We can look at a particular person's movements in depth. Sean is a guy on the move. If I pull up his name, you can see where he's been over the past few days. Most of the information is based on Tony's reports."

"Great job, Zach."

"One other thing. You can see who visited the stables during the day, not just at three o'clock."

He tapped the keys, and a list of names appeared. The horses were popular. It seemed odd that Janai and Lydia and Gloria were interested in the horses. She'd go up to the stables herself to see what the attraction was.

# #

Three men were sitting on the fence at the corral. As Hope drew closer, her eyes fastened on a skinny, long-legged colt, with a fluffy tail, romping next to its mother. The colt was light brown with a broad white streak on its face.

When she reached the fence, the colt sprinted right up to her. She slipped off her sunglasses and reached through the fence. The little guy nuzzled against the back of her hand.

A feeling of joy enveloped her, and she gasped. Hope glanced up at the man sitting a few feet away. Her mouth opened when Matt turned toward her. His eyes held a smile, but he pulled down his hat, shading his eyes.

"This little one's only a day old," he said, as if he felt a duty to be civil.

"He's beautiful," Hope said, still touching the colt's face, but the colt scurried back to its mother.

"Did you need something?" Matt asked.

Hope shrugged.

"Rio, there, was born a while before you were attacked. Sani and the others were inside and didn't pay attention to anybody walking by."

Hope lifted her head and looked into Matt's eyes. "Are you still upset with me over the attack at the cookout?" It was when he was watching over her in the night that his attitude changed.

His voice held surprise. "Upset with you? No, I wasn't upset, just worried."

"I'm sorry. I caused a lot of people to worry. It was thoughtless of me to go up there by myself." She took a breath and held out her hand. "Friends?"

Matt swiveled around on the fence, jumped down and took her hand, held it in both of his for a long moment. Hope trembled at the touch. "Friends," he said. He let go of her hands and walked away.

Hope spun around and put both hands on the fence. The movement jarred her head, and she groaned. The colt came sprinting back to her, and she petted it, murmuring sweet words.

She took out her camera and snapped pictures of the animal. The camera in her hand reminded her of the photographs of the footprints she'd taken at the cookout site. She'd ask Zach to upload them to his computer. She petted the colt and started back to the hotel.

Love was impossible. An invisible string attached her to Jake Sanders, a man she saw once in a blue moon. In a way, it was an ideal relationship. She liked her life in Los Angeles and was not prepared to give up her business. Jake felt the same about his life in Washington, where he rubbed elbows with powerful people.

Why, then, had Matt Dennison tilted her world? He was exactly as Jake described, a bull in a china shop. She looked down at her hands, but his touch was as tender as a kitten's paw.

Suddenly, Hope wanted to go home, wanted to get away from this sordid business, wanted to leave her feelings for this FBI man buried in the desert.

CHAPTER 29

Matt was standing outside the lobby, and Hope stopped beside him. "I forgot that I had taken pictures of footprints up at the cookout yesterday."

"You have photographs of footprints and you forgot to mention them? What's the matter with your head, Diamond?"

His harsh words stung, and she faced him squarely. "As a matter of fact, my head is exactly the problem, and you know it!"

"Sorry, sorry. I forgot."

"Yes, people do forget things when they are dealing with a concussion."

"No need to go on. I said I was sorry." He reached out and took her arm, "Let me see the pictures."

Hope threw out her hands. "Out here in the sunshine?"

"You're right. Come with me." He pulled her inside and whispered, "Don't say anything while we're walking. I don't want people to hear." Hope looked around. Nobody was in sight.

The man seemed discombobulated, and his tight grip pinched her arm. "Ouch," she said and pushed his hand. He loosened his grasp but didn't let go.

His room was at the end of the hall. When they reached his door, he opened it, and she went inside ahead of him. She breathed in the spicy scent of Icelandic Wind. He'd obviously been using products from Janai's gift set.

The drapes were closed, and Matt switched on the light. The room had a lived-in look. A jacket was slung over a chair, and a pair of boots tilted against the wall. She took in other details: a guitar case open on the bed. *Leaves of Grass* on the nightstand, a root beer bottle on the desk.

The painting on the wall stopped her. A beautiful Indian maiden in buckskin sheltered against snow in an aspen grove. The vivid details of the maiden's face stood out against the snow and the white trees, emitting a sadness that resonated with Hope. She rubbed her arms. Matt's voice interrupted her thoughts, and she turned.

"I can't believe you had the foresight to take pictures of the footprints," he said, shaking his head.

"You say the nastiest things and don't even realize it." His puzzled look proved her point. She gritted her teeth.

"If I had examined the prints yesterday, we might have known then who was trying to kill you." His words had a sharp edge, and he stopped, held his palms out, and said slowly, "I'm sorry. You had a concussion. I shouldn't have said what I did. May I look at your phone, please?"

"Yes, you may," she said, but her tone was biting. She reached into her pocket and pulled out the phone.

"Wait." He went to the bureau and tugged on a pair of latex gloves. He held out his hand, and she handed him the cell phone.

Matt took off his hat and tossed it on the bed. Then he sat down on the sofa and scrolled through the photographs. Ten minutes passed before he said, "I'm going to upload these photos onto my computer. I'll send them to Washington. The lab guys there can confirm what I think I'm seeing."

"What did you find?" She tried to take back her cell phone, but his fist closed over it. He moved to the chair at the desk. Hope pulled up a chair and sat next to him, watching him tap keys.

"The photos should get attention. I've marked them 'Rush, Urgent, and Confidential.' But to be sure, I'll call a friend." He pressed a number on his cell, stood up and paced around the room.

"Hey, Rose, this is your old pal, Desert Rat." He laughed at her comment and spoke for several minutes. "That long. Dang!" He disconnected the call.

"We won't get the results until late tonight. Rose has to pull in a photo evidence guru who's at his son's soccer tournament."

Hope's eyes stared at the picture on the wall. Scenes were flashing at her like the lights on a patrol car. Sitting beside Zach and viewing the timesheets. Sitting in her room reading the team's accounts in the dossier. Taking photographs of footprints.

The evidence was coming together. Some pieces were vivid like the Indian maiden's face in the painting, but some were obscure like the snow and the white aspen trees.

She looked up. Matt's eyes were watching hers.

He still held her phone and turned it toward her. "Nice photo of you and Jake." Hope was wearing a golden gown, and Jake was in a tuxedo with his arm around her bare shoulder. Matt's jaw clenched.

Hope's face flushed, and she stood and stretched across him to take back the cell phone. He caught her hand. "Sorry, but I can't let you have it. It's evidence."

The flush in Hope's face turned red with anger. "What do you mean? I want to show the photos to the team."

Matt stepped over to a drawer in the bureau and pulled out a clear plastic bag. He dropped the phone into the bag, sealed it and wrote on it with a black Sharpie.

"Look, Diamond," he said, pulling off his gloves, tossing them into the trashcan. "Two people know about these photos now. As far as I'm concerned, that's one too many."

His words struck like a match to a tinderbox. She should calm down before she said things she'd regret. Her tongue wasn't listening. "That's insane! You conceited, arrogant, smug, pompous, pigheaded, two-bit jerk!"

Moving quickly, she started for the door, but he reached it first. She tried to push him aside, but it was like trying to move a block of cement with a feather.

She stopped pushing and shouted, "Dennison, I will never forgive you if you don't apologize for that remark and give me back my cell phone." Standing in front of him, fists clenched, she waited for a response, her breathing erratic.

He stayed quiet until her breathing became regular. When he spoke, his voice was soft, placating. "I *do* apologize. I didn't mean what I said as a put-down. Come and sit down. I'll explain."

Fists clenched, she sat on the sofa. Her heart was racing. He walked over to the credenza and stood with his back to her. Then he set a bowl of almonds and a glass of fruit juice on the table. The gesture jarred her mentally. "I'm okay."

She was sitting on the edge of the couch, and her head was throbbing. At last, she picked up the glass and drank a little of the juice. She took a deep breath to relax the stiffness in her neck and shoulders. She nibbled some almonds and drank more juice. She was regaining her composure. She looked over at Matt, who had sat down beside her. He was leaning back against the cushion with his eyes closed.

"I'm listening," she said.

His eyes stayed closed, and his words caught her off guard. "You know who the killer is, don't you?"

The simple question drained away her anger as if a tsunami had washed over her, and she answered. "I think I do, but pieces are still missing, and I don't have any evidence. It's all guesswork from reading the reports, looking at the timelines, seeing the footprints, and letting my senses free float around impressions."

Matt continued in his lazy, rich voice she found so attractive. "I'm in the same boat. I re-read the reports and spent time on my own with Zach's algorithm. Then I looked at your photos. My conclusions are, obviously, the same as yours. The only thing we can charge the person with is the attack on the hayride wagon. That's because your photographs show clear footprints where they should not have been. Around the horses, up beyond the restrooms. In my opinion, the photos constitute hard evidence."

Opening his eyes, he sat up straight. His eyes held that mocking smile. "You're the goods, Diamond. You had the smarts to take those pictures yesterday. By the time I was ready to take photos, the ambulance had trashed the tracks. If the lab can estimate the size and weight of our suspect and we find shoes to match the prints, we'll have solid evidence that may allow us to make an arrest. I don't like admitting it, but you were a step ahead of me."

She gave him a warm smile. "What are you going to do?"

"I'm in a dilemma. I can't allow even a hint of what I've told you to leave this room. Professionally, I shouldn't have told you anything. Legally, what I'm saying is that I am no longer your friend."

"What do you mean?"

He opened his wallet and held out his identification card. "I am FBI Agent Matthew Lawrence Dennison. If you tell *anyone*, even Madison—" She started to protest, but Matt took hold of her hands. "I know how you feel about Madison, but hear me out. If you tell Frank or anyone else, I will faithfully discharge the duties of my office and charge you with obstruction of justice." He stopped talking for a moment. "I need your word that I can trust you."

She put her hands on her throat. It was tightening up, and she couldn't swallow. He was asking her to choose between giving him her trust and betraying people who would risk their lives for her. She looked in his eyes and knew he understood her misery, but he would absolutely arrest her for obstruction of justice.

"If you give me your word, I'll trust you completely, and that's the end of it."

"Tell me why it's so important that what we know—and you admit it isn't much—must be kept secret."

He chuckled. "You don't give up." She shook her head. "I'll tell you my reasons for secrecy, but whether you agree with me or not, the conditions won't change." She nodded, holding back tears.

"Our villain has antenna as sensitive as that of a butterfly. One wrong word, look or movement could result in another murder."

"But the team wouldn't say anything."

"When people know information, it can leak out unintentionally. I'm not willing to take that risk." He took a long pause. "How did I know that you knew who the killer was? I read it in your eyes."

He smiled. "Your eyes are beautiful. Deep blue like the Hope Diamond. But they can let out secrets unless you're on guard every second. Fact is, I think you've somehow conveyed to our murderer that you know something. That's the reason for the attempted break-in last night."

After a long minute, she reached a decision that pained her. "How do you plan to proceed?"

"You haven't given me your word that I can trust you."

She set down her glass, put her hand on her heart. "FBI Agent Matthew Lawrence Dennison, I promise to hold confidential anything you've told me or will tell me. Now can you tell me what you plan to do?"

"I shouldn't, but I'll say this much. I've ordered my team to be on call. I intend to take the person into custody if the results of the photographs show what I think they will show. I also requested search warrants."

"What can I do to help?"

"I'll be grateful if your staff continues protecting your clients."

"That's our job. You can count on us." She stood up to leave, and he stood beside her. He looked at her, and his eyes held the same surprised hurt as when Dimitri kissed her hand.

"By the way, Diamond, you didn't tell me how you knew Jake Sanders."

She frowned. *Why was she hesitant about telling him anything at all about Jake?* "That's my secret."

"Fair enough." He opened the door.

"Take care of my cell phone. I want those photos back." He recoiled, and she smiled. "You deserved that."

"Yes, I did." He laughed and closed the door.

As she walked along the hall, she hung her head in shame that she had to keep her team in the dark. Frank might understand, but the others would feel bewildered. She was their leader. She shouldn't be double-dealing behind their backs. If only she hadn't let Matt read her thoughts. It confirmed his reasoning as to why she couldn't tell anyone what she'd discovered. An unintentional look could be dangerous.

Even though she knew in her heart who murdered Meghan, she hadn't found any way to prove it. Conjecture, yes, but you could build a case against every person in the hotel based on conjecture.

As she was passing the Blue Spruce, Frank called out. Startled, Hope took a deep breath and entered the room. Coffee was brewing, and she inhaled the fragrant aroma. She picked up a purple mug and poured herself a cup. "Anything new?" she asked, sitting down beside him.

"Haven't seen you for a while. When you go dark, we worry. I thought we might have to call in the FBI to organize a search party." He raised his eyebrows. "Zach is out scouting for you now."

She reached for her cell. *Darn!* "I don't have my cell with me. Would you text him?"

Frank looked askance at her. They always carried their cells on duty. "Sure. By the way, Zach talked to the casino dealer. Dimitri got there at five, not four, as he said. He had a car and could have made a side trip to the cookout area about the time you were there."

Hope put her hand on her chin. "Did Zach tell Dennison?" Matt hadn't mentioned that fact to her.

"He texted him. Have you come to any conclusions about our murderer?"

The question hit a nerve, and she lowered her eyes. "I'd like to keep my ideas under my hat for the moment. Do you mind?"

"That's a new approach for us, Hope."

"I have to ask you to trust me." Her hand shook as she set the cup on the table. He must find her attitude baffling after she had confided in him about her confrontation with Matt.

"I trust you. I just don't want to walk into a buzz-saw."

"I will tell you everything as soon as I can." He reached over and squeezed her hand. His faith in her brought a smile to her eyes.

After leaving Frank, Hope walked outside and sat alone on her favorite rock ledge to keep her emotions from exploding. Things were moving, but she had to stay still, like this ancient rock. Isolated from her team. Shoved behind an ice wall by Matt. Battered by fear of the unseen chindi.

Voices were coming along the path. Tony and Sean. They wouldn't see her in the niche of the rock. She took a deep breath and called out in case they were looking for her.

"Hope!" Tony called back. "No wonder we couldn't find you."

She smiled and stood up. "Just enjoying the comforts of nature," she said, pointing to the rock ledge.

"You look much better than the last time I saw you," Sean said. He took off his hat and fanned his face.

She felt light-headed and sat down. "How is Ellen?"

"That Janai lady has her worn to a frazzle with all her meetings. Does she never take a break and have a little fun?"

"Sean, you're one of those guys who likes to have fun all the time," Tony said. "Talk about a kid in a candy store. You have the perfect job."

Sean grinned. "After Ellen and me were married and I'd finished with football, I started working at Old School—on the candy line, mind you. I ate more candy than we shipped. They had to promote me out of there to stay in business." They all laughed.

"The candy Ellen gave me is delicious," Hope said.

"I'll send you a sample of a new concoction our head candy maker came up with. It is to die for." Sean put his hand over his mouth. "Whoops! I won't be saying that anymore, but, truly, it will put us into the healthy snack business big time."

The sun drifting west told Hope it was time to go back to the room. She stood up to leave and put her hand against the rock. "You look shaky," Tony said. "I'll walk you to your room." Hope took Tony's arm, glad of his support.

"What have you been up to this afternoon," Tony asked as they walked along.

"I've been trying to wrap my head around this case," she said and kept her eyes on the path so they wouldn't reveal her thoughts. "How about you?"

"I went dirt biking with Sean."

"You and Sean seemed to have developed a strong friendship."

Tony shrugged. His voice was low and held a touch of melancholy. "I saw bike tracks leading to the cookout, and Sean admits he was in the area yesterday. He could have been your attacker."

Hope's heart beat harder. The sound of an engine revving before she blacked out crossed her memory. Tony seemed to realize his remark struck a chord. "Do you think it was Sean who attacked you?"

Hope closed her eyes and said she didn't know. When they reached her glass door, she pulled out her key. She stood still, looking at the door, her head tilted to the side.

"Anything wrong?"

She shrugged. How easy it would be to forget to lock the glass doors. She pushed on her door, and it was locked tight. She unlocked it, slid it open, and stepped inside. Last night, maybe the killer was checking to see if she had left her door unlocked.

Her leg shook, and she fell against Tony. He helped her over to the recliner, and she stared at the painting. The horsemen seemed to be jeering at her because they knew more than she did, but she was catching a few of the clues they kept juggling among themselves. *If only she could catch the essential clue.*

"*Mama mia!* You've figured out who the killer is!" Tony said, standing in front of her, his brown eyes as big as a coconut shell.

She gulped and shook her head. "Please, Tony, promise me you won't repeat that idea to anyone else." She reached up and clutched his hands. "I'm sorry, but I can't tell you anything more just now."

Tony's lips compressed into a straight line, and he pushed her hands away. "I'm sorry you feel you can't trust your team, boss. Obviously, the only one you trust is that FBI agent."

He spun around and left through the glass door.

Hope jumped up and ran over to make sure the door was locked. Her head rocked with pain. She looked across at the painting. She had a foreboding that she was one of the horsemen. She was trying to catch the evil in the middle, but it was reaching out for her.

CHAPTER 30

Hope was lying on the bed when the telephone rang. Maybe Matt had news about the footprints. She answered. "How's everything going out there, Babe?"

Usually, her heart quickened whenever Jake called. To keep her confused feelings out of her voice, she smiled. "Okay."

"I saw requests come across the wire. It appeared things were moving out on the desert. Thought I'd take a shortcut and have you fill me in."

Oh no! Another person to keep secrets from. Jake was FBI and could read everything in the reports, but she had promised Matt to tell no one, and he was trusting her to keep her word.

She delayed answering so long that Jake asked, "Still there?"

"Yes, I'm sorry. My mind has taken to slipping away in mid-conversation since the clout on the head."

"Oh, I'm sorry. I shouldn't have called. Are you okay? Is there anything I can do for you back here?"

"No, thanks. Dennison's coordinating with your people. The doctor says I have one of the hardest heads he's ever seen, so I'm fine. Just a headache."

"That's a relief. I was worried about you. I talked to Dennison the other night. Did he mention it?"

"No, he didn't. Was he supposed to tell me something?"

"Just that I asked about you. I guess he forgot."

"Probably. He's been busy, and I'm the last thing on his mind."

"Glad to hear that." Before she could comment, he said, "I've got another call. Let me know if you need me. Stay safe, Babe."

She hung up with a frown. Matt had known about her and Jake before he saw that photograph. That could explain the change in his behavior. She was too weary to worry about him. She had caused a deep rift of trust in her own team, and healing could take a long time.

It was time to dress for the evening program. She didn't feel like going, but she had no choice. She stood up, put on black stretchy pants and a thick wool sweater. They were going back to the campfire where they had watched the dancers perform the night they arrived. It was a tradition of the hotel to wish their guests *yá'át'ééh,* or "make today great!"

# #

The soft glow from the ceiling lights in Blue Sky provided a muted background for the splash of colors jetting out from the glass bubble sculpture atop the tall table. Matt was talking with George at the bar. He faced her and said, "Hello." She nodded but didn't speak. Her voice wasn't steady enough to engage in conversation.

"I am happy to see you looking better, Miss Diamond," George said. "Would you like a drink?"

"Ginger ale, please." He handed her an iced drink wrapped in a cloth napkin. She smiled. He apparently didn't want her hands to get cold holding the drink. She must look a wreck.

She sat down on a sofa. Matt stayed at the bar. They would all be leaving tomorrow. Maybe she'd get rid of the ache in her heart if she didn't have to see Matt again.

His attitude had been professional when they talked in his room about the photographs and the actions he would be taking. The ice curtain had been pushed aside, but the warmth he had shown her at the square dance was gone.

Janai arrived wearing a blue velvet jacket. "Have you identified the killer yet?" she asked Hope. "We're leaving tomorrow."

Hope swallowed. Before words came out, Matt reached out to Janai. "Hey," he said, "I wondered if you were going to keep the ladies in a meeting tonight." Janai smiled and took his arm. She had an easy way with him. "Sit down here," he said. "I'll get you a drink."

When he returned, Hope could see his face and hear the two of them laughing. Matt was used to covert action. That's why he studied drama. It was easy for him to hide secrets. She was glad her business didn't often require her to be surreptitious.

Chatter grew louder as people entered. Sean and Ellen stopped at the bar. Zach sat down with Margo by the window. Gloria stopped in front of Hope. "Our last evening at this amazing resort. Have you found the killer?" The question asked in that bubbly voice caused Hope to stammer, and Gloria went on. "I'm not sure you ever will. I mean, do you even know for sure how the girl died?"

Margo turned around and said, "We'd all like the answer to that question."

Matt stood up. "The investigation into the death of Miss Connors is continuing. As soon as the perpetrator is identified, you will be informed. Any questions?" No one spoke.

Hope looked at the colored glass bubbles to take her mind off the case. Tony sat down in the chair next to her. "I'm sorry, Hope. I had no right being rude to you." He looked down at his hands, and Hope cast her own eyes down. It wasn't his fault. It was hers. "I hope you'll forgive me," he said.

"Of course. We'll talk things over tomorrow." He met her eyes and nodded. Then he glanced over at Matt, shook his head, and went out to the patio.

She tensed when the Shadow Lady slipped onto the sofa. "Are you coming to the campfire with us tonight?" Hope asked.

"No. The first night was enough for me. Spirits and chanting make my skin crawl. I heard what the FBI said, but I'm asking you, Hope Diamond. Have you identified the killer?"

"Do you have any ideas?"

"Me? Why would I have any ideas about a killer? Frankly, I think Janai should find a more dependable security agency." She stood up and went outside.

Looking around the room, Hope counted heads. "Where's Lydia?" she asked Frank, who was close by, apparently standing guard over her.

His glance toward the patio showed that he had expected Lydia to be outside smoking. "I'll ask." He put a hand on Zach's shoulder. He and Margo were looking at the sunset. Frank stood behind their sofa, speaking in a low voice. He nodded at whatever Margo said. After a minute, he came back. "Margo's had her nose in the computer and hasn't seen Lydia. I'll go to her room."

Hope crossed her legs and squirmed on the sofa. She looked at Matt, and he raised his eyebrows. She shrugged. He stood up, said a word to Janai, and sat down at the other end of the sofa. "What's going on?"

"We're missing Lydia. Frank asked Margo, but she hasn't seen her. He's checking her room."

Matt kept turning toward the hallway and looking at his watch. "I'll go check." He stood up, then said, "Here's Frank."

"Lydia had a headache, took a couple aspirin, and fell sleep. She'll join us in a few minutes."

Hope's rigid shoulders loosened. "Thank you for checking." Frank squinted, looked at Matt and back at her. Tony must have talked to him, and now he detected collusion between her and Matt. She felt as though she were in the middle of a vice, and the two ends were squeezing the life out of her.

"What's the entertainment tonight?" Matt asked. "I forgot to check that fancy binder of yours, Diamond."

"The hotel does a special farewell for guests around the campfire." She pointed toward the hill. "We were there the first night. It seems years ago."

"It was the first time we saw the sunset," Frank said. "It was so beautiful. Everybody raved about it. Now, we take it for granted." He turned and looked out the window as the sky put on its magic show.

"You do take your blessings for granted." Matt looked down at Hope. She wrapped her arms around herself.

Frank glanced behind him. "Here's Lydia," He held out his arms, and she walked over to him.

"Are we any closer to finding out who our villain is?" she asked in her foghorn voice.

"I'm sorry. I can't give you any information," Dennison said.

Lydia looked at Frank and Hope and back at Matt. She mouthed quietly, "You didn't answer my question." He didn't reply, just shook his head. Hope held her breath. These women pulled a lot of strings, but Matt never seemed daunted by their influence.

"Shall we go out to the patio? Dinner won't be long," Frank said. Lydia raised an eyebrow at Matt, but she took Frank's arm and left. Hope let out her breath.

Zach and Margo stood up. "Dinner's ready," Zach announced as they passed, and others in the room followed.

Matt turned to Janai. "You go ahead. I'll catch up with you after dinner." She smiled and went outside.

He sat down on the sofa and slid over to Hope. The mocking smile was gone. His eyes held the look she had seen in the ambulance. "I'm sorry. I've treated you like a jerk."

Hope's throat choked up, and she swallowed. "Jake said he called you the other night."

"No excuse. Believe me when I say I never wanted to hurt you."

"I believe you. I don't think you'd deliberately hurt anyone."

He grinned. "Well, not anybody as beautiful as you, anyway." His cell phone rang. He said a few words and hung up.

He took a deep breath. "It's a go. The lab confirmed that your photos can be used as evidence. My team will arrive sometime after ten. It's later than I'd like, but there's no way our villain can leave."

Hope's breathing became irregular. She looked around, her head moving side to side.

Matt looked around, too. "What's wrong?"

"Chindi's close by." She held her arms tight against her chest.

"Diamond, when you woke up last night, you asked me a question. 'Why did you leave me with chindi?' I didn't understand what you meant."

Letting out a deep breath, Hope said, "Before the attack, I felt the presence of chindi, and I got spooked. Your face came into my mind, and I relaxed. Just before I blacked out, I thought, 'Matt, why did you let chindi catch me?'"

She felt him shudder. "Forgive me. I should have gone to the cookout myself. It was an inexcusable mistake."

"I feel chindi here now." The premonition was strong, and her arms, in spite of the sweater, had goosebumps. "We haven't heard the last of our murderer."

He wrapped his arm around her shoulders and pulled her close. "Then stay close to me every minute."

"No, we have to act natural. You were right. I have a strong sense that an inadvertent word, look, or action could provoke the killer to do something rash."

He nodded and moved his arm away. They sat together, silent, tense, watching the sky turn into a shadow, thoughts of a killer filling the space around them. A razor slice of moon appeared, and stars blinked in the blackness. Guests shuffled out of chairs on the patio.

Hope tapped his arm. "Janai is looking for you."

"Don't go getting jealous now just because a billionaire lady wants to do the two-step with me." He laughed, a croaky sound, not his hearty, carefree laugh. The tension was too thick to shred with a laugh.

"Go! Sitting here with you is the most dangerous thing I've done all week." Her words pushed through the disquietude, and he grinned.

"Aristotle said wise people should be willing to expose themselves to danger when they care enough. Otherwise, life is not worth living."

"Do you think love is dangerous?"

His eyes flickered. "Yes, I do. I deal with domestic violence. But maybe that's passion, not love."

She shivered. He lived in a very dark world.

"I'd better go. That lady is stomping her feet like a bull in the shoot." He stood up. Then he leaned over and whispered, "I'd like nothing more than to stay here with you."

Hope felt a surge of love flowing through her soul. She touched the back of her fingers against his face and smiled. Then he was gone.

When she walked outside, Tony was standing by the table. "Dennison went off with Janai. May I walk you up to the campfire."

"Thank you, Tony. I would like that very much." She held tight to his arm, frowning as Coyote preceded them up the hill.

CHAPTER 31

Hope sat at the edge of the bench around the campfire and sighed at the feeling of *déjà vu*. Although the *yá'át'ééh* was supposedly different from the first evening, the singing and dancing appeared much the same to Hope. With hands folded, she watched the moccasin-clad performers sway to the beat of the tom-tom. Their turquoise-and-silver jewelry flashed in and out of the firelight.

Meghan Connors had been sitting next to Lydia, smoking. The young woman was so sure of herself. She would be promoted or take a golden parachute. The fact that she might never be avenged frustrated Hope's sense of justice. She kept her eyes on the dancers. Otherwise, her eyes could betray her and expose the secret she had promised Matt to keep.

Matt broke the spell. He had not been at the ceremony that first evening. He was the wild card that could prevent another tragedy. At that moment, chindi brushed her shoulder, and she jerked.

Tony moved closer, put his arm around her and touched her hand. "You're cold. Let's go back to the hotel." She shook her head, but he pulled her up. "Come on. You're still dealing with that concussion."

They edged away, and Tony lit his flashlight and guided her down the path. Inside her room, he asked if he should stay with her or go back in case somebody else needed help."

"You go back, Tony. We need eyes on the women. Thank you." She kissed his cheek, and he left.

Hope put on a thick, fleece-lined jacket, slipped her gun in the pocket, and went back to the patio. Colored lights twinkled along the overhang. She gazed dreamily into the blackness. If there really were UFOs, the desert would be the perfect landing spot.

The dancers came back and passed Hope on their way inside, barely visible in their dark costumes. After some minutes, light from flashlights moved bumpily down the path. Margo and Zach arrived and sat down across the table.

"You cheated," Margo said. "I saw you and Tony sneak away."

"I was cold. I should have worn this jacket in the first place."

Margo wore a black woolen cape. "The air is chilly. I'll have a hot buttered rum."

George stepped out of the doorway. "I make a very good hot buttered rum," he said and switched on the space heaters.

"I'll pass," Zach said.

"I'd like a cup of hot green tea, George," Hope said. She watched the parade of lights coming down the hill. Two small red dots stopped midway. Must be Lydia and Gloria smoking. The sight sparked a memory. Her eyes snapped open. Those cigarettes. They were the elusive clue that had been taunting her.

"You look as if you've seen a ghost," Margo said.

George brought their drinks, and Hope wrapped her cold hands around the warm mug. She chuckled. "I'd been thinking about flying saucers and how they're always spotted in desolate areas. My eyes played tricks on me. I imagined that the beams from those flashlights were landing lights from a UFO." She smiled and sipped the hot tea. Other guests were milling around the patio.

"I understand what you mean," Zach said. "I've thought about UFOs since I've been here. I talked to Matt. He's from Clovis. That's not far from Roswell, where that alien spaceship controversy happened in 1947. It made me curious, and I've been reading stories about the incident."

"You can't believe all that nonsense," Margo said.

"The truth? Out here in the desert, in all this blackness, I have to admit UFOs are a possibility."

Everyone had come back, and Matt and Janai were standing nearby. "Matt, don't tell me you believe in extraterrestrial life," Janai said.

"Why not? Look at those stars over our heads. Carl Sagan and Stephen Hawking knew a lot more about galaxies than I do, and they both were persuaded that extraterrestrial life was a possibility." He shrugged. "Me, I have no clue, so I can't rule it out."

Hope looked at Matt. How little she really knew this earthy cowboy who talked about extraterrestrial life and traveled with Walt Whitman.

308

"My mind operates on a practical plane," Margo said. "If you can't put it under a microscope or in a test tube, I'm a skeptic. I'll leave you good folks to debate the mysteries of the cosmos. I'm going to bed." She shoved her empty mug away from her and stood up.

"Thanks for your company this week, Zach. Mind you don't get abducted by aliens on our last night." Everyone laughed, and she waved good night.

Janai said she was going back to the room, and Matt walked off with her. Frank and Lydia followed. Tony went with Gloria. Others began saying good night. Hope looked around. She was alone. Her Guardian Angel was tapping her shoulder to get out of there.

The twinkling lights went out. She'd waited too long. She drew the gun out of her jacket pocket. She tried to ease out of the chair, but it was too close to the table. She crouched forward. She felt a sharp prick in her back. She turned. Margo's face was close to hers, a savage pit bull, eyes bulging. Margo slashed out with a knife, but Hope was spinning out of the chair. She pushed it back against Margo, hitting her hand. The knife clattered to the ground, but the contact jostled Hope's gun out of her hand. It skidded under the table.

Hope faced the woman. She was in the karate horse stance. Hope slipped off her jacket and flung it aside. The women circled around, executing blocks, punches, elbow strikes, and flying kicks.

Suddenly the outside lights came on, flooding the patio. Hope heard a noise, but she didn't look away from the eyes of the pit pull. Margo was punching at her furiously. The adrenalin rush had helped Hope to fend off her opponent, but her body was tiring. She wouldn't last much longer. She took a deep breath, steadied her feet. Her arm and fist flew out in a fluid motion and caught Margo under her chin. The woman collapsed. Hope hunched over, hands on her knees, pulling in breaths.

Margo was quiet on the ground. Hope glanced around. Matt, gun in hand, jumped over the chair. He bent down and checked Margo's pulse. "She's breathing," he said and put his gun in the holster. He stood up and tapped his cell phone. In seconds, three men and a woman rushed onto the patio and took charge of Margo.

"Evidence bag, Carl," Matt said, pointing to the knife on the ground. "I'll be with you shortly."

Matt turned to Hope. "Are you all right?" She nodded. He picked up her jacket and wrapped it around her. "I turned on the lights, but I couldn't get a clear shot. There was no way to get in between the two of you, and I didn't want to distract you."

She nestled against him, and he held her tight.

"I have to tend to this business. I'm sorry." She gripped his arm. "Here's Frank."

Frank walked over to Hope, and Matt loosened his hold. "Take care of her, Frank. I have to see to Margo."

At the table, Frank shouted for George. "Hot tea, strong, and plenty of sugar!"

Suddenly, the patio was filled with people, all asking questions. Trucks smashed together inside Hope's head, and the bright lights blinded her eyes. She put her face against Frank's chest.

His voice was unsteady when he spoke to the crowd. "Margo attacked Hope, and officers have taken charge of her. We'll give you details tomorrow. Please, go back to bed."

The muttering continued, and Lydia raised her foghorn. "You heard Frank. Hope is in shock and needs all of us to go back to our rooms. Margo came with me. If I must wait until tomorrow to learn what happened, so do the rest of you. Now go!"

"Thank you, Lydia," Frank said. "If I knew anything, I'd tell you, but I don't."

"I know. Take care of Hope. Good night."

"My gun," Hope whispered to Frank, pointing under the table.

He picked up the gun and slipped it into his pocket. He checked her back and said she must have been moving as the knife struck. Her jacket was ripped, but he didn't see a wound.

George brought the tea, and Frank asked him to turn down the lights. He stirred several cubes of sugar into the cup and held it to Hope's lips. "This is a habit we have to break."

After drinking the tea, Hope brought her emotions under control. "I'm feeling better."

Frank beckoned to Zach, Lucy, and Tony, who were standing by the patio door. They gave Hope a hug and left. Frank pushed his chair closer to Hope and held her hand, but neither spoke.

Matt stepped out from the patio. "Here you are. I thought you'd be back in your room."

"Just waiting for you," Frank said.

Hope turned to Frank. "You're the best. You can go to bed. The threat has left the building."

Frank laughed and whispered to Matt, "Take her jacket into evidence. The knife rip's in the back."

Matt's eyes widened, and he nodded.

"Diamond, you were ace high with that *krav maga*," Matt said, sitting beside her.

She touched her head. "I never felt this bump the whole time. I feel it now."

"That's because your brain was busy with your survival. Let's get you inside."

An officer carrying a knapsack met them in the hallway and followed them into Hope's room. Matt helped her out of her jacket. "Evidence bag, Carl," he said. The officer took the jacket and stood by the window. Hope sat in the recliner, and Matt gathered up a comforter and tucked it around her. He sat close by and nodded to the officer. The man set a tape recorder on the table, turned it on and went back to the window.

"Miss Diamond, please tell me what led to the attack on you tonight."

"Good grief! I almost forgot. I know how Meghan was killed."

Matt's mouth dropped open. "You know what!" Hope tensed, but he said softly, "Tell me."

"First, let me ask you something. Did you bag the cigarette butts in the ashtray on the table where Meghan died?"

"That would be routine for the crime scene crew."

"Whew," Hope blew out a breath. "The lab should analyze them for enzymes that affect the heart. They may not have found anything if they weren't specifically looking for enzymes."

"Tell me more."

"Here's what I think happened." Wacky though the words sounded, she was convinced she was right. "Before leaving Chicago, Margo had doctored a cigarette with an enzyme that, when combined with nicotine, could cause a heart attack. When Lydia asked Margo to fetch her cigarettes at the reception the first night, Margo must have inserted the doctored cigarette into the open pack. It was apparently intended for Lydia, but Meghan smoked it by mistake. You remember, Lydia said Meghan had borrowed cigarettes from her."

"I remember, but why do you think the murder hangs on enzymes and nicotine? Enzymes aren't poisonous."

"Margo mentioned her work with enzymes and the diseases they might help. Heart disease was one. That was one of the clues I couldn't snag. She must have concocted a way of synthesizing the enzyme with nicotine, which has poisonous properties, to trigger a heart attack."

"That's an interesting theory, almost like science fiction."

"Science fiction! Are you kidding? It's a logical theory, based on empirical evidence."

He laughed. "How did Margo know you figured out what happened?"

"Just what you warned me about. When I saw the glow from the cigarettes up the hill, I remembered that same glow when Lydia and Meghan were up there smoking. That was the crucial clue I totally missed. Everything clicked into place, and my eyes popped open like a cartoon character's. I thought I'd fooled her with that talk about UFOs when Zach and you jumped in with comments, but Margo was too sharp."

Hope turned, and the pain in her head hit. "Ow!"

"That's enough for tonight." Matt nodded to the officer. The man walked over and collected the tape recorder. He gave Hope a thumbs-up sign. She smiled, and Matt shook his head. "Get out of here, Carl!" The man was chuckling as he carried his gear out the door.

"Carl will kid me about this interview forever. I'm not usually baffled by a witness."

She grinned.

"Diamond, as I've said before, you're the goods. I'd like to stay and make sure you're all right, but I can't violate a person's rights because I'd much rather be doing something else."

"I'm fine. Go take care of Margo."

"Stand up. I want to make sure you're not dizzy." Hope pushed the comforter aside. Her head was rocketing, but she stood up. "Can I get you any pills?" Matt asked.

"I can take care of myself, thank you."

Her smile was warm, and he put his arms around her. "I'm sorry for what happened to you. When Margo said she was going to bed, I thought it was okay to leave you and escort Janai to her room. Of course, that attack makes Margo liable for attempted murder. From that standpoint, it was a good thing. Not good for you, and I'm sorry."

"I know. We can talk tomorrow. I need to go to bed."

He kissed her gently. "Let me call Lucy to help, just so I know you're safe in bed."

"Dennison, I'm not too tired to execute another *krav maga*. Go!"

CHAPTER 32

"Sorry I'm late." Hope rubbed her eyes coming into the conference room at ten minutes after nine.

"How are you feeling?" Frank asked.

"Groggy."

"Is the FBI coming?" Tony asked.

The door opened. Matt entered and looked toward the refreshment counter. He stopped. "No coffee?"

"Oh, no! I didn't order any because we were leaving today." The team moaned. The door opened again, and in came Cecelia with the coffee cart.

"Cecelia, you're the best!" Hope said, and everyone clapped. The woman smiled and set out the coffee and rolls.

"Sit still, Hope. I'll bring yours," Frank said. Everyone else headed to the refreshment station.

Hope drank coffee and ate the roll. The fog in her mind lifted, and she said, "I want to thank you all for your vigilance in keeping the women safe. Lydia was in great danger, and thanks to all of you, especially Frank, Lydia is safe and will go home today."

She asked Matt to fill the team in on the search warrants executed by the FBI. When he didn't answer, Tony nudged him with his elbow.

Matt jerked. "What?"

"We'd like to hear about the searches."

"The searches, right." Matt took a drink from his coffee mug and sat up straight. "At five-thirty this morning, we secured a document from Margo Knight's safe believed to represent the motive for premeditated murder."

Hope's eyes opened wide, and she looked at Frank. He nodded.

"We also found a pair of shoes we believe match tracks made around the horses. At six a.m. Chicago time, agents searched her apartment and found a vial containing an unknown substance. It has been sent to the laboratory." He looked around the table. "Any questions?"

In the silence, Hope asked, "You found the motive?"

"We found an offer for employment that would put Margo in charge of a competitor's research labs around the world. Frank says it's a much more prestigious position than her current job."

"What does that have to do with the motive?" Lucy asked. "Couldn't she take the job if she wanted it?"

"Margo was under contract to Grand Med for another two years," Frank said. "Lydia wouldn't release her because of the FDA trials. Margo was the lead contact. Obviously, Margo was more determined to take that job than Lydia ever imagined."

"Was that ever on our radar?" Tony asked.

"If you recall, I 'accidentally' found an envelope from a competitor in Margo's trashcan. It occurred to me it might have been an employment offer, but I didn't attach much importance to it at the time." Frank pointed his thumb at Matt, whose eyes had closed. "Matt never got to bed last night handling all things Margo. I ran into him coming out of her room. He had the offer and asked me some questions."

"Have you talked to Lydia?" Hope asked.

Frank nodded. "She was shocked. She felt terrible about Meghan."

Hope took a deep breath. "I want to apologize to all of you for not sharing the photographs I took—"

Frank put up a finger. "Matt admitted he threatened to arrest you if you told us about those footprints. 'Obstruction of justice,' he said."

"Please know that I'm sorry. I never meant to imply that I didn't trust you."

"I should have known better," Tony said. "I won't make that mistake ever again."

"How did you figure out Margo was behind everything?" Lucy asked, looking at Hope.

Hope put things that had happened during the week into perspective. After several seconds, she said, "Facts pointing to the killer had been free-floating in my mind, but I couldn't nail them down and arrange them to fit into a pattern. Cigarettes mainly. Cigarettes underpinned the whole case."

"How do you figure?" Frank asked.

317

Hope recapped what she had told Matt the night before. "At the reception, when Lydia asked Margo to fetch her cigarettes, she sidestepped into her own room, grabbed the poisoned cigarette, and added it to Lydia's open pack."

Frank's hand shook, and coffee spilled onto his jacket. "The idea of Lydia smoking that cigarette makes my blood run cold. Of course, I'm sorry about Meghan. Her death was a tragedy."

"How did Meghan end up with the lethal cigarette?" Zach asked.

"Meghan ran out of cigarettes at the campfire, and Lydia handed her the open pack that Margo had doctored, unwittingly setting her up as the victim."

"Sounds like the perfect crime, but the wrong person died," Tony said.

"That's exactly what happened," Hope said.

"Other hints scattered throughout the dossier should have made us suspicious of Margo," Hope said, "but they were conjectures, not facts."

"What hints?" Lucy asked.

"The first telling point was that what happened here took a mastermind," Hope said. "Matt described Sean as a mastermind, and we all knew Margo was smart."

"She was a very bright lady," Zach said with sadness in his voice. Lucy reached over and squeezed his hand. "It's hard to believe Margo was behind all the bad stuff that happened here. Sorry, Tony. I was totally off base." Tony pressed his shoulder.

Hope took a moment and then went on. "The second point is that the person had to be a risk-taker. Lydia told Frank that Margo didn't balk at putting the company's reputation at risk."

"I was on the risk-taker track myself," Tony said, "but I was worried about Sean."

"Sean was smart and a risk-taker. But his risk-taking was more physical. Football, horses, and bikes, whereas Margo's risk-taking related to business and drugs. To me, Ellen didn't fit that profile at all."

"I admit defeat on the McKennas." Matt tapped Tony's arm.

"What about Sean's poisoning? We need to clear up that matter for Ellen and Sean," Tony said.

Hope shook her head. "I think Margo got scared when Matt said he was investigating the case as a homicide, and she tried to divert suspicion. I believe Margo slipped into Ellen's room through the patio door and planted the poisoned candy. I have no way of proving it. I'm sorry."

"Why would Margo drug Paco and ride in the same wagon?" Lucy asked. "She could have been killed,"

"As I said, she's a risk-taker. I don't think it was a very big risk for her after seeing her flip kicks last night. She wore jeans to the cookout and sat at the end of the wagon, where she could vault out if the wagon overturned. She apparently didn't care how many people were killed or injured in that little caper."

A stunned silence followed her statement. Tony finally said, "I can't figure out how Margo managed the attack on you at the cookout."

Matt rubbed his eyes. "I have a theory. It's one of the things that pointed me to Margo." Hope frowned. He hadn't explained how he'd reached his conclusion about Margo.

"From Zach's time machine, I picked up the fact that Margo was walking back from the stables in a long skirt and carrying a large handbag at roughly the right time."

"She often wore that outfit," Lucy said. "I don't see anything suspicious."

"You mentioned she ran ten miles a day," Matt said, pointing at her. "That outfit was a perfect disguise for a runner. She could wear shorts underneath the skirt and carry her Nikes in the bag. All she had to do was pass the stables in the long skirt."

"Did you have any other reasons for suspecting Margo?" Hope asked, putting her head on her hand and smiling, the gesture he often used to elicit information.

"The McKennas were top on my list, but I didn't ignore the fact that Margo was the most experienced person here when it came to drugs, and we had three incidents involving drugs— Meghan's death, Sean's poisoning, and the horse doping."

Lucy turned to Hope. "Why did Margo attack you again?"

The attack flashed past her eyes like a film on TV. "Matt's warning that any one of us could give away secrets came back to haunt me. At the time, I resented his attitude. What did I call you, 'arrogant?'"

He spoke slowly, his eyes on hers. "I think you *may* have said that I was a 'conceited, arrogant, smug, pompous, pigheaded, two-bit jerk.'"

"Sounds about right," Tony murmured.

"I'm sorry, Matt. I admit it before the whole team. You were right. I was wrong."

"Well, you were right in more important ways," Matt said. "We wouldn't be charging Margo with murder if you hadn't come up with what I called your 'science-fiction theory.'"

"How can we prove that Margo poisoned Sean?" Tony insisted.

"We need the arsenic or the needle, and we need to connect it with Margo," Matt said. The room became still, no shuffling of paper or rattling of cups.

Lucy jumped up. "I know! I know where Margo hid that stuff! It's on the trail that Gloria and I hiked the morning after Sean's poisoning. We ran into Margo, and her pants were smeared with dirt. She said she'd stumbled because of a bunny. I think she knelt down to bury the evidence."

The room held its breath. Then Tony grabbed Lucy. "*Lucia, mia ragazza! Ottimo lavoro!*"

Matt laughed. "Honey, I think he's happy."

"Honey, lucky for you I'm in a good mood."

"Good job, Lucy," Hope said. The girl had a flair for surprising all of them with some important, unknown fact that connected everything together.

Hope turned to Matt. "What are you going to do?"

"Take Lucy and Tony and go find that stash."

CHAPTER 33

Guests were coming into Blue Sky to hear why a sweet, little lady went off her rocker and tried to kill them. Tony had dug up the arsenic kit, and Matt turned it over to his team. He had a lot of paperwork ahead of him, but he was resting his head against the sofa, his eyes closed. He breathed in perfume and smiled. Hope said, "Matt, the meeting is about to start."

He squeezed his eyes. "Can you and Frank handle it? I'd like to get some shut-eye."

"Matt!"

He opened his eyes and smiled. "Diamond, you are one pretty woman. Remind me to play that song for you." He scooted forward on the couch and pulled on his hat.

"I'd love to hear you play," she said, pushing him back on the sofa. "Stay here. Frank and I will do the talking. It'll be quick. We're not giving out any details that could compromise the case." She smiled, and he felt as happy as a kid slapping at soap bubbles. His cell phone rang. It was Jake Sanders bursting the bubbles.

"Great job, Matt. Everyone was on edge thinking one of the ladies was either a killer or about to become the next victim. A job in foreign counterespionage has your name on it. When can you be in D.C.?"

"Can I let you know? I have to tie up loose ends," Matt mumbled.

"Okay," Jake said, but his tone made it clear it wasn't okay. Jake probably had a good idea what he meant by loose ends. "Don't wait too long. You know how the wind shifts in Washington."

"I do indeed." Matt hung up and looked across at Hope. His heart speeded up. He was staggered by his feelings. He wanted her to be a permanent part of his life. If that could happen, he'd ask for an assignment in L.A., where they handled counterterrorism.

Hope was wrapping up her remarks, saying that thanks to Agent Dennison, the FBI would be bringing charges against Margo for the murder of Meghan Connors.

When she finished, Janai trouped over to Matt. He stood up and accepted her congratulations as graciously as if he were speaking to the President. Who knew, Janai might be his boss one day.

"Matt, why don't you come out and give the FBI a hand in Los Angeles?" she asked.

"I've been offered a job in Washington."

"That could be fun, too. If you do decide to come west, my door is always open."

He smiled, and she held out her hand. He lifted it to his lips. "Go get 'em," Madam President."

Matt sat down, and his eyes followed Hope. She was smart, beautiful, sophisticated, but it was the fire she lit in his soul that made him want to marry her.

Suddenly, a wrecking ball exploded in his head. Why would this amazing woman want to marry a down-home cowboy like him? He played out scenarios in his mind where she laughed at the thought of marrying him. The pain was so intense that he clutched at his chest. He needed sleep. As soon as he was on his feet, he'd let Jake know he'd be heading back to Washington.

Hope gathered the four women together. "I want to tell you how sorry I am about the tragic events that took place here."

"You risked your life for us, and we are deeply grateful," Janai said and embraced her.

Then she held her arms out to the other women. "Your confidence in me has affirmed my decision to seek office in this country that we all hold dear."

The women clapped and began moving away. They would be leaving Secret Sands shortly. Janai had arranged with Dan Nakai to visit some tribal leaders, so her plane would arrive in the evening.

"I'm sorry about Margo, Lydia," Hope said, reaching out to the woman.

Lydia nodded. "I talked to Mark, and we agreed to stop squabbling and act like responsible partners in the business."

"I'm glad to hear that you and Mark are setting aside your differences," Frank said, stepping over to them. He took Lydia's hands, and she pulled him close. Hope had come to appreciate

Lydia over the week and would miss her. Frank would miss her more.

Gloria, in a lime traveling suit, shook hands with Hope and hugged Lucy. "We're going to move forward with our bid," she said. "Why fight now? We may not win the contract, but we'll get our feet wet for next time." She laughed her bubbly laugh.

"Come to Greece, Miss Diamond," Dimitri said. "I teach you *sirtaki*." Hope smiled, and he kissed her on both cheeks. Gloria's plane had arrived, and they hurried out to the van.

"*Mamma mia!*" Tony came over with a wide smile. "Ellen told me the real reason she brought Meghan out here. Ellen is pregnant! She wanted to throw that fact in the girl's face, but she couldn't do it. Ellen's expecting twin girls, and she and Sean asked me to be the Godfather of Antoinette!"

"That is great news, Tony!" Hope said, hugging him.

"I need to call Maria. Fingers crossed she answers." He laughed and pulled out his phone.

Sean walked over, his head down. "I'm sorry about Meghan," he said. "I'll feel the guilt for the rest of my life."

Hope put her fingers on her forehead and felt the truth of what she was about to say. "You don't know it, Sean, but you saved my life." She told him about hearing an engine at the time of the attack at the cookout site. "I think Margo left without making sure I was dead because she was afraid of being seen."

Sean's eyes lit up, and it was a moment before he spoke. "Thank you for telling me. That makes me feel better." He spread out his hands. "I've never spent time in the desert like I did here. It takes hold of you and makes you think about life in ways you never did before. It's made me realize how much I love my wife—

and my son. Now I learn I'm going to have two sweet baby girls to love. Thank you for uncovering the truth. Ellen and I will be forever grateful." Sean kissed her cheek. He walked back to his wife and wrapped his arms around her.

Hope understood Sean's feelings. One week in the desert had changed her thinking profoundly. She had come to value the traditions and beliefs of a culture very different from her own and to value and respect a man she didn't really know but who had taken hold of her heart.

# #

At six o'clock, Hope slipped into her one-shoulder black jumpsuit and spritzed on Icelandic Wind perfume. Without warning, she felt lightheaded and sat down on the recliner. Matt had avoided her after the talk. It could mean he was going back to Washington. She was determined not to put herself in another long-distance relationship.

She looked at the painting. The image that shot back from the horseman in the tan hat and blue shirt was Matt winking at her. She couldn't leave with feelings between them hanging in the air.

Hope knocked softly on Matt's door in case he was asleep. The door opened. He was wearing a white shirt with his gun in a shoulder holster. He was leaving without saying good-bye. She lowered her eyes like a schoolgirl sent to the principal's office and mumbled, "I came to hear you play that song."

He clenched his jaw. "Come in and sit down," he said in his icy FBI voice. She sat on the edge of the couch, folding and unfolding her hands. He walked over to the bed where the guitar case stood open. He turned his back to her, his shoulders stiff. She put her hands on the edge of the sofa and started to push herself up. She would leave without embarrassing either one of them further.

He turned around and grinned. "You really are something special in that outfit, lady." She smiled and sank back against the sofa.

Matt slipped off the shoulder holster and brought the guitar over to a chair in front of the couch. Roy Orbison wrote this song for you, pretty woman," he said, clicking his thumb and forefinger at her and laughing, a sound she was growing to love. He started strumming and singing "Pretty Woman" in his rich baritone.

He finished the song, but she turned away from the feelings in his eyes. When she looked back, he started picking and singing a ballad that, he told her, only Kris Kristofferson could have written, "Loving Her Was Easier (Than Anything I'll Ever Do Again)."

When the song ended, tears streamed down her face. Matt set down the guitar and walked across the room. He drew open the drapes and stood facing the desert. The lowering sun created an apricot glow across the sky that slid into the room.

Hope sat silent, searching her soul. She looked over at Matt, and the thought of losing him brought a deep stab of pain, and she winced. She walked over to the window and stood beside him. She liked the feeling of being close. He opened his arms, and her heart leapt at the smile in his eyes. His embrace, his cheek touching hers were electrifying. His kiss, passionate and tender, set her heart on fire.

"What are we going to do about this?" he asked.

"Are you going back to Washington?"

He pushed back and looked into her eyes. "What are you going to do about Jake Sanders?"

The answer came easily. "Whatever you'd like me to do."

"In that case, I'm going to request a transfer to the City of the Angels."

The End

Karen's "Old School" Fudge

Ingredients

- 2 cups sugar
- 1/8 tsp. salt
- 2 heaping tbs. cocoa
- 5 oz. can evaporated milk (in a pinch, ¾ cup regular milk)
- 2 tbs. butter (or peanut butter)
- 1 tsp. vanilla (or other flavoring, like almond or rum)
- 1 cup broken walnuts (optional)

Method

- Mix together sugar, salt, and cocoa. Stir in milk and cook at medium heat just until the ingredients warm up.
- Lower the heat. Fudge will bubble up the sides of pan.
- Stir occasionally, scraping the bottom to prevent burning. Fudge will boil down and become glossy.
- Fudge is ready when it reaches soft-ball stage (about 10 minutes). Use candy thermometer or test by dropping a little fudge into very cold water. Roll with fingers into soft ball.
- Remove from stove. Add butter and vanilla. Beat fudge until it thickens.
- Add walnuts and pour into a buttered pan. 9"x9" is a good size, but you can use different sizes and shapes.
- Cool on a wire rack. Store in a covered container.

Tip: Buy decorative tins, butter them, pour in fudge, and give as gifts.

Made in the USA
Las Vegas, NV
11 November 2021

LEGION

— *of* —

PNEUMAS

Book one The Condemned

LILY JOHNSON

CIRCLE OF SERPENTS

CONTENTS

A note from the Author

I want to thank my sisters Andolin, Callia, and Elena who in our early years played the games with me that helped inspire me to write these novels. I want to thank my friend and cover artist Don Delahunt who was the first to finish reading this book, and helped me through all the steps of publishing it. Without him I wouldn't have this cover that has helped me move forward to self-publish. I want to thank my English teacher Dawn Anthony, for helping me become a better writer and tutoring me all those years. I also want to thank my family and all those who supported me, with this journey. I couldn't have done it without you guys.

I also want to send thanks to the editors and to all the people at Book Baby, especially Mike Taylor. Not only did my editors do an amazing job, but they helped me become a better writer, making me able to write more smoothly, with fewer mistakes. Telling me where I could do better, and where my work was best. They have also helped me publish this book, and helped me through all the steps of getting there.

And I want to thank my brother Cody, who wasn't always happy to hear about my book all the time. But no matter what, he has been there for me, encouraging me, and giving me the best piece of advice that anyone could, that I take to heart every day. "You can do anything you want if you put your mind to it, and to always improve on yourself and everything you do."

Moving forward and continuing no matter how hard things get is what made it possible for me to make this book. And again, thanks to all who has helped me with the making of this novel.

INTRODUCTION

I am the cold breeze that passes through. I am the feeling that someone is there, but you are all alone. The fact is, you are never alone, for I am always there. I wait until we can be reunited through death. Death takes time; I have been waiting 18 years, but still you live.

Time is running out, and the world is becoming more dangerous for you. I cannot help you until you die because they will not allow it. They don't know us, and they are making a mistake, but there is nothing I can do about it.

The world has always been torn between good and evil, heaven and hell, life and death. We are the ones to find a balance through it all, in a dark, unforgiving world.

London, you know nothing of the perils around you. You cannot find your place until you find yourself. You believe that you are a mortal man, living a luxurious life, when really your life hasn't even begun.

I will continue to wait and learn. I will be ready when the time comes for us to be joined as one. I am not your enemy, London, but will you understand that? You have lived your life believing that I am of myth and that I was created by Satan. You yourself must find the answer to what I am. Am I your spirit, or am I your demon?

CHAPTER 1

Marriage

I take a deep breath as I look into the mirror. I smile, thinking I look good dressed in a fine suit. I have been nervous about this day for a while. I will be no longer a single man, but married to a beautiful woman. I do not know her as well as I would like; it is an arranged marriage although I have always been attracted to her. When we were young, we would meet in secret. She was the first girl that I kissed.

Time has passed since I last saw her. I will get the time to know her again after we are married. It helps me to know she is excited about our wedding; I am but I am also nervous about the whole thing. Sometimes, I wonder what I am even doing.

"I am so proud of you, London. This is a big day for you and the whole family," my uncle says, standing behind me at the mirror.

I know he means my family marrying into the royal line. I turn around to my uncle with a smile, "It is my honor to make this family proud."

"You are marrying a very beautiful bride. Be a good man to her now," he tells me.

"I swear my life on it," I tell him as I put my jacket on. "Is grandfather here yet?" I ask, looking in the mirror again.

"No, he is not here yet, but don't worry, he will be. You just worry about getting married; I will take care of everything else." I turn around to face my uncle, and he starts to fix my jacket collar.

"You never seem to get this right, London," he says as he fixes it.

"Well, I can't be perfect at everything," I reply with a devious smile.

My uncle shakes his head. "You are right. No one is perfect. Now get out there and greet your guests. There are a lot of people here for your wedding."

I swallow hard hearing that piece of news. I have been expecting it, but I am far from ready. I had no part in the wedding plans, so I have no idea how big it is actually going to be. All I know is we are getting married in the chapel of our kingdom's capital, Galencia. It is the largest and most spectacular castle where we live in the Sonara Plains. I would have liked to have had the wedding in my grandfather's castle, where I grew up, but it wasn't my choice to make. The king has chosen me to marry his daughter and wants us wed under his roof.

I walk out of the room with my uncle beside me. A few steps down the hall, I part ways with my uncle and go to check on my mother in her room.

There has always been a dark history between my mother and the family. I feel that in a way, they have disowned her. They are never friendly to her and have always treated her as if she isn't worthy. Yet in all these years, I have never found out why they are so cruel to her.

My mother doesn't have any friends, unless you count the housemaid who has worked here since before, I was born. She is the only other person my mother is close to besides me and my great-grandmother Anna. I still don't think the maid knows much more than I do about my family's secrets. My mother does not talk much, and I am one of the only people she will talk to. My mother has always been unhappy. It's as if she is missing something and waits for its return. I want to help my mother, but she won't tell me the reason for her longing, and I don't know if she ever well.

I never knew my father. People have told me stories about how he was a war hero. They said he died in battle before I was born, but I don't know how much truth is in that story. My mother has never talked about my father. I want to hear the story from her own lips, and because I haven't, I question it. I don't know what she is hiding, why I am not told who my father is. It is just another lie and mystery of the family that I am not allowed to know. I am determined to find out someday, even if I have to dig deep into my family's past.

I knock on the door to my mother's room, and I hear her voice from inside reply, "Come in."

I walk into the room. My mother smiles when she sees me, and we embrace.

We let go, and my mother holds me at arm's length, eyeing me up and down.

"You are too good for her, London," she says flatly, with no tone to her voice.

I look at her with a small frown. She lets me go and walks over to a small table with a teapot. I know my mom isn't happy with this wedding, but she won't just say it. I wish she would, but I already know why she doesn't like it, or at least I believe I know why. I could never tell anyone, but I am far from ready for marriage myself. Who likes the idea of marrying a woman you only knew a little in the past? As hard as it may be, though, I am confident that I can make things work. Sometimes, you just have to take one for the team.

My mother fills two cups with tea and asks me without looking, "Do you want one?"

"All right," I reply.

She walks over and hands me a cup, then sits down at the table. I sit down in a chair facing her. I watch my mother as she sips on her tea.

Many people have said my mother is one of the fairest women in all the land. Many men tried to win her hand before she settled with my father. She has long, black hair, which is usually braided. Her dark brown eyes miss nothing. When I was younger, there was nothing I could get away with. She always seemed to know when I was lying. People say I have my mother's eyes, I have no idea what I inherited from my father. No one ever mentions me looking anything like my father. Makes me wonder if anyone here even really knew him.

I take a deep breath, knowing one of the hardest things in the world is getting answers from my mother. She is a woman who says what she thinks is needed and nothing else. Even though she is my mother, I have always seen her as a mysterious woman. She is nothing like the rest of the family, except my great-grandmother, Anna. I would believe my mother isn't even related to them, but there is no mistaking that they share the same blood.

I was told my great-grandmother Anna practices magic, magic that she also taught my mother. My family looks down on my mother for it. My mother doesn't use magic often, but I just know she is powerful with it. It is kind of like a feeling I get around here. There aren't a lot of magic people around here, but one time someone else came to our castle who was, and I felt the same thing. For whatever reason I seem to sense those who are. Maybe everyone can, I don't know, for I never mention it to anyone. For whatever reason I feel it better not to.

My mother is a tall proud woman, who most people, upon first meeting her, respect. She has long black hair that comes down to her lower back. She has hazel eyes, that are captivating and a depth of mystery in them, that's beyond comprehension. Despite her serious appearance, she has a charming humorous side to her. When I was little, she was my best friend, I have never felt alone or unloved when she was around.

"What is wrong, Mother? I can see in your eyes you are not happy," I said, looking at her. I cannot drink much of my tea because I am nervous about the wedding. I am often the center of attention, but I don't like it. I don't like people thinking so much of me. It becomes stressful if I can't live up to their standards. I would rather not have that weight on my shoulders all of the time.

"I just wonder—is that really what you want, London? Or is it what your grandfather wants?" She says after a few minutes of silence.

I take my time to reply. She does have a point: my grandfather was the one who arranged this match with the royal family. My grandfather has always been my father figure. My mother and grandfather dislike each other, and they have different ideas about what I should do with my life.

I look back at my mom. I know that, to her, my silence only proves my uncertainty.

"I like Sara . . . she is a good woman," I finally reply.

"She is for show, nothing else," she tells me.

My frown deepens and I answer quickly in defense, "You don't know that."

"London, don't tell me otherwise. She has her looks, and that is all she's got. And I hope that is not the reason you are going through with this because I know I raised you better than that."

I immediately feel guilty. If I am not marrying Sara just for her looks, why else *am* I marrying her? I don't know her that well. I know it is not for her personality. I am not the kind of man to marry for show. No, I am not doing this for my grandfather. I am doing what I think would be best for my family.

I tell her truthfully, "I am going through with it because I am trying to become the man my family wishes of me."

My mother grabs my hand and looks deep into my eyes. "No, London, you can't care about what they want of you. You need to follow your own heart— what does it tell you?"

I grip her hand but look away. "I don't know."

My mother grabs both of my hands and continues, "Well, no matter what happens, I know you will. Just promise me something, London."

"What would that be?"

"Promise me that you will always be in charge of your own destiny. Don't ever let anyone else control you, or tell you what to do because that is no way to live." My mother said this holding my hands tight, our eyes locked.

I see the pain in her eyes. I feel she has never followed her own destiny. I know what she needs to hear.

"I promise to be the master of my own destiny."

She smiles, and I can tell how much those few words mean to her.

———•———

I stand up, feeling uncomfortable in the crowd. There are more people here than I have ever seen. I know a few of them. Among the throng are lords from neighboring towns, blacksmiths, traders, servants, knights, farmers—it seems the whole kingdom has been invited.

The main hall is decorated in white and red, the traditional colors of Sonara weddings. White symbolizes innocence, youth and passion. Red represents love and, in our customs, a long-lasting relationship. The bright red roses at the center of each table are a special variety with blooms as big as a human head, found only in the Sonara plains. They grow wildly here, and are known as the wedding rose; you will see them at every Sonara wedding.

The guests are all dressed in their finest clothes. It looks as though the ladies are trying to out-dress each other, each in her finest dress, lots of jewelry and an abundance of bright colors. The men dress in their finest suits as well, some in black, others in blue, tan and teal green. The warriors wear light armor, polished until it seems to reflect all the light in the room. The king's daughters, dressed beautifully, stand out among even the finest dressed ladies in the room. The king has six daughters and two sons. I will be marrying his youngest daughter, who is 18 like me. Her sisters all married much younger, roughly at the age of 16, but the king didn't seem to know what he wanted for his youngest. At one time, Sara was to be married to a duke from a neighboring country, but that plan fell through. My family has loyally served the royal family for years, and we have gained a noble rank. My grandfather, Richard, is the lord of a large piece of land, a site of his own castle and city. It is named Harvester's Field, for it has some of the richest farmlands on the continent. It is rich with volcanic soil. The king respects and admires my grandfather and has decided that this union is what my family deserves. I know my grandfather is very proud of this turn of events. When I glance in his direction, I can see him beaming with pride. As he moves, he receives respectful greetings and radiates goodwill in return.

Many people greet me as well as I stand and wait for the ceremony to begin. I smile and shake everyone's hands, thanking them, and make small talk. I hardly know these people. There are too many names to remember, and too many people in general.

My best man and childhood friend, John, walks up beside me. He seems to share my feelings about all these people.

John is 18 like me as well, and we always considered ourselves twins from different mothers because we are born on the same day. John comes from a well-off family, and his father is captain of the guards, serving under my grandfather in our hometown. John is planning on following in his father's footsteps as well, and becoming a soldier.

"Hanging in there, London?" he whispers to me.

"What do you think?" I reply through gritted teeth, smiling and shaking someone else's hand.

"It looks like you are surviving; that is what matters, right?"

"Barely."

"Well, think of it this way, the wedding will be over soon, then you won't have to worry about it anymore."

"Either way, I think this is going to be a long night."

"With someone like her, you hope, right?" he said, elbowing me.

I smile, shaking my head, and murmur, "We all have families here, John, it's probably best we don't talk like that."

He laughs, "Well, don't tell me you weren't thinking about it. I am going to go get something to drink. You have fun greeting people." He pats my back and starts to walk away, but before he gets far, I call, "Could you bring me a drink as well?"

He smiles and asks, "The hard stuff?"

"I need something."

"Just don't get drunk. You can't be stumbling when the king is giving his daughter to you."

"That would be a nightmare!" I agree, thinking about it.

Finally, the crowd quietens. We take our places, and the wedding begins.

I stand with Sara, holding her hand. I am nervous as hell. I feel hot, and the room is packed with people. My heart is pounding; I can hear it in my ears. Sara gives me a sweet smile and holds my hand a little tighter. I smile at her and hold her hand a bit tighter in reply.

She truly is beautiful. She has long, wavy brown hair. She has a few freckles on her face, perfect skin, nice lips, and a hell of a body. I love her smile, voice and laugh. She is what any man would want. She is a very polite woman and was taught proper etiquette. Some men say she knows her place, although, oddly, that worries me. I want a woman with a fire to her; I hope Sara has that. I don't want her to serve me, or only be the woman who raises my children. I want a relationship in which we truly connect on a personal level. I hope I can get that with Sara, but that is something only time can tell.

We say our vows, then we kiss. The crowd cheers wildly. When I pull away from her, her smile is bright. I smile in return. We face the crowd and walk down the steps hand in hand. People congratulate us, and the feast begins. Every delicacy you can think of is served. The finest meats, salads, breads, soups, vegetables and desserts, prepared by some of the best chefs in the whole country.

The king's family and mine sit at a special table. Sara and I sit in the middle, putting us again in the spotlight. The king and queen sit at the head of the table. Sara's brothers and sisters sit with their spouses. I sit next to Sara, with my grandparents and great-grandparents, my mother, and my uncle and his family. Other people eat at their own tables, or dance to fine music.

I talk with my tablemates and try to eat as much as I can. I can't eat as much as I would like, though; there is too much going on around me. Sara gives me cute smiles whenever she can. It will be nice when I can spend some one-on-

one time with her. I haven't been able to say much to her, with everyone trying to talk to us.

The king rises from his seat, and everyone goes silent. "I am overjoyed to see my youngest daughter married to such a fine young man. He is well known throughout my kingdom as one of the best sword fighters and archers. Above all, his family has been loyal and trustworthy to the kingdom and the throne for many years. I am honored that this bond will continue for many years to come."

People cheer with the king's speech. Then, as the crowd falls silent again, he continues, "However, London, before you can spend time with your bride, there is a duty the kingdom wishes you to perform."

I am caught by surprise, Not expecting any special requests. "And what will you have me do, my majesty?" I reply with pride.

"There has been a beast terrorizing the land. I want you to go with a group of knights and take out this beast. Return with its head, and you prove your strength as a warrior." The king says this, looking me dead in the eyes. He is expecting a reaction from me.

All eyes seem to be on me. In the silence, I look at my grandfather, his expression still proud. This is what he has always wanted of me. I know this beast is a big issue, or the king would not bring it to my attention. I am not afraid of any beast, and it cannot hold me back from what I must do.

This isn't a strange thing for the king to ask. Often when two are going to wed, it is common for the man to go on a hunt to kill some sort of beast. It proves strength and courage. Usually this is done before the wedding, but not always.

I look at the king and reply, "And it shall be done!"

Everyone cheers at my answer and raises their glasses. The king bellows, "To the young new couple, London and Sara!"

"To London and Sara!" the crowd shouts, and they all drink to us.

CHAPTER 2

Decisions

spirit

"Should we wait to go to London? Or go to him before death does?" Amias the sorcerer asks.

All of them sit at a table discussing what they should do about London. London must die, but he must be able to come back. They are already taking a risk, letting him go as far as he has.

"If London must die, it is not like we haven't been waiting for that," The Hunter replies. He is one I trust, probably because the rest *don't* trust him.

"If we step foot there, they will know about us. We might risk losing him by being there, and we risk being detected by our enemies. But if we are not there, I think the risk of his death is that much greater," Breccan interjects.

Breccan is known as a hero throughout many lands, from his fighting and his bravery in battle. He is a simple man, a true warrior, and a strong ally.

"Maybe we should see what his pneuma thinks of all this," Amias said, from under his hood.

The other people at the table look at him and consider what he says. Finally, the elf sergeant Livefen replies, "He would probably know more than the rest of us. And he wouldn't risk losing him forever."

I dislike the elf, and if I could, I would let him know. I make it clear to Amias how I feel about him, but he never passes the message.

Amias is a special mage, one who can talk to spirits before anyone else can. His eyes are different colors. It is rare, this trait; they say one eye has normal vision, while the other sees what the normal eye cannot. I don't know if that is true, but he can talk to me, so that is all that matters.

Amias looks at me and asks, "What do you think?"

I don't reply right away. I never give easy answers. Once I am finally with London, I am going to treat these people far from nicely. The only reason I am here is that I have nowhere better to be. I do plan to meet with London after this, his mission, I believe, could become fatal.

"I think it is best to be ready, but give him space. If you believe that London is to help you, you must believe he can take care of himself, or what would be the point of trying to help him?" I say to Amias alone.

Amias seems to agree with me; turning to the rest, he tells them my thoughts on the matter.

"I think it is too big of a risk. Someone should be nearby, ready if the worst is to happen," Livefen says.

Sometimes, I wonder why they ask for my opinion. They seem to do what they think is best, regardless of what I say.

"I will watch him," the Hunter says. He never seems to be afraid to do what he must; he too is tired of being here.

"No! If you do, then they will certainly find London. You are in their sights enough," Livefen said, dismissing the idea.

"I am not afraid; they are going to find out sooner or later. I think it is a risk we must take. I would rather they find out sooner than lose London altogether."

"He does make a good point," Breccan puts in, in his deep neutral tone of voice. Breccan, despite the fighter he is, is not a debater or arguer. He always offers suggestions, but never final decisions, or raises his temper when an idea he doesn't agree with is laid out.

"Someone should go, but I don't think it should be him," Livefen argues.

People continue to argue, and it becomes tiresome to me. How do they ever expect to get anything done, if all they do is argue?

Finally, they decide that The Hunter will go make sure that London stays safe. It took long enough.

I leave after hearing this. I go through the window and let the wind bring me somewhere new. I travel back to where London is. He leaves today. I don't know how he will fare, but I have a feeling this trip could change his life forever.

CHAPTER 3

A Fatal Ending

London

I ride out with other young men close to my age, who are here only to make a name for themselves. My grandfather rides ahead of the group with experienced fighters and monster hunters. I am known to be one of the best when it comes to fighting, but I do lack the experience that some of these other men have.

I am a little nervous. I know that this monster has been causing a number of problems. I recognize some of the guys here as the king's best fighters. I wouldn't be so nervous if I had some idea of what I am up against. The people who have been reporting it have different ways of describing it. We are assuming there is more than one beast terrorizing the land.

I ride near John most of the time. He is here as well, trying to make a name for himself like some of the others. I am already known in the kingdom, more so after marrying the king's daughter, so that is not why I am here. I am here because it is my duty and because the king requests it.

We travel through a land of grassy plains as far as the eye can see. Trees are sparse in this area. We ride up and down hills, careful with the horses over the rocks. The soil is hard and rocky, making it hard for the farmers to grow crops here. Some places in the Sonara Plains have very few rocks and are some of the best farming lands in the world. The Sonara Plains supply food to more places than any other country in the continent of Warlean.

Other than grassy hills and rocks, the landscape is featureless. We are heading southwest, toward a range of great mountains that reach high into the clouds. The mountains are bare. One of the mountain peaks is an old volcano, but I have never seen it myself. In many places, you can find volcanic rocks. I will travel and see faraway lands someday, but for now, I will only be able to hear about these places.

As we travel, we come across a few houses usually well-spaced between each other, spread across the land, all being ranchers and herders in these parts, since the land is good for nothing else. The houses are made from stone, since we are abundant in that resource here and the roofs of the houses are made of thatch.

We have been on the hunt for a week now. We have seen some of what the beast has been doing. We have talked to the people who live here, to find out more about this monster. People seem to be scared to death of this thing. Many have told us entire herds of sheep were found dead, often bleeding from the mouth or the eyes but with no other sign of physical injury. An alchemist has looked over the sheep and has seen no signs of disease. They were as healthy as could be, before they were found dead.

I can see that many of the younger guys are unnerved by this sight. I am as well, not just by the dead livestock but by the realization that the older monster hunters who have been doing this for years are as uncomfortable as I am.

We travel through the grassland, finding more people reporting dead livestock. Dead animals are stacked in piles for the farmers to use what they can from them.

Looking at all of the dead sheep, a cold feeling comes over me. I look at one dead on the ground. Its eyes are open wide and are completely black. It looks like its soul was torn from its body, and that is how death came to it. Flies swarm around the carcass. There are no wounds on the animals that we can see, and not all of the sheep have bled from the mouth and eyes.

I get down near the animal and try to inspect it a little more closely. I wrack my brain, trying to think of any creature that can do this to its prey. What beast would waste so much meat? I don't like this, and I know I am not the only one.

My grandfather shouts, distracting everyone's attention from the massacre. "We must continue on. Wherever this beast is, we are getting very close to it. We have to be always on alert. Whatever this is, it must be from hell itself."

We continue, getting ever closer to whatever has been claiming the lives of these animals. I wonder why we haven't seen any human victims yet, since there have been some cases of people going missing recently. I don't have any doubt the creature was responsible. Many beasts start hunting animals and eventually turn on man. Why would it not leave its human prey behind? Maybe it doesn't want anyone to know, for as long as possible. If that's the case, then we are dealing with an intelligent beast, and that will make this hunt much harder than we expect.

At night, I sit with the other young men around the fire. The older fighters and hunters take turns patrolling the area. There are 12 younger men and five experienced fighters with us on this hunt. I wish there were more experienced fighters. My grandfather might count as more than one man though.

My grandfather is one of the best fighters in our country. He was nominated the best fighter in our kingdom two years in a row, when he was in his prime. Now that he is older, he isn't any less of a man, although some unexperienced people might think so, for he has gained a little weight around the belt since he doesn't fight in large battles anymore or is as active as he used to. Nowadays, he spends a lot of days in his castle, working over papers, and enjoying good food that comes with being a lord of a castle. But he hasn't lost his strength; he could still beat most men in a single one-on-one combat.

We are camped on one of the many hills, surrounded by large boulders and a few groves of trees here and there. The trees are denser here than before, which helps us feel less exposed. Heading down the hill to our right, there is a little trail that leads to a sheep farm. The sheep will be used as our bait, in hopes of luring the beast. I don't feel comfortable being so close to the sheep, but we have to catch this thing, and this is the way we plan to do it.

"I don't like this," one of the younger guys says nervously. His name is Jessie.

"We knew what we were getting into when we came out here," John answers, trying to reassure us.

We all sit closely around the fire like we expect it to protect us from whatever is out there. Normally, we wouldn't sit so close to each other. We all are scared. I can't say otherwise. I have a bad feeling about this beast that I cannot shake.

"I feel that we are walking into a trap. Don't you guys feel it? It feels like someone is watching us out there," Jessie says, making us all look over our shoulders.

"Stop talking like that," John says. Jessie is saying what we all feel. We can't deny that.

"I have heard of something similar to this beast," Ronnie says. He is the youngest of all of us, only 16. He looks the most scared, but he is hiding his true terror well.

"What is it, then?" Jessie asks.

"It is one of those damned. They say that their spirits, named pneumas, take the souls of others to feed. They must eat, every living thing does. So, they eat the souls of the living. That is what is happening to the sheep and the other farmers' animals."

"That is crazy talk, Ronnie. The damned and spirits are those of legends. Folklore to scare children into behaving," John retorts, dismissing Ronnie's idea quickly.

Everyone has heard about the damned and their pneumas. They say they cannot die, and they walk a line between life and death. They say there is an up and down to everything, only two places things come from, heaven or hell. They say that the elves, fairies and other creatures of the sort came from heaven.

Werewolves and beasts of that sort came from hell. Man, dwarves and similar races supposedly came from heaven. Occasionally, the devil will plant his seed among us, turning men into creatures from hell. They say they are more of the middle ground. Elves—they are protected by God. The devil cannot have his hand in corrupting them like humans or similar beings. I don't believe these ideas. They are black and white, dividing people into believing that they are better than others. I heard the elves are known to think that egotistically.

Magic is the same deal. Anyone can learn to use magic, but it either comes from hell or heaven. Where you get your magic from depends on who you are and how you practice it. It isn't easy to do, and it takes mages years to learn and wizards even longer. Some people are born better at it than others. Sorcerers are already born able to use some magic. Plus, they can do things others can't, like seeing the future.

They say the damned are the rarest of beings and are the most powerful of all. They are immortals. Elves and other races can live for years, but they die, unlike the damned. They say the spirit of the damned—the pneuma—is torn from them, and it is a living thing that follows them around. The pneuma is the damned's only connection to life in this world. When the damned die, they return from hell because of their pneuma, which brings them back through the bright light.

For everyone else, that bright light takes us to the next world. Heaven or hell, wherever you believe you will go. Death is not the same for the damned and their pneuma. There is no end for them, until they lose their pneuma. They will be trapped in a special hell for all eternity, known as the Darkness. Maybe they are not afraid of death, but the hell they go to is worse than death.

The damned are only a legend, though. They are stories and myths, nothing more. What Ronnie is trying to say is crazy. Either he trying to scare us more, or really believes it and has a lot to learn.

"It is true. My father said he saw a damned once," Ronnie goes on, sounding more serious.

"Well, I don't believe you," John says, putting another log on the fire. "But if that is what you want to believe, Ronnie, then be my guest."

"You know just because you haven't seen it, doesn't mean it is not true," Ronnie insists.

"I think he does have a point there. There are plenty of things people tell us to be true but are not. I think I will keep an open mind about the damned," Jessie, says, looking like he is considering all this.

"I think you both are crazy, believing in the damned and their pneumas," John snorts, shaking his head.

It is hard to get John to believe in anything he cannot see. He is one of the most stubborn people I know, but he is a good man.

We all stop talking and look down the trail. We can hear the soldiers coming back, but from the sound of their voices, something is wrong.

I get up with a few of the other boys. We walk down the trail toward the voices. I don't have to ask to see what's wrong. My heart jumps into my throat as I see all the sheep are dead. All of them like the ones before, lying there lifeless on the ground.

I have an uneasy feeling. Something is watching me. Whatever killed the sheep is here. My grandfather yells, getting all of our attention, "The beast is here, everyone get ready!"

I duck down hearing a sudden scream. I feel a gust of wind blow over my head. I look up with my heart beating fast. Two of the men in front of me are picked up high into the air! The creature drops them. They scream as they fall, and hit the rocks below.

I get up and watch the creature in the air. I don't know what it is. It doesn't seem to have any identifiable shape, and it moves as if it is part of the wind. Like a mist or smoke. Its color is a grayish dark brown.

I pull out my sword, and my attention is drawn away from the beast toward the younger men at the fire. A man dressed in heavy armor has entered the camp. The man swings his hammer into one of the young men's chest, sending him backwards. Blood splatters from his chest, covering his hammer and the grass around him.

I run over to help, but I hear screaming again. I look up just in time to see that creature coming at me, with its claws stretched out to grab me. I stand my ground until it is right up to me, then I roll to my side, striking at it.

The creature screams horribly and flies back into the air. I quickly make my way toward the armored man. He is a fighter I have never seen before; no one seems to stand a chance. He hurls his hammer with so much force, crushing through armor, smashing skulls. I have no idea how I am going to defeat him, but I must try.

John tries to stand against him, swinging his sword at the man's head. He dodges the blow, as if he was expecting it. He hits John in the stomach with the end of his hammer, driving him back. He swings his hammer at him again to finish him off, but I push John out of the way and raise my shield. I feel my knees buckle as he smashes a death blow at my shield. My arm is hurt, and I don't know how much damage it took. I back away; I know I can't take a hit like that to the shield again.

I stand to face the man. To my surprise, he starts to talk with a little laugh, "So you are the one people have been talking about. Why, you are nothing more than a boy."

"Who are you?" I yell, holding my shield and sword, ready for an attack.

"You will find out soon enough, trust me."

Before I can do anything, something from behind me shoves me to the ground. I lose my shield as I fall, but I still have my sword, holding it tight in my grip.

The creature has attacked me from behind. It has legs now, and a large mouth baring its teeth. It claws my face. I yell with the pain and anger. I will not be finished this way. I feel the burning sting of the slices on my face. It tries to bite me, but I block it with my sword. It is not going to eat me.

The creature whacks me to the side, sending me rolling away. I quickly get back on my feet as the creature comes toward me, angrier than before. It walks on four long legs, snarling at me.

"Come on!" I yell at it.

The creature growls, then charges at me. I stand my ground, ready, and as it gets close, I swing my sword at its head. It hits me, and I fall to the ground again. I roll underneath it, and with all of my strength, I stab the creature in its stomach.

The creature screams in pain. It changes shape again and vanishes into mist.

I gasp for breath. I have no idea what that creature was. I try to stand up, but before I can, something smashes into my head.

I hear my skull crunch. My body goes limp as I hit the ground. The light fades away as my heart slows to a stop. Then my world goes black.

CHAPTER 4

Bright, White Light

"*Your time is not up yet, London . . . it has just begun, so get up!*" I hear a strange but somehow familiar voice in my head.

I feel cold, and there is only darkness. I cannot move; I do not feel my body.

Again, I hear the voice: "*London, you must get up.*"

"*Who are you?*" I ask, replying to whoever is speaking in my mind. I reply the same way it speaks to me. I don't know how I am speaking, though, for I don't think I am in my body.

The coldness is an empty feeling. I am scared; I don't know what is going on or where I am. Am I anywhere? If this is death, then where am I supposed to go? I don't see any light at the end of a tunnel. I just hear a voice that is strangely familiar to me.

"*You know who I am,*" the voice replies.

"*I don't think I do,*" I answer, feeling lost and confused.

"*I have always been with you, London. You couldn't see me, but you knew I was there. Now you mustn't talk, but get up. It is dangerous for you to stay here.*"

"*Where am I? Am I dead?*"

"Yes and no. London, I am here to help you. I would explain more, but right now you must get up. I promise in time I will tell you everything."

How can I get up? I don't know where I am. I can't feel my body. I can't even see. I don't know where to start.

"How do I get up?" I ask whoever is speaking to me. *"I don't know how."*

"You can, but you must calm down first. You have to find yourself."

"How can I do that, when I feel nothing?"

There is no answer. In the world of only blackness, a light appears in the distance.

"Follow the light, London. I cannot tell you how, I can only guide you. You must do this yourself."

I try to follow the light, but I don't know how. I don't have hands, feet, or anything to bring me to it.

"Tell me London, why do you want to live?" the voice asks.

"Because, I am not ready to die," I reply.

"Then get to that light! You must not be discouraged!" the voice orders.

"How can I? I don't know how to get to it. I don't even know where I am or how to move."

"You don't have your body, London, but you don't need it here. That light is your freedom. Now go for it! You must want it for it to happen."

I try to get to the light. It doesn't seem to work time after time, but I still try. Finally, I pause to gather my disoriented thoughts.

Why do I want to live? I want to live because I have more to offer the world, I cannot leave my mother, I cannot leave Sara and I cannot leave myself.

I move to the light, feeling like I have the weight of the world pushing me back. I don't let the weight stop me. The closer I get to it, the more I want it. I am close to the light, and a hand appears in front of me.

I reach for the hand somehow. I am pulled through the light, and I can feel my body again.

I sit up with a jerk. A small group of people leaning over me jump back with surprise. I look around to see that I am where I fell. My grandfather is near me. He is wounded and bloody. John is next to me with a few other men.

My head starts throbbing, and I can't help but cry out in pain. But I would rather feel this than nothing at all.

"London, you are all right!" John yells with happiness. He kneels beside me and looks at my head.

I lie back down, in pain. I touch my head and can feel dried blood. I know that hit should have killed me, but it didn't. Or did I came back from death? Was I dreaming what I heard? Who was speaking to me? I wonder.

"London, I thought you died. You weren't breathing, and your head . . ." my grandfather trails off as he looks at my head.

I feel my heartbeat start to race. I know something is up. My grandfather looks at me; everyone looks at me.

I sit up a little and look at them. They seem speechless. I take a deep breath and ask, "What's wrong?"

"London . . . you . . . you were dead," John says.

"Your skull was smashed in, but now . . ." my grandfather says, gazing wide-eyed at my head. "It seems to be fine."

I try to think of what to say. I don't know what to think of it myself, but none of us can explain it. "Maybe it wasn't as bad as you guys thought; I must not have taken the full force of the hit," I suggest.

No one seems convinced, but there is no other way to explain it, so they disperse.

My grandfather speaks, looking around him, "We did what we could tonight, and we killed the beast! We suffered a heavy loss. We will get what sleep we can and bury the dead in the morning. Then we head for home."

Almost the entire camp was slain by the beast or the man in armor. Everyone except my grandfather, John, Jessie, Ronnie and one of the experienced hunters is dead.

They get busy doing what they can. I slowly get up, with John not leaving my side. Looking around, I feel sick to my stomach. So many dead bodies spread out on the hilltop. Blood is puddled under their bodies. Many of the dead are missing limbs and heads. Some have their chests smashed in.

I look over at John and he tells me, "You are lucky to be alive, London, I thought we had lost you. That monster and man were demons."

"You guys really slayed them?" I ask.

"We slayed the human, but the creature took off after he died. I don't think it will be back."

I nod my head without replying. I think of that dark place I was in. I wonder who was speaking to me. I want to know who it was.

"Are you sure you're okay, London? You were hit hard in the head . . .. It is like you came back from the dead. Everyone thought you were," John says.

I look around as people work to gather what they can from the camp. They are watching me with sidelong glances. They can't believe I am alive either.

"I am okay, John. My head just hurts, that's all. I am glad I am here," I say, trying to pull off a weak smile.

"Yeah, we all are. You should take it easy. Why don't you go to bed? We can handle the mess out here, then we will turn in as well. That is if we can," John says glancing at the bodies.

"All right," I agree. Even though I should help, I feel I need to be alone and try to understand what happened to me.

I don't think anyone is getting sleep tonight, even though my grandfather said we should. The sheep farmer offers us shelter in his house or barn. We will take the offer, unable to sleep out here.

I walk into the house and am given a place to sleep by the fire. I lie down, wide awake and thinking of what happened. Who was speaking to me? Where was I? And all the bodies dead on the field. What was that thing that killed them? It seemed like something out of a legend. I have the feeling that even though they said they killed that human; it isn't over between us.

CHAPTER 5

A New Life

The Spirit

Finally, the day has come; London and I are free. Other pneumas and damned will find out soon, and they will come. London's life is in more danger than ever before.

Eighteen years I have waited, only able to observe. I could never do what I wanted. Now the world and the people who oppose us have awakened a beast. I will show no mercy to my enemies. We will gain the power that is rightfully ours.

London and I must come together first. London will fight it. He doesn't want to believe people like him and like me exist. This will mean the life he is living will end. When people find out who he is, they will not love him. He will be cast out. Life is cruel, and he will have to face that.

People are scared of us, and that is why they want to destroy us. London must be able to understand this, or he will not make it. Throughout these 18 years, we could not talk to each other, but I learned who he is. London does not know who I am, though, and I know he will fight me.

People talk about us. The elves know that I am a black pneuma, the most powerful magic on the other side of light. They do not like this, but I like that they are annoyed. I despise the elves. As long as they stay out of my way, I will do the same for them.

Before I meet London in person and turn his world upside down, I must try to build myself up. I am a shapeshifter, but I cannot shift into much until I consume the soul of what I wish to turn into. It is a nasty business taking souls from creatures, but I must.

The people from the Sanctuary are not happy with my disappearance. I have been with them for most of my time. But now that I am free, I go with the wind. To wherever I please.

The Sanctuary is a place where many of the kingdoms, friends and foes come together, to fight bigger problems at hand. Sometimes, the menace is invaders that come from the sea; sometimes it is an evil magic that has become too powerful to the world.

I drop by a little here and there, unnoticed, to hear what they say about us. They are worried about what I am doing, and what I plan to do. They don't trust me, but they want to use me. I laugh to myself; I have seen smarter people. Either they should trust us and allow us to help them or leave us to do our own things.

People look at London differently now. They wonder how it was possible that he came back from the dead. I never liked his grandfather much, and I don't trust him now. He has been acting differently ever since London came back. I will watch him closely and make sure he isn't up to anything. If he tries anything, I will be there. He will have to answer to me.

Rumors spread quickly about what happened to London, mostly because of Jessie. That boy has a big mouth, and he tells everyone. Now the whole town tells rumors about the man who came back from the dead.

I will try to let London know who I am before I start interrupting his business. If anything puts him in danger, I will be there. We have to stick together now; I depend on him and he will depend on me.

Life has brought us together, and if we cannot learn to work together, we will fall into a very horrible place. Death isn't the worse thing there is; in fact, sometimes it is a way out. For us though, there is only one place we could go to the Darkness, and it makes hell seem reasonable.

CHAPTER 6

Black Mist

London

Two weeks have passed since I returned from the hunt and its dreadful events. In the time I've been home, I have been spending time with Sara. So far, life with Sara has been good. It has been all love, and I can't complain.

Since my return, some view me as a changed man. Rumors have spread throughout the kingdom that I survived death. Rumors are just rumors, though, and I bring no attention to them. If anyone asks, I say that I survived a hit to the head, that is all.

We have come to visit my mother out in the farmland. Since my wedding, she lives alone in her house, which is much smaller than my grandparents' castle. Most women in our kingdom do not live by themselves; people seem to look down on women who do. My mother, however, is an exception. People think highly of me in this town, so they do not look down on her. Sara and I have a nice house near the castle. We had the choice to live in the castle, but I didn't want to. I just want a small place, with enough room for Sara, me and perhaps one or two more.

Sara, as a princess, is having to get used to living in a smaller house. I do not want servants and a huge house or I will never feel at home. I think she will learn to like a simpler life, but she will have to get used to it first.

Sara and I are sleeping at my mother's house tonight, in my old room. We spent a nice evening with my mother today, and now we are trying to get some sleep. I can't sleep very well. I have been restless all night. I don't know what it is, but something is keeping me from sleeping.

Ever since my incident at the hunt, something hasn't felt right. I haven't heard the voice again, but I know it isn't gone. I feel there is something out there but I can't find it. I don't know where to begin.

I distance myself a little from Sara as I try to fall asleep. I don't want my tossing and turning to wake her. Closing my eyes, I finally fall into a light sleep.

"London, if you want answers, then meet me out in the field," something says.

I jerk upright in bed and look around the room. It is still dark, and Sara is still asleep beside me. It is the voice that helped me out of that dark place. I wonder if it is just a dream. Either way, I am going to do what he asks. If he is really going to meet me on the field, I am going to be there.

It is strange that though I have never heard this voice before, it sounds like a voice I have known for years. It is not a stranger to me, nor is hearing the voice in my head, though I have never heard voices in my head before.

I get out of bed and put on some clothes and my boots. As I head out, I put on my cloak and my hood. It is a bit chilly tonight, so I dress warmly. I look behind me after opening the door. Sara is still asleep. I don't want to wake her from sleep, so I leave quietly.

I walk out into the cold, still night. The sky is clear, with many stars in the night sky. The moon is bright, and I can see everything around me. I make my way to one of the taller hills around me. I am assuming he—it? —will be able to find me up there.

I walk to the top of the hill and peer into the darkness. I don't see anything out of the ordinary. I can see the neighbor's house. Its residents are all asleep, and no light is coming from any of the houses.

I wait for a while, without seeing anyone or anything. I sigh; maybe it was only a dream. I don't even know what I am looking for.

I make my way back down the hill, and as I do, I feel the wind pick up. A cold breeze that came from nowhere. I look around, and I hear something moving through the grass. The grass is swaying widely from the wind now.

Finally, I spot something in the grass. I see a mist of black roll up over the hill toward me. Instantly, I am filled with fear. It looks just like that creature we killed on the hunt. Something tells me it is all right, so I do not move.

This mist is completely black, as black as the night. The mist comes up to me, lifting itself from the grass a little, and begins to circle me. I only move my head slightly, to keep an eye on the thing.

Finally, it stops in front of me and I hear his familiar, strong, and yet smooth voice; "It is strange for you to finally notice my presence."

I want to ask how long he has known me, but I feel like he has been around for a long time. I take a minute to think, then ask, "Who are you?"

"I do not have a name; normally people wouldn't use a name for me. I suppose I will have to find one. Unless you would rather give me one, I don't really care. A name is just a name to me," he replies carelessly.

The mist stays in front of me, waiting for me to talk. Looking at it, I ask again, "That doesn't really answer my question. What, or who, are you?"

"What do you think I am? I am your pneuma; at least that is what people call it. I have been here your whole life, waiting to meet you after death."

"What?" I say, not able to stop myself. "Those sorts of things don't exist!"

The mist takes a minute to reply. "I exist as much as you do. You may not like it, London, but deep down inside, you know it is true. You could never see me until now, but you know I have always been there. You know there has always been more to your life than what meets the eye. I don't have to explain this to you, London, because you already know it to be true."

My heart starts to race. This cannot be true. I don't know what to think or do. The damned cannot be true nor can pneumas. And yet, the form in front of me, the stuff of legends, is as real as anything else around us.

"You will understand in time. I know right now you don't know what to believe. We must work together though, if we plan to stay alive. You know this."

I nod my head. I cannot explain why, but I seem to understand what it means, even though I have never met it before. I seem to share some sort of connection with this thing, but I don't know how to describe it.

"I need time to think about this," I say to it, not sure what else to do. I don't know what to think of all this, or if this is true. I don't think he is my enemy, but I don't know.

"Time is something we are short on, but I cannot tell you what little time we have," it replies.

"What do you mean by that?"

"That creature you fought, that was a damned and his pneuma. Just like you and I. The man isn't finished; he will come looking for you again. When older damned and their pneumas discover a young pair, such as us, we will be the first on their list to go."

"Why?"

"That is just how it works. You have a lot to learn, London, if you plan to make it very far."

"It is going to be a little hard to do that; I can't even believe that you are actually here. So, are you telling me that you have been with me forever? When I died, you started following me?" I ask, needing answers.

"I have been with you for your whole life. Your very first thought brought me into existence. Pneumas live complicated lives, but in ways, we are like the damned. I didn't choose you, and you didn't choose me. I was with you from the beginning, by someone else's doing. But we are one; we will be together in this world now. Your death is mine, and mine is yours. The same for our life, we both have different parts to play, but each is as important as the other."

I take a minute to think about all he has said. I look around the hill, hoping somehow the answers wait for me there, and away from the mist. This is hard to understand. This changes everything; this changes my life forever! What is going to happen if he is telling the truth? What am I supposed to do?

"There is much for you to learn, London. I know you are on the fence about what I say," the mist says, all its attention on me.

"Well, I am not comfortable with this whole thing, if that is what you mean. I need time to think," I say, not able to stand still.

The mist moves around me, and I stand facing it. I don't think this thing will try to do anything to hurt me, but I am ready just in case. I don't know what is true, but I do know this creature and I share some sort of bond. I believe it when he says our lives are in each other's hands.

"I cannot explain everything so that you can fully understand. You don't know me very well yet, so I don't expect you will believe what I tell you. In a few days, a damned will be here. We can trust him, but be on guard. He will explain to you what must be done, and he will tell you more about the damned and their pneumas. And someone else must speak to you as well."

"Who?"

"Someone you know. You will see soon enough." The mist rolls away from me. It floats like fog, as the wind bends the grass.

"Wait! I need to know more! Where are you going?" I call out. I start to follow after it, but I know I will not be able to.

"I know how you think, London. You will find out, just not from me. You and I already have plenty of things to sort out."

"But, wait!" I shout, and watch it disappear into the night.

I feel more confused than ever. I am lost, and I don't have any idea what is going on. I stand on the hill, trying to understand everything that just happened.

I walk back to the house. I quietly walk into the room.

Sara is awake; she sits up when I enter the room and asks in a concerned voice, "Are you okay, London? Where did you go?"

"I just took a walk. Don't worry about me. I am fine," I reply, getting ready for bed again.

I climb into the bed beside her, pretending everything is fine. I feel lost and confused on the inside. I am not going to say anything to Sara, not yet, anyway. Not until I know what is going on. I don't know her that well yet, and she doesn't need to wonder if I am crazy after only three weeks of marriage.

As I lie down, she snuggles up close to me and shuts her eyes. "Are you having trouble sleeping tonight?" she asks me.

"I did, but I will be fine, you just go back to sleep," I tell her, kissing her gently on the head. I put my arms around her, hugging her back as she falls asleep again.

I cannot sleep at all though, not with everything I talked about, and not with that mist creature in my mind. What is going on, and what is going to happen?

CHAPTER 7

Visitor

I haven't heard from or seen anyone new since meeting the black pneuma. Nothing out of the ordinary has happened. Sara and I are back at our own home now, and I have received a letter from my mother, saying she wishes to see me. This time I am going to make the journey alone.

I ride my horse down a little path to get through this rocky country. I am near my mother's house now, and many things are running through my head. I know something is up, and I get the feeling it has something to do with the black pneuma. Why would my mother be involved? Has she been hiding something from me my whole life? I don't want to believe so, but I feel that is the case. What don't I know?

Unlike some places in the Sonara Plains the soil is ideal for growing here. The land that I live in is also owned by my grandfather; Harvester's Field has the best fertile soil in the whole country. My mother and many others who live here, however, made their homes on the hills and slopes, overlooking their gardens. The houses all have space around them; the only tightly packed buildings are those in the small town, where most of the buildings are shopping places.

I pull on the reins once my mother's house is in view. I frown; there is a stranger's horse outside. My mother doesn't know a lot of people, so I do not know who could be there.

I get off my horse and lead it down to the house. I tie him next to the other horse. They smell each other and seem to get along. I wonder if my encounter with the stranger will go as well.

I walk into the house without knocking. My mother is sitting at the dining table with a man whom I have never seen before. The stranger looks middle-aged. His light brown, nearly blond hair is short and uneven; he must cut it himself. He has dark brown eyes that seem to say a lot about him. His face is scruffy but looks well-groomed compared to his hair. He has a cloak on, and I see that he is armed. He carries a strange-looking bow. I have never seen one like it. There is a large sword attached to his belt. He looks like a warrior and is muscularly built. A large scar stretches from one cheek to his chin. He looks like a man who knows how to fight, and you wouldn't want to be his enemy. You can tell he doesn't work for anyone but himself.

He smiles at me, a smile of welcome that contrasts with his rough, tough appearance. In his eyes, you can tell he has a sense of humor. I don't know if I trust this man yet. There is nothing that tells me he is bad news so far, but I am going to be on my guard nevertheless.

"You must be London. I go by many names, but you can call me Sully," the man says, rising from his chair to shake my hand.

I shake his hand in return, and he sits back down at the table. I sit down as well. I look into my mother's eyes and ask, "What is this all about?"

My mother looks at Sully and asks, "Do you mind giving us a minute, Sully? I must speak to London about something."

He smiles politely and replies, "Sure, I will be outside waiting." He gets up and leaves the table.

I wait until the door closes, then, turning to my mother, I ask, "Who is he?"

My mother takes a deep breath and pours me a cup of tea. I take the cup as she gives it to me. My heart is beating fast, clueless about what she needs to talk to me about. I am almost afraid of what she might say. Perhaps, I will finally know the reason for the distance between my mother and the rest of my family.

"London, I should have told you sooner. I didn't know if you were a damned or not, so I didn't think I had to until now. London, your father did not die in battle. Your father was a damned. He did not know this until later in life. He left us because we thought it would be the best way to protect you. The damned can find each other, and their pneumas, through dreams. If you were to become a damned, we wanted to protect you. He left so that no one would find you," mother says slowly and deliberately, watching my eyes as she speaks.

I don't know what to say or think. This whole time my father was never dead, and she never told me. My father is a damned, and this means I truly am one.

I take a deep breath and ask her, "Why? Why have you never told me this, Mother? This changes everything!"

"I wanted to tell you, London, but I had no idea you were one until recently. When I heard the rumors about you coming back from death, I knew that you were a damned. I am sorry to have to tell you this now."

I stand up, unable to sit still. I run my fingers through my hair, not believing what I am hearing. I look back at my mother and ask, "Who is this Sully?"

"He is a damned, like you."

"Where is my father now?"

My mother looks into her tea, "I don't know, London. I think he is with other damned, but that is only what I've been told. His pneuma used to visit me from time to time, but he has not done so for a long time now."

I sit back down, "It is not fair that you have never told me all of this. You should have."

She looks at me with sadness in her eyes, "I wanted to, London, but I didn't want that weighing on your mind all the time. Just because your father was one, didn't mean that you would be; there was only a chance. I did not tell you because I wanted you to live a normal life. Maybe I should have done things differently, London, but I was only trying to do what I thought was best. The kingdom—I have no idea how they would react if they discovered a damned living here."

I am upset, but I am not mad at her. Some people would have been angry. I have a right to be; I have been lied to all of my life. Even so, I am still not mad at her. My mother raised me mostly herself, and she went through a lot to make sure I was okay. If she thought that concealing the truth was better for me, then I won't fight her about it. I don't think she was right for not telling me, but I respect her and the decisions she made raising me.

My mother grabs my hand and I grab hers in return. I cannot look at her directly yet.

"I am sorry, London. I hope that you can forgive me."

I try to give her a smile, "Of course I can; I will not hold this against you."

She squeezes my hand tight. There is silence for a little while, and I finally ask, "So why is there a damned here? Do you know Sully?"

"No, I only met him yesterday. If you want to know why he is here, we should probably let him in to tell you," my mother replies, letting go of my hand.

I nod, and my mother calls him back in. I jump as I see him enter with a black mist beside him.

The black mist moves toward me, and I back up a little. What on earth is he doing here?

Sully laughs, "Young people first meeting their pneuma make me laugh. He is not going to hurt you, London." He sits down in his seat after saying this.

The pneuma speaks to me through my mind. *The Hunter has more sense than you do sometimes.*

"What are you doing here?" I ask, trying to reply through my mind like it did, but mumbling instead. I don't know how he does it. I don't want to say anything wrong. He seems to understand, regardless of how quietly I speak.

"I am here so we can get used to each other, London. Expect to see me more often. Just don't jump with fear every time I enter the room," it says, moving away from me.

"I am not afraid. I was just surprised to see you here," I reply, as bravely as I can.

I walk over and sit down in my chair. Then suddenly, the mist changes into a human. I expected him to be a shape-shifter, but it is weird watching it happen. My pneuma has become a young man around my age. He looks like a normal person. His hair is black, but his eyes are even darker. I think I see something wild in them, something that makes him look less human. Looking into them, I see the eyes of a predator.

"What do you think of your pneuma?" Sully asks, after I sit down. My pneuma is wandering around the house, checking everything out. He seems to mind his own business while Sully and I talk.

"Strange," I reply, not knowing any other word for how it feels.

"I feel the same about you. You are one of the strangest humans I have met, I must admit. Out of all of them, I am stuck with you," my pneuma says aloud. Everyone can hear him now.

"Well, I am glad to see that the feelings are mutual," Sully smiles, and continues, "Now, I am sure you want to know why I am here."

"Yes," I reply. I wonder how much the pneuma knows.

"Well, London, I am with the Sanctuary right now. Usually, we don't agree with each other, but we both have a common enemy at the moment," Sully starts.

"Are you talking about *the* Sanctuary?" I ask. There is a place that all the kingdoms formed, called the Sanctuary. Great warriors, wizards and all kinds of powerful people go there to fight enemies who are threatening the world. Kingdoms unite, despite their differences, and work together to protect the land from invaders across the sea.

"Yes, I am," he replies.

"Then why are you here?" I ask. I don't like where this is going, but I realize there is a side of me that does. I don't mind the life I live, but it wouldn't have been the life I would have chosen. I want to see new things and travel the world.

"I am here, London, because we need your help," Sully says.

"This is where it gets interesting, London. People don't like pneumas, but they will help us if there is trouble," my pneuma says. He is looking at some books on the shelf. This time he talks in my head, so I alone can hear him.

Sully continues, "I don't know if you noticed, but I am a damned just like you. I lost my pneuma, to a mage, though. A few very powerful mages are taking the pneumas of the damned. They do not kill them, for I would be dead if they did, but they capture them and use them. You are one of the few left who still have their pneuma, London. The other people who have them are on the mages' side, or won't help us."

"So, what am I supposed to do?" I ask.

"We need you to help us set the pneumas free. You are still young. It would be hard for you to face mages and other damned alone, but you have your pneuma. Your pneuma is the most powerful spirit of dark magic. The only one who would come close to him is another black pneuma, or a white pneuma, the most powerful light magic. There is one who has a white pneuma, but he is no help to anyone. His name is Tellabore. He hides in a forest and pretends that no one else exists. There is, however, another damned with a black pneuma. He is known to be one of the most powerful damned around, and he is involved with the mages. His name is Damon and his pneuma is Talon. It is a name that many people know and fear," Sully tells me.

"So, the Sanctuary wants my pneuma and I to take out Damon and save the pneumas?" I ask, feeling a little nervous about the whole thing. I am known in my land for being one of the best fighters for my age, but that doesn't mean I am the best. Plus, I don't know my pneuma that well, and I am going to be relying on him to do this with me. I don't feel confident about this.

"Well, you couldn't have said it much better than myself. London, you must come back to the Sanctuary with me. We can help teach you and your pneuma all that you need to know, so you can start your mission."

I think about this. They don't sound like they are giving me much of a choice. I don't know why, but I want my pneuma's input on this. I know he knows a lot about this, so I want to know what he thinks.

I talk to my pneuma, still figuring out how to speak to him in my head. *"What do you think? It doesn't sound like we have much more of a choice."*

He puts a book down and replies in my head, *"We always have a choice, London, but right now, there is only one way we can go and stay safe. Other damned know we are here, and they will find us. Either we can go to the Sanctuary or go with another damned who would like to use us. They would do this for any damned who is new, but because I am a black pneuma, they will not leave us alone. Either you are with the other damned, or you are a threat and they will hunt us down."*

I take a deep breath. It sounds like there is only one way for me to go. Speaking to my pneuma again, I say, *"So, the Sanctuary it is?"*

He turns to me and answers, *"It sounds like the best option."*

My mother and Sully remain still and silent; they seem to know when I speak to my pneuma. I wonder if it is considered rude to do that, but I have the feeling many of the damned do it.

I take another deep breath, looking at the both of them. "I will go to the Sanctuary then."

Sully smiles and speaks. "We will be glad to have you. We could use someone like you; too many people there think too much of themselves."

I smile, thinking I have met plenty of people like that.

"So," Sully asks, "does your pneuma have a name yet?"

My pneuma is standing near the table facing me now. He shrugs his shoulders, "I don't care what name I am given. London can give me a name."

They all turn and look at me when he says this. I wrack my brain, trying to think of a name. I am naming him something he will be called from now on, so I want to make sure it is a good one.

Finally, I think of a name I have used many times in my life. Since childhood, I have called any animal I catch by this name. If my pneuma knows the history of the name, I don't know how much he will like it; I am sure he doesn't want to be seen as a pet or to see me as his master. But he left it up to me, so I will name him what I want.

"I will call you Brian. Unless you will not take the name," I reply, looking at my pneuma.

Sully shakes his head, "Strange name, I don't know if it fits. I suppose if London says you are strange, then maybe it does."

My pneuma seems to think about this and says, "Why not? You don't hear it often nowadays, and it isn't out of the ordinary. A lot of people try to name their spirit something everyone will remember. Normally, the names are unnecessarily long. I don't need a name to make an image; I can do that without one."

"I guess it is settled then," Sully says, with another smile. He seems to be a happy person, or at least he has a good sense of humor. If I will be working with him as well, it will be nice to know someone who doesn't think like some of the other people I have met.

I hope going to this place with them is the right thing to do. I am still having a hard time believing all of this is really happening.

CHAPTER 8

Good byes

I am back home, packing a few things for the trip to the Sanctuary. Sara will not be coming with me. This is mostly because she has no desire to. She does not want me to go, and would rather have me stay.

I am in the living room with Sara and Brian. Brian has decided to come with me. He is a little frustrating because he doesn't listen very well. He seems to think he has no boundaries.

When he is around other people, he must stay in human form. Turning into mist form could get us both killed.

We told Sara that Brian is an old friend of mine. The story is that he works for the Sanctuary now, and I will be doing a mission with him. No one knows he is a pneuma, and that is how it must stay. Nobody in this town believes they exist, and if they were to find out, there is no telling what they would do. Sara doesn't know either, and I am afraid that I cannot tell her. I don't think she would understand.

"Can I see you in the other room, London?" Sara asks. I can tell Sara isn't happy about this whole situation, and I don't think she likes Brian either. I follow Sara into another room, leaving Brian in the living room

As soon as we close the door, Sara starts. "I don't like this, London. Who is this old friend of yours? And do you have to leave? We haven't been married very long, and you are already gone so often."

I take a deep breath. "Sara, I do not want to leave, but I have to. I didn't plan to leave like this, but I must. Brian is just an old friend of mine. Sara, you can come, but if not, then I promise I will visit."

I feel horrible inside. I have only been married for a few weeks, and I am already disappointing her. What else can I do, though? I didn't plan for this, and there is nothing I can do about it. I like Sara, but now I wish I hadn't made that commitment. The last thing I want to do is make this marriage hard on Sara. I feel I am not the same man I was a couple of weeks ago. My whole life is changing before my eyes, and I wish she didn't have to be involved. I have a feeling deep down inside that she is not going to like it when she finds out I am a damned, and that Brian is my pneuma.

"I do not wish to go," Sara said. "I have too many things I will need to do here. I just don't like this. Ever since you came back from that hunt, things have changed." She says this looking like she doesn't really know what to say.

She has no idea how much changed, but I can't just tell her that. I want to find out a little of what she feels about the damned, though. I want to know if she would ever accept me if she knew.

"Sara?" I ask.

"Yes?"

"Do you believe in the damned and their pneumas?"

She looks at me with confusion, and asks, "What does that have to do with anything?"

"I just want to know."

"I don't know. Maybe they could exist," she says skeptically.

"What would you think of them if they do exist?"

"Why?" she replies, obviously having no idea why we are having this conversation.

"I just want to know."

"I don't think I would like them. They are demons from hell. You never hear anything good about them. The devil himself created pneumas, placing them in the world to make it unbalanced."

I didn't think her views about them would be that dark. I can hear it in her voice. She believes what she says. I don't know how easy it would be to change her mind. Even if she were to know, I feel she will stay with me. I cannot see her liking Brian. It seems that Brian is never going to leave. Even if he wanted to, I don't think that he could.

"Why did you want to know?" she asks, this time wanting the answer.

"I just wanted to know your thoughts about it."

We hug each other, and I continue to say, "I promise I will visit often, Sara, and I will try to be done with this mission as soon as I can."

I won't tell her I am sorry, because there is no reason for me to be. It is a job I must do, and she knew who she was marrying. I cannot apologize for who I am.

After spending a few more minutes together, I go back into the living room to see Brian. He isn't here anymore. I wonder where he has run off to. I look for him in the house, and it doesn't take me long to find him. Brian is looking in one of the cupboards of the house to find old heirloom weapons that have been passed down through my family for many years.

I am annoyed with Brian. He has no respect for my things. Just because he is my pneuma doesn't give him the right to do whatever he wants in my house.

"Brian, what are you doing?" I ask, stepping up to him.

Brain turns to me holding one of the blades and replies, "This sword was built to kill spirits. It is old and small for its size, but nevertheless, it did its job. Some spirits met their fate with this blade. I did not know your family line had a spirit killer."

I don't know what to say—I'm just as surprised. If that is true, I had no idea either. "How do you know that?"

"Because for 18 years I have been only studying and observing, unable to do anything else. I have seen many weapons and been to many places. Trust me when I say this weapon was used to kill spirits." Brian puts the sword back in its case.

"Brian, you cannot go through everything in my house. It isn't yours," I say, trying not to sound too angry with him. I don't want to start a fight, but he has to know his boundaries.

Brian doesn't look at me or acknowledge a word I said. Instead, he just closes the cupboard.

"Brian," I say firmly. I am feeling more annoyed now.

Brain turns to me, "Let's get one thing straight, London. I am not your pet, and you are not my master. We work as a team, as pneuma and damned. I will respect you if you respect me. I know everything about your house. I am just seeing what some of these things are when I am actually able to touch them."

"First off, Brian, I never thought of you as a pet or myself as your master. But if you want respect, then you show me some first. So far, you haven't shown any," I said, stating the facts.

Regardless of what Brian says, I don't think he knows how to show respect very well. He wants to be the head man. The man who gives orders, but doesn't take them. That isn't going to happen with me. Like he said, either we are a team or nothing.

Brian smiles slightly, "I will show you respect, but remember that I am unlike anything else you have met before."

In a blink of an eye, he becomes a black mist. He flies down the hall, knocking over everything he passes by.

"Brian!" I yell. I am pissed now.

I run to the end of the hall. When I look back, everything is fine, and Brian is still a person in front of me. I take a step back, putting my hand to my head. What's going on? I look at Brian and he seems fine, but I can tell by the small grin, he knows what's going on.

"What is going on, Brian?" I ask in an unfriendly tone.

"I wanted to show you how much you need to learn, London," Brain says in his sinister, calm way of speaking. "What you saw was all in your head. You don't know how to defend your mind very well. I am here to protect you. No one will be able to do that to you when I am around. I am your protector. I am the one who brought you back to life when you went to that dark place. I know how you felt when you were there; it is the worst feeling imaginable. You should respect me because no matter what happens, I will be there to watch your back. Where you are going, you are going to need me."

I stand there for a minute while Brian walks away. Sara comes in and asks, "Is everything okay? I heard you yelling."

"Everything is okay," I reply. Still thinking about this. Maybe I misgauge what Brian can do, and what he is. He is powerful, but I think he is a lot more powerful than I ever thought.

I finish packing the rest of my stuff, and it is time to leave. Brian and Sully will be accompanying me to the Sanctuary. We are taking a carriage the whole way. I would rather ride my own horse than take a carriage. They want me to keep hidden. I don't think it will make a difference, but I am not going to argue.

There are some more people from the Sanctuary here who will be escorting us there. Someone puts my stuff in the carriage. Brian, Sully and I will be the only ones in the carriage. Eight other people will ride on horseback.

John is here, along with my mother, uncle, grandfather and Sara. I saw the rest of my family the day before to wish them goodbye. I spent the rest of my time with Sara yesterday. The remaining people are the ones I am closest to.

I say goodbye to my uncle, and then to John.

"You take care of yourself out there, London," John says, shaking my hand.

"The same for you John," I reply. We hug goodbye, then I walk over to my grandfather.

We stand there looking at each other for a minute. Then he says, "Make us proud, London. Promise me you will come back in one piece."

I smile, "I will try my best." I know my grandfather expects something. He isn't happy with this, but there isn't much I can tell him. I want to tell him more, but I don't think it is a good idea, nor would he understand.

I hug my mother, and she whispers to me, "You take care of yourself out there, London. Remember, you and Brian have to watch out for each other now." My mother is the only one here who knows the truth. Everyone else thinks I am going on a mission to slay a beast and win a war.

"I promise I will do my best," I reply, kissing her on the head.

I let her go, and stepping back we smile at each other. I slowly walk away from her and go to Sara. Sara and I look at each other and I tell her, "I will see you soon."

She smiles and replies, "Just make sure of it."

We hug, and I kiss her on the lips. The kiss is short and sweet, to respect everyone around us.

After saying my last goodbyes, I take one last look around. I know when I get into this carriage and leave, everything will change. This place will not be the same anymore, and I know this. In my mind, I am saying goodbye to the life I've known. I know everything is about to change for me.

I get into the carriage on the left side. Brian sits next to me, looking through the window. I wonder what he is thinking. I wonder if we will read one another's thoughts someday. I hope not because I wouldn't want him to know what I am thinking all of the time.

I lean back in my seat, and sigh. Brian speaks to me in my head: *"I don't think you will miss it as much as you think, London. We both know adventure and danger is what you really want."*

Sadly, I can't argue with Brian. I wish it wasn't this way. I feel like I am making a choice between this new life and the one I lived. Although in reality, I had to go down this path regardless. I chose this one instead of battling other damned by myself.

"Let's hope I didn't make this trip for nothing," Sully says with a smile.

"Let's hope," I reply, with the best smile I can pull off.

I am not planning on going down anytime soon. I am ready to fight till the end because I will never yield to anyone. I guess Brian and I have something in common after all. The end is only the end for us, when we have nothing left to give.

CHAPTER 9

The Sanctuary

W̲e have been traveling for several days now, and I am getting tired of sitting in this carriage. We can only sleep a couple of hours each night, and then we must keep traveling. We are in a hurry to reach the Sanctuary and are getting there as fast as we can.

I have been in the carriage with Sully the whole time. He looks as tired of it as I am. Brian has not been in here at all. He turns into a black mist when there aren't any towns or people nearby. I don't know what he does, but he eventually returns.

We stop occasionally, to stretch our legs. I can't say I will be disappointed when this trip is over.

I start to doze off, still tired. There isn't much else to do but sleep. It is early morning. The sun is warming everything up; it is a bright and sunny day.

Sully sits on the seat across from me. Brian is out doing what he wants.

I look through the window, trying not to fall asleep. I don't have much to talk about right now. We are traveling through lush, green forest. It isn't enough to wake me up right now.

"London, that is not how you want to look when they open the carriage, is it?" Sully asks.

I sit up quickly, not realizing that I fell asleep. I look around, interested now. "We are here?"

"Thankfully, yes," Sully sounds just as relived as I feel about it.

I peer out the window to see a castle of gold. I am in awe. This place is in the forest, with castle peaks high above the trees. There are many guards patrolling the castle gate. They let us in when they see us.

We arrive in front of the castle. This place is beautiful, with plants and trees everywhere. It looks like it has the taste of many cultures.

"Let's go, shall we? I don't think I can sit another minute," Sully says as the carriage door opens.

"The same here," I reply, following him out. As I step out of the carriage, I see that there are a few people waiting for us.

Sully and I walk toward them. Brian joins us, taking human form again to walk beside me. He says in my head, *"I do not like the elf. He doesn't like damned or their pneumas. I wouldn't trust him. The girl, Jennifer, she is a damned like us. Her pneuma has been captured, like The Hunter. The big guy is Breccan; he is known for his fighting and is considered one of the best fighters. The last one is Amias; he is a sorcerer. He can talk to the pneumas when others*

cannot."

"They sound like nice people," I think to him. We stop a few feet away from them.

"Just wait until you get to know them," Brian says with a bit of irony in his voice. Brian then turns into a black mist again.

Brian is very fast when he changes form. When he is in his mist form, he cannot be hurt. He cannot hurt others either. He must become a solid form first, or be partially solid. Brian is strange, and I am still trying to understand all that he can do, but it isn't that easy. He doesn't tell me much, so I am learning from Sully, or on my own.

"London, these are the people you are going to be working with. They are Jennifer, Breccan, Amias and Sergeant Livefen of the elves. And, of course, I will be helping you as well," Sully says, introducing them to me.

"It is nice to officially meet you, London," Livefen says, and shakes my hand. That isn't normally how the elves introduce themselves, but I am sure he has gotten used to it, working with men.

Livefen is tall and built like a warrior. A lot of people think elves have perfect skin and are the fairest race of them all. If that's true, then he is not one of them. He is a big guy. He looks fit, but not massive. He is wearing light armor and carries a long sword at his hip. He has green eyes, long ears, like all elves, and blond, short hair.

The rest of the people shake my hand. They already know my name, so I did not have to introduce myself.

Jennifer, the other damned besides Sully and me, seems like a nice girl. She is slightly shorter than I am. Her hair is long, curly and bright red. She is part fairy, but looks more like an elf to me. She does not have wings. Maybe she is only half fairy, or never grew any. Yet again, maybe she can fold them up. I have heard some people with wings are able to fold them flat. Jennifer fits the elf description. She has perfect skin and is very beautiful. She is also a fighter. She wears a nice sword on her hip. It is not a sword you can get around here. She looks young, maybe around my age. But the damned are immortal. I wonder how old she really is.

Amias keeps more to himself. He is covered in a cloak and hood. He seems friendly though, but I can't tell much more about him than that. The most noticeable thing is his eyes. They are two different colors—one is blue and the other is brown.

Breccan is a warrior, and there is no second guessing that. He is the biggest guy here. He seems friendly and is more welcoming than some of them. He looks like a man who has done a lot in his life and has seen many battles.

"It is nice to finally see you in person, London, and your pneuma as well," he says, watching Brian.

Brian, in a mist form, can't seem to leave anyone alone. He is in everyone's face, then gone, then comes back, doing whatever he wants.

I would think this would annoy more people, but most of them don't seem to care much. Maybe it is something pneumas just do. Livefen doesn't seem to like him, and I feel that Brian doesn't like him much either. I think Brian dislikes more people than he likes.

"It is nice to finally meet you guys," I reply, trying to be polite. How I feel about this whole thing isn't clear to me yet.

"I am sure Sully has already filled you in on some details. There is a lot for you to learn, and in only a small amount of time. I heard you are trained well for your age, but there is still more you must learn. Mostly, you and Brian must learn to work together. I am sure there are things we can teach you as well," Livefen says.

"I didn't know I was coming here for training," I reply.

"Having a pneuma isn't simple, and yours looks like a handful," Jennifer says, watching as Brian bothers a few guards.

I smile, "I suppose you are right."

"Well, Jennifer, why don't you show London where he will be staying? Let him get settled in, and at dinner we will discuss things. As for Slayer, please follow me. There are things we have to talk about," Livefen says.

I have noticed that Sully goes by a lot of names. A few I have heard so far are The Hunter, Hunter, Slayer, and Sully. I have a feeling Sully has a big reputation and has been around. He has probably gotten nicknames from many different places.

Sully doesn't look thrilled that they wish to speak to him. It seems like he doesn't like the elf much either.

Jennifer smiles brightly turning to me, "Follow me. I will show you to your room."

"All right," I reply, but she has already walked off. I walk fast, until I am beside her. We go through the doors of the castle and make our way up a staircase. Brian follows, in human form.

"So, Jennifer, how long have you been here at the Sanctuary?" I ask. It is a good idea to get to know these people, since I am going to be working with them.

"I have been here for a few months now, but I have been here many different times."

"Are you here because you are looking to get your pneuma back?" I assume that is the main reason why she is here.

"Yes, but I am also here because I want to help all of the damned. I want people to know that the damned are not what they think. We are people too, and not all of us are evil. Nor do our pneumas come from hell. You know many people call them demons instead of pneumas? People like to judge what they do not know or understand," Jennifer says, with a strong opinion on the matter.

"*She is very likeable, isn't she? A very headstrong woman. I can see you two getting along very well,*" Brian says through thoughts.

"*Is there anyone else you like besides her?*" I ask through my mind the best I can.

"*The Hunter is all right, but not many others. Many of the people here are only here for themselves. Others are here to use us. They need our help, so they will ask for it, but they also don't like the damned. They are lost, stupid and confused for the most part. Jennifer, I think, is here for her own reasons as well, but at least they are for the damned.*"

Brian isn't shy about saying what he thinks. I wonder if that will get us in trouble in the future. Sometimes saying whatever you think isn't the wisest thing, as I have learned in the past.

"Is that what you fight for—the damned?" I ask her.

"Yes, mostly. How much do you know about the damned and their pneumas, London?" she asks.

Before I can reply, Brian speaks up, "Not a lot, I am afraid."

She laughs a little "Well, don't worry; you have come to the right place. How are you two getting along anyway? Have you got a name yet?" She asks Brian.

"We haven't killed each other yet, so there is that. And his name is Brian," I answer for him.

"Brian, huh?" she says, thinking about it. "It is unusual for a pneuma's name, but not bad."

"Well, what is your pneuma's name?" I ask. I wonder if it upsets her to talk about her pneuma when it is not here. I will have to learn what not to say around here. I could always become like Brian and not care what people think.

"Her name is Vixy."

"She sounds nice," Brian says with a smile.

I wonder if pneumas can form relationships. I never thought about it, but why not? I wonder if it is at all like people's relationships. I truly don't know very much about them, and Brian hasn't told me much.

"She is nice, but she is mean as hell. So, when I get her back, I would leave her alone if I were you, Brian."

Brian's smile only widens "I will judge that for myself when I meet her."

We stop at in front of a room. Jennifer looks at Brian and me, "If you have any complaints, take it up to Amias, Breccan or Livefen. Your room is behind these doors. This is where you will be staying while you train."

"Sounds good to me. Thank you for showing us the way," I smile.

"No problem. I will see you both at dinner. Someone will come and get you when it is ready. Until then, settle in. I will take my leave," she then walks away.

"Bye, Jennifer, see you at dinner," I say after her, then I walk through the door.

The room is big, with windows that light up the whole room. There are shelves full of books. There is a large bed, and a table with fresh fruit. The room is kept very neat and clean. It is one of the biggest rooms I have probably ever seen in a castle. It is warm and cozy, and there is a balcony that leads outside. I could get used to a place like this.

I sit down on the bed, with not much to do. My stuff was already moved in. Sitting there, I think of Sara. I wish she were here with me right now. I enjoy her company, and I like sleeping beside her at night. Once you're used to sleeping with someone every night, it feels very lonely without them. You realize how nice company really is.

"What's on your mind?" Brian asks. He is sitting down on one of the chairs, still in human form.

"I am thinking about Sara. About other things as well. There is a lot to think about right now," I reply.

He shrugs his shoulders. "Sara is nice, I suppose. You know she will not take you now."

"What are you talking about? You do not know that," I say defensively.

Brian looks at me seeming a little carless in his tone. "I am not trying to make you mad, London, but I am telling you the truth. Look at it this way—even if she does still want you, she is mortal. You will stay young for years to come. Sooner or later, time will get the best of her."

I don't say anything. Brian is right, and it is painful. I never thought about that. I sigh, not knowing what to think now.

"I am sorry, London, but life is cruel. It is better for you to find out now."

I sit and think. Maybe there is a way to fix that. The world is huge, and there are a lot of things out there. Maybe I can find a way, but I don't know where to start. Brian doesn't know everything, and I don't think he cares much about Sara. It doesn't matter what he thinks of her though—it is my business and my choice. I don't know all that goes through Brian's mind, but I hope he knows he is not going to control my life.

CHAPTER 10

Swords, bow, and an axe

I follow Sully as he leads the way. He told me that all damned have special weapons, designed especially for the damned or for people with great power. We walk through a bright hall, with windows down the left wall. Brian follows as a mist, going whatever direction he pleases.

It is my second day at the Sanctuary, and I have mixed opinions on this place. Last night during dinner, I didn't say much. I mainly just observed. Brian talked often to me in my head about what he thought about everything. I don't want to believe everything Brian says though. I don't know what his or anyone else's intentions are.

I think Brian is right on one thing, though. I don't know what they plan to do with Brian and me if we succeed. I know Livefen and his people do not like the damned and their pneumas. And I don't think I will change his mind, even if I do help. I can't help but feel there is more going on than what they are leading us to believe. I will find out what they want, sooner or later.

The three of us stop in front of a large doorway. Sully turns around to face me.

"London, behind these doors are more swords than you have ever seen in your whole life. Now, choosing one won't be as easy. You will have to make sure to choose one that will fit with you and won't betray you," Sully tells me.

"What do you mean by *betray me*?" I ask, a little confused.

"You will find out," Sully replies with good humor like always, then opens the doors.

We walk into the room, and my breath is taken from my lungs. Looking around, I have never seen so many weapons in my whole life!

The roof is very high. It rises up and up until it ends. All of the walls are lined with weapons. There is every kind of weapon here, from bows and crossbows to axes, swords and much more. Just glancing at the weapons, a little closer, I can tell they were made by blacksmiths from all over the world. I don't even know where to start.

"I spent a lot of time in this room before I could do much. This is where I learned about most weapons," Brian says to me through thoughts. Brian is admiring the weapons.

"Well, being in here for 18 years isn't the worst place to be," I say, still very surprised by all that I am seeing.

"You should try it before you judge."

"Are you impressed?" Sully asks.

I turn to face him with a smile on my face, "This place is amazing! But with so many weapons, how I am supposed to find the right ones?"

Sully walks away and picks up a weapon.

"It is just as much them picking you, as you picking them. The weapons will be able to talk to you in your head, London, a little like Brian can. This is why you will have to choose carefully, because some of them are liars. They will betray you if given the chance. We tried to get rid of any that could, but some may do so because they do not like you, not because they are an evil weapon," Sully says to me.

"In my whole life, I have never heard of weapons that are able to talk to you," I say, a little shocked.

"Well, there are a lot of things you don't know about yet. That is why you are training rather than going straight to fighting with Brian."

Sully offers the sword to me, which I slowly take. As soon as my hand touches the cold blade, I hear in my thoughts, *I am not fond of the damned. You will have better luck choosing a different weapon.*

I let it go, surprised, even though I have been told it will speak to me. I look at Sully and say with some of my surprise creeping into my voice. "I don't think it likes me very much."

Sully smiles. "I already knew he wouldn't, but at least he is honest. I will leave you to decide which weapons you want. When you have found them, come meet me on the training grounds." Sully puts the weapon away and leaves me with Brian to find my weapons.

I look at Brian and ask, "Any suggestions?"

"I will not be the one wielding the sword. So, I cannot help you. I could make suggestions, but I want to see what you choose. What you get will determine how good your judgment is."

"I feel like I am being tested on everything I do," I say quietly, but Brian hears me regardless.

"Pretty much. Now, you better get started. People will be waiting for you. The longer you wait, the more unsure you will appear to them. And that is not something you want them believing. You must become a very well-respected warrior whom everyone will know by name."

Brian says this as if that is a goal we are aiming for. I don't know what Brian wants, but my goal is not to be known throughout the land. I would rather live a life that is a little simpler than that. I want to leave people alone to do their own thing, and for them to do the same for me.

"You seem to have an idea of what you want me to become," I say. I hope he knows that I will do what I want, and I am not going to become what he wants.

"We are damned and pneuma because we share more than you think, London. Pneumas think what a damned one thinks. A pneuma is just more honest about your own thoughts. A damned may not see it yet, or they are not open about it," Brian says, as if it is a matter of fact. I don't believe that a pneuma speaks for the damned. Brian doesn't seem to think anything like me, and I nothing like him.

"I don't believe that."

Brian looks at me, "London, I am not like another human being. I am not anything you have met before. I take the form of a human because that is how you want to talk to me. That is how most people would. I am called a pneuma for a reason. There is a reason why we are stuck together like we are."

Some people say that they are demons, who share the soul of a human. That is how they walk on earth like the rest of us. I don't think I believe this, but I don't know what to think about the spirits or pneumas yet. That is, if Brian is really a spirit. I do not believe they are the honest side of a damned though. Brian seems to have a dark, sinister side to him. It always seems like he is up to no good, and he talks like he has a sinister purpose he is getting at. Brian hasn't done anything evil, as far as I know. He seems to have a side of him that I just don't trust.

"I don't know, Brian. I don't know how much I should believe you." I say this, not trying to start a fight, but simply to be honest with him.

Brian smiles slightly a smile that never meets his eyes "I do understand. You know, London, the sooner you trust me, the sooner we can start working together. Until then, I am afraid there is only so far, we will be able to make it. Now, you better get to choosing your weapons, as we are being waited upon." After saying this, Brian takes his spirit, or mist, form again. He goes about the room and does what he pleases.

I turn my attention from him and look around the room. I take in a deep breath. There are so many to choose from—where do I start? Do I have to touch every single one to find what I am looking for? Or will it just come to me?

I start to walk around the room, looking at all the swords in front of me as I do. There are ladders on each wall to get the weapons that are higher up.

I pass the bows and stop when one of them catches my eye. It is a dark bow, nestled amongst the bows made by elves and other creatures of the sort. I grab the bow and examine it up close, running my hand along the string of it.

"Usually, people pay attention to the other bows. They think bows made by elves and fairies will somehow serve them better than ones made from the dark creatures of life," the bow says in my head.

"Who made you, then?"

It is a nice bow, the color black and gray. It has markings up and down the wooden part—carvings of vines and a giant bird of prey. The bird's eye is very detailed. I have never seen this kind of wood before, and I assume it is from a land very different from here.

"I was made by an orc. Normally, fine weapons are not made by them. At least that is what many think. My maker was a very talented one. He learned how to make weapons from man when he was young. He was raised by a family of humans and learned from their father. He was very well known for his skill where he lived. Many people didn't like him though because he was an orc. I fell into the hands of a wizard for some time, until he met his fate with a dark sword. Since then, I have been here. I have only had one master not including my maker, but I served him well when he did live. I will be willing to serve another just as well."

I think about it, looking at the bow. So far it seems nice, and I feel willing to give this bow a shot. I am still having a hard time getting over the idea that the weapons can talk. I wonder why. Have they trapped souls in here? No one seems to want to tell me. I probably won't find out the answer from Brian, even though I am sure he knows.

"All right, if you promise to serve me well, I will choose you," I decide.

"I promise that you won't be disappointed," the bow replies.

I put the bow over my shoulder, along with its matching quiver. The arrows are made of the same wood as the bow. It is a hard wood, and I have a feeling it can work well.

I continue to wander the room, hearing distant voices entering through my thoughts, trying to grab hold of me to draw me to them. I stop as a see a small axe that's beautiful, if you can call a weapon that.

It is a small one-handed axe, with the blade on one side. The color of the weapon is what caught my attention. The handle is smooth, with purple and dark green and the carving of the wood is that of a serpent. The serpent goes around the handle and its head points up at the top of the axe, with the snake's mouth open, and it looks like it is spiting either poison or a purple flame from it. The blade itself is bright silver, polished until it shines.

I run my finger carefully down the blade to test its sharpness. I pull my hand away quickly as I feel it cut. I look at it and see a few drops of blood run down my finger from the open cut. I smile to myself, thinking well now I know.

"You are interesting, young damned." I hear a woman's voice enter my thoughts, coming from the axe.

"You look like a very fine axe, who made you?" I ask, speaking aloud, but like Brian she understands either way.

"I was made by a very old race, someone from the far north. You interest me, for I sense something about you. Yes…but I don't know if you are the right one."

I am not sure what she is trying to say. Right one? Maybe she doesn't like me, what's still odd to think, that a weapon doesn't like you.

I reach out and touch the handle of the axe. I put my fingers around it, but as soon as I do, I feel a burning pain. I yelp and draw my hand away quickly, even taking a step back with the surprise.

"Watch yourself, London, I don't think she likes you." I hear Brian say, followed by a low chuckle.

I am annoyed that Brian is finding pleasure from my pain. He won't help me, but he is happy to laugh when I don't get it right.

"I am sorry, but you are not the damned for me. However, I sense a future that you can bring me to someday. Someone that will mean something to you, someone you will share the same blood with. Bring this person to me, for I will serve them forever, or until their last breath. My name is Venom, do not forget. Someday I will see you again, when you bring my master to me," the axe says. Then I feel her mind leave mine.

I frown. I don't see why I would bring anything to her. This is strange, so I move on, with a bleeding finger and a hand still numb from the burning pain I felt from Venom. Next time I am going to be more careful before I reach out and touch any weapon here.

I continue to walk around the weapons. Many of them seem to be reaching out to me increasing their thoughts to get me to come to them. I hear them in my head, but they are quiet voices. Finally, I hear one whose story interests me, so I walk over to it.

A small one-handed axe has caught my attention. It is with other blades that look fine as well, but this one still holds my attention. It is a brighter color than the bow, almost a gold color. The marking on the handle is that of a big cat.

I grab the handle of the blade this time being a little more cautious, and it speaks, *"And what do I have the honor of calling you?"*

"London."

"Well, London, I am ready to kill and defend again. And promise to always stay loyal. Many warriors that are great will choose an axe like me, for I kill like the pounce of the cat. One swift strike is all it takes to lay my enemies to rest."

"I could use an axe," I begin, but before I can finish, he speaks, *"I will not go without my brother though. We were made from the same steel, and I am only half as good without him."*

I look at the many blades and ask, "Who is your brother?"

"He is a bit higher than me. Climb up the ladder, and I will tell you which one he is."

I don't know about this weapon. I don't know if I can trust him. What can they do, if they are an evil blade? Is burning your hand the worst, they can do? Can they make you kill yourself, or what? I feel I am going to go ahead and listen to it though; it seems like a fine axe. This axe feels a lot happier with the idea of serving me than the last one.

I start to climb the ladder, hearing many of the weapons' quiet voices enter my head. The bow and the axe talk to one another. They seem to get along, I guess. I still find this strange. Brian stays on the other side of the room, examining blades himself, but doesn't bother to help me.

I stop climbing when the axe tells me to. On my left, there is a steel blade. It looks similar to the axe, but darker in color. This sword has a wolf etched into it.

I grab the blade, and it speaks in my head, *"I fight as good as my brother, and I want blood all the same. If you choose the both of us, we swear to be loyal to only you. No one would be able to use us against you. I bite like the wolf, and at night the call of the wolf and moon shall be known."*

I have no idea what it means by *the wolf and moon shall be heard*, but I do like both the axe and the blade. I think I will pick them, along with the bow. I am more into one-handed weapons than two-handed, anyway.

I start to climb back down the ladder. I put the sword in a sheath on my back along with its brother. Just as I start to climb down the ladder, I hear a voice in my head that says, *"Your choices are smart, London, but only a weapon as legendary as I am will put fear in your victims."*

Many of the weapons try to say what they can, to get me to notice them. Unless they do not wish to have a master. I have been ignoring most of them, but I am curious to know why this weapon thinks he is legendary.

I climb up the ladder and stop when I see the blade. This sword is larger than the one I already have. The handle looks like scales of dragons, bronze in color. The sword has colors in shades of blood red, light blue and silver, depending on the light, woven into the blade. I have never seen anything like it before, and I am intrigued to know where it has come from. So, I ask.

"I have been around for many years and have slain beasts that no other weapon could. I was made many years ago by a cavern dwarf. But later, finished by a man and an elf. I have battled dragons, trolls and ancient beasts that came from hell. I haven't had a master in some years now. Others that have entered this hall, I have found unworthy of me. But you are something new, London. I wish to join you in your battles and fight your enemies."

This weapon I can tell holds a lot of power, but I am interested in it. I think it could serve me, and seeing how it looks, I have no doubt it is a powerful sword. I grab the sword and reply, looking at it in the light, "Then you can accompany me."

"I promise that your choice will not be in vain," the sword replies.

I climb down with the sword in hand and jump the last few feet off the ladder. Hitting the ground, I land on my feet. I tie the sheath of the blade on my belt, and carefully slide the sword in.

I have the axe and the smaller sword he calls his brother on my back. They are easy to reach and don't get in the way of my cloak. I also have my bow swung around my back, while the new sword hangs on my hip.

Brian faces me, in human form again. "Are you ready then?"

I walk toward the doors and reply, "Let's see what they want to teach us."

"Well, it is about time you are ready," Brian replies. He turns into mist and follows me out the door.

CHAPTER 11

Training

Brian

Training has not been easy. London and I have different ideas, or at least that is what he thinks for now. I know he doesn't like that he is a damned, but fighting who you are is not going to get you anywhere.

London doesn't trust me right now, although a lot of people feel that way. He is listening to what other people have told him, not to what he really feels about me. Black pneumas are the most powerful, besides the white. But being known as the evilest of all pneumas—I think London believes that.

People have already influenced him as to what he thinks about us. I will have to change his mind on that, but I have found him more stubborn than I expected.

We are at the training grounds, and London is working with the weapons he has chosen. It will take time for him to get used to them, as he is not used to weapons talking to him and helping him fight like they are.

I watch but don't do much. I am supposed to be training as well, but I don't want people to know what I can do. The elf would love to get rid of me, if given the chance. We are just too important to everyone for him to try anything now. I don't trust any of them; anyone who works for the Sanctuary is an enemy to me.

The Hunter is out there with him, along with Breccan. They have been the main ones to teach him how to use his new weapons and see how good he is. He is learning quickly. He was a well-known fighter to begin with.

I move along the training grounds as mist, watching the three as they practice. I have been learning how to shape-shift better. Consuming more and more animals has allowed me to be more than just a human. I don't show these people that I can.

"I thought we were supposed to be training together," London says through thoughts. I smile to myself as I notice he hasn't mastered it very well. He must speak with his lips when he does it. I guess it isn't easy to learn for some, like him.

"You are training, and I am learning. I would say that is working together," I reply, staying in one spot of the field now.

"I am being serious, Brian. I don't know much about you, and you are supposed to be my pneuma. If I know nothing about you, how are we supposed to work together?" London tries to stay calm, but I hear the irritation creeping into his voice.

I find London's complaining annoying. If he wants to train with me, then we shall.

I rush toward London, still in spirit form. I pick him up in the air, bringing him higher and higher. London yells in surprise, not expecting me to do this.

"What are you doing, Brian?" he yells at me.

I drop him close to the ground, so he will not be hurt very bad. But he will still feel it.

He gets up quickly, very pissed off. He asked for it. The other two stay out of this.

"Why did you do that?" London demands, looking at me.

I circle around him quickly, "You told me to train with you, and you lost. If I were an enemy pneuma, you would have been dead by now. It would be left to me to fight it on my own. You must always be ready for the enemy's pneuma, even if I try to take him out for you first. There is that chance he can come after you first. So, do better!"

London tries to ready himself with two weapons. These are not the ones he picked up, but ones that are meant for training. They hurt like hell, but they cannot kill. It is a training axe and sword. They are similar to the weapons he will be using to battle.

I move around the field once again, as London keeps his eyes on me. Breccan and The Hunter stay on the outside of the training grounds and watch. I know many eyes are on us, wondering what we can do.

I rise high into the air as a black mist. Then, faster than a blink of an eye I charge at London. London holds his ground and tries to hit me, but I am quicker than he is. He misses me, and I come back, hitting him hard to the ground. Then I go back to where I started.

London gets up quickly, after hitting the ground as hard as he did. He repositions his shoulder, which I know he hurt in the fall. I can feel that he is angrier now. It is not anger at me though, but himself. He wants to do better. Every time I knock him down, he knows that is every time he could have been killed.

"You must do better, London, if you ever want to survive an attack by another damned," I say.

"I know," London replies, still watching me.

I go after him once again. When I get about halfway, I shift into a black wolf and approach him a bit more slowly.

London watches me with his weapons ready, expecting me to do something. I bare my teeth at him and move in closer. London needs to know that the closer you let a pneuma get to you, the greater the risk.

He tries to strike at me when I get close enough, but I jump back quicker than he can strike, growling as I do so. I watch his eyes, as he watches mine. I can tell he is ready for anything, but sometimes being ready isn't enough. He must be light on his feet and be able to make decisions within a split second.

One slip up and he will be dead. I will have to try and protect his body battling a damned and his pneuma, while he comes back. They call us an immortal race, but we are not completely immortal. If a pneuma dies then so does the damned, and damned can be killed, it is just hard to do, and must be done a certain way.

I jump at London, and he tries to strike me, but at the last minute I jump back from the attack and shape-shift into a creature. This creature I consumed the soul of a few days ago. He was strong, but I was stronger. It is a creature about as tall as a human. It has two legs and two arms. It has a snout like a dog's, with big teeth and ears. I stand on two legs. The talons on my hands are little knives themselves.

London is taken aback by what I have become. I knock him off of his feet with my long tail. London hits the ground, and I jump after him. In a real fight, this would be his end. But London is quicker than I thought. He is on his feet again, and he stands his ground.

I come for him, but London defends himself. He doesn't let me get that close again, but I am not trying that hard. I torment him. I pretend I am going to strike, but I don't at the last minute. I move around him quickly so he constantly has to rotate.

"People say you are one of the best fighters for your age. Prove it, London!" I yell at him.

London doesn't reply, but looks determined.

He moves toward me as expected, and then strikes at me. I try to avoid the hit, but he is able to hit me. I move away with an angry growl. I want London to do his best, but I don't want him to win.

I turn into a mist and come for him, knocking him down again. Once he is down, I hold him down. He resists, but every time he tries to get up, I push him back down. I am faster than London could ever wish to be. By keeping him down, he knows there is no way he can win.

London tries to protect his head and still holds onto his weapons. He stays low, trying to avoid my knocking him down again.

As I try to batter him down once again, London throws a strike at me. I cannot avoid the hit. He hits me in the side, and I back away, feeling the pain. It is a good strike, and I will give London the credit.

He gets up slowly, watching me. I turn into a human and say, "You finally landed a hit. That would have been worth something, if we were up against another damned and pneuma. But with how long it took you to hit me, you could have been dead in that time."

"Well, since I never had to deal with pneumas until now, I would say I am doing an okay job."

"Doing just okay will not keep you from dying," I reply calmly.

London shrugs his shoulders, but does not reply. I think it annoys him slightly that I am so negative about his fighting skills. I do it to get on his nerves. On the other hand, it is because I am telling him the truth. Those pneumas and damned, some of them have been around for years, and experience is something you cannot gain easily. If London wants to win his battles, he has to fight the best he can.

"Then we will just have to continue to train," London says, turning away from me.

I watch him go. There is a lot of training to be done.

CHAPTER 12

London's choice

London

After I am done training, I am worn out and pissed off. Trying to work with Brian is a lot harder than I thought it would be. I am sick of the whole thing. It is turning into a nightmare. Everyone is relying on us to do this, and Brian and I haven't moved very far. There is a battle between us, and I don't know how it is going to end.

I take my helmet off and set it down beside me on the bench. I take a deep breath in and put my hands together. I am going to take a bath after this. My hair and clothes are a mess. It has been raining the last couple of days, making the training ground a muddy mess. It is sunny today, but it wasn't enough to dry out the mud.

I look up as I hear someone walking over to me. Sully walks to me, "You look like a mess."

"Well, this is what happens training in mud all day," I grumble.

Sully sits down beside me on the bench.

"You and Brian, I see, are having a hard time getting along."

"He does not listen. What am I supposed to do? I don't know much about the pneumas. So far, I know they are more stubborn than any human I have ever met. I think he and I have different ideas on how we want to do things," I said, just going ahead and telling Sully what's wrong. I trust Sully, and I don't have many other people to talk to about this. There is Jennifer, but I don't want to tell her all those things. I am becoming closer to her, and we are friends, but I don't need to unload on her the problems I am having.

"I know pneumas can be a pain. Pneumas want to be treated equally, London. Do you think you treat him that way?" Sully asks.

"I don't tell him how to do things, so yes. It is more like we disagree on what we want. Can it be that a pneuma and a damned don't agree on things?" I ask. If that is true, it would suck, but I don't see why not.

"Damned and pneumas do not have to agree on the same things. You both will have to come to some sort of agreement, if you want to work well together. You are stuck together whether you like it or not. There is more to Brian than meets the eye. I think you two will get along in time, you just have to come to terms with each other. When I first met my pneuma, it took some time to get along. Once you become friends, it changes everything. Pneumas are not like people. You will see sooner or later what I mean. The younger you are when you first meet your pneuma, the faster you usually get to trust each other," Sully said with an encouraging smile. Sometimes, I wonder how he can always seem to be in a good mood, despite everything that is going on.

People keep on telling me that, but I don't know. I will try to believe them.

"There is always another way, though," someone says. I look up to see Live-fen walking toward us.

"And what do you mean by that?" I ask.

Sully looks annoyed with Livefen here; he obviously doesn't agree with what the elf has to say.

"After you do this job for us, London. If being a damned is not what you wish, then there is something that can separate you. Both of you will live and be able to do what you please. The elves have had it done, but I would only be able to give it to you once the job is done."

"Separating a damned from a pneuma should never be an option," Sully snapped, quickly pushing that idea away.

"Well, it is not your choice, Slayer. London has a lot to lose if he stays as a damned. If he decided to split, he could get back everything he would be losing," Livefen says still calmly, but the irritation with Sully is there.

I think about this before saying anything. I don't know what to think. Brian and I have different ideas, but for some reason, the thought of being separated from him sounds cold. Ever since Brian has come to me, I feel I am never without him. At any time, I could reach out to him and talk. I can feel his pain, anger and sadness. I don't know what it would be like without feeling him there anymore. Knowing what I know now, I doubt going back the way I was would fix anything.

"It doesn't work that way, Livefen. You do not know what we feel as a damned. Brian and London will learn to trust one another," Sully argues. They both fight hard for it like they are the ones to determine it. It wouldn't matter which one won the argument because I will choose whatever I think is the best.

"I am not saying they will do it. I am giving London a choice to choose what he wants to be. If he does this for us, I think it is only fair to offer him what we can," Livefen says, looking at me.

"*He only wants this because he does not like the damned or their pneumas. Less of them is what he wants,*" I hear Brian say in my head.

Brian comes to us in mist form, and I can tell the elf didn't expect him. Sully doesn't look surprised, though. I think he is well aware a damned is never far from their pneuma.

"*I can't disagree, but is there ever a time I am without you?*" I ask Brian. I don't think I have any privacy anymore being with him.

"*You can do what you want, London. If you wish to take something to separate us, I am not here to stop you. I am here to help you, not to control your life. I do have my own ideas and opinions. You do whatever you think is right, but don't expect me to like it."*

"I didn't expect to see you, Brian, although I should have known. Damned never travel far without their pneuma," Livefen says, looking at Brian.

"I didn't come here for London. I thought I would come by and pay a visit to my favorite human. All pneumas have words for you, Livefen. You don't know how popular you are," Brian says sarcastically.

"Well, I don't have to do what pneumas want, nor am I trying to."

"I know. Just don't ever be surprised if you meet your fate by one."

"Is that a threat, Brian?"

Brian comes near me as a spirit, "Why would I threaten my favorite elf? You can trust that I don't intend to harm you."

"I don't know how much I believe that," Livefen says, laying it thick in a sarcastic tone. It is obvious Livefen hates Brian, as much as Brian hates him.

"*I am glad to see you getting along with someone,*" I communicate sarcastically to Brian.

"*That should make you happy.*"

"Well, I will take my leave now. Both of you, do more training if you can. We will head out as soon as the both of you are ready," Livefen says, then leaves us.

"That elf has a lot to learn. For being the warrior, he is, I don't think he knows enough," Brian says to Sully. Brian isn't shy to let people know when he dislikes someone.

"He does," Sully agrees.

"We should probably train more before we are finished," I say stepping to my feet.

"Probably so, but not because the elf says so. I do not serve him," Brian replies, moving around the place.

We are in a little garden that is in one of the outside hallways. It is a little place, with lots of flowers and vines growing up the walls.

"Nor do I," I reply. I follow Brian back to the courtyard. I do think of what Livefen said, though. I don't want to throw any idea like that out the window. I just wonder what he means by it, and what it would be like to lose Brian.

"Well, I think it is something we can all agree on, then," Sully says, following us to the training ground as well. Sully continues, "I am here because I have to be, not so much because I want to be."

"I am the same way," Brian says as a mist moving around us.

I don't answer, but I believe it is the same for me as well.

CHAPTER 13

A battle of shifting

Training is becoming most difficult, with Brian and me still not getting along. Sully encourages us to work together, but it isn't working out very well. Some say that it is my fault because I am refusing to become a damned and accept Brian as my pneuma. I don't know, maybe that is slightly true. After living the life that I had, then being thrown into something completely different, people can't expect me to take to it like a fish to water.

"*Keep fighting like this, London, and we will both be in trouble,*" Brian says in my head, none too friendly.

Brian and I got off on a bad start this morning when he took out a coop of chickens. The sanctuary isn't happy about it, but there isn't much anyone can do about it. I understand that Brian must eat, but he doesn't have to take people's animals. What annoys me the most about all of this is I know he did it to cause problems. Brian is happy to get on people's nerves, making it hard on the both of us.

"I am trying my best, Brian," I reply, readying myself for another attack.

Sully and Breccan are nearby to help me, adding in some hints on counterattacks. They can be of help, but this morning, I am finding them more unhelpful than useful. I am not in the best of moods, and being yelled at about what to do is pushing me to my limits.

Jennifer is watching us outside of the training grounds. I have trained with her some, but she isn't here for that. She is here to help fight with me and to make sure I don't fail in the process.

"If that is your best, then I don't want to see your worst," Brian says, moving in as a spirit.

I don't reply, but continue to stay ready for another attack. I have noticed that this morning, he is a lot harder than he normally is. I am not going to bring it up because I don't expect an enemy pneuma to be easy on me. I have the feeling it's because Brian is angry with me. He wants to make the training as unpleasant as he can. Every time he hits me, he makes sure it is going to hurt. In return, I make sure it is the same for him.

"You guys keep fighting as if the both of you are enemies," Sully calls to us, as Brian once again wins the attack on me.

I pick myself up again after being thrown back into the dirt. I hate it when he does that; I don't like having to pick myself up so many times. Being knocked to the ground is a bad place to be if you are fighting. Every time I hit the ground; I know that is a time I could have been killed.

"And it will stay that way until London knows what he wants," Brian answers, changing into a human. He isn't far from us.

"You can't blame this all on me, Brian. It is not like you are perfect. You don't make anything easy when you fight with everyone and listen to no one," I tell him. I throw my helmet down. I have had enough, and so has Brian. Maybe we should really fight and get it over with.

Brian stands there with his arms crossed, watching me. I watch him back. Finally, Brian replies, "You can't expect me to listen to you when you don't even want to be what you are. As soon as you accept your fate, I will listen better."

"I do accept my fate, Brain," I snap raising my voice a little.

Brian shakes his head, "You can't lie to me, London."

"Maybe, the problem isn't me accepting my fate but accepting you. You came into my life, changing everything. You are nothing like me. I didn't ask for this." I started with my voice rising, but I begin to talk in a quieter tone towards the end. Maybe Brian is right, I can't accept it, at least not yet. I just wish I had some time, but that is not something I can ask nor get.

"Well, what are you going to do about it now, London? Are you going to listen to that elf? You are who you are. This is what you were meant to be," Brian says.

Sully and Breccan listen. They want to stay out of it. This is between Brian and me, and they know this.

"I am not going to listen to the elf. Let's just get back to training," I sigh. I don't know how much good it will do to keep fighting with Brian. It probably won't do anything. I am angry, but unlike Brian, I know when to give it up. Fighting with Brian won't solve anything, and probably just make it worse.

"If that is what you want. Now, tell me London, how much do you trust me?" Brian asks through thoughts, turning back into a spirit.

I have a bad feeling about the way Brian said that. I don't know what he is up to, but I have an uneasy feeling about it.

"Why do you ask?" I watch him closely, as he circles the training ground. Brian moves around in his spirit farm, one that makes me uncomfortable when he is in this kind of mood. I never know what to expect from him.

"Because I think it is something we need to find out," he replies.

Brian quickly moves up the wall toward a guard and grabs the guard by the leg. He takes him across the field to me. Holding the man some feet above the ground, he will die if dropped.

The man yells frightfully as he dangles upside down. The other people quickly react to Brian. They aim their bows and crossbows at Brian. Breccan and Sully come running over to us. People are yelling, confused and ready to fight Brian.

"Brian, what are you doing?" I yell at him.

Brian stays put, holding him in the air. Livefen comes fast through the doors into the training grounds. "Put him down, Brian! We will take you down if you harm any of the guards," he shouts to Brian.

Everyone stands ready to fight, but it does not seem to faze Brian. He seems to just keep his focus on me.

My heart is pounding, and I breathe harder. What in the hell is Brian doing? Is he trying to get himself killed? If he is, then he is trying to get the both of us killed. Why he would do that?

"Do you trust me, London? What do you think I will do? Do you believe I am a dark evil spirit or will you learn who I am? Brian asks through thoughts.

"I want to believe that you are not evil," I reply, telling him the truth. But I don't trust him yet, even though I want to.

"Then what do you think I will do with this guard?"

I look around, not liking this. Everyone is ready for what Brian might do. I don't know what he is going to do, but I don't think he would kill the guard. I believe he is crazy enough to do something like this, he is not afraid of the other people, but not to hurt in this way. I don't see him killing the guard because that is not who he is. At least I hope to God he is not.

"You are putting me through a test, and I don't think you plan on killing him," I think to him. I mean what I say.

Brian still holds onto the guard and does not reply. I believe he is thinking about what I said, but who knows. I haven't figured Brian out yet.

The people around us are anxious and confused. They do not know what is going on, and look nervously at their captains, waiting for orders.

"What is going on, London?' Sully asks me, under his breath. Sully is closer to me than anyone else.

"It is a test," I reply in the same quiet voice he uses, not keeping my sights off Brian.

Sully doesn't reply. He looks nervous like the rest. No one likes this. I just hope Brian doesn't make this into a huge ordeal.

Brian drops the man, and he yells as he falls. Before the guards can react, Brian has a hold of him again. He sets the man on the ground. Then, faster than the eye can follow, he knocks over all the guards who are near us.

He stops in front of me. Brian is now a human, and everyone is pissed about what he did. Brian doesn't care.

"What in the hell was that about?" Livefen yells, walking to us.

We don't answer him, but instead Brian telepaths, "*You trusted me better than I thought you would.*"

"*Maybe so, but you will never pull another one of those here ever again*", I tell him, looking him in the eye. I don't care what he is trying to prove, he almost got us killed. We are in for it now.

Livefen walks over to us. Brian and I turn to face him. Sully and Breccan are behind us, also ready for what the elf has to say. The guards around us seem angry about what Brian did to them. I am not sure if Brian did it to cause bigger problems or because he didn't like them pointing their weapons at him.

"What do you think you are doing?" Livefen demands, stopping a few feet in front of us.

"We were training," I reply. I know it was a bit more than that, but I will play it off like the both of us were in on it. I may not fully trust Brian, but I won't point fingers at him when speaking to the elf.

"That did not look like training to me. You make sure that something like that will never happen again. You both are working for us, so don't push it. There are punishments for those who disobey," Livefen replies, with an air of authority about him. His attitude is like he is speaking to a species lower than himself.

I don't like what he said, but I know it is getting to Brian more. I sense his anger, and I hope he doesn't do anything too crazy.

"You are not the only one who is in charge here, elf. To lay that remark out, I think you are walking yourself into something you should keep out of. I do not serve them, and I do not serve you," Brian snaps. He turns around to Sully and Breccan and continues, "I do not serve anyone here. We are here because we all share a common goal." Brian walks up to Livefen, then lowering his voice says, "The moment you think you control us is the moment I am out of here."

Livefen and Brian both stand staring at one other, both pissed about what the other thinks. I watch, but I do not do anything. I am on Brian's side with this one. If I know anything about Brian, it is that he hates nothing more than other people who think they control him.

Sully steps up beside me, and I know he is about to say something. Before he says anything, a loud bell begins to ring.

We all look at each other. We see a guard running toward us across the training ground and yells, "We are under attack! A damned, his pneuma and a group of men are attacking the castle!"

"Men, get to your battle stations!" Breccan yells, reacting quicker than the rest of us.

The captains begin shouting out orders to the soldiers.

"London, you and Brian must make your way into the castle," Sully said urgently in a tone that left no room for debate.

"What?" I ask in surprise.

"We cannot risk you fighting a damned and his pneuma yet. Now go, there is no time to argue!" Sully makes his way to the attack and yells at some guards, "Make sure London and his pneuma make it into the castle. Protect them with your lives!"

Guards come to Brian and me and one of them says, "Quickly, this way, London."

I want to help fight, but I will obey. Even though my heart is telling me otherwise. Brian and I start to follow the guards into the castle with Jennifer, but before we can get far, one of the guard's yells, "The pneuma!"

We all look up to see a grayish red spirit in the sky. It is the one I fought on the night I was killed.

They continue trying to get us into the castle. As we get to the door under a railing, the pneuma attacks.

It grabs one of the men in the back and drags him backwards. The man yells, trying to claw at the earth, anything to escape from the pneuma. The soldier's screams are cut off as the pneuma breaks the soldier's neck, twisting his head, until his bones snap.

The pneuma is about to strike again, but Brian beside me turns into a black spirit and going over the guard's heads, he hits the attacking pneuma.

"Brian!" I yell, not expecting him to fight.

Brian and the pneuma face each other, back from the rest of us. They take a second before fighting. They make all sorts of angry sounds I have never heard before. Brain stays between us and the pneuma, planning to defend us. I think the other pneuma is nervous to attack Brian.

They stand watching each other, then in a flash it all changes as the other pneuma comes in for the attack. They both lunch for each other, with teeth and claws. It is two large animals in a brawl, trying to overpower the other with their strength, or tear their opponent open to bleed out. I try to keep up with the battle, but they are constantly changing, making it almost impossible. They move so fast, and all the while shapeshifting into all sorts of things.

With every cut Brian gets and every hit he takes, I can feel his pain. I cannot let Brian fight alone. Regardless of what the guards told me; I will help.

I pull out my axe and smaller sword and start to walk over to the pneumas. The axe speaks in my head with excitement. "*Finally, I get to taste blood again!*"

"*Just make sure not to kill yourself before you can land a strike,*" the sword adds.

The guards call out my name, but they don't do anything to stop me. I hear someone walk up beside me and I see it is Jennifer.

Jennifer meets my eyes in return. I know she is here to help me, not to stop me. I feel a new respect for Jennifer, but I don't have much time to think about that. Brian and the pneuma are at each other's throats.

They both circle each other, with blood covering them. They are in human form right now, neither of them looking away from the other's eyes. The other pneuma glances my direction when he sees me approach closer. I want to help Brian, not make things worse for him.

We all here fighting over at the castle wall. Shouting, yelling, screaming of dying men or battle cries. Also, the clanging of swords, and steel on steel. I have no idea how that fight is going there. I know if we don't take out this pneuma, he will kill all the men that are with us.

They both turn into spirits and the other pneuma comes rushing toward me before Brian can get to him. Jennifer holds her ground beside me as the pneuma comes for us and reaches out to grab us.

I move to the side faster than he can grab, and I swing my axe at his side. The pneuma screams, but so does Jennifer as the pneuma digs its claws into her arm.

Brian is a second behind, and he and the other pneuma are locked in combat again. I look at Jennifer and she says through her teeth, "I am fine, London, help Brian." She says this holding her arm where she was cut. I want to help her, but Brian is the one who needs helping right now.

I go to help Brian, but stop as I feel a burning pain in my chest. Brian makes sounds of pain, and I know the other pneuma has landed a powerful strike at Brian. The pain is so intense, but Brian is doing this for the both of us, so I press on.

Brian is in the form of a black panther, while the other pneuma in red is a huge serpent. They both hiss at each other, moving in for the fight again. The other pneuma coils around himself, with his open mouth revealing two large fangs and dripping salvia. Brian stays just outside of striking distance, waiting for an opportunity. The snake is as large as Brian as a panther, so they are more than evenly matched.

Brian lunges at the snake. The snake strikes, but Brian throws his shoulder in the way, knowing the snake would aim for his neck. As the snake sinks his fangs into Brian's shoulder, Brian shuts his powerful jaws down on the serpent's neck. Brian stands on his hind legs and tries to tear into the serpent's flesh, using all of his strength to do so.

For a second, Brian looks like he has the upper hand, then it all changes. The other pneuma lets go of his grip, and almost turning his head completely around, he latches on to Brian's face. Then he quickly coils himself around Brian's body. The snake tries to wrap himself tighter, but Brian fights him, struggling to keep the pneuma from choking him out. Right now, it is a race for both of them. Can Brian keep the pneuma off of him enough to tear him open, and can the serpent choke out Brian and his strength before Brian tears him to bits? Blood shines in the light where Brian has inflected large wounds on what would be the snake's neck, and where the snake has left two huge gash marks on Brian's shoulder. Brian will probably have another two of those on his face, where the other pneuma got him. Also, they have many wounds already on them from their previous little fight before they got locked as snake and cat.

I run over there with weapons in hand. Upon seeing me, the pneuma tries to get away from Brian. Before he can, I swing my sword and cut him deep in the side. As soon as I do, I am angry with myself. I know it hurts him, but I didn't deliver any fatal blow; his scales are a lot tougher than I expected them to be, making my strike not as effective as it could have been. Brian and the pneuma let each other go, with the pneuma screaming a high-pitched scream. Some of the people hold their hands over their ears.

The guards have been staying out of the fight. I don't think they know what to do, and it is probably better that they do. I know I am taking a risk trying to help them. Their battle is not like others, and even Brian could hurt me without meaning to. Constantly shape-shifting is a dangerous fight for anyone around.

The other pneuma turns into a spirit again, with Brian having to take a minute to get his breath back, then quickly goes high into the sky flying away from us. Brian watches it leave, and I know he wants to take it down, but he is not in good enough condition to. Brian turns into a spirit and rising over my head, he leaves as well.

"Brian!" I yell, watching him leave. I cannot follow him for he moves too fast. I don't know what he is planning on doing. He is hurt and is going to need help.

Brian saved Jennifer and me. Brian isn't as heartless as he pretends to be, and maybe I have been judging him too harshly. I need to find him, and I need to set things right.

I go to Jennifer who is up and ready. She has cloth wrapped around her arm, but she didn't do more than that. I believe she is all right, but she needs a better bandage. I already see the cloth turning to a light red, as blood seeps through her wound. The cut is about a three-inch-long gash.

We look at each other as I get closer and I ask, "Are you okay, Jennifer?"

"Don't worry about me, I am fine. What about you?" she replies.

"I am fine, but I need to find Brian," I said a little out of breath, with the excitement that just happened. "You get that arm checked, and I will be back."

Without waiting for a reply, I start off on a run, trying to follow where I saw Brian go. Jennifer watches and calls, "Be careful, London."

I continue to run, trying to talk to Brian in my head. He is hard to talk to; he can speak through thoughts better than I can. And if Brian doesn't want to talk to me, he won't; too bad I can't do the same to him, at least not yet. But right now, that is all I want from him. I wish he would say something so I know he is okay. At least I still sense where he is, I seem to feel where he goes, and that is what I follow now.

It sounds like the battle is beginning to die down at the wall. I am sure the damned and his pneuma are both still alive. Today, I got a taste of how the pneumas fight, and what they can do. I know the battle with Brian and me has only just begun.

CHAPTER 14

Excepting fate

I head out of the castle wall to find Brian. I know people are going to be worried, wondering where I went. I haven't told anyone except for Jennifer, but she does not know where Brian is.

I know that they won the battle, but I don't know how many losses they took. From the sounds of it, we didn't get off easy.

The area around the kingdom is beautiful. Wildflowers are all over the fields of tall green grass. But there are not a lot of trees, as the Sanctuary's castle doesn't want invaders climbing them to get in. Beyond the small field that surrounds the castle, it is thick, lush forests all throughout the terrain.

Following Brian, I go past the castle and beyond. There is a cliff on this side, and a waterfall. I know Brian is there.

I jump from a rock and land on flat, hard ground. I walk over to the edge and look over. It is a breathtaking sight. I can see for miles around in all directions. I can see faraway mountaintops and vast lands of thick forests. To the east, I see the valley terrain of my homeland, the Sonara Plains.

I look at the rocks. I know Brian is hiding somewhere in them. I take a deep breath and say, "I think I have been judging you too hard, Brian. What you did back there . . . you saved a lot of people's lives."

"It doesn't look like I am an evil demon from hell then, does it?" Brian says, a hint of sarcasm in his voice. Brian comes to me in his black spirit form. I know he is hurt, but I can't tell how badly when he is a spirit.

"I have been told that all my life, but after meeting you, I don't think it is true. I know that we must work together, Brian, and I know who I am." I say this truly, accepting the facts. It is hard to accept, and finally admit, that I am not who I thought I was. I feel I will have to start my life over to figure out who I really am in this world.

Brian stops in front of me and turns into his human form. We both look at each other and he says, "Well, now we are finally on the right track. I just want you to remember this, London: No matter what happens, I will always be there, regardless of if you make the wrong decision. Your pain is mine, your shame will be mine and all that affects you will also affect me. And it is the same with you."

I nod my head and stick out my hand. "I think it is about time we start to take fate into our own hands."

Brian smiles. "It's the only way."

We shake hands.

"How badly are you injured?" I ask him after letting his hand go.

"I will live." Then he turns back into a spirit.

"Would you like me to help you?" I assume he will take care of himself, but I offer.

"No, I will have Jennifer do it. Now let's go. People are going to be thinking we left them."

We both start to head back to the castle. As we walk, I say, "So, I want to know." I take a second before I continue, thinking he is probably going to find this question very dumb. I don't know much about pneumas and don't know anything about their love lives—if they love at all. He seems to talk about girls like any other man would, so I assume he has feelings for them. I wonder if it is for any woman, or only pneumas.

"*You tend to ask a question, but never finish,*" Brian says with thoughts. He is running through the grass and flowers as a little fox. If I couldn't feel his location, I would probably have no idea where he is. He jumps above the grass, and I can see him when he does.

"*You never gave me time to finish,*" I retort.

"*Maybe because you take so long to. Now, what do you want to ask?*"

"*Are you attracted to women? Like, women who are not pneumas?*" I ask, waiting for Brian to come back with, "That's a stupid question."

Brian catches a butterfly off a flower and bites it, killing the little thing. We are in front of the castle, and I can see the guards on the wall. I can see some running off to tell people about us.

Brian eats the butterfly. Then he looks at me, his brown eyes with a hint of gold in them meeting mine. "*I can see why you are attracted to them, but I do not feel it for human women. I want to get to know Jennifer because I have a feeling Vixy could be a real catch. Usually, a pneuma mirrors their damned. If that is so, I am looking forward to meeting Vixy*".

I smile slightly, not sure about his strategy. "*Have you ever met a female pneuma before?*"

"*I have not met many other pneumas in my life, but what sort of question is that?*" Brian says, continuing our conversation through thoughts. Then once again he moves through the grass and out of sight.

"*I am just asking.*"

"*Now one more question.*" I said, thinking it is probably another stupid one to him.

"*Yes?*"

"*When you shape shift how are you able to keep your clothes?*"

Brian takes a secant to reply. Just when I think he isn't going to, he tele-paths. *"It is a special material, that is able to keep with us. It comes from a different realm, but can be found in a few places here. The Sanctuary has a whole room of armor kind of like the weapons room you visited, that's strange and unique. There is where I found my clothes."*

I nod finding it all strange, and still have more questions to add, but don't have the time for we are at the castle now.

We go through the gate as the guards open it for us. As soon as we come through, Sully heads towards us. As Sully gets close, Brian shifts into a spirit again and roams the area.

"The both of you okay?" Sully asks, concern in his voice, as he runs up to us.

"Yeah, we are. Brian has a few wounds, but he said he will get them fixed later. How is everyone here?" I ask, shrugging his worry to the side.

"Besides a lot of people freaking out about not knowing where you were, it could be worse," he responds.

"It is nice to know we are missed if gone for very long," Brian says sarcasti-cally to the both of us. I have noticed that sarcasm is Brian's favorite way to reply.

"I wish people cared about me that much," Sully smiles, playing along. He looks back at me and continues, "You two get yourselves cleaned up and your wounds fixed. Then come meet everyone tonight at dinner. There is a lot to talk about."

I nod, then ask before Sully walks off, "Is Jennifer all right? She got a bad cut on her arm."

"Don't worry about her; she is one tough woman. It is going to take a lot more than one cut to keep her down," Sully says, a touch of pride in his voice, before he walks away.

Brian enters my thoughts as we start to head toward our room. *"It looks like you feel something for Jennifer."*

"I am married to Sara," I say bluntly.

"*Just because you are married doesn't mean you never notice other women anymore*," he replies in a calm manner that gets under my skin sometimes.

"*You seem determined to make me say I feel something for her.*" I watch Brian as we start making our way into the castle.

He is in spirit form now, traveling a lot faster than me. Sometimes he is behind me, beside me or in front of me. I walk at a normal pace.

"*I am only saying what you are thinking. It is fine if you want to be a loyal husband to Sara, but you don't have to hide what you are feeling. I know anyway, so why bother?*"

I guess Brian is right. But Jennifer is a friend, and that is how it is going to stay. I don't know her that well, anyway. Obviously, Brian doesn't wait long when he decides if he wants a girl or not. I guess I am like that too. But I am a married man now, and a loyal one. I hope that Sara will be just as loyal.

CHAPTER 15

The Journey Begins

I sit at the table with Amias, Breccan, Livefen, Jennifer and Sully. We had a small dinner together, but now we talk about what we should do. Brian is in the room, but he never sits at the table with us. I don't know why; I guess he doesn't like having to sit with other people. He usually comes and goes as a spirit.

"It is no longer safe here; we will have to move out," Breccan announces, starting the conversation that we all knew was coming.

"Do you think you are ready to take on a damned and a pneuma?" Sully asks, looking at me across the table. "You and Brian fought a pneuma earlier. How do you think that went?"

"We can handle another damned and pneuma. It is about time we fought them; training how we are can only teach us so much," Brian answers for me. He does what he wants in the room, but I know he listens to every word that is spoken at this table.

"That is the kind of spirit we are looking for," Breccan cheers, raising his glass and taking another drink from it.

Sully still watches me, wanting an answer from me. Brian will never say he is not ready for a fight, but I am a little more cautious than he is. That is a good thing because if I were just like Brian, we would be in constant trouble.

"I feel we are ready just the same. Brian is right; the only way you truly learn is by going out there and doing it," I reassure them. I take a drink from my own glass, feeling my throat's dryness. In truth, I am nervous about the whole thing. I wish I was as confident as Brian, but after fighting a pneuma for the first time, the idea of doing it again isn't very appealing. I know I will. I am not a quitter, and this is something I must do.

"That is good because we all need to be ready. We know what your first target will be. We will help you the best we can, but you will have to be the one to take out the damned and his pneuma," Livefen says, his eyes meeting mine as if he is trying to find some weakness there.

I don't think he has much faith in us, but I don't really care. I don't need his faith.

"When will we be leaving?" I ask, trying to take the reins in this conversation. I don't want them to get the idea that Brian and I are serving them, but that we are benefiting each other.

"In a couple more days, it will no longer be safe here. The sooner we leave, the better," Amias speaks up. Amias doesn't talk much. I don't know him well, but I know he is powerful at what he does. He has gained the respect of a lot of people, including Breccan. I like Breccan. I believe he is a trustworthy man. He respects Amias, so I do too.

We talk for a while longer, then we all leave to do our own things. I go back to my room to write. I write letters to my mother, Sara, my grandfather and John. I miss all my family back home and wonder what they are doing. My heart feels heavy, and often my eyes water when I am alone thinking of them. This is the longest and farthest I have ever been away from the people I love.

I feel horrible inside that my family has no idea what I am really doing or what I have become. I am scared to tell them. Brian said—and I am afraid it could be true—that they will not accept me for what I have become. It breaks my heart thinking about it, so I try not to. I don't know how they will act, and it isn't fair to judge them before I know. I am happy to know my mother loves me, though—no matter who I become.

I have always felt I owe something to my mother. She went through a lot to raise me and I want to pay her back for that, but I know all she wants in return is my love for her. I want to make her happier and give her a better life than what she has lived. I promise myself that I will.

Brian jumps on my bed as a small dog and asks, looking over my shoulder, "You seem to write a lot, don't you?"

"Well, when you love people that is normally what you do." I continue writing, not looking up from my work.

Brian doesn't answer, but jumps back off the bed. Then through thoughts, he says, "*We have company*".

"*Who?*"

"*Jennifer*". Then he turns into a man.

I put my letter away and get up as I hear the knock on the door. I open it, not bothering to say anything, as I know who it is.

Jennifer smiles. "Hey London, are you busy right now?"

I am a little taken aback by how pretty she looks. Normally she is dressed in armor or pants and a long-sleeved shirt, which is unladylike in my country. But right now, she is wearing a light pink dress that comes down to her knees, with a slit on the right leg. Her curly red hair is down, and I can tell she has made an effort to fix herself up. She isn't wearing shoes.

"You look very beautiful tonight," Brian says, giving her a charming smile and being polite for once in his life.

Jennifer can't help but smile, and her checks blush a light pink. "This is nothing, I just threw it on." She is shyer talking about herself; she obviously isn't used to being called pretty. She is beautiful regardless of how she dresses.

But men don't normally bring to her attention that she is beautiful when she's dressed as she usually is.

She looks back at me and says, "I came to ask if you would walk with me to the town. They are having a party tonight, and I have no one else to ask. Everyone else is doing their own thing. I didn't bother asking them."

I smile, looking at her. I can't say no, especially with her already dressed up for it. I take a deep breath, delaying the reply just a little. I enjoy keeping her hanging; she does it to me enough when we hang out. "I will be more than happy to accompany you."

Her smile brightens in return, and I quickly get my jacket on. I walk through the door, and Jennifer and I start to make our way out of the castle. Brian follows us as a spirit. He doesn't have to worry about the little town, for it is aware of spirits. This castle is its castle. When in danger, the townspeople retreat to it for safety.

We leave the castle walls and walk on the trail that leads us to town. The grass sways in the wind and from the bright moon tonight, I can make out the wildflowers dotting the grass.

I walk beside Jennifer as Brian plays in the grass. I am surprised to see how playful he is. Brian is never in one place very long. When you first meet him, you would think he was some creature from hell. Once you get to know him, you find that he is very different from that. He is constantly shape-shifting into something new and playing around us or by himself.

"Vixy is just as playful as he is," Jennifer says.

"Pneumas are nothing like I expected," I reply, watching Brian come in and out of the tall grass.

"They are very different from anything else I have met before. They are like people, but in so many ways they are not. What I do know is I wouldn't change it for the world. I can't imagine being different from a damned."

I look at her, a little surprised with her answer. "Being a damned means that much to you?"

"I am what I am and I wouldn't change it. Would you?" she asks, looking over at me. Jennifer and I walk side by side. I enjoy walking this close to her, but I try not to get too comfortable. She is just a friend, and that's all.

I smile to myself, "I still can't answer that question. I don't know how much this will affect my life yet, and I am afraid to find out."

"I hope it will turn out well for you," Jennifer responds.

"Thanks."

"I wish I could help you fight that damned and his pneuma. The Sanctuary doesn't want us damned helping until we have our pneumas back," she says with a little bit of heat behind the words—not toward me, but obviously the others.

"I am sure Brian and I will be able to handle it," I smile reassuringly.

"Well, that is good. But when I get Vixy back, we will help you fight them every step of the way. I am here to guard you and Brian from everyone and everything. And once I start something, I always finish it."

"You don't have to guard us."

"I must. I already decided that," she says with determination that will not be rebuked.

"But why?"

"Because I want to help the damned and their pneumas. I cannot do it myself, though. They need someone like you. Brian is a black pneuma, and black and white pneumas are the dominant ones. Occasionally a gray pneuma, but that is rare because they are usually unbalanced with their magic. They are in between dark and light magic. If balanced, they can be the most powerful."

I think about everything she says. Jennifer is not joking around. I have a lot of respect for Jennifer. She is a determined woman. She is not afraid to fight, and she does what she sets out to do. I am happy to have someone like her by my side, and I want her to know that.

"I am happy that I have someone like you to help me, Jennifer. I can use all the help I can get," I give her a warm smile.

"It is my honor to help you," she says proudly, and I see a hint of a smile behind those lips.

We continue to walk together to the town for the party. We spend a lot of time together, along with Brian. The night continues, and the party starts to wind down. Jennifer, Brian and I sit on a roof. We hear the party below us and watch the stars in the sky.

We don't say much while sitting on the roof; we just enjoy each other's company. And for once in quite some time, I am happy. I forget about the troubles ahead and enjoy life for what it is in the present.

CHAPTER 16

Fear of Death

Brian

We left the castle a week after we were attacked. Now, we are camped out close to where the damned and his pneuma are waiting. We believe that Vixy and Sully's pneuma will both be there.

We have been talking about the plan, and it is simple. They will attack the kingdom, while London and I take out the damned and his pneuma. The simpler the better, but I worry if London is truly ready for it. He says that he is, and he is determined. But I can feel that he is hesitant.

The only way we will ever win anything is by trusting each other and relying on one another. So many young damned and pneumas die because they cannot work together. All damned will fight another damned in their lifetime. Me being a black pneuma means we are going to fight even more. We need to be ready for it.

The pneuma and damned we will be fighting, have been around a lot longer and have more experience than we do when it comes to war. This damned, however, is cocky and thinks way too much of himself. He could have killed us for good the first time; he knew London was a damned when he first killed him. I know what he is doing though, and he is playing a risky game.

There is a way for damned to become more powerful, and that is by consuming the souls of other damned, like their pneumas do. It is a nasty business, but the strongest of damned come from this. And whether London likes it or not, he will have to do this, so we can become stronger in a shorter amount of time. The damned we are going to fight is waiting. He could have taken London's soul on the night he killed him, but he is going to wait until London has died several times. Every time London comes back from death, it hardens his soul a bit more, making it more powerful. That is when our enemy will try to take it. It is like that old saying: What doesn't kill you makes you stronger. Every time London comes back from death, the stronger he will become.

London is sitting away from the camp, in deep thought. We have to stay off of the main road. The people of the fort would know what we are coming for and they would tell the rest, making it more difficult for us.

The surrounding forest isn't as thick as the one outside of the Sanctuary. It will help keep us hidden though, including from unfriendly eyes in the sky. The ground is mainly dirt and leaves, with little grass and other plants growing. The trees grow high, getting whatever light they can. It is hard for the plants below to get the sunlight they need to grow.

I go to London and make a few circles before settling down. I usually circle a few times, so I can check out the surrounding area before resting myself. I don't trust that anywhere is safe, and it is my job to make sure we are always safe.

If I die, there is no coming back for me. If London dies, he can come back with my help, but that is easier said than done. It isn't easy finding him when he dies, and it becomes even harder if he leaves his body and must restart. The worst part, though, is that if London dies, that is everyone's chance to finish both of us off. I am only half as good when London isn't with me, and other damned and pneumas know this.

"What are you up to?" London asks, watching me.

"I was checking out the area. As you can see, now I am with you. What are you doing is the question?"

London shrugs. "Nothing very useful to anyone but myself. I am thinking."

"Thinking about what lies ahead isn't going to help you that much either. You think too hard on it and it is only going to fill you with doubt. You know we will win this, but that is only if we do one thing . . ." I let the sentence hang to pique London's curiosity.

"What is that?"

"We are going to have to work together and trust each other. If we can do this, we will win."

London nods. "I know, and I will."

"That is good, but there is one more thing we should talk about."

"And what is that?" London pulls out one of his blades to sharpen. His weapons are able to talk and demand a lot of caring from him.

"Were you or were you not killed by this damned?" I know that he was. But just in case, I want to hear it from him.

"Yes, I believe so. I was smashed in the head by a hammer. He was the one running around with one," he responds. He cringes a little, thinking about when he died. That is exactly what I am afraid of.

"How do you feel when you think back on it?" I speak softly, for I know it is not a topic he wants to discuss. No damned or pneuma likes to think of the dark place our damned can go to.

"I feel cold. The place I went to is somewhere I do not ever want to go again. It was very cold and lifeless, and I did not feel anything," London says, thinking back on the memory. I can tell he can't stand the thought. I know how he feels. I do not ever go to such a place, but I know what he feels while he is there, and it is a horrible feeling.

"Well, let us hope that you will never have to go to a place like that again, although I think we both know that probably isn't the case. I am asking these questions because often when a damned is killed, he will develop a fear of whatever killed him. The only way to beat that fear is to face it. I don't know if you will have this fear, but if you do, it will be a problem for the both of us."

"Well, what do we do? Is the fear usually easy to beat?"

"That depends on the damned. I believe you will be able to do it though. You will just have to be careful because he will expect this and use it against us."

"I will be ready for it, but let's just hope that it isn't the case." He sounds confident, although I catch the doubt in his voice. He is nervous about the whole thing. I see him rub his hands together or fidget with things, a sure sign that he is. Although I can't blame him, he just better lose that when we face our enemy.

"Yes," I reply, making sure to keep the doubt from my voice. I must show I have faith in him or we have already lost. I need to make sure that I can keep him from giving in to fear. I would take on the damned myself to make sure that problem wouldn't happen, but I don't know if London can take on a pneuma by himself yet. Pneumas have been known to take out whole groups of men before. Hearing how these two act, I think the pneuma is worse than the damned in this case.

"Let's go back to the camp; I am sure people will have words to share with you. And it will help you think of something else," I suggest.

"All right, I could spend some time with Sully and Jennifer." London gets up and we start making our way to camp.

I follow him as a spirit. At night is when I become a scary sight. Due to my dark color, you can barely see me as I move through the dark. Pneumas with lighter colors can't pull that off as well.

We go into camp with the rest of them. London goes to talk with Sully and Jennifer. They both are starting to like him a lot. Sully looks at London as a friend, and I know he has a lot of respect for him. I think Sully used to be in it for himself, but after meeting London that has changed. I lot of people have come to like London quickly. They like his personality, charm and his good sense of humor. He has this friendly way about him. Most people are going to take a quick liking to him. It is good that London has these traits, because I certainly lack them.

With Jennifer, it is the same way. I believe they will become even closer as friends, both being around the same age. She is a bit older than him, but in the damned world, she is just as young. I can see in her eyes her loyalty to him only grows stronger, and that loyalty will never die. She is a very loyal person. Gaining her respect is something that is hard to do, but once gained, it is never lost. There is something else there too—I see she likes him. She will hide it because London is married, but he can decide how he feels about that. Even though London doesn't want to admit it, he will not be able to stay with Sara. No matter how much he wants to.

CHAPTER 17

Bitter Defeat

London

"What do you think about all this? Do you think that they will find out before we make it there?" I ask Brian, stepping between two trees that are growing close together. It is a tight fit, but nowhere in this forest is it easy to move around.

We have been traveling through the forest since four this morning, leaving the group behind. We decided that they would cause a distraction while Brian and I take out the pneuma and damned. This will be going on tomorrow, but I am trying to get as close as I can to the fort. I will sleep when it gets dark, then attack in the morning. I don't know how I will be able to sleep being so close to the enemy, but I will try. I will need all the rest I can get.

Brian enters my thoughts. *"Well, I hope everything goes as planned, but do not count on it. More often than not, something goes wrong along the way."*

I have noticed he is more negative than positive. Maybe he is being more realistic about things, but I don't think being negative all the time helps very much.

Brian is in his spirit form. He stays low to the ground as he moves effortlessly. He can cover ground very quickly this way. I wonder what it is like being a pneuma. At times it seems a lot more fun than being a human. You have no boundaries when you are a mist. I don't think he can get tired when he is one.

I jump over logs and step through the brush, all the while trying to remain undetected. I don't know if there is anyone in this forest, and I cannot afford to get caught.

"*Stop!*" Brian warns, coming to a halt himself.

I stop as soon as he says to, feeling my heart start to race. He obviously senses something, and I am probably not going to like what it is.

"*What's the matter?*"

"*Something is out there,*" Brian creeps forward, still staying low to the forest floor, making him hard to spot. He moves like a shadow, and only his movement gives him away as something sinister moving along the floor. I stay where I am. I don't think he wants me to follow.

Brian stops, then he enters my thoughts once again. "*It is just a bear.*"

"*Well, a bear isn't a good thing.*" I feel my heart beat faster at the thought of fighting one of those. I move a little forward to see if I can catch sight of it. After a few minutes, it comes into view. It is a large brown bear with its head up, smelling the air. I have a feeling it already knows I am here.

"*A bear is nothing to a pneuma,*" Brian snorts, sounding insulted that I would think the bear was ever a danger.

I guess that is true. I know that before, the bear would have been a bigger deal, but not anymore. I wonder if there is anything that Brian fears.

"*Are we just going to continue then?*" I ask uncertainly, still staying low where I am.

Brian doesn't reply, but goes up into a tree. The bear seems to be minding its own business. It puts its snout to the ground and smells around. It looks in my direction. Before it can do anything, Brian jumps out of the tree. He hits the ground hard, making a loud noise.

The bear and I jump at Brian's entrance. The bear takes off running in fright. It looks back to see what the sound might have been, then quickly moves on.

I am breathing hard and my heart is beating fast. I wish Brian would tell me before he does something like that.

Brian laughs. *"Did that scare you, London?"* He circles me once, then moves ahead.

"I wish you would have given me more of a warning before you did that," I say through gritted teeth, then start to follow him.

"I got rid of the bear, so that should make you happy." Brian moves ahead once again, keeping low.

"At least there is that." Secretly, I am relieved the bear is gone. Brian is right though; I don't think there is much to fear anymore, now that I am a damned and Brian is my pneuma.

"I can't wait until we fight again. So far, not much has happened," the axe whispers into my head.

The weapons will randomly start talking to me. I am getting to know them, having been with them for a while now. My bow wishes to be called Raptor. He says he is a hunter, and he kills as swiftly as birds of prey. Bone Crusher is what the axe wishes to be called and his brother is called Wolfbane. The sword that tells me he has slain dragons and other damned is named Misery.

"Don't worry, you will get your chance soon enough," I say cheerily. It is ironic because there is nothing cheery about killing anyone. The only thing the weapons talk about, when they do talk, is killing. I guess they weren't designed for anything else, so it only makes sense that they do.

Brian stops again, lower to the ground. I get down as well and wait. I believe this is Brian just checking our surroundings, but I will be quiet.

"I don't like this," Brian whispers through thoughts.

"*What is wrong?*" I whisper back, even though we're speaking through thoughts and no one would hear us anyway. Maybe the bear is back and Brian isn't happy about that. But seeing how Brian acted earlier, I don't think he cares about the bear.

"*Something doesn't feel right. Just be on the lookout,*" Brian thinks to me, then slowly starts moving forward.

I start to follow Brian, going slow as well. I don't like not knowing what is out there. My heart is beating faster, but I keep my breathing under control. I feel how Brian feels, and I know he is worried about something.

We stop as we hear a loud noise coming through the trees. Something tries to come for me, moving extremely fast.

I get down low to the ground, quickly jumping off a log. I look up after it passes and my heart skips a beat. It is a pneuma.

Brian is already up and ready, watching the pneuma now. He is not going to let the pneuma get that close to me again.

I am up and ready now with Bone Crusher and Wolfbane. We see the pneuma's damned walk out of the woods. His helmet is up, so we can see his face. He smiles at us and speaks. "Well, well, well. Look what we have here. I believe we have met before. How did being hit in the head with a hammer feel?"

Looking at him, I feel a fright that I have never felt before. It is taking all my effort just to stand here and face him. This must be what Brian was talking about, but I had no idea it was going to be like this. I feel like running and hiding, but I am not going to do it. I am not that kind of man, and I will not abandon Brian. I must beat this if I ever plan to get over it. I hope that if we start fighting, the fear will start to go away.

Brian stays near me, ready for anything. He watches the pneuma. The pneuma is what he will fight, so I will have to take care of the damned. I think Brian can take the pneuma. The last fight did hurt Brian, but I think he would have killed it. I just need to make sure I can take care of this guy.

The other pneuma is nearby, also waiting. Unlike Brian, he is moving around. I can tell he doesn't have much patience and wants to fight. If he were human, I believe he would be pacing.

"I think I see some fear in your eyes, is that true?" The damned laughs, then continues. "Don't worry, I promise to make this as painful as I can."

"Whatever you do, London, don't back down. You will overcome your fear as you face him. Just don't get killed," Brian thinks to me.

"I will try my best." I grip my weapons tighter.

The damned walks toward me. Brian and the other pneuma launch toward each other. Their fight sounds terrible, but I don't have time to pay attention to them. The damned comes for me.

As he gets closer, he raises his hammer. I feel stuck to the ground. Fear has taken hold of me, and I don't know what to do. My mind goes blank.

The damned swings his hammer at me, then I hear Brian yells in my head. *"Duck!"*

I duck as the hammer goes swinging over my head. I am up quickly, but the damned is already trying to swing at me again. I try to defend myself with my weapons, but I have to keep walking back to avoid getting hit by him. I haven't been able to throw one hit at him. Again, and again, he tries to hit me. I know I won't be able to avoid getting hit for much longer.

I back up to a big tree. As he swings his hammer, hoping to finish me off, I bring Bone Crusher up to try and stop the attack. Our weapons collide, and with all my effort I slice his side with Wolfbane.

He backs up a little, and I slip away. I am now behind him in more of a clearing, and this time I am not backing up. Doing that is only going to get me killed. I am lucky I have survived this long doing that.

We are both ready to fight, but we both wait for the other to make the first move. He holds his hammer, while I have Bone Crusher in my right and Wolfbane in my left. This fight will not last long. Neither of us has good weapons to block off a hit. We are going to fight, and one of us will be going down.

He runs at me, and we both swing at each other. I first try to hit him, but I know I must defend myself. As he brings his hammer down, I use my weapons the best I can as a shield. He hits them, and I can feel how hard that hit is. If he would have hit me, it would have been all over. I cannot get hit by this guy or I am done for.

We back up and I come at him this time swinging Bone Crusher at his arm. He yells, as he is not able to defend himself and I land a strike. It hits him hard, and I feel it cut through his armor, smashing into his arm and hitting flesh.

He shoves me away with his hammer and arm. I stumble back, losing my balance. Before I can recover, he swings his hammer at my arm.

The hammer goes smashing into my arm, making me yell from the pain and shock. I drop Bone Crusher. I have never felt pain like this before, my arm is broken and the pain is intense to the point I don't know how much of it I can take.

I don't have enough time to do anything as he swings his hammer at my leg. I hear the bone break and the hot burning pain as the hammer hits it. I fall over and yell in pain once again. I try to move, making sounds of pain I cannot help. The pain is so intense my eyes are watery and every breath I take seems to be difficult. My stomach is in knots, and I think I might be sick.

The damned stands over me with a smile. I try to crawl away, but I can't. There is nothing I can do. I feel weak, vulnerable, and I failed. My heart is beating so fast I can hear it pounding in my ears, and I can't take control over it.

Before he can get very close, Brian as a mist comes over me and knocks him back. The man stumbles back. His pneuma tries to go for Brian again, but his damned stops him.

Brian stays with me, making sure that no one else can cause me harm. The other pneuma circles us, but makes sure not to get that close to Brian. The damned stays where he is and watches us.

I cannot move; the pain is too much. I try to move, but I cannot. I let Brian down, and now there is only him. If they decide to attack, I don't know what we are going to do. I try to control my breathing and grab Wolfbane, I don't really know what I can do with him right now, but I feel better at least holding a weapon.

"You are a pathetic excuse for a damned. Not just any damned, but you are the one with the black pneuma. I thought you guys were supposed to be the most powerful." The damned smiles, reviling teeth, that remind me of a wolf's, with large canines.

We say nothing. We both know that we are at the mercy of this damned and his pneuma. I never expected it to turn out like this. I did worse than I thought I could.

"You know I think I am going to leave you like this. To see you suffer, and continue suffering like this makes me happier than if I were to just kill you. But next time we meet it will be for the kill, and I will make sure the suffering will be even worse. The only difference is you can find comfort in that it will end because I will not give you another chance." The damned still smiles as he says this, and I can see the delight dancing in his lifeless eyes as I lay here in pain.

The damned and his pneuma start to leave us. Brian stays where he is. I feel horrible. I cannot move, and the pain is the worse I have ever felt before. I cannot move my right arm and leg. I try to roll more onto my back with a yell, as I try to put less weight on broken right limbs. I clench my teeth tight, trying to fight the waves of nausea hitting me.

Brian moves, so he isn't above me anymore and turns into a human. He gets beside me and I know he can feel the pain as well. I don't know what to say, and I am pissed at myself and ashamed. My first battle and I really screwed it up. I know I can do better than this, so why didn't I? I close my eyes tight and turn my head from Brian, as I feel tears in them. It would be no good for Brian to see my cry. They are tears of anger, mostly for myself. How could I screw up so bad?

CHAPTER 18

Personal hell

B rian is beside me, looking over my wounds. I feel sick, and I don't know what to think or do. The pain is so intense and nothing makes it better. I try to move, but I'm not getting anywhere.

"It doesn't look good," Brian says to me.

"I'm sorry, Brian. I should have done better," I say through clenched teeth. I close my eyes, trying to cope with the pain. I don't know what we are going to do, but I can't fight like this. And I don't know if I will ever heal completely from it. I take a look at my arm and leg, and they are far from good. I don't know if I could ever be okay after that kind of break.

"I was hoping that it would be a long time for this to happen, but you are going to have to die, London," Brian says softly. He is being nicer than he usually is to me, but that didn't sound so nice.

"What do you mean by that?" I am barly able to get out, opening my eyes to look at him.

"Well, look at you! We cannot fight like we do, with you looking like that."

I get what he means, but I don't like it never the less. I don't want to go to that dark place again, but I guess it's better than being stuck like this.

"I guess we don't have much of a choice," I say in agreement, closing my eyes again. I just want the pain to go away.

"No, we don't. London, this will not be like your first death."

"Well, how is it going to be different?" I am getting the feeling I am going to like it even less than I thought.

"I cannot describe it to you, for I have never been there. This time, you will be going to a different place to return to your body."

"So, what does that mean then?"

"You will come back, but you will have to find your way out. I cannot tell you much more, London, but you are going to have to trust me. I promise I will get you out of there. Down there, you must protect yourself. That is when these weapons become so important to a damned. The weapons will be able to follow you down there, where no other weapon would be able to go."

I nod, and grunt a little—even that small movement makes my head spin. I am just trying not to pass out. There is nothing Brian can do for me. Brian stands up and looks around into the forest.

"We are going to have to find something to finish you off," he says, looking as if he is thinking out loud.

"What?" I yell through clenched teeth. I guess I can't expect anything else, but hearing that makes my heart beat faster. Even if I can come back, the thought of dying is a nasty one. How is he planning on killing me? It isn't pleasant dying.

"Something is going to have to finish you off. I don't like this any more than you do, but I know what we must do. I am afraid it won't be a quick death either. Your body must not be able to take you back, so you can restart."

"Well, can't I be killed quickly first?" I ask, breathing harder. I try to move, but only make a sound of pain.

Brian looks shaking his head slightly, "I am sorry, London, but I don't think so. There is no one here but me, and I cannot kill you."

"Why not?"

"Because a pneuma should never kill his damned. There is a chance you can develop a fear of me, and I don't know how we would break that. That is something we cannot afford, so we will have to find something else to do the job."

I sigh, feeling like shit and hating this situation. Why, out of all the ways, did this fight have to end like this? I guess it could have ended worse. I just want to be killed and get this over with.

"Let's just get me killed, so we can move on," I say, closing my eyes and trying to relax the best I can.

Brian gets down beside me again and says in that sinister-like smooth voice of his, "I cannot help you; you will have to die. But I can make it easier for you though."

"How can you do that?" I ask, not bothering to look at him.

"I can put you to sleep."

I think about it, then nod slightly. I would rather not be awake for my death.

Brian stays with me as I grow more tired and feel weak. He must be doing it, but I don't know how, neither do I care right now. With this pain, I am glad I am going under. Finally, my world goes black....

———◆———

I scream as I feel horrible pain! I can't move, but I try to lash out at whatever is hurting me, to only find that I can't. All of a sudden, all my feelings are gone. As suddenly as the pain arrived, it vanished.

I open my eyes, feeling the same cold feeling I have felt before. I know I am dead. Whatever that pain was that I felt must have been something finishing me off.

This place is different. I don't feel right. Unlike last time, I can feel my body and I can move. I am in a place unlike before, where I feel like I am nowhere and nothing at all. I get up and look around. I am in a dark place that looks like it has no beginning or end. Ahead of me, I see a glowing light, like that of a fire. I don't like this, and I have a very bad feeling about this place. I feel cold. All the warmth of my body is gone and all sense of feeling. I can feel Brian now, I sense where he is, and that is where I will be going. It leads me to where the glowing light is, but that is where something tells me I don't want to go. I want to listen to that instinct, but I must find Brian if I want to get out of here.

I start moving forward, where the glow is. I step onto a road. This is no place I have ever seen before. It has a glow that comes from the land itself, where there is a broken-down town. The city is very large and the buildings are bigger than any I have ever seen before.

I walk down the road, but I stop as I see two men walking down the road where I came from. They only look up at me as I get closer.

One of the guys is tall and skinny, probably just adding visually to his height. This guy has a hat on, and his nose has obviously been broken a few good times. He looks like he is a man who doesn't have a lot of patience. The little guy is shorter than me, but unlike his friend, he seems to have a lively personality. I heard them while they were talking. The little guy had a lot to say, and the tall one seemed to just listen.

"Who are you? You seem to be new down here," the tall guy says as his greeting, sounding a little disinterested. They both stop walking.

"I am new, and was wondering if you guys know the way out," I ask, trying to be friendly.

"What's your name, kid?" the shorter one asks.

"London."

"We have a boss who mentioned something about helping a kid named London," the tall one said.

"What is your boss's name?" I ask, wondering if it is someone I know or not. I don't know how many other people are named London.

"He goes by a lot of names; Sully, Hunter, Slayer."

"I know who Sully is." I sigh, happy that these people have some connections.

"Well, since this is your first time, we will help you get out. Normally, people figure out this part themselves. That can take a while, and I don't know if you will survive the night. Now, come on," the tall guy says, waving at me to follow.

I quickly start to follow them. I am glad these guys are so quick to help; they sure don't wait long. I am going to be cautious though. They look safe, but it is always better to be on your guard.

"So, why do you guys think I wouldn't survive the night?" I ask as I walk to the town with them.

"Because kid, that is when they come out," the short guy replies.

"When who comes out?"

Both guys look at each other.

"I guess it is a very good thing we are helping him out," the tall guy said to his friend.

The shorter guy meets my eyes, "I don't know how much you know about this place, kid, but it is pretty much hell. It is a place where damned and ancient creatures go, when they are slain. There are seven different levels of this place, and you are in the first. You can only make it back being on the first level. If you go any further down, you would have to make it back to this level before coming out."

"What brings you to these other levels of hell? Does it depend on who you are?" I assume being like hell, the seventh would be the worst place. Looking at their expressions after saying it, I don't think that is how it works down here though.

"No, that is not how it works. Why do you think the night is so bad down here? It is because that is when they come out. If you get caught by one—well, you will be lucky if you can fight him off and at least only be dragged down to the second level."

"Who is they?

"Trust us, it is better you never find out," the tall guy replies.

I swallow hard, not liking this place. I feel uncomfortable being down here. I would rather not come back to this place again, if I can help it.

We walk through the town. There are other people down here; many of them have weapons, which must be similar to mine. People watch as we walk by, but none of them says anything to us. I would rather just get out of here, and not have to worry about other people.

After getting through the city, they take me to a large pool of water. It is as black as night. They don't get very close to it. The taller one says, "If you feel your spirit calling to you, go to the pool. If you see a bright light in the water, it means he is summoning you out. If you don't see anything, back up quickly. Water is the key to life, and it still is for you. However, if you don't see that light you will get a nasty surprise, so don't ever go into a pool of water down here unless you see your light."

I can believe them, for it was a light that got me out of a dark place the first time. I have no idea what could be lurking in the water that they are afraid of, and that is making me nervous.

"What is in the water that is so dangerous?" I ask, looking at them.

"Let's just put it this way, kid, everything in this place is trying to get you. The water is no exception. This place is meant to drag you under. Further and further down you will go, until you hit the bottom. And once you are there, it is almost impossible to get back out. You will have every evil thing imaginable keeping you there," the short guy says.

I look back towards the water. I feel Brian calling for me, so I shall go. I hope that there is a light there, and I won't meet anything else, but I won't know until I am there.

I start walking to the water and the shorter guy calls, "Good luck, kid."

"Thanks for the help, and the luck. I am going to need it," I reply. I continue my way slowly to the water.

"You are telling us," the tall guy says, not making me feel much better about this.

I approach the water's edge with much caution. I look to see a bright light in the water below the surface. I believe this is when I am supposed to jump, but it isn't as easy as that. Not in a million years would I want to jump into that black abyss. But I need to get out of here, and I must trust Brian.

I close my eyes and jump into the black water. It is freezing, although being cold already it doesn't affect me like I thought it would. I don't need to close my eyes or hold my breath, for I don't seem to need air. So, I swim. I head to where the bright white light is. As I get closer, the bright light seems to sink farther down, the more I try to reach it.

I follow this bright light. Nothing else is around me but water and darkness. Finally, the light seems to make it out. I swim faster, wanting nothing more than to get out myself.

I make it out of the water, throwing my head up with a splash, loving nothing more than to be out of that place. I seem to be home, but I feel nothing. I am cold and dizzy all at the same time. I start to slip back under, unable to help it, but Brian grabs me and drags me out of the water.

I try to move when I make it to the shore but have a hard time doing so; I feel so strange. I can't see either, well at least not how I normally see. I can still understand everything around me, from light to color, but just not in a normal way. It is like my other senses have taken over, allowing me to hear, smell and feel my surroundings making the perfect image my mind needs to see where I am.

"You are okay. London," Brian says reassuringly.

"I can't feel anything, Brian. What is wrong with me?" I ask rolling onto my back.

"Well, you did just come back from the underworld."

I put my hand on my face and sit up. I can't believe what I am seeing. Is it real?

There is no flesh on my hand, nothing but bone. I start to panic. What is wrong with me? I feel around to find my whole body is bone, and I am dressed in nothing. I try to get up, but can't seem to find my footing.

Brian pushes me back down, "Calm down, London. This is supposed to happen."

"I am supposed to have no more flesh, and be a walking skeleton?!" I yell. I am looking at him, my voice rising with the panic I feel.

"Yes, now lay back down, you have to rest for a second. We are in a bad spot. We have to find the others. Bringing you back has worn me out, and you are in no state to defend yourself."

I lay back, listening to Brian. I put my hand on my head and try to calm down. I need to get control of myself. Panicking isn't going to help anything.

Brian stays beside me and neither of us talks. Finally, I calm down a little, putting my hand on my face. "So how did I die, Brian?"

"Let's just say that the bear helped out," Brian's says, irony heavy in his voice.

I take my hand from my face, and turn my head to him with shock, "You had the bear eat me?"

"I didn't know any other way to kill you," Brian retorts calmly.

I close my eyes again. Brian is right, I guess. I just find it a bit ironic.

Brian drops my clothes on me and continues, "You might want to wear this. Being a skeleton, you don't have anything to hide anymore…although I don't think you ever did, anyway."

"Thanks for kicking a man while he is down, Brian," I say, slowly starting to put my clothes on.

We rest a little more, then I get up. I don't feel well. I feel strange, not myself, only bones. I am going to trust Brian though, he has helped me this far, and he seems to know what he is doing. We need to make it back. I can see how tired he is. We need to find the group and talk about what has happened.

We start to move. Brian having a hard time too. Brian ends up turning into a fox, and I just carry him. He helped me back, so I will do the same for him. We walk through the forest in the dark. I listen to his instructions, and we continue to get closer to the others.

CHAPTER 19

Skeleton

Since we got back with the others, Brian has been sleeping in our tent. Bringing me back took a lot out of him, and he now has no choice but to rest. I, on the other hand, get no time for that. All of them want to talk to me, and many are not happy. I am not happy either. I didn't plan for this, and I am already angry with myself for failing so miserably.

"You cannot die again as a skeleton or you will stay dead next time," Livefen starts, not being able to sit down. They are all unhappy how this turned out, but the elf makes it more obvious than the rest.

I sit on a log facing Amias, Jennifer, Sully, Livefen and Breccan. Jennifer isn't saying much, but is just here. Jennifer's job is to protect me, she says, not to tell me what I am doing wrong or what to do. Sully doesn't seem mad, just concerned. Breccan looks concerned as well. I have no idea how Amias is feeling, as usual. Livefen is pretty pissed about the whole thing. He doesn't like anything that interrupts his plans.

"We will have to get you fixed up before we continue forward," Amias says, agreeing with Livefen. I don't really know what they mean by that, but I am assuming there is a way to make me not a skeleton anymore.

"I will help him out with that and I will have him back as soon as I can," Sully said.

I watch all of them talk, thinking I truly am working for these people. It is not about what I want. It is all about what they say. I am the one with my life on the line, and there is nothing I can say about it. It is not going to be that way forever.

"No!" Brian shouts. They all stop talking as they see Brian walk over to us. He is a human right now, and he doesn't look too happy.

"It is best for you guys to do that before anything else," Livefen says, looking at Brian.

Brian looks around at all of them, "London and I will decide what is right for us, by ourselves. So, the rest of you can screw off," disregarding what Livefen said.

I know that pissed a lot of them off, but Sully and Jennifer look like they didn't take too much offense to that. They know who Brian is, and that something like this is to be expected from him.

"You are here because of us, Brian. Don't think that you can go rogue now," Livefen shot back.

"Maybe it is best to let them decide if London thinks he can do it," Breccan says, trying to ease things up a little bit.

Brian looks at me, "If you plan to go as a skeleton, there is a risk. If you die, there is no coming back. On the other hand, we have no time to waste. They know that we are coming for them, and the more time we give them the more they will benefit. You will not let him defeat you, and you will prove that to everyone."

I have a feeling he isn't really giving me a choice, but I think Brian knows what he is talking about. He brought me back, and made sure that we made it back safely. I think I owe it to Brian to trust him.

I look at them all and getting up from the log, I say, "Brian and I will face them in the morning. We are not going to wait until I am human. It doesn't matter how many lives you have. Either you are going to fight and win, or lose and die."

That damned already said he was going to kill me regardless, so I don't think it matters if I can come back or not; I need to face him and get it over with.

"This decision is going to get both of you killed," Livefen protests, but I think he knows it is in vain.

"Have more faith in us than that," Brian says with a ray of a smile, "I don't believe you will die tomorrow."

The elf only glares. Giving in, he turns on his heel and leaves.

"You really know how to get on his bad side, don't you?" I say, with what would be a smile, if I could smile, to Brian, watching Livefen leave.

"I don't think I could do otherwise."

"I hope you two know what you are doing," Breccan says getting up. Then he and Amias leave. I don't think they are mad, but I don't think they are completely happy with the decision either.

"Is this really what you want, kid?" Sully asks, stepping closer to me.

"It is. Do you think this is the wrong way to go?" I ask, looking at him. I respect what Sully says and would like to hear it from him.

I like Sully and I think he is smart. He knows more about damned and pneumas than anyone else here. I am sure Jennifer knows a fair amount, but she hasn't been a damned for as long as Sully has. I also know that Sully is working for himself and not involved in it like the rest. He is here for his pneuma, and I believe that is it.

"Really thinking about it, I don't think either of you is wrong. You are doing what you have to do. Just be careful, we don't need the both of you to die," Sully says placing his hand on my shoulder.

"We don't plan to," Brian replies in his calm voice.

We say goodnight to him, and Sully leaves like the rest. Jennifer walks over to us, as we start to walk back to our tent.

"Well, look at you now. All bones, huh?" Jennifer says with a cute smile.

Brian turns into a spirit and thinks to me, "*I think you have an admirer.*"

I feel like Brian is constantly encouraging me to put a move on Jennifer. He seems to ignore the fact that I am a married man. He doesn't really care for Sara, and thinks that I shouldn't either. He and I don't have to agree on the same woman. Jennifer is a wonderful woman, but I can't think of her as anything more than that. I am a loyal man regardless of what Brian thinks.

"Don't worry, it won't affect my good looks in the long run," I say, trying to smile, which I can't do very well being a skeleton.

She laughs, "I don't know what good looks you are talking about." Jennifer walks passed me, still wearing that smile.

"You must be blind if you don't know what I am talking about," I say keeping my pride.

"I must be blind then. Goodnight, London. You should get some sleep. It will be good for you."

"Goodnight," I reply. I watch her go to her tent, then turn in to mine.

Brian turns into a black panther and comes into the tent with me. I lay down and he says through thoughts, laying down at the opening of the tent, "*What was that all about? Decided to flirt a little, did you?*"

"*That wasn't flirting, and is there any time you are not involved in what I am doing?*" I turn away from him, trying to get comfortable.

"*I was there before she came. If you want to be alone with her next time, then all right. I just thought you didn't feel that way about her,*" Brian says, looking out of the tent, seeming a little too innocent.

"*You know what I meant, Brian. I am not saying I want alone time with her.*"

"*So, you are telling me you never dream about her? You never think unpure thoughts about her?*"

"*That is none of your business in the first place,*" I snap.

I can tell Brian would be smiling if he were human. "*Fair enough. Good-night, London.*"

"*Goodnight Brian.*" Then I turn over once again, feeling like I can't find a comfortable spot. In truth, I have feelings for Jennifer. I will never act on them, and I wish Brian wouldn't suggest so. It is not something I want to talk about. I am already uneasy about Sara and me. I have no idea what she is going to think about what happened. I am a bit nervous about finding out. Thinking these thoughts, I soon fall into an uneasy sleep. The closest thing to sleep. I find I cannot sleep being a skeleton, just rest.

CHAPTER 20

Revenge

What happened yesterday with that damned and me is not going down the same way today. I am out for blood and he is on my list. Brian and I are ready to finish this and there is nothing that is going to stop us.

The rest of the group is nervous about it. They don't like the fact that I won't regain my flesh first. They know there is nothing they can do to change our minds.

We are all going for the attack. Like last time, Brian and I will be taking out the damned and his pneuma.

Brian and I are in the forest on a hill, starting to watch the battle unfold. As soon as we see them, we will go for the attack as well.

There is a small castle in a clearing far from any trees being too close to it. Surrounding the little castle are a few houses and shops. It is not very well protected here, but maybe they thought the forest would help them with that. The forest is thick all around, making it hard for a very big army to attack.

The battle is taking place in front of the buildings and the castle on a large dirt road. The road is fairly wide, allowing a small army to fight each other out in the open from both sides.

"Are you ready for this, London?" Brian asks. We keep our eyes open looking for the other damned and his pneuma.

"I am ready. I will not lose this time," I say this holding onto the hilt of my sword. This time, I am going to be fighting with Misery. He says that he wants to, so I am giving him that chance.

"Well, if we lose again, then there is no second shot at it. We won't lose though. You are a fighter, London. You and I are here together for a reason. And it sure as hell is not to die from this guy."

We don't say anything else, as we see the damned and his pneuma are now involved in the battle. There are Livefen, Breccan, Jennifer and Sully fighting on our side. Some soldiers who work for the sanctuary have joined us also. The enemy has soldiers fighting with the other damned and pneuma.

Brian and I look at each other and I say, "Let's go set things right."

I jump up from where I am, with Brian following. I pull Misery out as we start to get close. I am dressed in a black cloak and hood. I don't wear armor like the other damned. Being a skeleton, I don't think it would fit well, anyway.

The damned and his pneuma stop fighting when they see us. People clear a path for us, regardless which side they are on. No one wants to be involved in a damned and pneuma fight.

I feel the same horrible fear that I felt last time facing him. This time, I will not let it destroy me. My life depends on it.

"I didn't expect you to come back so soon," he says with a smile, but I can tell he is a little nervous.

People back away from us and watch. The winning side depends on if he or I win. Brian is beside me as a man. I stand ready with Misery in my hand. The other pneuma is a man as well, watching Brian. The other damned watches me, holding his hammer. He is wearing his armor and looks more protected than I am. That doesn't faze me. This time, I am out for blood.

"I am surprised you would come back as a skeleton. Although, this time I am going to kill you either way. We can't keep this fight going forever, even if we are immortal," the other damned says, getting ready for the attack.

"No, we cannot," I agree coldly, as I start to walk toward him.

Brian and the other's pneuma change into spirits and attack each other. The other damned and I swing at each other. The sound of steel on steel rings throughout the land as our weapons collide.

The damned backs up a little, seeing that as much power as he put behind his strike, it didn't faze me.

I don't give him much time to think on it, and I come at him again, swinging my sword surely. He avoids my hits, but each time I am closer to striking him. He backs up as I come at him, still swinging my sword.

Brian and the other pneuma force people to give us more space. Their constant shape-shifting puts everyone at risk of being killed by accident.

The other damned swings his hammer in an overhand swing at me. I move out of the way just in time, quicker than he can expect. I step to the side, then bring Misery down on him, cutting his hand clean off.

He screams as his hand hits the ground, and blood pours from the wound. He grabs his hand with his good one as a look of shock and confusion fills his eyes. I don't give him time to recover or think, and drive Misery through his chest.

I hear his pneuma scream in anger and pain, but it is quickly cut short by Brian. Brian won't let him go to his damned; Brian will not let him get away this time.

The damned falls to the ground. He is still alive, but in pain. I don't find comfort in someone's misery, but he did worse to me. I don't feel sorry for him as he moves around on the ground moaning with pain, as tears fill his eyes, blood covers his hands, and now his chest.

Blood comes pouring from his hand onto the ground and drains out of the wound on his chest. He looks at me, breathing hard. He puts his arm in his cloak to try to stop the bleeding.

Brian gives the pneuma he is fighting a large cut in the stomach. He's bleeding everywhere, unable to fight. He is on the ground, trying to keep himself together.

The damned looks up at me as I look down at him. I feel as cold as ice. Nothing fazes me right now, as I watch them suffer.

"Let us finish this scum. Drive me through his heart!" the sword thinks to me.

Brian stays near the other pneuma, but we both know he isn't going anywhere. Brian watches me as a human, letting me decide how I want to drag this out.

"You should have killed me when given the chance," I say coldly to him. I drive Misery through his chest. He starts to scream something to me, but the blade goes through his heart, killing him.

The pneuma dies as soon as his damned does. I pull Misery out and look around me. Now that I have slain their captain, the soldiers of this kingdom try to get out of here. They no longer feel they can win with him gone. Now they must save themselves.

"Take the soul of the damned, London. It is a nasty business taking the soul from something, but it will be for the better," Brian says through thoughts, walking up to me. We don't have to worry about anyone else trying to fight us, for that is the last thing any of the soldiers here want to do.

"Why?" I ask. I am learning to trust Brian, but I won't just do something unless there is a good cause for it.

"It will make us stronger. Damned do it to gain power. We lack the experience, so we need all the strength we can get."

I nod my head, not really liking the idea. I will do it because I trust Brian. I walk over to the dead body of the damned. I don't really know what I am looking for and am about to say it to Brian, until I hear what sounds like a heartbeat. I don't know how, but I know that sound is his soul.

I extend my hand to try to grab it. I feel it come towards me, as if it is ripping away from the body. I feel the life in my hand. I bring it to me and I feel the soul go through me. I consumed it and now I will gain whatever power he has.

I turn to see Sully. He looks at me, "You are learning quickly."

"I am just glad I finished what I set out to do."

"And you did it well," Sully smiles.

"Now, I think it is about time we set your pneumas free," Brian says to us.

Sully looks happy with those words. After all, the reason he is here is to get his pneuma back.

Amias, Breccan, Livefen, Jennifer, Sully, Brian and I all go inside the small fort. There was a mage here, but he has already been slain. Amias takes the mage's staff, so he can try to set the pneumas free from within it.

The rest of us wait patiently as Amias holds the staff, and speaks in a language I do not understand. The staff is a white long stick, with a large top that almost looks like some strange crown. It is transparent, and inside there are many different colors that move around. I assume those must be pneumas.

Amias says a few last words, then taking the staff, he smashes it on the ground, shattering the top piece of it. The pneumas are set free from it, rising up from the ground and scattering around the room. There are five of them; one goes to Jennifer and another to Sully. The rest leave through open windows, trying to get back to their damned.

Sully and Jennifer look overjoyed to be back with their pneumas. Their pneumas swirl around them and shape-shift into different creatures.

Brian and I keep our distance. I smile, happy that we could reunite them again. I haven't been with Brian that long, but I can understand what it would be like without him. I know that it would feel as if I were missing a part of me.

I would not be whole without him. It is amazing how fast that feeling came, for just a little while ago, I would never have even dreamed of such a thing.

Both of the pneumas take human form, and slowly approach Brian and me.

Sully's pneuma, as I know his name to be Danny, is about as tall as Sully. He wears a dark green cloak. I am surprised to see that he also has a bow. I didn't think the pneumas used weapons very often. He looks a lot like a hunter from the way he dresses. His clothes are camo, his boots look designed to be silent and stealthy. I assume, looking closer at the bow, that it is used for hunting. Maybe he is the reason why Sully is also known as The Hunter. As a spirit form, I see that he is a dark green color. I wonder how powerful green-colored pneumas usually are.

Vixy, which is Jennifer's pneuma, is a dark red color as a spirit. She dresses in a red skirt, and an orange long-sleeved shirt. She has short, bright red hair. That would look unusual for most people, but it looks good on her. She looks a lot like Jennifer. If I didn't know she was her pneuma, one would assume they were sisters. I wonder if Brian and I look very similar, I never thought about it.

Both Vixy and Danny stop near Brian and me, and bow their heads. Then raising them, Danny says, "We are in your debt for saving us. We swear to serve and honor the both of you."

"And the same for me. Although, it looks like Jennifer had plans to serve the both of you regardless," Vixy says with a friendly smile, and a look of joy in her eyes.

"I am just glad we could help," I reply, and bow my head in return.

They return back to Jennifer and Sully.

"I am glad that things went smoothly after all, but there is still something that needs to be done," Livefen says looking at me.

I know what he is talking about, but I will be more than happy to be back. I feel cold as a skeleton. I cannot feel my own heart. I do not breathe, and it is driving me a little crazy. Now that the battle is over, it is starting to weigh heavier on my mind, the state I am in. I seem to notice people's breathing more and the pounding of their hearts. It is frightful to hear it; I don't like it and would be happy not being able to hear them again.

Sully walks over to me and says with a cheerful smile, "I will help you with that, London. We should do it soon. I am sure you are tired of being a walking skeleton."

"You have no idea," I reply, meaning it.

CHAPTER 21

In the flesh

I follow Sully and Danny. They are taking Brian and I to a place where I can regain my flesh. We have left the rest for now. They are back at the king-dom we took over.

We are traveling through the forest. We have gone up and down hills and through meadows, wildflowers dotting the fields. This place is beautiful, since its full spring now. Everything is so lush and green.

Brian and Danny are quickly becoming friends. They run through the meadow together, playing games and shape-shifting all the while. They will come back to check on Sully and I, then go back to their games. They keep close enough that we see them pretty much the whole time. Occasionally, it will feel like there is only Sully and I.

Danny is older than Brian, but I know Brian is the dominant one. They are like people in some ways. Then again, they seem to arrange themselves like animals rather than people. For the pneumas, there always must be a dominant male and female. Brian quickly took the place of being the dominant male, and Danny doesn't fight him for it. Vixy is the dominant female I assume, but she also doesn't have any competition.

People talk about the pneumas being like demons, and how they are from hell itself. Or that they are Satan's offspring. I don't see any of those things in them. If you didn't know them, you would believe these things. When you get to know them like I do, you find they are nothing like that. Watching how they play and communicate with their damned, they are very far from being the offspring of Satan.

"How much farther?" I ask.

"Not much now. We don't have to be in a specific place, but it is better we go here," Sully replies. Sully walks ahead of me, while I follow a few feet behind.

"How do I actually become human?" I look at my skeleton hands, and try to comprehend how the change will be or work.

Sully slows down so we can walk side by side. "You will have to consume souls to become human again. I know you can do it because you did it to the damned yesterday."

"He was not innocent, though. I mostly did it because Brian said I must. I didn't know consuming souls was something I had to do," I say, not liking this. Now I am starting to see why they think the damned come from hell. I am not an evil person, though, and I will not do evil things.

"Well, that is why I am not just taking you anywhere. I am taking you to a prison. That is where I go if I must consume souls. You are a lucky kid to have someone to guide you through this. I had to find out for myself. You will have to consume souls; it's not really a choice. You can choose who though. If you don't, you will start craving them, and feel pain no man can withstand," Sully tells me.

I don't like this piece of information. Who am I to say who is guilty or not? If they are in prison, more than likely they deserve to be there. There is a chance they don't. Do I want to be responsible for their deaths?

"I know it is hard, but we do what we must do. It is a bad prison and everyone there is on death row, anyway," Sully says with a slight smile, trying to lighten the mood.

"I just never thought I would be doing anything like this," I sigh.

"Most of the damned don't know when starting out, unless your parents happen to be damned as well. Even so, there is never a guarantee that you will be one."

"How do people become damned, then, if it is not carried by your parents?"

"Most people don't really know. I guess it is something you will have to ask the pneuma about. Although, you will find there isn't anything private in your life to them, but a lot of their life remains a mystery. I have known Danny for many years now, but I don't know everything about pneumas. I know pneumas can form relationships and have children, but I don't know much about that. We don't know from our pneumas. Brian is young and Danny never settled with a female pneuma. At least not for very long."

"Pneumas sure are strange creatures," I say, watching Brian and Danny play around in the grass.

"No kidding."

"So, when you die as a skeleton that is it then? You are dead, dead?" I ask curious with all that goes on in skeleton farm.

"Yes, you see, a pneuma is actually the soul, while the damned is the spirit."

"I never thought of the spirit and soul being two different things."

"Well, they are. It is easier to see in a damned since our soul is separate from us, but for most, it is harder to explain."

"So, what happens if I don't get souls to feed on?"

"You will lose control of your body. You must have them, if you don't soon, you will lose all since only the craving of souls will be what you want. Being a skeleton, the perks are, you can sense heartbeats and life around you in a whole new way, but you can only be a skeleton for so long, and you don't get any second chances."

I nod, "It defiantly enhances the senses, but I don't think it is worth the cost."

Sully shrugs, "Possibly, but you never know. You have proven today that being in the flesh or bones, you can still defeat your enemy."

I would smile if I could at his words. "Let's just hope I don't have to die and become bones before defeating my enemy every time."

"You will learn, kid," Sully said, placing his hand on my shoulder.

We continue to travel, and soon we are in a town. It is a small town with a little fort, and a wall around it. The people here look poor and hard-working. Their prison is quite big for this little town. Sully tells me that this prison holds many of the county's prisoners, who have done enough bad to be sentenced to death. The prisoners are gathered up all around the county and brought here to be tried. It is a harsh time, and people don't like taking chances, if you are guilty, they believe better to finish it now than wait for another crime to happen.

We stay outside of the town, for I cannot fit in as a skeleton. The four of us will have to wait until nightfall.

I sit on a rock, cleaning my weapons. I have always been good at taking care of my weapons, but these guys will insist if I don't do it enough. The weapons constantly want to fight and be used.

Brian is with me now. He sits nearby, talking to me here and there. He mainly watches the town.

We continue to rest, until night finally closes in. The four of us, with Brian and Danny in their spirit forms, make our way into the prison. Sully knocks out the guards in the front, and we go through.

The prison has about 20 people in here. It is a big prison compared to what I have seen before. There is one walkway down the middle, with cells on both sides where the prisoners are kept.

The prisoners look scared of us, as we go in, shutting the door behind us.

"No one says a word, and we might let some of you live," Brian says coldly, going down the hall as a spirit, checking them out.

I can feel their heartbeats, and they are beating fast. They know why we are here. I do not want to do this, but I need souls. I know it is too great to ignore those needs.

"I will let you do this part yourself, London. I will meet you outside when you are ready," Sully says, and then he and Danny leave.

I look at Brian and he thinks, *"I can help you find the evilest in here. I can read people, and I will know who has sinned the most in their life."*

I nod, appreciating his help. If it weren't for him, I wouldn't know where to start. I just want to do this and get it over with.

Brian slowly goes down the rows and stops at one of them. He stays by the cage for a minute, then thinks, *"This man here."*

I walk over to the cage and see a man standing there watching us. He looks scared and his heart is racing. He knows what his fate is.

I extend my hand and feel his soul. Without touching him, I start to pull it out. The man falls to his knees and stops breathing. His soul is in my hand, and I can feel the heartbeat. It is the heartbeat of life.

"You need two more before we are done," comes Brian's voice in my head. *"You will have to consume more of these souls than if you consumed pure souls."*

I nod and he shows me the next cage. This man is more freaked out in his cell, seeing what I did to the last guy. He starts to cry and begs for me to spare his life. I know he is evil. Brian tells me he is far from an innocent man. His pleading doesn't sway me, and probably only encourages me to carry on my task.

I take his soul, like the last, then collect one last soul. Now that I have what I need, I leave. The guards are still out, so I have no problem leaving undetected. I walk back to the field where Sully is waiting.

"Did what you had to do?" Sully asks me as I get close.

"I got the souls, but I did not consume them yet," I reply.

"No reason to wait."

I have been dreading it, but he is right. The sooner I get it over with, the better. The souls are still in my hands. I put them in my mouth, and I breathe them in.

I fall to my knees as soon as they are in me, severe pain all over my body. I fall to the ground and don't even know what's going on anymore. The pain is intense, and it is the only thing I feel.

"You will be all right, London. This is how you are supposed to feel," Sully says in a soothing voice. I know he is no stranger to it.

Finally, the pain dies. I slowly get up, feeling week and shaky. I smile despite myself, seeing that I am human again.

"How do you feel?" Sully asks, looking at me.

"Human again," I reply with relief in my voice.

Being a human again, I realize how much I missed it. I can feel things again, I can breathe and I feel the beat of my own heart. I didn't like being a skeleton. Things seemed so cold and I did not feel alive. It is a dark feeling that I don't want to feel again.

"Well, I am glad to hear it. We should probably make our way back, unless you would rather make camp somewhere," Sully stands with his hand on his sides as he looks around.

"I would rather make it back." I have no problem traveling in the dark, and I don't want to be near that place anymore.

"Then let us go."

We all start to head back. I walk beside Sully, as Brian does what he wants. He leaves all of us now, including Danny. I don't know what Brian is doing, and probably will not find out.

"You did good tonight, for your first time," Sully says, putting his hand on my shoulder.

"I just hope I don't have to do that again," I reply with a small smile.

"Trust me, kid, this probably will not be your last time. Maybe you have learned something about it, and you will try harder not to die," Sully responds with a smile.

I shake my head. "Don't worry, I think I have learned my lesson."

CHAPTER 22

Home once more

As time passes, Brian and I become closer, and I also really start getting to know the rest. We continue to take over areas that Damon and his pneuma, Talon, control. We are starting to become well known at what we do, and people are starting to know us by name. I don't personally know what to feel about this, but I will do what I do and try not to worry about it.

I never expected anything like this to happen. If anyone had asked me what I would be doing now, not in a million years would I come to a conclusion like this. Life has its ways of changing your plans though.

I am happy, but also a little nervous. I will be able to visit my mom, John, Sara and the rest of my family. I am a little nervous because they may have heard what has become of me. They need to know, but I would rather I break it to them, than them find it out any other way.

We are in the forest. Our camp is cleared out, so there is only dirt where we set up our tents. There is a stream right by our camp, which we are taking advantage of. It is not every day we have running water on hand. So, we have been taking turns washing up and cleaning our things.

I am sitting around the fire with Sully, Breccan, Amias, Livefen and Jennifer, along with our pneumas Brian, Danny and Vixy.

Usually, the pneumas will hang out with each other away from us when they are not with their damned. Tonight, though, they are with us as humans. I sit next to Jennifer, while Vixy sits nearby on the other side of her. Brian sits on my right, but he isn't very close to me.

We are eating our dinner and just hanging out. It is nice being able to do this. We work all the time with each other, but don't have much time to sit back and really get to know more about each other.

So far, I like all of them. Even Livefen isn't awful once you get to know him. I am probably becoming closest with Jennifer and Sully, but I think I am beginning to make friends with the rest as well. Breccan is one of the best fighters and is a good man who loves to tell a joke when he can. Amias is not the most talkative person I know, but he is smart and trustworthy. Livefen isn't as bad as he was when I first met him, and shows he has a good personality when he wants to. But I can't trust him. Brian really doesn't trust him either, and I must go with Brian on this one. It feels like he is hiding something.

I am really beginning to like Sully. He has been helping me a lot, and he is always there to lend a hand if I need one. He has probably helped me out the most when it comes to learning how to be one of the damned. Every mission I do, he is there to help, and I know I can trust him. I see Sully and me staying friends for a long time. And I am glad to have someone like him here.

Jennifer is the person I am the closest to. We get along extremely well, like we have known each other for years. She is a bright spot in my life, having to go through what I do. She seems to understand me, and I never have to explain myself to her. Like she said she would, she makes sure to always be there. She says she is my bodyguard and she takes that job very seriously. I know if she is around, I don't have much to fear, because I know she has my back. I really like Jennifer and admire her. Not too many women where I come from are as strong as her. Most women from the Sonara Plains do not fight, in fact it's pretty much unheard of. Although I believe it's a mistake on the kingdoms part.

"Well," Amias said to get all our attention. "We have been doing good recently, and I am sure we really have done some damage to Damon. But we promised you, London, that you could visit your family before we continue farther. When you come back, though, we are going to have to start going into more dangerous territories."

"I think we are ready for that," Brian states.

I have noticed that Brian will never say he can't do something; he never wants to look weak in someone else's eyes. He always wants to be the top man, the one who answers to no one. He obviously makes an impression because Vixy and Danny seem to respect that.

"I think we are too," I said, meaning it. The last camps we have taken out went very well. There is never such a thing as being too ready, but I don't see why we are not in good shape.

"That's good. I guess we can expect a lot when you guys come back then," Livefen says, rising from his seat with us near the fire.

"I already thought we were doing quite the job," Brian smiles.

"Of course, but there is worse to come," Livefen responds like he doesn't have the time to talk to Brian. Livefen hates Brian just as much as Brian hates him, I am sure.

"Well, I will be going to bed now, the rest of you have a good night," Amias gets up, drinking the last bit of his coffee.

Many of us start to turn in after Amias, except Jennifer, Vixy, Brian and me. We stay siting around the fire, talking.

"So, excited about visiting home?" Jennifer asks me.

I smile, not able to help it. I can't wait to see people back at home again. I just hope they are as happy to see me.

"Yes, I am very happy to be visiting them. I am a bit nervous though. I will have to tell them the truth about who I am unless they already know, then I will have to see what the outcome is," I watch Jennifer as I speak.

"Well if they truly love you, then they won't care what you are. It shouldn't matter to them if you are a damned or not."

"Where I came from, though, we have always believed the damned were just people in myths or legends. And they were always seen as something from hell."

"I know what you mean. A lot of people think that. Where I came from people knew they existed, but they also believed they came from hell," Jennifer stares at the fire as she speaks. I have the feeling that people didn't treat her very well when they found out what she was.

I smile and gently place my hand on hers, in a sign of friendship. "And it is amazing how wrong they are. Some of the nicest people I know are damned."

Jennifer smiles slightly, "I never thought of myself being that nice of a person. I kill people for a living."

"A lot of people do. I know you have a big heart, though, and you are very caring."

"You seem to know a lot about me," she says with a half-smile, and the attitude that I am full of shit.

"I am telling you the truth when I say it. I don't say things just because." I drink some more of my coffee.

Jennifer stares into the fire again with a slight smile and puts her hands together gently, "I guess you are right. I believe what you say, even if I am not sure about it."

"Well, don't doubt me. I promise I don't tell lies." She looks back at me, that pretty smile of hers still on her face.

Brian and Vixy talk a short distance from us. I bet he is trying to flirt with her again. Since they met, he is constantly trying to get on her nerves or flirt up a storm with her. She is no easy woman though. She is extremely sassy and can be harsh to him sometimes, although he probably deserves all that she gives him.

"I am glad to see Brian getting along with Vixy so well," Jennifer says, looking over at them.

"Yeah, Brian doesn't know when enough is enough."

"I guess not."

There is a pause. We both glance around until finally Jennifer breaks the silence. Taking a deep breath, she says, "Sara is lucky to have a man like you."

"I don't know. We weren't married very long before I left to do this," I reply, still not meeting her eyes. From where I stand, Sara is very unlucky to have me. I am nothing like she thought I was, what even I thought I was.

"Maybe, but that doesn't make you any less of a man. Well, goodnight, London. Sleep well," Jennifer gets up.

"Goodnight, Jennifer," I watch her as she and Vixy go to their tent.

Brian moves to sit beside me. After a few minutes, he thinks, *"That Vixy sure is a stubborn one."*

"Maybe you should give up," I suggest, taking another sip of coffee from my cup.

"All pneuma women play difficult, but I know she likes it. You know that Jennifer really admires you, although I do not know why." Brian throws a small branch into the fire, as he telepaths to me.

"She is a good woman. I am glad that I am able to be friends with her," I think, with a slight smile.

"Yes, it is good we are friends with her. We have a lot of enemies; we need people like her. Well, we should probably get our sleep. We will be heading out early tomorrow."

"All right. I will just finish my coffee first." I take another sip, trying to finish quickly.

Brian and I stay by the fire, talking about all sorts of things while I finish my drink.

It is strange, for I feel like Brian is my best friend, a brother, someone I have known forever, but I found out only a couple of months ago he even existed. I guess that is just the way having a pneuma works though. Brian knows all about me, so I am sure it feels even more that way for him.

We finally turn in for the night after I finish my coffee.

CHAPTER 23

Paying the Price

Brian

I worry about London. Word has spread far and wide about us, and I don't think London is going to like what he finds. His country hates what we are or refuses to believe we even exist. I hate to tell him, but I don't think Sara is going to be the loving wife he thinks he is going home to.

I don't know everything, but I know his marriage to Sara isn't going to last. She is a woman just for show. A prize to be won, nothing else. Her looks are deceiving and she is no woman for London. If she knows who he is, she will not take him.

I don't know about the rest of London's family. I think John, his friend, will accept him. They were practically brothers growing up. I think it is going to take a lot more than London being a damned to break their friendship.

London has been close to his grandfather, who has been like a father to him, for all of his life. To me, though, his grandfather seems to do things because that's how he wants them, not because it might be best for London or because that's what London really wants. I think his grandfather likes London so much is because London is the only grandson he has. He has put all of his hopes and dreams into London, and he wouldn't do that for a granddaughter. He does have a son, but his son committed some sort of crime when he was younger, keeping him from moving any higher up the rank. That leaves only London to be the one he has put all of his dreams into.

London doesn't have the best family in the world, but at least he has his mother. His mother will love him no matter what London is or does. I know that London has a very close relationship with her, and it is going to do him good now. He will need someone like her for what he is more than likely going to face.

Only London and I will be making this trip, which is probably for the best. I don't know for sure how things are going to go, but I think even London is a bit nervous about everything.

I will not tell London what I think, because if I am wrong, I don't want to put those thoughts into his head. And besides, I think he is already aware that things could go very wrong on this trip.

Everyone pays a price for what they do. The damned often pay the biggest price in return for immortality. London will find that being who he is; it means that he will have more enemies than friends wherever he goes. There is no such place as home for us. I will never turn on him, though, and will be there regardless of what he faces. We must live together, and at the end we will die together.

CHAPTER 24

Never again

London

I ride up the green slopes of my old homeland on a horse. I follow the dirt trail that will lead me into town. I am sure Sara and the rest of my family will be at the castle. It is my grandfather's after all, and they know I am coming home. I have sent a letter a couple of days prior to this.

Brian rides on a horse near me. It is best that he stays a human and does not change while we're here. He rides a horse to fit in more.

So far, Brian has been quiet on this trip, making me nervous. It is never very good when Brian is too quiet. Maybe he knows something I don't. If he does, I wish he would speak up because he isn't making me feel too well. I am already a little nervous to see my family and friends; he doesn't have to be so silent, making it worse.

"Are you tired of riding?" I ask, trying to start a conversation. Never having ridden a horse before, I assume he doesn't like it very much. He can travel a lot faster than any horse can in his spirit farm.

"It is all right, but I will be happy to get rid of it. I don't need a horse or any other creature," Brian replies.

"Well, in a little bit here we should be in the castle and be done riding them," I try to act cheery, even though I don't feel like it. But with Brian sounding like he doesn't really care to talk; it isn't working too well.

"You have been nervous these past two days. What do you think will happen when we make it there?" Brian asks, not looking at me or betraying anything he might feel about it.

I notice he doesn't hold anything back. I think we both know why I am nervous. I love my family, all my cousins, my uncle, aunt, my great grandparents, grandfather and my friend John. There are also lots of other people I know and care about here. At least I know my mother will be there for me though. She already knows who I am, and I don't think anything could make her not love me.

"I don't know. I hope for the best, but life usually gives you the opposite of what you want, Brian. What do you think? Do you think I will be tossed out? Forgotten?" I ask, worried about what he is going to say.

"I don't know; the only thing we can do is find out. Remember this though, London, you are who you are supposed to be now. Before this, you were in a life that wasn't you. A damned is what you were always meant to be, and life didn't change that," Brian says, finally meeting my eyes.

I guess Brian is right. I have always been a damned, even when I didn't know it. It is hard, but I will finally learn the truth about the people I love. Either they will love me or I will be met by how they really felt the whole time. I just wish it didn't have to come like this.

Brian and I enter the city, and as soon as we do, I find the worst that could be expected. As Brian and I walk down the streets, there are no smiles, no greetings, just looks of disgust and fright. All these people I have known since I was a child, now look at me with hate and fear. They know what I am, and they don't like it.

I feel my heart sink, and I try not to catch people's eyes. I feel dirty, unwanted; like I have done something terribly wrong. Brian seems to ignore them all, as we pass them. Nothing ever seems to faze him though, and he doesn't know these people like I do. He didn't grow up with them.

As we approach the castle, I don't feel much better; everyone seems to look at us. We are getting the feeling that we are not wanted here. Looking ahead at the castle door, I see my mother and John. I smile despite myself.

I get off my horse when I am close enough and walk up the steps to the both of them. Looking at my mother I see the sadness in her eyes, but she smiles as she sees me and calls, "London."

We embrace each other, and I whisper to her, "I missed you."

"I have missed you too. How are you doing?" she asks, pulling away a little from me.

Brian comes up the steps and stands a few feet behind me. He doesn't know these people like I do. He will give me my space, but he doesn't want to be with the rest of the others either.

My mother and I try to pretend that things are normal. But we know everyone around us is watching. No one wants me here, and they make that more than obvious.

"I'm doing okay, mom," I say, trying to pull off the best smile I can.

I look at John and I let go of my mother to walk to him. John tries to give me a smile, but I know it is hard for him too.

We both stand there at first, until John finally breaks the awkwardness, "It's good to see you again, London." We both embrace when he says it and then let each other go.

"It is nice to see you. How have things been going?" I ask.

"They have been all right," John says, trying to sound friendly. He is uncomfortable though. So am I, but I am trying not to let the atmosphere of the town get to me.

"Where is Sara and Grandfather?" I ask, looking around.

"Grandfather and your uncle are on a hunt; they will be back soon. Sara is in your old room in the castle," my mother answers. I see in her eyes though, that what I will find I am not going to like.

I swallow hard, getting ready to expect the worst.

"I am going to go say hello to her." I start to walk to the doors of the castle, with a heavy heart.

Before I can walk through the door, though, John grabs my arm.

I look at him and he says in a low sympathetic tone of voice, "London, I have to warn you…"

He clears his throat and I know he doesn't want to tell me.

I don't let him continue; I take a deep breath, and place my hand on his arm.

"I understand, John. But I need to see her."

John nods and lets me go. My mother grabs my hand tightly, and I grab hers. My heart is heavy and my mouth is dry. She gently lets me go and I walk through the door. Brian follows me in.

We walk a little down the hall, being the only ones in here. I stop feeling weak, and don't want to walk up the stairs and through the doors to Sara because I know only heartbreak is there.

Brian walks up to me. He stands beside me, then thinks to me, "*I will be waiting here for you. If you need me just say my name and I will be there. Good luck, London.*"

I nod and reply, "*Thanks.*"

I start to walk up the stairs and go to the room, where I know she will be. I stop at the door and take another deep breath. I love Sara. We haven't been married for long, and I don't know her as well as I could. But I do love her. Ever since I was younger, she has been my dream girl. When we were fourteen, she came to this little place for a while, to get some extra tutoring. When she came here, it was the best thing that ever happened to me. We have always known each other, so her being here was everything I wanted. We would spend long hours together. After a while of her being here, I remember her daring me to kiss her under the huge oak tree out in the castle's apple orchard. I remember before I kissed her, I was so nervous I thought I was going to pass out. After that we had kind of a secret romance thing going on until she had to leave. And from that day forward I knew I had to have her. So, when I found out we could get married, it felt like a dream come true.

Dreams don't last though. I know that it is not going to be a happy reunion. I am going to have to be strong and accept whatever happens.

I open the door and walk through the room. Sara looks at me as I come through the door. We both look at each other. I see she has all her things packed.

I feel my heart sink even lower seeing this, and a lump in my throat. It is true then; she wants to leave.

Neither of us knows what to say. I see she has sadness in her eyes, but they are also cold. She is angry with me, and it is not even my fault. I didn't choose to be a damned, that is just who I am.

"How come you never told me?" Sara asks bitterly, sounding cold and distant.

"I didn't know I was. Sara, look—just because I am a da-"

But she cuts me off before I can finish, "I am sorry, London, but I can't live with one of them."

I am filled with grief, but I feel anger as well now. None of us planned for this, it is not like I did it because that is what I chose to do.

"I am not what people say I am. I love you, Sara, and you are my wife. I thought we were supposed to stay together through all the ups and downs in life," I said, trying my best to reason with her.

"I am not your wife anymore, London. Death do us part, and I am afraid you have died. So, I am no longer your wife, and you are no longer my husband. I leave today, London. I am just here to say goodbye. So…goodbye London," she says, with tears in her eyes, but her voice remains just as cold.

I am not going to beg; I will not make her stay. She does what she wants. If she can't love me, then there is nothing I can do. So, I just stand where I am, feeling like I am in a nightmare where everything I knew and loved is being torn from me.

I look at Sara and reply, "Goodbye, then."

She grabs her things and starts to walk out.

She stops as she gets close to me and tearfully now says, "I am sorry, London. I just can't stay with you." Then she kisses me.

Her kiss doesn't make me feel any better, but worse as I feel her tears on my face. She pulls away from me, then she places her wedding ring in my hand and leaves without saying another word.

I watch her leave, feeling heartbroken. I feel numb. Can this really be happening? I sit down on the bed and put my hand on my face. I have tears in my eyes but I won't cry.

Brian was right; he knew this would happen to me. I can't blame him for anything though; it is not like this is what he wanted to have happen to me.

I put my hands together and think with a heavy heart. I wish I could have done better. I feel like I failed as a husband, but was that really my fault? I think the truth is, Sara really didn't love me that much.

I hear a knock on the door, and then John opens it.

We each exchange looks and he says, "London, your grandfather is here, and he wants to see you."

I get up, feeling like I must pull myself together. I am not ready for my grandpa, either. Grandpa is the man I have always looked up to, the man who has been pretty much my father for all these years. Will he betray me too? Will he look at me as the townspeople do? I don't know if I can take that.

I walk out the door and John follows right beside me.

First, there is only silence between us; then he starts, "London, I want you to know, I don't care what you are or who you become. We have been friends ever since we were kids, and I will always remain your friend. I will never treat you how this town is treating you. And I want you to know that if there is anything you ever need; I am here for you. For I am one friend that will never turn his back on you."

I smile looking at John, "Well, I am glad to see I will always have a friend here."

John puts his arm around my shoulders as we walk, "Well, after you are done talking to your grandfather, do you want to get a couple of drinks? We haven't done that in a while; I am sure that old bar is missing us."

"Do you think they will want me back?" I ask.

"Those guys are always so drunk in there, a horse on two legs would be able to buy a beer, and they wouldn't notice anything different."

I laugh a little despite myself, "I guess you are right."

We stop when we get to my grandfather's door. We each exchange looks once again and John sighs, feeling nervous for me.

"Good luck, London. Just remember it doesn't matter what people say you are. You are a good man, and I know that wouldn't change just because you became a damned."

"Thanks, John. You are a good friend and I don't know what I did to deserve you."

"Hey, I know you would do the same for me. Just hang in there," he says, then grabbing my shoulder, he walks away.

I take a deep breath, then knock on the door. I hear my grandfather's voice from inside ask, "Who is it?"

"It is London."

There is a pause, then I hear him say, "Come in."

I go through the door and my grandfather has his back turned towards me, looking at the large window that overlooks the town. I stand there after entering the room, feeling uneasy and not sure what to do.

It is a large room, with books lining most of the shelves, and a large disk towards the window. There is a large stone fireplace that adds most of the light to the room and the warmth.

"You can sit down, London; there is a drink on the table for you," my grandfather says, not bothering to look at me.

"That is all right, I prefer to stand," I reply. But I do take the drink. My grandfather finds things easier to say as long as he has a drink with him.

"I wish your mother could have told me. My own daughter wouldn't even tell me what man she had a child with," I hear his voice sounding weak like he is about to cry.

I feel a lump in my throat upon hearing his voice. He is a strong man, and I have never seen him cry. To know this subject is almost bringing him to tears tells me how emotionally torn he is about this. I don't know what to say. It wasn't right for my mother to do that, but I am sure she had her reasons.

"Maybe she was afraid of this," I say, sounding as upset as he is. What would really change if he knew this was a possibility, anyway? No one planned for me to be a damned as far as I know.

"Well, at least we would have known this could have happened." My grandfather now turns to face me.

I shrug my shoulders, "No one could have guessed."

"There is a way to get you back again, London. I heard there is a way to get rid of your pneuma without you dying." My grandfather steps closer to me as he says it.

I will not do it though. Brian is right, I have been a damned all my life; I just didn't know it. And if I could be normal again, what good would come from that? Now that I see how the town treats me, I don't think I want anything more to do with them either.

"No, I cannot do that. Look, I am sorry things didn't turn out the way you planned, but there is nothing we can do about that now. I will not give up my pneuma, even if that means I will stay a damned forever. I am who I am, and nothing is going to change that." I look my grandfather in the eyes when I say this. I love him and I don't want to lose him, but I can't do something if my heart isn't in it.

"But, London, you could have a chance to get your life back," my grandfather protests, sounding more desperate now.

"No, I am a damned, and that is how it's going to stay. If I come back, what am I getting, anyway? Sara doesn't love me, and I wouldn't want her back if the only way she would love me is to be something I am not. I wouldn't do it for the town because they betrayed me as well. My mother understands. And I hope you will too, grandfather," I start talking with some anger, but I end it being calmer. I don't want to fight him about this; I already have enough killing me as it already is, with Sara leaving me, and the town hating me.

"But, London, everything you have worked for and done; do you want that all to be in vain?" He asks me like he cannot understand why I don't get it.

"I don't think it was all in vain, but if that is how you want to look at it, I guess so. The only thing I want, Grandfather, is for you to be there for me, regardless of what I choose. I want to make you proud, but I also have to do what I feel is right."

My grandfather sighs, then takes a gulp of his drink before answering. "London, I am not happy about all of this, but you are my grandson and I could never disown you. I feel like I have made a mistake with my daughter, I have never been that close to her. But I will not make that same mistake twice. I am not happy about this, London, but I love you and that will never change."

I smile despite how I am feeling right now. I know he isn't that happy with me, but he will not toss me out because I am a damned. It is more than I can ask for.

"Thank you for the drink," I say, placing the now empty glass on the table.

My grandfather watches me. "How long will you be staying?"

"Not for long." There is a lot to do, back with the rest. Besides, seeing how this place is, I would feel strange staying too long, anyway.

My grandfather tries to give me a smile, and we both give each other a hug. I know things are going to be different between us, but I hope not too much. I know he isn't happy with my decision, but I cannot do anything else.

As we let each other go, my grandfather says, "You should probably get your rest, London. I am sure you had a long day and need it."

I nod, thinking he has no idea. This pain in my heart is killing me, and I need some time to get away from all this. There is a lot to think about, and a lot to say goodbye to.

CHAPTER 25

Moving on

I sit at a table with my mother sitting by me. Brian stays at my feet as a fox. He stays with me, but when he doesn't want to be noticed or talk, he usually takes the form of an animal. I guess that is his way of giving me space. We are in my room. The room is warm and lit by a few candles, but I feel cold.

My mother and I are having a couple of drinks as I try to work through all that has happened. John still loves me, my grandfather accepts me, but I know things will never be the same between him and me. Sara left me, the town hates me and my uncle and his family lost respect for me. When I talked to them, I can see in their eyes they no longer trust me.

I lay my head on my hands on the table. I drank quite a bit and don't feel well. My mother drinks some, but she holds her liquor better than any other woman I know.

"Where do I go from here?" I sigh.

"You will finish what you set out to do," my mother replies. She doesn't sound comforting but harsh. My mother loves me, but it has always been tough love. She doesn't do much sympathy unless she truly feels it is needed. I don't mind this, though. By raising me by herself, I think she feels she needs to do this. And it probably helped me become a better man. I feel lost now, not sure where to go or who I am anymore.

I put my hands down and look at her. "I know."

It is still the same night when I arrived at the castle, or should I say morning. It is about 1:30 a.m. now. My mother has always been a night owl, so she does not mind staying up late.

"London, I know it is hard to believe, but you will find living like a damned is what you truly want and love," my mother says, holding my hand.

I look at her, wondering to myself if that true or not. It is not like I truly enjoyed the life I had, but it wasn't a bad one. Maybe this one will be better. It is something I don't think I could ever get tired of.

"You belong with the damned. And you will be happy knowing you belong somewhere. London, I have never told you this, but I am a type of witch. The genes of a witch always stay strong in a generation, unless they are watered down enough. Your great grandmother was one. I never belong anywhere because of this. And I was afraid, London, that something like this would happen to you. That is why I let your grandfather take you under his wing, and help raise you to become what he thinks you should be. I was hoping that no matter what, you would have a good life, but now you can have one being a damned."

I smile despite how I am feeling. My mother would do anything for me, and I feel someday I will pay her back for all she has done for me. I do want to know more though. Even though she is my mother, there are a lot of secrets I don't know about, concerning her, and my…father.

"Where is my father now?" I ask.

"I believe he is with other damned, but I am not sure where."

"Do you still love him?" I ask, knowing I am crossing into an area that is more than likely sensitive for her. I don't want to ask her this, but I do feel it is my right to since he is my father.

"That's complicated. You are his son, just as much as you are mine. It is not something I can explain very well. Those are feelings I keep to myself."

"Do you think he ever wanted to see me?" I don't know why I am even asking these questions. I guess because I am already hurt and depressed, so I am just saying what I want to, not caring if I get the answers or not.

"Yes, I am sure. Now, London, we should probably turn in, it is growing late even for me. Try not to worry yourself anymore. I promise things will start looking up for you soon." Then she kisses me on the head.

"Good night, Mother," I reply, giving her a weak smile.

She gives me a smile in return. "Good night, London."

She starts to walk away, but before she can get far, I say, "Sorry, talking about my father like that. I am sure it hurts."

"It is okay, London. You have every right to know. I should have told you more about him a long time ago. I promise I will tell you everything I know soon enough; I just need time to say it."

"I understand. I love you."

"I love you too, London."

Then she leaves Brian and me.

I sit straight in my chair, realizing that I am getting tired now. I drink the last bit of what was in my glass and set it back down on the table, upside down.

Brian gets up from lying by my feet and turns into a human. I look at him as he sits down in the chair facing me. Brian helps himself to a drink and then says, "Your mother is a smart woman, London."

"I know." There is a pause. Then I continue, "I will be better tomorrow."

He probably is a little annoyed with me. We have a lot to do and many more people to fight, and I don't look much like a fighter right now. But I am not made of stone; I can't ignore how I feel.

"At least once in their life everyone goes through something like you are. And what is so bad about getting drunk occasionally? It won't help your problems, but you can pretend. Someday, London, you and I will be known all throughout the lands for what we are going to do," Brian says, pouring himself another glass.

"What are we going to be known for, then?" I'm a little intrigued now. I know Brian has plans, but he never really cares to tell me about them.

"We are going to be known for changing the world, and how the damned and their pneumas live in it. Look at them, London, they are not living the life right now. No one likes them, and today you experienced that first-hand. Wouldn't you like a place where you can be what you are, without people looking down at you for it?"

"Well, I am sure all the damned want that."

"Well then, what do you think? Do you think you can and will be able to change things, or is that something you just don't have in you?" Brian asks this looking at me in the eyes.

I take a deep breath thinking about it. Why not? If a damned I am, then I should be the best damned I can be. And if I am supposed to be one of the most powerful ones, having a black pneuma, then that is what I should be. I see how these people treat me here. The people I once cared about and considered a part of my home. Why should other damned have to suffer like me?

I take a deep breath and start, "I don't think I know. Maybe you are right, Brian, maybe you are wrong. But from now on, I am going to be a different person. I have entered a new life being a damned, and it is time I owned it."

Brian gives a slight smile, "And I am sure you will."

CHAPTER 26

Adapting

"*This fight will be quick and easy,*" Misery says in my head.

I take a deep breath looking ahead of me. I haven't fought too much more damned, after the first one, but today I will be fighting another one. I am ready, though.

We are out in the middle of an open field. I have been back with the rest for two weeks now and have been pushing all those sad thoughts of what has happened to me aside. I have grown numb to those feelings, and only now try to do my best and take out this damned, Damon, and his followers.

It isn't easy trying to ignore what happened back at home. I keep waking up in the morning, thinking it's all a bad dream, that it didn't happen and I could go back and it would all be different. I guess I still haven't accepted what really happened to me yet, I just wonder when I will. And when I do, will I feel some new kind of pain? I just don't know what to think about the matter of home anymore.

The damned and pneuma I am fighting now are a little unexpected. He just showed up and wished to fight with me. Normally, when the damned fight, everyone else seems to stay back. Sully and Jennifer now have their pneumas back and could fight another damned as well, but they normally leave that part up to me. Plus, the damned we have been fighting are hard to beat, and they believe I am the one most suited for the job.

The field is in somewhat of a slope. I am at the higher end, while he is towards the bottom. There is a pond nearby at the bottom of the slope. It is dawn and the first birds are starting to sing their songs. It seems too peaceful for what is about to go down between us and this stranger here outside.

The rest don't know about this, for I was taking a walk, and this damned showed up. I know he is an enemy from the start, he makes that quite clear. I believe he wants to kill me, and then brings that news to Damon himself. He wants to come higher up the ranks and thinks he can do that taking me out. Although, I believe he is mistaken.

Brian is beside me as a human. He looks at the damned and his pneuma like they are not worth the effort. Brian is good at making people feel like they are not worth much. He is too honest sometimes, and he never holds back from saying what he thinks.

"So, London, the boy who has grown a name overnight. It will be an honor killing you," the damned says, pulling out a carved small sword. His sword is a bright red color, catching the light from the early sun, as he pulls it out of its sheath.

"I expected more," Brian says, sounding uninterested watching him. "Either the damned for Damon are the weaker damned, or we are just getting the weaker ones."

I normally don't like to judge how good someone is at fighting until I get into it, but in this case, it is a little different. From the way he holds his blade and his nervousness he feels even though he tries not to show it, gives him away. He looks muscular and powerful and that's usually how he probably wins his fights. He uses strength and speed to knock his opponents out quickly; I don't think he is accustomed to a good sword fighter. I do believe I am above average.

I smile at Brian's last comment, without any humor, "Who knows, let's just finish this. Can't keep them waiting."

The damned and his pneuma are waiting for us to make the first move. So, we might as well give it to him.

We walk down the hill. I hold Misery in my right hand, keeping it low. Brian turns into his spirit as he follows beside me, keeping his attention focused on the other pneuma.

The pneumas go at it first like they normally do. They shape-shift into some sort of creature and fight with each other.

I swing first at the damned, and he is barely able to avoid the hit, moving out of the way just in time.

I stand where I am watching him. He looks at me, trying to figure out what my next move is going to be. I will let him try the second strike.

His pneuma is a rusty red-colored one, which means he is a powerful damned. Any color could be, but the red are known for it. It is most common for the damned to have any shade of red, but showing how powerful the magic could potentially depend on the color of the red. All red-colored pneumas are powerful but the lighter the red, the more power they use from light magic, a darker red means they use more magic from dark magic. Although from what I have been told, often the darker ones are the more dangerous ones. This is how it works for most colored pneumas, although some are only light and some are only dark. For example, purple pneumas are on the darker side of magic, while yellow pneumas are on the brighter side. Gray pneumas are the only ones who are completely down the middle between both magics, while black are pure dark magic and whites are all light magic.

The damned comes at me swinging his sword. I block it with Misery and kick him back. I can see he is getting a little nervous now. He isn't much of a match for me, and he is quickly learning it. He has the disadvantage of being on lower ground then I do, but either way his odds don't look good.

I am quickly done with playing this game. I come for him, swinging Misery at him over and over again, in quick snake-like swings and strikes, keeping them small but fast, so all he can do is try and avoid the blows. He keeps trying to avoid the hits with his own weapons, but every time he does a little worse, and I know he can't avoid them for much longer.

Finally, I can land a hit, and I stab Misery through his chest. The damned falls to his knees, dropping his sword. His pneuma screams and I jump back quickly as Brian tells me to. But it isn't good enough, for the pneuma grabs me, knocking me down as he digs his claws into me. It is half-spirit, but he uses long arms with claws to try to take me out.

I try to get away, but he drags me closer and tries to tear into me. I dropped Misery when I hit the ground. I try to grab the hands, as he attempts to tear my flesh with them.

Brian grabs him as the creature that he shifted into once when we were practicing in the arena together. The pneuma is forced to fight Brian now as Brian tears into him.

The pneuma turns into the same thing Brian is and tries to bite him but Brian grabs ahold of his neck, with his powerful jaws. The pneuma tries to put up a hell of a fight. But Brian breaks his neck twisting it far enough, with a crack.

Brian lets him go as soon as he does, turning back into a human. The other pneuma does, too, but lays there, not moving. Brian has blood all over him, some his own but most of it being from the other pneuma.

I get up. I have some cuts on my arms and a few on my face from that pneuma, but I am okay. My heart is beating so fast I can hear it in my ears, and I am a little shaky. I didn't expect that pneuma to come after me like that. If pneumas expect that their damned is in trouble, they become crazy, and that is when you have to be most careful. They will do crazy things to ensure the survival of their damned, but in this case, it wasn't enough for these two.

I walk over to the damned, who lays there dead now, but I can still take his soul. I catch his soul in my hand and consume it.

"Sorry about the pneuma coming after you like that. He was stronger than I expected," Brian comes over to me.

I walk over to the pond and start to wash my hands. "Don't worry about it. I am still here."

Before this fight, this would have been a big deal to me, but I am starting to adapt to such things. This won't be the last time I fight like this, might as well get used to it. It's because I have finally accepted what I am and what I must do.

"They didn't put up much of a fight, did they?" Brian says, looking at their lifeless bodies.

"Not really. I expected a better performance. I think this damned was working on his own though. He probably thought killing us would be a stepping stone for him, so he would be able to become someone in Damon's eyes."

"It sounds like something, some would do. Now it looks like we have company," Brian changes the conversation to thoughts.

I stand up from the pond. Looking where Brian is looking, I see Livefen walking toward us.

"I wonder what he wants," Brian doesn't sound too thrilled about seeing the elf.

"Well, I think we are about to find out." I am better at talking through thoughts now, but I could be better. If someone were to watch me, they would notice my lips were moving, but I don't make it obvious.

"It looks like he didn't stand much of a chance," Livefen says, as his greeting, stopping short of us. He looks at the two that we killed, then turns his gaze back to me.

"What do you want this morning? Have another thing you want us to do?" Brian asks none too friendly.

Figures that Brian would start out that way. Livefen seems used to it by now though.

"I don't want anything. I just noticed the fight you guys had. Many of the other damned don't seem to stand much of a chance anymore."

"I suppose," I reply.

Livefen nods his head like he is thinking and then continues, "Food is done at the camp. I will expect to see you guys there soon."

"Soon enough," Brian sounds a bit happier that the elf will be leaving. Livefen turns after saying this and walks back up the hill.

"*He tries to talk to us, but none of us like each other,*" Brian thinks, once Livefen is gone.

"*Yeah. I don't like the way he looked though; I think he is planning something.*"

"*Well if he is, then we will find out soon enough. Now let's get breakfast.*"

"*Sounds good to me.*"

Then the both of us make our way back to camp.

CHAPTER 27

Jennifer and I

I am sitting out in one of these pretty meadows, with wildflowers all around in the tall green grass. This will be the last time we camp out in this sort of scenery for a while. We are going to be attacking one of the damned, one who is very well known on Damon's side.

Brian is around me, jumping around in the meadow as a fox. Anything he turns into always has a black coat. After he jumps around for a while, he comes back to me, turning into his spirit form.

I am sharpening my weapons as I sit in the grass. Right now, I am sharpening Bone Crusher. It is bright and beautiful today. The sky is clear with a few puffy white clouds here and there. Brian is low to the ground. I think he would be lying down if he was anything else, but as a mist, you wouldn't be able to tell.

"How does it feel to be a spirit like that?" I ask, looking at him from my work.

"I don't think I could describe it to you. I guess it is almost like being in water, but freer," Brian replies.

"Did you have to consume the soul of a human to become one? I know you had to for all the other animals you can turn into."

"*No, a human is one thing I am able to turn into before anything else. It is more a part of me than any of my other forms.*"

I nod my head, thinking. I wonder if it annoys him that I ask all these questions. I don't think so, but you never know about Brian.

"*Now what about you and Jennifer? You know she likes you, so when do you plan to put a move on her?*" Brian asks, always getting straight to the point. He seems to forget that it was only a month ago that Sara left me.

I guess I have to answer him since he has been answering my questions. I put Bone Crusher back in its holster, then think to him, "*Jennifer is quite the woman, but I don't know when I would put moves on her like you say. You know I did about a month ago just lose my marriage.*"

"*True, but what quicker way to recover than having another woman's company?*"

"*I wouldn't want to use her just as a way to recover from the last woman I had. I think you are a little woman- crazy.*"

"*Maybe, or maybe I am just being realistic. A lot of woman are just there to break men's hearts. So why stress over one woman so bad?*"

"*I am not stressing over any woman; I am just recovering from Sara leaving me. Maybe she is a bad woman. She sure as hell didn't care about me as much as I cared about her, but it still takes time to heal from something like that.*"

"*I suppose so,*" says Brian, "*but the sooner you get over it, the better.*"

"*I know, and I will.*" I reply with more conviction than I feel. "*What about you and Vixy? You don't seem to leave that girl alone.*"

"*She is being stubborn, but she will give in. She likes me, but she would rather not admit it.*"

"*I think a lot of women like to do that. Anything they can do to keep the game going.*" I pick a flower beside me and admire its bright blue, as I speak to Brian through thoughts. Something as simple as this flower makes life worth living.

"*But that's what makes it interesting, right?*" Brian continues. "*Now besides talking about women, I think there are more important things to talk about.*"

I take a deep breath, thinking about where to begin. There is a lot that needs to be done, and I am nervous about fighting this new damned. He has a golden pneuma, and I heard he is known for being a hell of a fighter. What makes me most nervous is that too many people are mixed into this whole thing. People like Sully don't think I am ready for it yet. Then there are those like Livefen telling people I am. They debated it but decided to go with the elf's plan. Not everyone is happy about it, but that's what we are doing.

"Do you think we can beat this damned with the golden pneuma?" I ask Brian, looking at him, this time not bothering to speak through thoughts.

"Well, we better. We lose this battle, we lose altogether. He isn't like the first damned we fought—he isn't going to give us a second chance. The first damned we fought was arrogant and cocky. This damned with the golden pneuma is older and isn't a fool."

I nod then reply, taking a deep breath while looking out over the meadow. "I will be ready for it."

"You have come a long way in such a short time, London, you should be proud of yourself." Brian then moves away from me, and through the grass, as if he is part of the wind.

I get up, wondering if I should really feel proud of myself or not. I am not doing badly I suppose, but there is always room for improvement.

I go back to the camp where everyone is busy with work. They are all preparing for when we leave tomorrow to battle. My main mission will be to take out the damned with the golden pneuma, while the rest will be fighting his men.

We are on a hill with most of our camp being in the woods. We normally seem to camp this way. I go to find Jennifer. With not much to do right now, maybe she will be able to hang out and if not, I will give her company.

I find Jennifer by her tent, messing with her stuff. I smile to myself and say, "Hey Jennifer, busy?"

Jennifer turns to look at me. As a small smile appears on her lips, she gets up from her stuff and asks, "Why? Do you want to hang out?"

I can't help but smile myself. "If you have time."

"I think I have some time. What do you want to do?"

"Well, we could take a walk. I would take you out somewhere better, but there isn't any place nearby that's friendly as far as I know."

"Sounds good to me. Let's go."

We leave the camp together to go take a walk in the woods and meadows. We are not going anywhere in particular, but just enjoying each other's company.

"So how are you coping with all that has happened?" Jennifer asks gently as we walk through a meadow. She knows it is still a touchy topic for me.

"I am doing okay; I suppose it could be worse. A damned is always what I was meant to be. The life I was living wasn't very real, I guess you can say. But it is hard getting used to it."

"I know what you mean. Back where I come from, people didn't like me anymore when I became a damned. My parents still love me, but our relationship isn't the same."

"That is how it is for some of my family as well," I sigh, looking at her.

"Well at least we have friends like each other," and she meets my eyes in turn with her pretty brownish-green eyes. Her eyes always stood out to me. They are a brown shade, with a hint of green to them that seems to hold so much mystery. They always remind me of the color of spring leaves, when the first rays of the day shine on them.

"Yeah," I smile.

"I wonder how far we are from camp," Jennifer stops as she says this, looking back at the path we walked.

I know Jennifer likes me, she makes that obvious, but I feel there is a wall between us. She has her place and I have mine. I know that no matter how much she likes me, she will only go so far. I am going to try and get a little closer to her anyway though. I can't keep ignoring the feelings forever and neither can she. It will just be between me and her, and however she wants it.

Brian is right that I feel something for Jennifer. I have for a while. It has been hard ignoring those feelings, even more so when I know deep down inside, I should continue doing so. But some things are easier said than done.

"We are probably pretty far," I say, watching her closely.

Jennifer turns to me and we both stop looking at each other. She takes a deep breath. "When do you think we should go back?"

"I don't know."

I step a little closer to her as she watches me closely in return. I gently put my fingers through her hair and put my lips closer to hers. My heart starts beating faster being so close to her, and I know my breath is becoming a little heaver.

Jennifer watches me. "London, I do like you, but I have a job to do. I am supposed to be guarding you."

"And you have been doing an amazing job." I smell her neck and gently give it a small kiss. Her skin is soft and warm. I am so close I can feel her heart beating faster like mine.

She is trying not to smile but can't really help it. She puts her hands on me like she is trying to restrain me, "London, I don't think we should, and then there are our pneumas. I don't want them to be around."

"Brian is not here." I place my hands on her hips. She says no, but when I place my hands on her, she leans towards me.

"I guess Vixy and Brian won't bother us," she says her voice quieter now, as she watches my eyes.

I gently start kissing her neck up and down, feeling that she likes it. Her skin is soft and she smells good. Her lips find mine, and we slowly start to kiss. She puts her arms around my neck as we kiss. Her lips are warm and soft. She doesn't hold back when she kisses, and our breaths quickly start to come in heaver. We kiss for a few minutes, then she lets me go.

"Let's lie in the grass for a while," she says quietly to me, keeping her lips close to mine. "I don't want this going far. You have your place and I have mine. But I do like you, and I can't say no forever."

"I understand. Can we forget about our places for now, and just enjoy each other and how we really feel?" I quietly say back to her.

She gives me a smile. "All right, but just keep in mind, this won't happen again."

"I will try to," I smile.

We both lie in the grass, giving each other small kisses and touching each other. She only lets me get so close, but I enjoy it and don't push to go any further. It's all sweet stuff, and we act more like we have been lovers for a long time, just giving each other companionship. I like it though. It's peaceful out here in the meadow with her, and it takes me away from reality, to a place were I don't have to worry about all that has happened.

I have always had feelings for Jennifer. Now that we are kissing, I realize how strong those feelings are. I know I can't get ahead of myself though. She wants this, but I can tell she is also holding back a little. She doesn't think we should date, so sadly I know she means it when she says that this won't happen again. I wish it would though because I don't think I have ever been this close to a girl and have it feel so right like this. With Sara, I thought it was great and that our love was becoming something, but I know this is different. I really do have very strong feelings for Jennifer on so many levels, and I know it is the same for her with me. I am kind of wishing she wasn't in this spot, that she wasn't trying to follow her strict rules to protect me. Maybe if she wasn't, she would consider dating me.

She gently runs her fingers through my hair, as I lean over her. I put my hands on either side of her. As she places her hands on my chest, we are both kissing, and I have forgotten about everything right now except for Jennifer. We have been mainly kissing, enjoying each other and some flirting between the kissing.

"We should probably go soon, London. It is getting late," Jennifer said, through breaths of kissing me.

"I guess so," I said, stopping the kiss for a second to answer.

I give her a kiss again, as she kisses me back. I place my hands on her hips and get on top of her. Before I can do anything else, she flips us, so she is on top. I take a deep breath as she pulls her lips away from mine when she flipped us.

I smile at her and ask, "Don't like it when I am on top?"

"No, I like it, but it is time we go back. I know as long as you are on top of me, that wouldn't happen."

"I guess I had no intention of getting off," I admit, with a guilty grin.

"I know how a man's mind works," she said with a smile that probably looks a little like mine. She bites my lower lip, then kisses me. I kiss her back, but shortly after, she pulls away and gets up.

I get up slowly after her, knowing that she has had enough, "I suppose we are heading back now?"

"Yes, it's better that we do."

We walk back, keeping our hands to ourselves. Jennifer is sweet to me as we walk back, but she doesn't want to get very close. I don't push for anything and talk to her on the way back. A couple of times I give her a kiss, but they are small, and she doesn't want any more than that.

It is dark now; we were out later than I thought we would be. I think she is a little worried about what people will think of this. She doesn't want people to know she was kissing me like that. We enter the camp and Livefen walks to us.

"Where have you guys been? We have been looking for you. We are in dangerous territories, and you need to tell someone before you go wandering off," Livefen starts, sounding irritated like he normally does when speaking to Brian or me.

He may tell us what's next, but he doesn't control everything I do. I reply with a little attitude, "I was taking a walk with Jennifer, and I will go when I want without asking." With that, Jennifer and I walk away from him. I don't feel like arguing with him, so I won't. I know this annoys him even more, but there is nothing he can do about it.

I walk Jennifer back to her tent. We both look at each other and I say, "Well, you have a good night, Jennifer. Thanks for hanging out with me. I enjoyed your company." I smile as I say it.

"I enjoyed hanging out with you too," she smiles in return.

I step a little closer to her, but she looks down. She doesn't want a kiss, I can tell. She looks back up at me. "I liked the time we spent together, London, but I don't want it becoming public. We shouldn't do it again."

"I understand. I enjoyed it even if it was a one-time thing. There is nothing wrong with doing what we did."

"I guess you are right." Her smile is back, and she gives me a quick kiss on the lips.

"Good night, London. Sleep well."

"Good night, Jennifer. The same for you."

Jennifer goes to bed while I sit by the campfire thinking. Everyone else soon turns in. I wonder where Brian went. He isn't with Vixy, who was at Jennifer's tent. I don't have to wonder long though as I hear him in my head. *"You spent a long time with Jennifer in the grass. I thought you weren't ready for that."*

"I don't think that is any of your business, Brian. And how do you know? Do you spy on me?"

"No, I just know where you are at all times. Besides, I don't think Vixy approved of it. She is a bit protective of Jennifer."

"We didn't do anything more than kiss really, and just lay close to each other. It is not like Jennifer didn't like what we did."

"She feels it's her job to watch Jennifer though. If you plan to get closer to Jennifer, you should have Vixy like you first. She won't have any problem hurting you if she felt it is needed."

"*That sounds nice. No need to worry about that. For now, Jennifer and I are just friends, who have a bit of a romantic side to our friendship. We both are attracted to each other, but there are reasons, at least for now, why we should keep a distance.*"

"*If that's how it is,*" Brian replies.

"*Well, I will be going to bed now. Goodnight, Brian,*" I say, getting up. I go to my tent and lie down. Brian turns into a black cat and lies at the foot of the tent like he normally does.

I am awake for many hours thinking about all that went on. I question how much I really did love Sara and if I would have been a good husband to her in the first place. She hadn't been out of my life that long before I am already kissing and loving another woman. I know I would have never done that if we were married though. I can't blame myself. I really like Jennifer, and Sara left me in a very cruel way. I don't think it is wrong for me to move on as quickly as I am. It is better this way. I shouldn't be upset over a woman who doesn't feel the same about me.

Soon, I fall into light sleep thinking about Jennifer and the damned.

CHAPTER 28

Purple and gold

B rian flies high above the place. He is a small dragon, but big enough to carry someone. I ride him, standing on him, but staying low, not wanting to lose my balance and fall off. We are going to bypass everyone and land in the castle.

The castle is built on both sides of a giant river. The river is fast flowing. If I fell in, I would be swept away by the current. The castle is mostly on the west side of the bank. There is a large bridge across the river, which connects directly to the castle. After walking across the bridge, you get to the big open room with many glass windows that I will be in.

I am ready for the damned we must face. I have fought a few damned now, and I understand a bit more of what the pneumas can do, and what the damned are capable of. I have heard the damned can also be very powerful sorcerers, but I haven't met one of those yet.

"*Just take care of yourself when we face him. I don't want to have to save your ass again,*" Brian thinks to me.

"*Don't worry, I will,*" I reassure him.

As we enter the castle, Brian flies low enough for me to jump off, landing on my feet. As I stand up straight, Brian shifts into a human beside me.

In front of us is another damned. He is bold and wears a long, dark, purple cloak. His pneuma is also a dark purple. I don't like seeing this, there shouldn't be a purple pneuma. We were told he was golden.

"*I thought we were supposed to be fighting a damned with a golden pneuma.*" I do not look to Brian as I think this.

"*That's what it should be. Be ready. I think we have stumbled upon something bigger than we thought it would b*e."

Brian and I slowly start to approach the damned with the purple pneuma. I don't know who he is, but I am assuming he knows a lot of magic. I heard the purple pneumas are known for their dark magic. His damned doesn't carry many weapons, which makes me think of dark magic some more.

The damned stands where he is, as his pneuma turns into a man as well. His pneuma as a human is taller and slimmer than his damned. He has black hair, with a streak of purple through it. I notice pneumas either have their hair the same color as when they are a spirit, or will have a streak of that color in their hair, like this purple-colored pneuma.

"I had a feeling I would meet this new damned, London, and his black pneuma, Brian. You guys are building quite the reputation, but then again, most people with black or white pneumas do, and occasionally gray pneumas as well," the damned said, seeming very collected and calm.

I don't like that he is so cool about me being here. I am starting to get a bad feeling, almost as if they have been expecting us, and we are in for a nasty surprise.

"Well, you know why we are here," I say, sounding cold and emotionless.

"Maybe you should tell me. Why are you here? Is it to help the elves, some other kingdom or are you wanting to take over for yourself?"

"I am here to help the damned."

"What makes you think that Damon isn't doing that already?" he asks, sounding intrigued.

"Because he isn't helping the damned by taking their pneumas away."

"There is a reason for everything, London. Now before we fight, you should think about this. Is this what you really want? You might find that you are on the wrong side." He watches me closely. His pneuma just stands there, waiting for whatever happens.

"You cannot trust anything about these damned, London," Brian thinks.

Sometimes I have asked myself, "Am I really on the right side or not," not knowing much about the two sides. But I know I am not going to make a decision here.

"I am here to take you out, and that is what we are going to do," I said sternly, meeting the damned in the eyes.

He looks a little annoyed now. "Well, you can't say I didn't try."

Brian and I both look as we see another damned and his pneuma emerge from the shadows behind us. This is the damned with the golden pneuma.

This damned is dressed in golden-colored armor that looks like it was made from the scales of dragons. His pneuma turns into a human like the rest of the pneumas here. He has golden hair and dark eyes. He has an evil smile as he follows his damned. Instantly upon seeing these two, I have the feeling they are the bigger ones to fear.

"Good luck, Brian," I say as I start walking towards our enemy with Bone Crusher and Wolfbane in my hands.

"The same to you, London." Brian then shifts into a spirit.

As we get close, as is normally the case, the pneumas go for the attack first. Both pneumas go for Brian, all shifting into spirits to start their attack. I don't like the fact that Brian will have to face off with two pneumas at once. I cannot help him, since I myself have to face the damned.

Both the damned approach me, with the bold one not getting too close. He holds a small sword in his right hand, but keeps his left free. I don't know a lot about magic, but I am aware that magic is conjured and farmed by the hands. Magic can be transferred onto a staff or some other object instead, but I heard most damned use their hands. The other damned with the golden pneuma uses a long two-handed sword.

The golden-armored damned wastes no time and takes a swing to strike at me with his heavy sword. I bring up Wolfbane to stop the blow. As soon as I do, the other damned says words that I do not understand, and a bolt of purple leaves his hand.

Jumping back from the golden one, I use Bone Crusher to stop the magic from hitting me. I have been told the weapons we use will either store magic in them or reflect it, which I am hoping for now. It works, and Bone Crusher consumes the magic, but I am far from all right. These damned know more than I do and facing both at once is going to be more difficult than I thought.

The golden damned shows no mercy, his blade as quick as a striking snake. It flickers in and out, and all I can manage to do is avoid it with my own weapons or move out of the way just in time. The purple damned keeps close, ready to take over as soon as he sees his chance. While fighting the golden damned, I see the purple damned's hand light up with some sort of purple flame.

I start to throw some of my own strikes with Bone Crusher and Wolfbane. The golden-armored damned is a hell of a fighter, but I feel some of my confidence return. I am a match for him. The bold damned walks over, swinging a machete. I put Bone Crusher up to block it, but as soon as our weapons hit, I am thrown back, hitting the floor.

I quickly get up. I am shaken up and my head is spinning as the damned start to approach me again.

"Magic on his sword. We have magic as well, but unfortunately for us, you don't really know how to use it," Bone Crusher interrupts my thoughts.

He is right, it does suck that I don't know how to use it, but I wasn't completely taught everything about being a damned. I heard it takes years of practice to get good at it, anyway, and that is time I just don't have.

I glance over at Brian to see that the purple pneuma is not fighting now. Brian must have temporarily knocked him out of the battle, but that golden pneuma is proving to be a hell of a fighter, just like his damned.

I strike first when the damned are close enough again. I strike at the bold one, who doesn't dodge the hit as well as the golden guy would have. I hit him on the side, a little above the hip. He screams and backs up, as the golden guy quickly takes his place. He is angry now that I have hurt his comrade, and he gives me no chance to hit him. I am forced to walk back from the onslaught of blows.

Finally, I stop and stand my ground. Walking back will not save me and I will have to face him. The golden armored damned doesn't come straight for me like I thought he would. Instead, he says, "You are a good fighter for a young damned. Maybe some day you will be the leader of the damned and overthrow Damon, but until then, all damned will be your enemy."

I guess it is a compliment, but it is a strange one. Before I can do anything else, I see the purple spirit as a mist coming for me out of the corner of my eye. I try to react, but I don't have enough time before he grabs me and I am pushed through a glass window. The window shatters and I am thrown from the hall. I yell as I go falling, but before I hit the water, Brian grabs me, as a griffin. I try to hold on to him, looking down at the fast-flowing river below me. Brian brings us up higher. As Brian tries to bring us even higher, I hear him scream the high-pitched scream of a griffin as he drops me.

I fall, feeling horrible pain in my chest as I hit the water. The water is so cold. I take in a huge gulp of water by accident. I was not ready for it, so I took a deep, sharp breath when I went down.

I get my head above water, trying not to drown as I am dragged down the river. Coughing, I try to get the water out of my lungs. Brian has shifted into something else I know and falls into the water with me. I try to call his name, but I feel I am not getting through to him, and I am only getting more water into my mouth as I try to do so.

CHAPTER 29

A Trip Down the River

I feel cold. Just trying to keep my head out of the water is difficult. I feel horrible pain and I know it must be from Brian. I need to find him, but I can't.

I drift farther downstream with the water pounding me, making it hard to breathe without taking a mouth full of water with each breath. I grab on to a rock for dear life, trying not to go any farther down the river. I look up as I see the purple pneuma coming down the river. These guys are just not going to give up.

The purple pneuma comes as a mist with long claws stretched out for me, but I let go of the rock. I would rather be swept down the river than go with him. The current takes me and I am again at the mercy of this freezing river.

The purple and golden pneuma try to get me, but find it hard. Also, I know Brian is near, and he is still battling them. He is in the water as well, but I can't keep up with him or determine where he is. I am coming closer to the bank, as I try to grab on to what I can. Finally, again I grab a hold on to a rock, closer to the shore. I don't know how long I can hold on though. My hands are so cold they are numb. My teeth are chattering, and the pain is now intense. I don't know why it is so bad for me. Maybe Brian is somehow giving me more of his pain or something. I know that he is hurt, but I have no idea how bad. Just when I think I can't hold on anymore, Danny comes. Danny grabs me as a spirit and puts me down on the shore.

Danny turns into a dog and shakes himself out on the shore beside me. He must have been in the water helping Brian, for he is all wet as well. He turns into a human and comes beside me.

"London, are you all right?"

I am far from all right. I am frozen from the river, but I am cold from more than just that. I feel the cold of death and it's coming from Brian. I need to find him. I am in intense pain and can barely move. I shake from the cold and pain, and I don't know what to do. I call out to Brian, but he does not answer me.

"Brian, where is Brian?" I am barely able to ask Danny.

"I don't know, but Vixy is looking for him," he replies.

Sully comes over to us and gets down as well. Danny looks at him. "He doesn't have any wounds on him, but Brian is gone, and he is injured."

"Damn! I knew that this was a bad idea." Sully then looks at me, "Don't worry, kid. Everything will be okay."

I don't reply, but close my eyes and try not to move. That only seems to make the pain worse. Ever since I have become a damned, I truly know what pain feels like.

"London!" I hear Jennifer yell.

I open my eyes and she kneels beside me, with Danny being his spirit form again. She puts my head in her lap and says, looking at Sully, "Is he all right?"

"Brian is gone, so I don't know," Sully replies, the worry of the situation creeping into his voice.

Vixy is near Jennifer and she looks upset, although she is trying hard not to show it. Maybe she really does care a lot about Brian. Sully gets up as the rest start to come. I can tell by the way Sully looks; he is pissed. He isn't happy about how things went down, and I know he blames the elf.

Jennifer stays holding me, gently putting her fingers through my hair. I am glad Jennifer is here. This pain is intense and I feel so cold. It is nice to know I have her.

"Is he all right?" Livefen asks.

Sully looks at him and replies none too friendly, "No, he is not okay. We cannot find Brian and he is injured. We should never have done this. We knew that it was a bad idea, but we did it anyway. We keep this up and they are not going to live long!"

"Don't blame what happened on me, Sully. I did what I thought was needed. We must take out Damon, and we don't have the time to wait. None of us could have known there was a trap waiting in there for him." Livefen said, getting offensive.

"Well, he is no good to anyone if he is dead, is he?" Sully retorted, sounding more pissed now.

Livefen walks closer to him and replies, matching Sully's anger, "Things can always go wrong in a battle like this. It just so happens that's what happened. Now, why should you blame me for it? I didn't want this to happen."

"We all thought it was a bad idea. You are the one who pushed for it, and the one to bring it up. You don't care what happens to them, you only want Damon gone, regardless of the price. Next time you should keep in mind, elf, that without London and Brian, you are not getting rid of Damon."

They both glare at the other, with Sully's anger matched by Livefin's. Finally, Jennifer snaps, "Enough with the fighting. If we don't find Brian, he will die. We need to move London somewhere safe and look for Brian. He has to be somewhere around here. He is going to want to come back to London."

"Jennifer is right. Jennifer, a couple of guards and I will help move London to a safer place," Breccan said. "The rest of you should look for Brian."

"I will cheek the other shoreline," Sully volunteers.

"I will help too," Vixy says, sounding determined.

Sully only shakes his head. "I think you should stay, Vixy, just in case those pneumas or damned come back. We need a pneuma and damned here to help keep them at bay."

Vixy nods her head, not arguing with him. The ones looking for Brian leave, while Jennifer, Vixy and Breccan stay with me.

Vixy looks around and says, "I can take London to a safe place, you guys can follow after. Then you can set up camp while I stay as a lookout. He needs to get off the shoreline before he, or one of us, is spotted."

"All right," Jennifer says. "We will be right behind you."

Vixy turns into a reddish horse, and Breccan and Jennifer help me on. Once I am on, I try to hold on. I feel incapable of doing many things, but I must hold on. Being as shaky as I am though, it's going to be hard.

"Just don't fall off," Vixy quietly says to me.

I say back through chattering teeth, "I will try not to."

She takes off at a run, after walking a few feet away from the rest of the group. She runs through the forest, jumping over rocks, fallen logs and running faster than any horse I have ever ridden on. I just try my best to stay on.

Finally, Vixy comes to a stop. We stop at a little clearing, where there is long green grass, a forest and rocks scattered around the place.

Vixy lays down slowly so I can get off from her. I half fall, but that's okay, for I am off now. I lay there, still trying to call out to Brian. I am freezing and not sure what to do. I feel hopeless, but I can't move. Vixy turns into a human, "You need to get out of those wet clothes if you want to live."

I look at her and reply, "I don't have any other clothes."

She gives me a bag of clothes. "You do now. I know you hurt, but get yourself dressed anyway, and then you can rest. You will find I am not as nice as Jennifer, but I will help you never the less."

I take my clothes and pull out a pair of pants. She minds her own business while I get dressed. It is hard to do, shaking as bad as I am, hurting and feeling

I am in the open. I wouldn't want to be walked in on while I am getting dressed. Vixy stands guard though, so I don't think she will let that happen.

Finally, now that I am all dressed, I lay back down, feeling less cold. The breeze here is cold though. Even with the sun out and shining on me, it is still cold. Vixy turns into a red wolf and lays on me, to try and keep me warmer. Brian will often sleep half on me, as if trying to protect me, depending on what kind of animal he is. I shake while trying to close my eyes. She keeps her head and ears up, listening for any sound indicating that there could be danger.

"You really care about Brian, don't you?" I whisper, but like Brian, she hears regardless how quiet I speak.

"I care about him, but I don't look at him any more than that. You shouldn't look at Jennifer that way either. You both have your places, and it would be best if you guys didn't go there."

"I respect Jennifer and whatever choice she makes, but I cannot pretend I don't have any feelings for her. They just don't go away like that."

"Maybe not, but you shouldn't act on them. It would be the best for the both of you," she says coldly.

I don't say anything else. I get what she means, but that doesn't make things any easier. I close my eyes and try to rest and call out to Brian. I know he is out there somewhere, and I need to find him. Both of our lives rest with him, and if he doesn't make it, that will be our ending.

CHAPTER 30

Old friends

Brian

I have been battling those two pneumas long enough, so when I know London is out of the water and safe, I let the river current take me downstream. I go for miles downstream. I'm not sure how many miles I travel, but when I feel it is safe enough, I make my way to the nearest shore.

I climb on to shore, feeling worn out and not able to shift due to the arrow through my chest. I know I am being risky by giving London all the pain I can give away while at the same time taking his energy for my own, but if I don't, we would both be dead by now.

I must be careful, for London cannot die. In some cases, I would let him die if it was a choice between me and him. It is not like I want him to die, but he can come back. I cannot. In a case like this, however, I am too injured, and without help from London, we will both die. I cannot heal as well as he can, and he must heal me once I have taken too much damage. If he dies now, I will not have the strength to bring him back, and our lives will be very short ones.

I need to find him, but first I must take care of my wounds. Those pneumas know I am hurt, and they will continue looking for me. I must avoid them, and take care of myself enough so I can make it back to the rest of my group.

I take a deep breath and grab the arrow that is in me. I need to take it out or I won't be able to shape-shift. This will increase the bleeding, but I have made my choice. The arrow went all the way through. I will break the end of the arrow where the arrowhead is, for I can't just pull it out. After breaking it, I will pull it out. Doing it this way, the barbed arrowhead will not rip me up more inside as it exits my body.

I break it, trying my best to make no sounds of pain. I am pissed off that things turned out this way. London and I can do better. I take deep breaths as my heart beats fast. I pull out the arrow with a sound of pain and then throw it down. I put my hand where the wound is. It only takes a couple of seconds before my hand is covered in blood. I cope with the pain better, giving half the pain to London. I am sure he hates me right now, but he can live with it.

I turn into a fox and painfully go walking into the grass and up the hill from the river. I need to get away from the shore and to a place where I can help myself without being found by the pneumas or their damned. I stop as I hear something. I know it is a pneuma, but it is not the ones from whom I am trying to get away. This one is in inactive pneuma, meaning her damned hasn't accepted death yet. I know who she is. People cannot see inactive pneumas, but some people like Amias can, as well as other pneumas.

Her name is Cassandra. Before I could talk to London, I spent some time with her. She is a white pneuma, making her currently the only other known white pneuma. Her damned is with the elves, but the both of us have kept our damned a secret from each other. I liked her, she liked me, but we are both dominant pneumas. Usually, that has a way of getting ugly fast. That is not how it always is, but I know she is just as competitive as I am, and that makes for a strange relationship.

"It looks like you have run into some trouble," she says.

"I can say I have had better." I don't know why she is here, but I am sure she has her reasons. I don't have much time to talk though. I need to find someplace safe and stop the flow of blood.

"Well, I think I can help you out of this jam if you do a favor for me," Cassandra says, in that sweet, rich voice of hers. I am wary. I know there is a lot more to her than meets the eye.

"How can you help me?"

"I know where there is a place you can stay to keep yourself out of trouble. While there, I can find you help. I know who is accompanying you." She comes closer to me and looks where I am hurt. As in inactive pneuma, there is not much she can do besides what she offers.

I don't know if I should trust her, but I guess I am at her mercy. She could just as easily tell the pneumas I am trying to get away from where I am. I suppose I don't have any other choice but to trust her.

"Don't tell me you don't trust me. Trust what you used to know about me. I have never done anything to hurt you before."

What she didn't add was that she also couldn't have hurt me even if she wanted to before. I look at her and sigh, "I trust you."

I know if she was not currently in a mist form, she would be smiling at me saying this. I think she enjoys the fact that my life is in her hands. She doesn't waste any time and starts to lead the way. I follow her, still in pain, but trying my best to keep up and not show how bad I am hurting. She is already helping me. I don't want to give her any more than that.

She brings me higher up the hill. Just when I think I won't be able to keep up anymore, she stops at the mouth of a small cave located on the side of the hill. The entrance is small. It doesn't look like more than a crack with some bushes in the way. Once inside, I see that the cave opens a little wider, making it a cozy fit. There is enough room that I won't be too cramped.

I go into the cave and flop onto the ground. I start to lick my wound. It isn't the best way to deal with it, but I can at least keep it clean. If I were still human, I wouldn't even be able to do much to help myself. Hopefully, Cassandra will keep her word and bring help back to me.

"I will go now. People are looking for you already, so it shouldn't be long," Cassandra says. Without waiting for a response, she leaves. I watch her go and then go back to taking care of my wounds. The biggest wound I have is from the arrow that went through me. I also have plenty of other cuts all over me from the fighting I did with those pneumas. I clean them the best I can and stay as a fox. I think it is the best choice for now. In the cave, I am not very noticeable. I try to close my eyes and conserve my strength. I don't like having to wait this out, but I don't have much of a choice.

CHAPTER 31

Search and rescue

Sully

"We have got to find them before it is too late," I say, still pissed off about the whole thing. That elf didn't take things into consideration. This was risker than we even realized, and now we are paying the price.

London is young and he hasn't been a damned for very long. In the time he has been a damned, he has impressed the hell out of me. I want to make sure to help the kid the most I can, so that is what I am going to do. Danny and I are on the other side of the shore trying to find Brian. I have the feeling that he will be on this side, but there is no guarantee of that.

"I am sure we will find them. Brian couldn't have gone far," Danny replies, scouting the area as a mist.

"I hope not."

Danny stops, and I know something is up. I look around but do not see anything. Looking at Danny I think to him, *"What is it?"*

"There is in inactive pneuma here. She claims to know where Brian is."

"Do you think we can trust her?" I ask Danny in my thoughts.

"Well, if she really does know where Brian is, then we can't miss that."

"Then let's follow her."

I follow Danny as he follows the inactive pneuma. I cannot see her, but Danny would never lie to me. We head up the hill from the bank. I start to see signs myself that Brain has been here. I see prints of a fox. All young pneumas turn to a fox at first, when they are unsure of their truest animal form. There is also some blood following the trail, which I assume is Brian's.

We finally make it up the hill and Danny stops.

I stop as well and ask, *"What is it now?"*

"She tells me that Brian is in a small cave or hole, just up the hill. Now she will take her leave of us."

I take a deep breath, hoping that this inactive pneuma isn't about to lead us to our death. If Danny and I were to run into one of the damned that London was fighting, I probably would be able to take him out. But if there were both of them, I don't think we would have much of a chance. I am tough, but I know my limits. I have lived long enough to know what I am capable of and not.

Danny and I casually approach the little cave. Some relief washes over me when I see Brian in the little cave, right where she said he would be. I set down in front of the cave and Brian looks at me. I say reassuringly, "Come, Brian, I am here to take you back to London."

"You couldn't have come at a better time," he replies. I hear how weak he is though, and I know this is not over yet. I have to get him back to London before we lose both of them.

London

I toss and turn. Where is Brian? I need to find him, but I know I will be no help in my current state. I don't know what to do, and that cold feeling is only consuming more of me. It is horrible, but all I can do is try my best to fight it.

Jennifer stays beside me, and through all this, I think my respect for her grows that much more. She doesn't have to be here for me, but she is.

Jennifer grabs my hand and I grab on to her. She leans closer to me, putting her fingers through my hair and says softly, "This is the downside of having a pneuma. If they are hurt, the damned is often down too. This will get better with time. You guys will learn how to determine how much pain you should share, and when to take it."

"It will be nicer when we figure that out," I reply through gritted teeth, as I turn to look at her. I am worn out and feel like I haven't slept for days. I know it is from Brian stealing my strength, but I think he has to right now or we would both die.

"Well, after he gets here, you need to sleep for a while. This has drained a lot of energy from you."

"I am looking forward to it."

She gives me a small kiss on the head and continues to stay with me. I soon fall into an uneasy sleep that doesn't seem to make me feel any better.

I jerk awake saying Brian's name. Jennifer tries to calm me down. "He is here, but you stay right here. Sully is bringing him in. He isn't in a good condition, London, so you will have to help him."

"How will I be able to do that?" I ask.

"It's not something I can explain to you. Trust me though, London, you will. This is what makes the pneumas really need us, and death is why we really need them." She then gets up and leaves the tent.

Brian comes into the tent as a spirit. I smile seeing him, never feeling happier to see him. Brian comes and stops in front of me. He stays close to the ground and I know he is hurting.

"How have you been feeling?" he asks, his voice sounding far too weak.

"Like shit."

I know he would smile if he wasn't a mist right now. He continues, this time through thoughts, *"Healing me will be the only way to ensure that the both of us won't die."*

Brian turns into a fox and lays down beside me, too weak now to stand and to worn out to do anything else.

"I made a mistake, I think, taking too much of your strength, but we are going to need it now. If you can't heal me enough, then we both die," Brian continues.

Our life now rests in my hands, the opposite of what it was before. I saw how Brian looked after he brought me back from hell. He was worn out and slept for several days; the same thing will probably happen to me. I just hope I have enough strength to give to heal him. I look at Brian's wounds. I see that Sully tried to take care of them, but he has a couple of big ones that no one could do much about unless they operate on him.

I take a deep breath and put my hand over his wound. I don't know how to explain it, but Jennifer is right, it is not something you are taught, it is something you just know. I take a deep breath and close my eyes. It almost feels as if I leave my body, and even with my eyes closed, it feels as if I am seeing his wound and everything that is hurt and wrong with him. Not quite understanding what I am doing, I start to fix the muscle that was damaged by the attack. I work on the inside first, then move out. Once the muscle is fixed, I start to seal it up by pulling the skin together. I do this to his main wound first, which is a wound to the chest from an arrow. After this, I move on to some other deep cuts he got from the pneumas. He has lost a lot of blood and I try to make up for that by giving him more of my energy. I know it hurts him, for he moves uncomfortably and makes small whimpering sounds of pain. Hearing this, I continue, knowing I am doing him more good than harm. Finally, I fix all that I am able to fix. I don't have the strength to do much more.

I open my eyes, then fall back. I don't even have the strength to support myself. I try to move, but I can't. I don't know what is wrong with me; I have no strength, not even to lift my hand. Brian shifts into a human and looks at me. *"It looks like you and I are even now. I bring you back once from death, and you did the same for me."*

I can only say something through thoughts, not being able to talk. *"What is a matter with me, Brian?"*

"It took a lot of strength to heal me like that. You might have done more than was needed, and I had already taken so much from you before you did this. You are tough, London, tougher than I ever thought. I was meant to be your pneuma, and we are meant to help the damned and their pneumas. We are meant to take out Damon and change the lives of many. You have my undying respect. Now, you rest. You may need to rest for several days, but I will be here."

I close my eyes and slowly breathe. I don't have the strength for anything, and sleep is the only thing I can do now. Brian turns into a black panther and lays down near me. I slowly start drifting into sleep. I hear Jennifer walk in and Brian says to her, "The both of us will be okay, but London needs lots of sleep."

I feel Jennifer sits down near me, and hear her whisper, "I am more than glad to hear that."

I feel her grab my hand, and she leans closer to me and continues, barely above a whisper in my ear. "No matter what happens, London, I will always be here for you. There is nothing that can stop you, and nothing I won't do to help you." Then she gives me a kiss on the lips. Her soft kiss puts warmth through me, and with that I drift into a deep sleep, leaving the rest of the world behind me.

CHAPTER 32

Recovery

Brian and I are feeling better after a couple of days, although most of that time, I was asleep. Everyone has been staying put while waiting for us to get better. Jennifer and Vixy are often in the tent to see how we are doing. Usually, Jennifer and I hang out, making jokes and having a good time. I don't know how it really is for Brian and Vixy. I know they like each other, even if Vixy fights it. They seem to fight a lot though. I don't know what they are fighting about, and I think it is Brian pushing her buttons and that makes her angry.

I just woke up and feel more refreshed than I have these last couple of days.

"You are looking better. It is about time we start heading out. One or two more days wouldn't hurt. It is better to be completely ready than only halfway there. We will need all of our strength for what's to come," Brian says as a mist moving around our tent. He is usually active in the morning and evening.

Our tent is bigger than normal. You can easily walk around and fit several people. We use it sometimes when we need a meeting place and it's raining or very cold outside. For now, it is being used as a recovery tent for Brian and me.

"Brain, I have been meaning to ask you..." I hesitate a minute, then continue, "Do you think we are on the right side? I know that I trust Sully and Jennifer, and the rest. But do you think we are doing what is right?"

Brian jumps up on the small table in the room and turns into a black cat. He looks at me, meeting my eyes. "It is never that simple, London. I believe there is always a good and bad to everything. It just depends on how you react to it."

"Well, what do you think though? Are we doing the right thing?"

"I think so. This is the path that is laid before us. If we are wrong, then someone better give us a sign. It is still iffy on where we truly stand though. Everyone wants something else, and in this case, depending on what we do, we will either lose friends or make them."

"I guess once Damon is overthrown, there will be a battle to determine what to do next."

"That is a big question for us. What will they want from us after we deliver to them what they want the most—Damon dead?"

"Well, I hope we can trust them enough by then, and that they won't do anything to betray us," I say, knowing it is wishful thinking and Brian will call me out on it.

"We cannot live with that mindset. The people who accompany us are our allies until Damon is done. Then we will see how everyone's true identities emerge."

"What about Sully and Jennifer?" I don't think they would turn on us. I would still have a hard time believing it, even if Brian thought they would.

"I don't think we have to worry about them. The damned and their pneumas want a dominant damned and pneuma in charge. You can see in Jennifer's eyes she will follow you to the end, and I don't think Sully is far behind her."

"Brian, what makes the dominant damned and pneuma so special, anyway? I know that being a black pneuma, you are the most powerful of the dark magic, and the white pneuma are the most powerful in light magic, but what else? Why are we held to such a stature?"

"You sure are asking a lot of questions today," Brian says jumping off the table and brushing himself up against the tent as he walks. "I guess that means you are feeling better."

"These are all questions to which I should know the answers," I retort.

Brain looks back at me. "That is true. But to tell you the truth, London, I think only a few know those answers. There aren't many white and black pneumas. It usually takes many years before a damned comes around with a pneuma that is one of those colors. I am sure Damon knows, but I don't think he is using this knowledge as he should."

I don't know what Brian means by that, but he probably doesn't know the answer to that either. I've come to realize that he knows a lot more than me about this kind of stuff. However, he still doesn't know enough compared to what he needs to know.

Jennifer walks into the tent. I smile thinking she doesn't ever bother to knock. I don't really mind though; I have nothing to hide from her. We haven't known each other that long yet, but she and I "click".

"Good morning. You look better this morning," Jennifer says with a warm smile.

"I feel better. How is everyone else doing?" I ask.

"Everyone else is fine. Do you want to take a walk with me? It would probably be good for you."

"I would love to."

I get ready, and Jennifer, Vixy, Brian, and I all leave the tent for a walk together. People say "hey" to us as we pass them. Jennifer and I don't start talking until we are away from the camp, and Vixy and Brian are off playing around, like the pneumas love to do.

"Do you think people in the camp are annoyed that Brian and I have been down for so long?" I ask, looking at Jennifer.

"I don't think so, and they shouldn't be annoyed. People who are not damned would be down a lot longer than you and Brian were. I was almost getting worried about you though. You slept for about two whole days without waking."

I shrug my shoulders with a smile, "It beats going to that one place we go to when we die."

"Anything beats that. It's like a Hell especially designed for the damned and creatures like us."

"Have you ever been down there before?" I ask.

"No, I haven't yet, and I hope to keep it that way. I have heard enough stories to know that it is no place I ever want to be."

"Well, trust me, you have that thought right."

We both walk in silence for a few minutes, deep in thought. There are a lot of things to know. So much of the future is hidden from me. I wish my road was a little more paved ahead of me, so then I can at least see a little of what is around the bend.

"It is probably about time we head back. They are going to wonder where we went off to," Jennifer says slowly, coming to a halt.

"I suppose so. I hate feeling like I am monitored though. It seems like I can't do anything without them needing to know about it first."

"That is what comes from being in the spotlight."

"I suppose that's one of the downsides," I agree. "I wish I wasn't there though. But I think Brian has a different opinion about that."

"Brian looks like the type who would want to be there, not trying to put him down or anything," Jennifer says.

"That's probably very true." I stick my arm out for her, and say with a smile, "Shall we walk?"

She can't help but smile at me. "You know, you can be a real rascal sometimes." She grabs my arm anyway, and we slowly start to walk back.

I can't help but feel an attraction towards her, but I will not act on it and neither will she. I know she wants me though, and if I pushed hard for it, I could probably talk her into being my girl. I won't do that, at least not now. I am in no state to have a woman like her right now. If I had a relationship with Jennifer, it would not be a short-term thing. She is a woman who wants a long-time relationship and kids. I wouldn't mind that myself, but not for a while. I think in the future, Jennifer and I could become more than friends, but for now, that is how we are going to keep it. That time we did get a little close, I think it was us not wanting to contain how we feel any longer, but I don't think that is happening again anytime soon.

We make it back to the camp, and Brian and I spend a little time with the others before going back to the tent. I am exhausted again and I know Brian is too. As soon as we are in the tent and I lay back on the bed, I feel a lot better. I am surprised that I am still recovering from all that happened. I guess healing someone like that takes a toll on you.

Brian turns into a human and sits down on his bed. Sometimes he will be an animal and sit near me, while other times he will be in his own place. I close my eyes and think of all that is going on. Soon, I fall into a light sleep.

CHAPTER 33

Lies and trust

Brian

I wander wherever I please, checking up on people, listening to conversations and trying to find out what I can. There is nothing anyone can hide from me when it is about London or me. I am currently following Breccan and Livefen. Livefen brought Breccan away from the rest of the group to talk with him privately. I follow because I have the feeling, I will want to hear this. The elf is the last person I trust and I have a feeling he is up to no good.

I am in the treetops above their heads. I am a mist, but I stay so close to the bark and move so stealthily, they have no idea that I am here.

"I don't like how things are going, Breccan," Livefen says quietly to him.

"Neither do I. We should have never sent Brian and London into that mess yet. If they were to get killed, then we are all damned," Breccan replies, putting one hand in his pocket, while using his other hand to smoke a pipe.

"I wasn't talking about that, although that was a disaster as well."

"What are you talking about then?" Breccan asks, looking at the elf.

They are walking on a road through the forest. Trees grow so thick on either side and above them that most of the sunlight is blocked out.

"I am talking about London and Brian, and what they plan on doing. I do not trust Brian. I think he has his own ideas about how he wants things done."

"They are their own people. London and Brian do have their place helping us," Breccan says casually. This is how he always acts, as if he doesn't have a care in the world.

"I know, but I am afraid of what they really are, besides what we know. Brian is known for being the most powerful of dark magic. That is the magic that came from Hell itself. I don't know what he plans to do, but I bet he has something nasty up his sleeve for us."

"I understand your concern, but you are sounding like the people who know nothing of the damned and judge them as if they are creatures from hell. We know that is not true though. They are still people, and the pneumas are not what they seem."

"I am aware how the damned and the pneumas are, but there is good and bad to everything. Brian is not from the light, Breccan, you know this. I know we need him. I have the feeling, though, that his idea of winning is very different from ours."

"I don't think we should put Brain in that position, just because he is a dark pneuma. Often misjudging like that is where you make a mistake. We shouldn't be blinded by what stories and our eyes tell us. I think there is more to Brian than meets the eye, and it is not all bad," Breccan suggests.

They have both stopped walking to talk to each other. Breccan stays in one spot smoking his pipe, seeming calm. Livefen is a little more on edge. He seems bothered by something. He probably just can't make up his mind about us.

I don't think much of the elves altogether. They think they are the superior race because they believe they are from God. I believe they can be some of the most cold-hearted out of all the races. At least with some races, you know what to expect. Elves, on the other hand, seem to be always wearing a mask.

"Maybe you are right. I shouldn't assume the worst, but I would rather be safe than sorry. Tell me though, Breccan, if Brian and London were to get out of hand, would you help me stop them?" Livefen asks, looking Breccan in the eyes.

"I am here to help people, and all countries, from someone like Damon. I am here to help London overthrow him. If London and Brian were to become a threat, like Damon, then I will have to do the same to them."

"Well, I am glad to hear that. Not that I assume that London and Brian will go down that path, but we must be ready for anything," Livefen replies, rubbing his chin like he is in deep thought.

"I understand, but let us hope we won't ever have to worry about that," Breccan says, being his optimistic self.

"And I will."

They continue their walk, while I stay where I am. There is nothing more I can learn from them. I wish I could find Cassandra, but I don't know where to begin looking for her. It just seemed strange. After not seeing her for a while, all of a sudden, she was there, and then she was gone as quickly as she arrived. What I want to know most was why she arrived in the first place. She must be following us, for I don't believe in coincidences.

I go back from where I came, staying in the trees now as a crow. I land on a high branch and look around. I can see far and wide while perched up here. I can see the tops of all the trees and the river farther off in which London and I took our nasty ride. Beyond the river, I can see flatlands and then mountains north and west of us. It is a beautiful land, and with the sun going down and cool breeze in the air, it makes it even better.

Vixy comes and lands in a higher branch near me as a red falcon. She folds her wings in and looks at me.

"What are you doing up here, Brian? Spying on people?" she asks, looking at me.

"That is actually what I am doing. I am surprised you are up here. I thought you would be with Jennifer. You know she is with London," I say, looking at her in return. I know she is protective of Jennifer. She does not want London and Jennifer becoming anything more than friends. Truly I don't care what London does with his love life. I do what I want with mine and wish the same for him.

"Jennifer can take care of herself. She and London are friends, and nothing else," Vixy snaps.

"I am pretty sure that isn't true," I smile. (well, the best smile a crow can give).

"It is right now. Anyway, who were you spying on and why?"

I turn into a spirit and make my way down the tree, with Vixy as a spirit right behind me.

"Are you the police now?" I ask sarcastically. Once I am on the ground, I turn into a human. I turn around to see that Vixy is now a human as well.

Vixy has a look on her face that is a slight smile, but she is also a little angry as well. She is normally angry with me though, so it isn't anything new. She is always cute though, no matter how angry she is.

"No, I am not, but I do have to watch you."

"Well, I am glad to know you care," I give a slight smile as well.

"I don't care. It is just my job," she says, crossing her arms and throwing her hip to the side.

I walk up to her, looking at her. "You are good at pretending not to care, but I know you do."

She tilts her head slightly at me. "I do my job and that is it. If it makes you feel better, then go ahead and think differently."

I circle around her while she is watching me and reply, "You know you are very stubborn."

"One of us has to be."

"So, you do like me, but you feel that it cannot happen. It doesn't matter if London and Jennifer feel that way, does it? Why must we feel the same way they do? No one can say what we do or don't do with our lives."

We both watch each other and she takes a deep breath, not meeting my eyes. "For Jennifer, I will keep my space, Brian. I can't trust you, and not because you are a black spirit, but because I cannot trust anyone. Too many people have betrayed us and I don't want to fall for it again."

I grab her hands, and she holds mine back gently. I put one of my hands on her face, as she leans into it. We both look at each other and I say in a smooth voice, "To love someone is easy, to trust someone is hard. If you never trust anyone, Vixy, then how are you to ever live? Your happiness is just as important as Jennifer's. People have their opinions of me. I will always be put on the stand, where people and pneumas will try to challenge me. But it will forever be worth it if I have someone like you in my life."

I can tell this really gets to her, but I don't know if it is enough to change her mind. I am crazy about Vixy and I cannot help it. My only weakness is her, which I hate. There are times when I need to be thinking of something else and she is on my mind. How can I go through with my plans if I have a distraction like her in my life? I cannot ignore her either, for that only seems to make things worse. Maybe if I know she is mine, then there would be no more reason to worry. Instead of having her be my Achilles' heel, she can be my strength. How can I make her see that? I don't want to look weak to her, but I will reveal my weakness to her, to show her how much I care.

"I don't know, Brian. We are here together, but you belong in a different world than me. I am nothing in your world. People and pneumas pass me by as if I were nothing. My life is to protect yours. We do not belong in the same picture together, Brian. It would be better for the both of us if you started treating me that way," Vixy says, although I know that is not what she wants.

"I don't belong anywhere, Vixy. I make my own place, and you can do the same. Why should you not be in the same place as me? I want you, Vixy, and I will not hide that anymore."

She doesn't reply, but looks like she is thinking. I don't think she knows what to make of all this. I understand why it is hard for her to say yes, but why say no? I always keep my word, and I will treat her well.

I take a deep breath and kiss her. She does not kiss me, and backs up. We both look at each other and she says quietly, "I am sorry, Brian, but it cannot happen. Please don't push for it anymore."

I let her go, feeling heartbroken. I don't ever get sad, I get angry. I am not going to get angry with her though. I don't need to make it worse, even though I feel like losing my temper.

"If that is truly how you feel about it, then I'll stop. Just so you know, Vixy, just because you say no, doesn't mean that this is all over. I cannot help how I feel about you."

"I understand, Brian. I like you, too, but it is for the best." Then she turns into a spirit and leaves me.

I stand where I am for a few minutes, feeling more and more angry. I am sad about what happened between Vixy and me, but I use my anger to cope with it. This is how I deal with things, and after hearing what the elf and Breccan said, it only feeds the fire.

I walk back to the camp and see the elf at a table set up to talk about plans. At their last talk, Breccan acted like he wouldn't judge us until he knew what we were up to, but I know that he is a liar. He has his own plans and I will learn about them soon enough. Until then, I will do what I can to annoy him. London may not like it, but I want the elf to know that we are far from allies with him. We are only neutral for now because we will both benefit from that.

I go over as a spirit and flip his table over. Jennifer yells my name angrily, but the elf doesn't say anything. He knows that I heard him, and I am letting him know how I feel about him.

"Brian, what is a matter with you?" Amias says, sounding annoyed that I knocked over their table. I couldn't care less though. I am angry right now, and I could do worse than knocking over a table. He better stay out of my way.

I go find a place where I can think alone for a while. I know London will be here soon enough, but I will have some time to gather my thoughts.

CHAPTER 34

Taking Matters into my own Hands.

I walk over to Brian. He is on top of a hill looking out. He is a human right now, and is looking over the land. I know he has a lot on his mind. Then there was his sudden outrage in the camp. I wonder why he would do that. Maybe he is just trying to cause problems or was pissed off with someone. Whatever the reason, I need to know.

"All land is owned by someone, but in truth, the land owns everyone and everything. We must be like the land if we ever wish to accomplish what we want. We cannot trust anyone and must be ready for anything. There is only you and I, London, and if we don't watch each other, then we shall die," Brian says, not bothering to look at me.

He makes me a little uncomfortable talking like that. He makes it feel like we are going to rule one day, and that is not what I plan. I plan to help the damned and their pneumas. I don't think I need to rule to do that.

I sit down near Brian. "There are some to trust though?"

"Not really, London. We shouldn't truly trust anyone. Look at who turned on you. Your own family and wife. What makes you think the people you are with now won't?"

I take a deep breath, wishing he wouldn't mention that. It has torn a hole in my heart, and saying it like that doesn't help.

"What about Jennifer and Sully? You said we could trust them." I can tell he is in a pissed-off mood, and that is probably why he is acting the way he is. But it is not fair to throw in my family like that.

"We can trust them for now. Sully is only here to help us, and Jennifer just wants Damon to be overthrown."

"It's not that I don't believe what you are saying, Brian, but don't you think you are being even harsher than normal? You had a talk with Vixy and it didn't go well, did it?" I ask looking at him. I know he has feelings for her. He tries to pretend he hates everything and everyone, but I think Vixy stole his heart.

"Vixy is only a woman, like any other woman. You can't trust them, for they will suck the life out of you. No matter what kind of man you are, you will always fall victim to a woman's beauty."

"Maybe you are being too harsh about that, Brian. She probably feels like Jennifer does. I really like Jennifer, but I don't want to move forward with her, for I don't even know who I really am yet. I am sure Vixy likes you. She is just doing what she feels is best."

"I don't really care anymore. They are more than likely like everyone else, London. Everyone doubts us. They don't trust us, and if we were to defeat Damon it will not be over for us."

I don't think the girls believe that, but I am sure it will be far from over even when we defeat Damon. I don't think with Brian's burst of outrage helps much either though.

"I believe that as well, Brian, but we need to think about things differently. Let's turn the tables on them. I think we are both ready to take this matter into our own hands. It doesn't matter what anyone thinks of us, it matters how they respect us. It is probably about time we become more like what people expect of a damned and a black pneuma."

Brian smiles, "Then we are on the right track." Brian then turns into a mist, *"Sully is coming."*

I look to see Sully coming to us. He wears a friendly smile, and as he gets closer, he calls, "What are you and Brian up to?"

"Not much. What is everyone else doing?" I ask.

"Nothing really, still just trying to figure out what is the best next course of action."

"I would actually like to talk to you about that. Would you like to go for a walk?" I ask, getting up. Brian and I want to have control over what we do. We think it is about time we do. If we are one of the only ones who can defeat Damon and Talon, his pneuma, then why shouldn't we be in control of what needs to be done next?

"Sure," Sully replies. "I could use a walk."

We start to walk with Brian and Danny following us. They play around as animals near us, but in the forest. Most of the time, pneumas just play around when their damned are talking, but I am sure Brian is talking to Danny about more important things. I think the whole thing of playing around is just staying up to date on their shape-shifting.

"Well, what do you want to talk about, London?" Sully asks, starting the conversation.

"How do you feel about this operation? Do you think we are running it the best we can?" I ask. I am going to tell Sully first about Brian and I wanting to take things into our own hands; I would like to hear what Sully thinks about it before announcing it to the rest of the group.

"I don't think it is run the best way. People all seem to have their own ideas on the matter. You and Brian are thinking about running it yourselves, aren't you?" I figured he would come to find out before I even said it to him. He is smart, and the fastest to realize when something is up or wrong.

I nod to his answer, but don't have to say anything else, for he starts to talk again. "Well, if you want my honest opinion, then I think it is the best way to go. I don't trust all the people here and what they want. I do trust you, London, and I have faith or I wouldn't be here. You know, I was planning on leaving once I got Danny back, but I decided against it."

"Why?"

"Because I see potential in you. I think if anyone can defeat Damon and Talon, it is going to be you and Brian. Because I believe this, this is why I stay. You have a long road ahead of you and Brian. Friends will be in short supply, but I will be one of them. I think it is about time you take matters into your own hands."

I smile, glad I have someone like Sully here to help me.

"I promise, Sully, I won't let you down, or anyone else who chooses to help me. I will do whatever I can to help the damned and their pneumas. I am glad to know I have someone I can trust, no matter what." I stop and look at him, as Sully does the same.

Sully smiles. "I promise, kid, I will do whatever I can to help you. As long as you keep true to your word, I will keep true to mine."

"Then the truth between us is all that will be." We then shake hands.

We go back to the rest. Everyone is here. Some are talking or doing their own things, but they look at us now as we enter the camp. Brian is a human near me. Sully steps near the fire to get himself another cup of coffee, knowing what Brian and I want to say.

"Better now, after your sudden outrage from earlier?" Livefen asks Brian. I can tell he is still annoyed with how Brian acted earlier.

"You were lucky it was just that, Livefen," Brian said watching his eyes. I know Brian means it too. Brian only says what he means.

"We actually have something to announce to all of you," I say looking at them all.

They all listen more intently now, wanting to hear what I have to say. I can tell people like Livefen are a little afraid though, of what we might say.

"If we are the ones expected to kill Damon and set the damned and the people suffering from him free, then from now on the battle will be under Brian's and my orders," I say it stubbornly, not planning on backing down from anyone. This is what is going to make or break us. Either Brian and I take over our lives or remain under the Sanctuary and everyone's thumb forever.

"This really is an outrage. We are the ones to get you to do this, not you asking us. We know what to do next. You haven't been here very long. We all have a common goal, London, so why try to take something into your own hands when you don't know enough about it yourself?" Livefen protests. His protest was expected though. It is the reaction from the others that I want to see the most.

This may not be the best time for Brian and me to try and take control, considering we are here because Brian and I almost died. It has to start today though. We are here because of bad planning. We could have died, and maybe even worse. We could have all have been defeated, and what are people going to do about Damon then?

"If we don't know enough about this, then why are we even here?" I ask Livefen. He doesn't answer me, looking like he has to think about this one. I continue anyway, "Taking down Damon and Talon rests in all of our hands, so I want all your opinions on what we do next. However, because Brian and I have been dragged into this, to be the ones who have to slay Damon and Talon, I think it is only right we have the final say in the matter."

They all seem to think about this. I watch them all, waiting for their replies. Amias is hard to read as usual. Breccan seems to be considering any possibility that could happen. Livefin is hard to read as well. I don't know if he is really pissed about all of this or maybe actually thinking about it. I already know what Sully and Danny think. Jennifer, I think, will agree with me, but you never know. She might think the idea of Brian and me completely taking over is not the best one.

"I hope they know we are saying how it is from now on, not suggesting. Unless they have one hell of an excuse," Brian thinks to me.

"Let's just hope they don't."

"I am with you no matter who is making the choices, London. If I didn't believe you could make the right one, I wouldn't be here in the first place," Jennifer says, looking at me in the eyes, breaking the growing silence between all of us.

I smile, feeling happier than I thought I would be hearing this from Jennifer. I feel if I have her and Sully, that is all I need by my side to win.

"If I thought you guys weren't worth anything, I wouldn't be here. I look forward to seeing what plans you guys have," Vixy smiles. I notice the smile is directed to Brian. He has a faint one in return, but I know what she says means more to him then he lets on.

The rest start to agree, until it is only down to Livefin. He looks around him, then settling his eyes on Brian and me he finally says, "It looks like you two get your wish no matter what I say. If everyone believes that it should be up to you two, then who am I to say otherwise? However, remember that sometimes it will be a bit harder than you and Brian just having the last word on a mission or a problem."

"I guess we will cross that bridge when it happens," I reply, leaving it as that.

With all that now over, Jennifer asks, "Then what do we do now?"

Brian and I look at each other, then we begin to talk to the rest about our next course of action.

CHAPTER 35

Growing

Brian

Now that we have taken matters into our own hands, things are quickly starting to change for the better. We have accomplished more, with fewer losses, and London and I are becoming more and more powerful. It is getting harder and harder for our enemy to defeat us.

London and I have continued training as well. The elf (even if I don't like admitting it) is one of the best archers I have seen along with Sully. They both teach London to get better at Raptor, his bow. He always practices sword fighting with Breccan, and how to use his mind better with Amias. Damned can visit each other in dreams. Many learn how to use their mind, or use magic to read others, so they are trying to teach London some of this. Although it will most likely take him years to get good at it. For now, the main thing is to teach him to defend his mind from others. Jennifer teaches London how to use magic, along with teaching him more tricks with the sword. I have to hand it to Jennifer; she knows how to fight. She is light on her feet and a hell of a fighter. I know she puts hours and hours of practice into it. Everything Jennifer does, she wants to be the best at, and I think she accomplishes that.

I train as well, but a lot of it I learn myself. There isn't much the damned, people or other pneumas can teach me here. I will practice fighting with London to get better at fighting with the damned, and teach him to get better at fighting pneumas. But I can only learn so much from that.

I have noticed a change in Vixy. I think she doesn't like that she turned me down that day. I know she wants to keep it that way, but her heart is telling her otherwise. I am going to wait for her to decide. My plans are coming to play now, and I can't mess them up for anything.

London is becoming who he is meant to be. Our names are starting to spread more and more throughout the land. I know if Damon didn't know who we were before, he knows now.

People have mixed opinions of us, some good and some bad. Some people think we are the savior, while others think that we might be another Damon. We are going to be someone of power. No matter how much good we do, I think it will never be enough to show the people who we are. Because he is a damned and because I am a black pneuma, some people think we can never do good. I don't care what the people think though. I care much more about the damned and the pneumas. We are fighting for them right now, and it is their respect we want to win.

We are getting closer to the time when we will meet Damon and Talon face to face. We cannot challenge his throne and then not expect to see him soon. I don't know how he views us now. Maybe he thinks we are quickly becoming a threat, or maybe he doesn't think much of us at all. Either way, he will soon find (if he does not think so already) that he should take anyone like us to be a threat.

CHAPTER 36

Spirit Mountains

London

I am sitting on a rock, trying to eat my lunch. It is about midday, but with all the fog it is hard to tell. We are making our way up the Mountain of Spirits. It is bone-chilling up here with so much fog you don't know where you are going most of the time, and with it being an eerie place altogether.

Brian is a mist right now. He is staying near me, but is very alert. He doesn't like it up here anymore than I do. I always wanted to see the mountains, but not ones like these.

There are spirits up here who are similar to Brian, but a bit different. They are pretty much a pneuma who doesn't have a damned. They are not as powerful as Brain, and most of them can't hurt people. I don't know much about them, but I think Brian does, so I will quiz him later about it.

"You should hurry and eat, London, because we should be moving out. The spirits don't really come out until nightfall, and it will be better if we have a place to stay by then," Brian says, interrupting my lunch.

I put the last remaining food I had into my mouth then reply, after I swallow. "Can they really hurt us?"

"Not really, but some can. It really depends on the spirit. We can talk more about spirits tonight though, when we make camp. For now, we should continue." Brian starts to move more up the mountain.

I get up and start to walk up the mountain, following Brian. No one else is with us right now. Brian and I took the mountainside, while Jennifer and Sully make their own way to the castle. We want to take this place out without being noticed. The damned and their pneumas are all we need if we play this right. Brian and I will take care of the master, while Sully and Jennifer make sure to take out anyone who could be a threat. We decided to split up because the smaller the group, the less of a chance they will notice us. We heard there are spies all over, so we have to tread very lightly here.

We continue to travel during the day. When it starts to get darker, Brian says we should make camp. I listen to Brian since he seems to know more about this place than me.

The terrain is rocky and steep here. I must watch my footing, for the rocks are loose. There is not a lot of green here, but some manage to live in this harsh place. Trees are few and far between, but some types of bushes with small leaves seems to like it, along with a few other types of plants I don't recognize that grow through the crakes in the rocks.

We make camp in one of the flattest parts we can find. I set up my bed and put together a cold meal. We can't make a fire because it is too risky out here. I eat my food sitting down on a rock looking out, while Brian eats his, not having the slightest of manners with it. I don't think he cares. I don't really care either, although I generally have little patience for people who eat obnoxiously. I am glad he likes to eat by himself because of this.

Our camp is near a steep part of the mountain to my right. It is a fifteen-foot drop, from which I would like to stay away. It is little denser here with foliage, and there is a tall green plant with large purple flowers making its way through the rocks. That adds color and some brightness to a dark, lonely place. The fog that has been here all day has cleared up some now, and I can see the sky. It is going to be a clear night tonight, and I can already see some of the stars starting to come out. I lay back in my bed and put my hands behind my head, looking up at the sky. With nothing else to do, I just watch the skies for a while.

Brian is asleep, but I know it is an uneasy sleep. If we are somewhere where it is not safe, Brian will not have a good night's sleep. Usually, he will sleep near me as an animal, but right now he is away from me, curled up as a small fox. He is asleep, but his ears are perked up to catch the sound of anything that can pose a threat.

I watch the sky as it becomes darker, and more stars start to fill the night sky. The sky is beautiful tonight, and nights like this I am glad I don't have a roof over my head to block the view. I feel slightly lonely though. On nights like these I wish I still had Sara. I enjoyed waking up to a beautiful woman by my side, and liked having someone to whom I was close. I wonder if Brian ever thinks about that. I know that pneumas can and do form relationships with each other, but I don't know if they think of marriage or staying with someone forever.

I close my eyes, trying to get into a more comfortable position. I open my eyes once to see Brian still laying there, then fall into a deep sleep. When I open my eyes, I find I am in a warm bed in a room. I look around to see there is no roof over my head, so I can still look at the stars. It is a small room, but a cozy one. I take a deep breath and look to see a beautiful elf woman sitting at the foot of the bed. I sit up quickly and watch her as she turns to look at me.

She has long, straight, perfect blond hair, high cheekbones and nice lips. She is tall and fit. I have never dreamed of a woman like her before, but I don't think I ever had a dream quite like this in the first place. Even though it feels dreamlike, I feel conscious and know I am not just dreaming about this woman.

She has bright blue eyes that stare hard back into mine. A small smile crosses her lips, and she says with a voice as sweet as honey, as powerful as the wind and calm as the flow of smooth water, "Having good sleep?"

"Who are you?" I ask.

"Someone who has decided to drop by for a visit," she replies.

She comes and sits beside me as I lay back. I am not afraid of her and don't mind her getting close. I am in a dream, anyway. I think the only difference is, she is a real person and she is really visiting me. I heard that the damned can do that.

She gently runs her fingers through my hair and leans closer to me. I watch her as she keeps her lips close to mine.

"London, I have been wanting to meet you. There has been a lot of talk going around, and I wanted to see for myself who you are."

"Who are you? Are you a damned?" I ask.

She puts her soft hand on my cheek and gets closer to me, so we are practically breathing the same air. I take a deep breath, looking at her. I want to put my hands on her and kiss, but I am a little hesitant to do so, having no idea who she is. I do feel an instant like for this woman.

"I am a sorceress with the elves. I am very interested in you, London. Many people go through rough lives, but you are having the weight of the world put on your shoulders, after seeing only eighteen summers."

"I don't know if I would say that."

She gently leans closer to me and we kiss. Her kisses put a warm feeling through me. We start to kiss a little harder, and I put my hands on her. She doesn't kiss very long though and slowly pulls away from me. We both look at each other, taking deep breaths.

"You have a long journey ahead of you, and I want to help," she says.

"How will you be able to help me?"

"You will find out soon."

"When?"

"We will be meeting soon, and some things are better left said in person. I came here because I wanted to see you. I wanted to look into your eyes and see what kind of man you are. Many will try to crush you, London, but I will be your ally because we both want similar things."

"When will we meet?" I ask her again, having the feeling I will be getting no answer.

"Soon enough," is all she replies. She puts her hand on my cheek then we kiss again.

———•———

I jerk awake, breathing hard. It feels like I have been pulled from a whole different world. Who was that girl? What did she want from me? I don't think normally on a first meeting I would have kissed a strange girl like that, but because it was in a dream, I didn't see anything wrong with it.

"Had a bad dream?" Brian asks, looking at me. He is a black panther right now, laying in a crouched position. I can tell he is irritated. Those spirits must be keeping him up. I don't understand. If they are not much of a threat, what is he worried about?

"I was having a strange dream. In fact, I think it was more than a dream," I said looking at him.

"Who did you dream of in your sleep?" Brian comes to me and lays down. He is now looking at me, but his ears twitch a lot, meaning he is still on the lookout.

"There was an elf woman who was there. She was friendly and claimed to be a sorceress. She said she wanted to help me." I don't think I have to tell Brian I kissed her, for I don't think that would make a difference. It was still a dream after all.

"I wouldn't trust anyone who enters your dreams unless you know who they are. Have you ever seen this woman before?"

"No, never, although she told me we would meet soon."

"Our name is starting to get a lot of attraction. All sorts of people are going to start knowing about us. Many of them we will want to avoid. Did she say anything else?" Brian asks, looking into my eyes like I might lie.

I shake my head. "There was nothing else. She just claimed she wanted to see me with her own eyes. Now you tell me why you are so paranoid about these spirits." I said this, for Brian has gotten up, and I know he is thinking about going after one of them.

"There are two reasons why I do not like them." Then Brian leaps into the bushes and I see a spirit run off as a ghost-like, pink rabbit. Like the pneumas, they are all some sort of color. But unlike the pneumas, their animal still has the appearance of a mist or ghost when they shape-shift.

Brian walks back to me, then continues, "First, some of these spirits could be spies for the castle we are about to take over. He is a mage and a damned, a pretty powerful combination."

"What's the second reason?" I ask.

"Sometimes spirits of the same color as a pneuma will try to take control of their damned. It is rare, but I do not take chances."

"Could that happen to you and me?" I assume it could, but I don't see how. Brian tells me he has been my pneuma since I was born.

"It is possible, but like I said, rare. It would have to be a black powerful spirit. Either way though, it is my job to consider all possibilities, and overall, I do not care for these spirits." Brian goes back to walking around and listening after saying this.

"So where do these spirits come from? Are they a soul to someone, or just born the way they are?"

Brian sighs, but he answers. "There is two different kinds of wild spirits. One of the wild spirits, actually do have damned, but they are very different then us. They are known for being wild because often they will leave their damned for long periods of time, and are less human then normal pneumas. Then there is the other who are really called damnato, which means lost souls. They are ones who either lost their damned before they became one, or actually survived after their damned passed, which is most rare. There is another why a pneuma becomes a damnato, and that is when their damned is so far in hell, their pneuma cannot get them out, and get lost."

"Does the damnato look like these wild spirits we have been seeing?" I ask.

"Not all of them, but you will defiantly know there is something different about them, when you meet one."

I nod as I start feeling tired again. I am about to lay my head down when I hear a neigh. I jerk my head up and get out of bed staying low. I have no idea who it is. Brian doesn't seem concerned.

Brian walks to the north of us and gets down. He is a man now. He looks at me, and thinks, *"It is just more spirits."*

I walk over to him and get down beside him. I look at what he is looking at, and it takes my breath away. In front of me there are some dead trees with many spirits all around them. The spirits come in all colors, including green, pink, red, white, blue and even more colors. Most of the colors are all in different shades as well. The spirits are in the form of horses right now. It is a beautiful sight, and many of them sing in voices I can compare to nothing else. It is sort of like a human's, but yet so foreign to my ears. They run around playing with each other and dancing. Some of them in the trees take the form of humans. They are the ones to play and sing the music.

"It is beautiful. I have never seen anything like it before," I say, watching them.

Brian seems a little less impressed. "Beautiful maybe, but deadly even more. Beauty has a way of deceiving people. Some of the most beautiful things are the worst."

"It seems like most things have a way of deceiving you," I reply, thinking about it.

We both continue to watch the spirits dance under the stars. I move my bed so I can watch them. I lay there for a while with Brian near me, watching them and listening. I soon drift off into a deep sleep.

CHAPTER 37

Stranger in Black

I move quietly with Brian. Everything is dark, since it is just after midnight. We are walking stealthily along the castle wall, making our way inside. Sully and Jennifer are here, making sure the path stays clear for Brian and me.

We keep out of sight. Only a few torches are lit. There aren't a lot of guards out, and the ones who are seem tired. Brian and I can easily avoid them. We make our way into the castle. Brian moves first as a mist, quicker than any man can move. I follow behind him, keeping back, letting Brian lead the way. We make our way through the halls, with one side being nothing but the wall, and the other side filled with windows that let the light of the moon in.

"How much longer before you think we are at his room?" I think to Brian.

"We are almost there."

We make our way down a hall and stop before rounding the corner. There are two guards watching the door to the master's room. Brian and I exchange looks. *"I will take them out. I can do it without letting them know I was even there,"* Brian instructs me.

I nod. Brian moves away, staying out of the light from the torches and goes to the two guards behind them. Brian breaks one of the soldier's necks, then the other's before either had time to even scream.

I walk over there, as Brian is a man now. He looks at me. *"If the pneuma belonging to the master of the castle is any good, he will know we are here. Be ready."*

"Then let's not keep them waiting," I reply steeping to the door.

We both get ready. I hold onto the halt of my long sword Misery, ready for a battle. Brian is still human beside me, but more than likely when the door opens, he will change.

We both nod our heads to single that we are ready. We believe this should be the damned with the purple pneuma we fought at the castle with the golden dammed. I don't know if we will see him or not, though I learned that I should be ready for anything.

I open the door and Brian and I walk into the room. We see a younger man, probably just a few years older than me, looking at me from where he sits by a desk. His pneuma is the same age as well, and takes the form of a man. The damned's pneuma has black hair with a purple stripe through it. Like all pneumas, his hair represents the color he is as a pneuma, and the level of magic and what type it is.

We all stand facing each other. We are in a large room. There is a bed up against the right wall and a desk near a window at the back of the room. There is also a stone fireplace on the left wall.

I see that he is not the same guy I fought before, so the owner of the place must not be here. I am surprised to see that the young man carries no weapons. The weapons are all sitting on the bed. His pneuma also doesn't act aggressive. Upon seeing us, they act as they normally would. I don't think they want to fight.

"We knew you would be coming," the damned says, breaking the silence of the room.

"It doesn't look like you were prepared for it," Brian says as he glances at them both. He watches the pneuma more though. I think he is ready for the other pneuma to try something.

"I do not wish to fight with either of you. I have seen what you guys have done. I have been training most of my life as a sorcerer and a damned, and I cannot do what you did."

"So, you are a coward then?" Brian asks, sounding harsh and cold. It figures that Brian would behave that way. It wouldn't have been my approach, but Brian isn't wrong.

The other man doesn't seem to take offense, however. "I wouldn't say I am a coward. I just know what I am. I could fight, but I have no desire to fight with either of you. It seems that for the damned, there are only two sides from which to choose. You or Damon, and I can't say I am one that would die for Damon. I am here because I was being trained as a sorcerer under Bellmore, who I believe you have met before."

"I assume he is the master of this place, the damned with the purple pneuma," I say, just to ensure that it is the damned I had fought before.

"Yes."

There is silence for a few minutes, then I continue, "Well, there seems to be a bit of a problem here. We have come to overthrow the master and claim this place under a different authority." I don't have any idea where this damned and his pneuma stand, but I know I don't trust him.

"I do not wish to serve Damon. I do not want to betray my master, but I will not fight for what I don't believe. I would like to help you." He talks like there is no lie to what he says. I highly doubt that any of it got through to Brian. He doesn't have sympathy for most people, nor does he forgive easily.

"You betray your own people, and expect us to trust you? I don't know what false world you are living in, but it is not ours," Brian snorts

"I have been here since I was five. I have only trained while I was here. Many damned are starting to make their choice and choose a side, and I would like to choose mine now. I knew that you guys were coming, I could have made it difficult, but I didn't. I am hoping to help and not be an enemy."

Brian and I glance at each other slightly. I ask Brian, *"Well, what is your opinion?"*

"I don't particularly like him, but there is always the chance he is telling the truth. Although you know I don't like taking chances if they can be helped."

"I understand, but I think we can trust him." I can usually read people well, and I don't think he is lying. If we wanted to, we could take care of him, probably easily as well, but if we can avoid it, that would be better.

"I can help you guys even now," he says looking at the both of us. I think he knows we are considering if we should believe him or not.

"What can you help us with?" I ask before Brian can.

"I am not the master of this castle. I would not be left with that kind of responsibility yet."

"So, is Bellmore here then?"

He is already shaking his head before I finished the sentence. "No, but there is another who watches the castle in his absence."

"Are you saying you would help us fight him?" I ask, a little skeptically.

The damned looks me in the eyes, "I will. We do not like each other. I haven't wanted to be here for some years now, but had no opportunity to leave until now. I will help you, for even as good as you are now, I am sure you will need help. He is a mage and a very powerful damned. He has a way to make the wild spirits listen to him."

"Why should we trust you? That is the biggest question," Brian says, not looking convinced.

"If I hadn't said anything about him, you wouldn't know there was another damned here. I could have made a fight happen, I knew you guys where coming, but I didn't."

"I think we should go ahead and trust him, Brian. If things go awry, we can take care of him. If he is telling the truth, I would rather have someone as an ally than an enemy," I think.

"All right, but one false move from him will be his end," Brian replies, and I know he means what he says.

"All right, we believe what you say. If you help us with this mage, we will consider taking you in," I say to the damned and his pneuma.

"But keep in mind that we are far from allies at the moment. We are just neutral," Brian adds, keeping his tone unfriendly.

"I understand. I didn't expect more than that." The young man gets up and looks over at the bed. "Can I get my weapons now?"

I make a hand gesture for him to go ahead. He walks over to grab his weapons, then turns to face us again.

"Lead the way," I say, stepping away from the door.

He walks through with his pneuma, and Brian and I follow. He takes us farther into the castle. Soon the walls fade into rocks, and there are no longer any windows. We are heading into the mountain beside which the castle was built.

Little is said as we continue on this path. There are a few lanterns that light up the place, but that is it. Brian and the new pneuma follow us as humans. The new guy is dressed in robes like many of the other mage-type people I've seen. To me what stands out is how he styles his hair. He has both sides of his head shaved, except for down the middle like a mohawk. Either it is just his style or it means something to these mages.

"What are your names?" I ask the damned and his pneuma.

"My name is Samuel and my pneuma is Taylor," he replies. We keep our voices low, just in case someone is nearby.

There is no reason to say Brian's or my name, since they already know who we are. We don't say anything else. I just needed their names, so I know what to call them.

We head down and stop as we get to a strange room. There is a large bridge with deep slopes on either side that leads to a black abyss.

I stop as Samuel and Taylor do too. Samuel looks at me. "He is down here."

"For your sake, you better be telling the truth," Brain says, none too friendly.

"You do not have to worry about that. You will find that we are true to our word," Taylor the pneuma says, speaking to us for the first time.

Brian looks at him unfazed. "We will see."

We start to walk on the bridge, and before we get too far, we see someone making his way towards us on the other side of the bridge. He wears a black hood and a robe as well. His pneuma follows as a dark blue mist beside him.

"He looks ready for a fight," I think sarcastically to Brian.

"We must be careful. I don't trust who we are with, and the one with the blue pneuma is a damned to be reckoned with."

I pull out Misery, holding him low, but ready to use him. Samuel pulls out a black axe and a shield. This is not what I expect a mage to use, but whatever works for him.

The damned with the blue pneuma comes closer to us and says to Samuel, "I thought that you were never to be trusted."

"We all have to choose a side in the end. Mine is not with you," Samuel replies.

The pneumas go on the attack. I can't tell what they turn into. Changing from a mist to another form happens quickly, so it is difficult to keep up with them. The blue pneuma is quickly proving to be a challenge. Even with Brian and the new purple pneuma, Taylor, helping him, they still are having trouble.

I can tell the damned we are facing wants to take out Samuel. He comes for Samuel swinging a giant staff-like weapon at Samuel. I bring Misery up to protect him and both of our weapons ring out with the hit.

We back up and he says some words I do not understand, lighting up his staff a fiery blue.

Samuel and I stand together as the damned tries to swing his staff. We both defend ourselves, but with his magic, it makes it difficult. The damned's power is incredibly strong.

"I was designed to defeat swords of magic and mystical creatures. Take out his weapons and there won't be much more he can do," Misery screams through my thoughts.

I do as he says. Swinging Misery hard at the damned, he brings up his staff, and Misery goes smashing through it, breaking it into two. He backs up with surprise in his eyes, unbelieving what Misery just did.

He throws his now broken weapons down, backing up as Samuel and I move forward. His hands light up with blue magic, and I get ready for whatever may come next. From the corner of my eye, I see a black spirit come to his side. My heart skips a beat. This may be Talon. I don't know of any other black pneuma besides him and Brian.

The black spirit comes for me. I swing my sword at him, ducking as the black spirit flies over my head. He is smart though. He misses the blow and now comes back.

Samuel is now facing the damned alone, for I must face this black spirit. He is powerful and I need to know where the damned is. He comes at me, and I try to slice him, but he goes through me as a mist, making it impossible for me to hurt him.

He comes at me faster than I can react, knocking Misery out of my hands. He throws me to the ground. As I try to get up, he grabs me, dragging me across the bridge. I try to pull out a weapon with which to stab him, but I am not able to.

He lets me go once we are some distance from the others. I get up and face him. Seeing him better now, I know he is not a pneuma with a damned but just a black spirit. I wish I still had Misery with me, for that weapon is meant to take out spirits.

We stand facing each other, with me ready to grab Bone Crusher and Wolfbane. I know as soon as I do, he will attack, so I must be ready.

"I was wondering if I would ever meet you," the spirit says in a lifeless cold voice. A chill runs down my spine.

"I believe a lot of people are starting to wonder about that," I reply. The more I do, the more people want to get to know me.

"It will be different for you and me though. I need you."

I don't know what he means by that, but I don't like it. I try to come at him bringing Bone Crusher and Wolfbane out of their sheaths.

I can't seem to hit him. He is always a second ahead of me, or forms into a mist where he cannot receive any damage.

He comes swiping under me, so I hit the ground hard. I try to get up as I see him standing over me as a dark human-like figure.

"I see potential in you, but right now you are still too inexperienced and young," he says in that cold voice.

I try to rise but before I can, I feel a horrible burning pain in my chest like my soul is being ripped from me. I scream in pain, not being able to control the agonizing pain. I keep my hand on my chest, breathing hard, with my teeth clenched.

I look up to see that the black spirit has his arm stretched out like a damned would do to take someone's soul. I try to rise despite the pain. He kicks me down before I can. I roll around on the ground as the pain starts to spread through my body. The pain is intense, and nothing makes it better. The pain just increases.

Just when I think I can't take any more, the pain stops. I feel Brian near me, and the black spirit leaves. I open my eyes to see Samuel, Taylor and Brian.

Breathing hard, sweat covering my face and shaking, I slowly start to rise to my feet. Samuel looks concerned and asks, "Are you all right?"

I nod my head and ask, "What happened?" I was in so much pain I lost awareness of what was even going on.

"We defeated the damned with the blue pneuma. We did not defeat the black spirit, for he got away, but we saved you from him."

"Turns out they were worth keeping alive after all," Brain said, glancing at Samuel and Taylor.

Samuel smiles. "I told you we would be."

I nod, taking a deep breath. I feel better now, but I am trying to understand what just happened.

"You did well. I am glad we don't have to kill you," I say, pulling the best smile I can. "Come on then, it is time to meet up with the rest."

I take the soul from the damned with the blue pneuma and retrieve Misery, then we all start to leave this place.

There are things I want to say to Brian about what happened. I know he has things to say as well, but they probably will have to wait until later. I would rather just talk to him then, instead of doing it all through thoughts.

I know that black spirit, whatever it was doing to me, was affecting Brian as well. I think I have an idea what it was doing, and I believe Brian does too.

CHAPTER 38

Finally, Yes

Brian

I watch London, Jennifer, Sully and Samuel as they sit at a table drinking and talking. It is early in the morning. Earlier, we fought the damned with the blue pneuma. I haven't been able to talk to London since then, but I know he wants to talk to me. Right now, though, I think he drank a few more then he thought, and I know Jennifer sitting beside him is the only one on his mind. As long as he doesn't make a fool out of himself, I don't care.

I am with the other pneumas. We talk and spend time amongst each other. Taylor, the new pneuma, doesn't seem bad, and his damned is quickly getting along with people. I will keep an eye on him. I think Vixy and Danny have already accepted him. We are all in the same room as our damned, shape-shifting into different things, playing around and talking to each other. I am a cat sitting on one of the barrels in the room, watching everything. Vixy, in the form of a fox, jumps onto the barrel next to me.

"Hello, Vixy," I say, watching her.

"Hello, Brian. How are you doing this morning? Are you getting tired yet? You have been up all night," she says.

I jump off the barrel and turn into a man. Vixy jumps off and turns to a human as well. I face her now with a smile and say so only she can hear, "Sure, I'll go rest up, if you are willing to come with me."

Vixy shakes her head. "In that case then, you can stay up."

"Are you saying you will keep me up?" I ask with a hint of a smile.

"No, I am saying you can continue staying here, for I am not going anywhere with you." She walks past me like she has nothing more to say about the topic. I know she likes me, but she is too stubborn to give in.

"That is all right. You know you are a lot stricter than Jennifer is. She isn't that hard on London."

"Well, one of us has to be. Besides, Jennifer and London do keep their distance as well," she protests, turning back to me.

"I didn't think they kept too big of a distance from each other. If I recall they do have a romantic side to their friendship."

We are in the same room as everyone else, but it is a large room, so we are farther away from the rest. We talk quietly so no one can hear our conversation.

"That was only once, and they both agreed not to do it again," she says looking as stubborn as ever. I find that both attractive about her, and annoying. Sometimes she can be just a little too stubborn

I shrug. "If you truly believe that. It is better that way. We need to focus on our plans, not him thinking about Jennifer."

"If that is true, then why do you pay so much attention to me?" I can tell in her eyes she is anxious for my answer.

I smile slightly. "For fun, nothing more than that. I have things on my list more important than how you feel about me, Vixy. Besides, you made it clear a while ago that I am only someone you were protecting, not much more than that."

"I didn't say it quite like that." Vixy obviously doesn't like my response. I see a frown form at the corner of her mouth.

"Well, that is what you want, isn't it?" I ask. I turn into a mist and go through the window and on to the roof.

I turn into a man again and smile seeing Vixy follow me up here. I know she has a few words to say to me. This is serving her right though. She previously turned me down. If that is not what she wants then she better make it clear, or I will move on. I am into Vixy and I want her, but I will not bend over backwards for her. If she wants me, she will have to make it obvious as well.

"I never said that is what I wanted," Vixy says with her arms crossed, her hip swung to the side, and giving me a stern look.

"Then what did you say?" I ask, staring her down just the same.

"I said it would be for the best."

"Would it? I don't know how it would be for the best, but I am not thinking of that, Vixy. There are many things at stake right now, and London and I are only getting dragged further into the mess." I step away from her and look out away from the kingdom then continue, "Either we will make a change or die for it. Our fate is tied with that of Damon's and Talon's. We will either be the ones to bring them down, or no one will for many years to come. I don't see anyone else challenging them the way we are."

Vixy comes to stand beside me looking out as well. After taking a deep breath, she says, "You are right, Brian. That is a long road, and you are not even halfway there."

"I hope for a long life though, although it will be quicker than some think when Talon and Damon face London and me. Everyone who knows anything knows it is coming. It is just a matter of when, not if."

Vixy nods then looks at me. I look at her in return. "Brian, I am here because I admire you. As a loyal servant I will follow you to the end, but as something more to you, I don't know if I can trust you. I am strong, but I don't want my heart torn from me."

"Well, Vixy, I have told you what I think. It is up to you if you trust me or not. I must do what I do, whether you are by my side or not. Don't expect me to wait forever if you can't make a choice. You know what I want from you, now it is your choice to figure out what you want from me."

We both look back out, with Vixy thinking heavily on this. The options are laid out for her. She can choose, and I will accept what she does. Vixy grabs my hand. "My devotion to Jennifer comes first, but what I really want from you also comes first. I want to be more than just your protector, but I will also take care of Jennifer in what I think is the best for her."

"Well, if you are talking about her and London, you can lead her into whatever you think is right. What we want doesn't have to be the same as theirs."

We turn to face each other, and she gives me a kiss. I kiss her back and put my arms around her, as she does the same. I can tell she has wanted this for a while, but so have I. Our love would only help encourage Jennifer's and London's, since their spirits will be together, though it doesn't mean they have to have each other. Their feelings for each other will just be stronger.

Vixy and I stay on the roof for some time, enjoying each other. We only leave when we know our damned finally turn in to sleep.

London

I was very exhausted, and drinking so much didn't make me feel any better. I know Brian ran off with Vixy. I thought she turned him down, but I guess that is not how she felt after all. Brian comes into the room as a spirit and moves around the room before he settles down. I watch him come from behind the bed as a black cat.

"You are aware that it is five in the morning, right? I am surprised you stayed up this late," Brian thinks.

"The same for you. I shouldn't have drunk so much." I look up at the ceiling.

"It is all right to do so once in a while," Brian says, jumping onto the bed as he changes into a black panther. He lays down at the foot of the bed and looks out.

"So, I didn't know you and Vixy are together." I know she didn't turn him down again, for he is in too good a mood for that.

"We weren't until a little while ago. She has wanted me, but she has been think-ing it is not for the best. She finally gave in. Vixy is a good woman, and I am happy that she finally did."

"So, what does it mean when pneumas like each other? Will that have any effect on Jennifer and me?" I ask.

I feel dumb asking questions like this. It is probably one that all damned know, but I do not. I think Brian understands though. I did jump into this life head first, so I am learning as I go along.

"It can, but it doesn't change anything drastically. Your feelings for Jennifer could increase, but that is all. It is not like you don't already have feelings for her."

"Well, I do, but we are not in a relationship as you know. I just need sleep," I say, rolling over on my side.

"Then good night London, or good morning," Brian lays his head down.

I cannot close my eyes, thinking about that black spirit. I don't know what he was doing to me when I felt that pain. He could have been trying to take my soul from me, but wouldn't that be Brian? I guess I need to know more. Is a pneuma really your soul and spirit, or something else that's just a part of you?

I open my eyes and think to Brian, *"Brian, what was that black spirit doing to me?"*

"I wondered when you were going to ask me about that. We need to be more careful, London. I made a mistake. That spirit wanted you to be his damned, he is one of the lost souls damnato. That pain we were feeling, he was trying to separate you and me, so he would take my spot. Spirits normally get that way when their damned dies at a very young age before they are born, or when he is so little that they didn't bond that much yet. Sometimes, the pneuma is able to live. When that happens, they try to find another damned. Which, in this case, was you."

"What would happen if he ever succeeds?" I ask.

"We cannot let that happen, or that would be the end for us. We will both have to be on our guards now. We were lucky we had Samuel there, or things could be very different right now." I know he is annoyed with what happened. It could have been the end of us today. I am glad that Samuel was there as well. It is nice to know there is another damned we can trust.

"I will be watchful for that black pneuma. Do you think we will see him again?"

"I would be surprised if we don't," is the only thing Brian replies, laying his head back down to sleep.

I close my eyes and let my thoughts wander. Soon I am in a deep sleep, dreaming of faraway things.

CHAPTER 39

Bones Again

I look at my hands with no flesh, just bones. It is uncomfortable being this way, not being able to feel. I need to learn to be more careful. It is a scary thought. How many times have I died already? I wonder, does that mean I really am not that great at what I do, or is it just the way the damned work?

I died this time being pushed off a high cliff. It was a nasty death, but at least it was a quick one. I fell fighting with a group of mercenaries who work for Damon. They had with them a big, bulky, horned creature who pushed me off the cliff. After they were all defeated, it came up quickly, hitting me, and I did not react fast enough. Brian battled it, though, and took his soul, so he could take the shape of it. I left the underworld quickly, thanks to Brian. I met those two guys again when I was in the underworld. I think I am becoming friends with them.

I am sitting on a rock, near the edge of a fast-flowing small river. It is more like a little creek, not being very deep or wide. There are trees around us and it is dry here. Now that it is summer, things have been hot and dry wherever we are. There are no longer beautiful wildflowers all over the place, although we are not in exactly the same area, they were in.

Brian seems to jump around, shape-shifting to whatever he wants to be, having a lot of energy this morning.

I look up at Brian as he turns into a man now. "We should probably find a way to turn me back soon."

Brian sits down on the rock facing me, "That would be a good idea. You are not as strong when you are a skeleton. I think we are really ticking off Damon now though."

"Well, I am sure we are, but are we just a nuisance right now, or do you think he is starting to be threatened by us?" I ask. Brian will be very honest about this question.

"I don't think we are the only ones in his sight, but we are making an impact. When he does reach out to us is the time, we know that we have officially moved up. Once we become a big enough problem to him, I think he will want to talk to us first before he decides he wants to get rid of us."

"Do you actually believe he might want us to join him at some point?" I ask, a little surprised.

"It is highly likely. How do you think Damon got some of the best fighting damned to work right beside him? Many of them fought against him at first, but he has his way. Many of the great ones seemed to join him at the end. It will not be us though. We will be the first to finish what we set out to do. We came to slay Damon and Talon, and that is what will be done."

I wonder about what Brian says. Sometimes, I wonder how bad Damon is, and wish I knew more. I wonder why so many damned who set out to fight him changed their minds and turned to serve him. Sometimes I wonder, does Brian want to take out Damon because he is an evil ruler like everyone says he is, or does Brian just want Damon's throne?

"Why do you think so many damned went to serve Damon and Talon? Do you think he offered them something they couldn't refuse, or did they decide that they and Damon have something in common?"

Brian shrugs. "I do not know, but trust me, London, Damon needs to be overthrown. He has committed many crimes and has killed hundreds of people. For whatever reason, others have decided to follow him. I am sure it was for their own selfless purpose."

"Probably so," I say, but I still think about it.

I am tired of being a skeleton. Not being able to breathe, feel or eat is a horrible way to be. I will be better once I am human again.

Brian turns into a mist moving, around the rocks I am on. Moving forward, he thinks, *"It looks like company has arrived."*

I am about to reply but decide against it when I see Vixy as a mist come over to us. She and Brian circle around each other as spirits as a greeting, then she goes back to Jennifer as Jennifer comes into view along with the rest. Brian comes beside me, turning into a man once again.

There has been a change with Vixy and Brian since she finally decided that she loves Brian as well. It is all a secret though, except from Jennifer and I. I don't think there is any secret I could keep from Brian, and there is none he can keep from me. Well, at least as far as I know. Most people wouldn't be able to see the change in Brian and Vixy when they are near each other. They are very good at masking their feelings. I know Brian well though, and I know how he feels. Plus, when it is just Brian, me, Jennifer and Vixy, they are not afraid to show their true colors. It is a little odd though. Jennifer and I haven't talked about it, nor do we bring it to the attention of the others. I don't know if I should be concerned about it, but I don't think there is anything wrong with it. I am going to leave Brian alone on what he wants to do with his love life, as long as he does the same for me.

I have noticed that Vixy doesn't seem to like me too much, as she is a little cold towards me. I do not know why this is. Maybe it is because she knows I have feelings for Jennifer, so that makes her concerned. Jennifer and I are in a good place right now, and I wouldn't do anything to hurt her. I think Vixy probably thinks it is just her job to make sure that Jennifer stays safe.

Jennifer, Vixy, Sully, Danny, Samuel, Taylor, Livefen, Amias and Breccan are all here.

"It looks like you weren't being very careful," Sully says with a smile, seeing me as a skeleton.

We have all been taking out these mercenaries who work for Damon for about a week now. They were finishing up taking a group of them out, while I left to finish off some who escaped. It was on that last mission that I ended up as a skeleton.

"I try, but trying isn't always good enough," I reply. They all stop some feet from me. The pneumas stay as people this time, so that we can all talk. Usually, the pneumas will play amongst each other, while their damned are together, but for now, they keep to themselves.

"Well, we can tell," Jennifer says, giving me a cute smile.

I try my best with a smile, which is hard to do when you don't have lips. "Thanks for pointing that out."

"Well if I don't, who else will?"

"Well, enough of that, for there is something important we must announce to you," Livefen says. I can see in his eyes—whatever it is, he seems to think it is a privilege.

"I don't know what is so important that he must tell us, but I hope it is something useful to us," Brian thinks, not sounding all too thrilled about it.

"Who knows?"

"What is the important announcement?" I ask.

"The kingdoms will be coming together in a couple of days. It is one of the biggest parties of the year that takes place in the elven kingdom. London and Brian will be their guests of honor. Even your home kingdom will be there!" Livefen says, sounding rather thrilled by it.

I don't know what to think. I don't think I will be a very honorable guest to my home kingdom. After all, I did marry the king's daughter, and then she left me, saying she couldn't stay with someone who was a damned. I don't have any idea what that kingdom thinks of me now. You could say I didn't leave on the best note.

"You will have to become human again though. I don't know what kind of talk you would stir up going as you are," Sully says with a slight smile.

"Yeah, I don't think that would be a good idea." I look down at myself as I speak.

"No, so I guess you can deal with it yourself. Will we be seeing you at the party?" Livefen asks.

"Yes. I will turn myself back into a human and will meet you guys there. I think that is the best thing to do. There is no reason for you guys to continue to stay with me while I do that."

They all agree, and we continue talking for a little longer. We talk a little about the battle we just won, what effects we are starting to make on Damon and a little about what we should plan to do next. Most of them seem to be excited about the idea of this party. Sully doesn't sound too thrilled about it, but then again, it doesn't sound like his kind of thing in the first place.

We spend the night together, for they will leave in the morning, and I will visit someplace I can consume souls.

I lay on my bed watching the stars. I only prefer a tent when the weather is bad or it is cold outside. As a skeleton, I don't have to worry about the cold. Brian has been around the stream, catching fish or something.

After a while, Brian comes back to me. I don't know what he is right now, staying outside of the light of the fire, and moving fast through the night. Brian likes the night. He often runs around doing who knows what until he turns in. I do not think he needs as much sleep as I, for he never seems to sleep as much as me. He will occasionally sleep during the day when he can. He probably just assumes that the worst will come at night, and if I am asleep, that means he has to watch out for the both of us.

Brian turns into a human and kneels by the fire. He doesn't look at me, but thinks to me, *"Many pneumas are out tonight. It is amazing; all of you can stay in bed on a night like this."*

I don't see why tonight is any different. Perhaps it is an especially full bright moon.

"What is so special about tonight?" I ask Brian.

"To a damned, maybe there is nothing special, but to a pneuma, it could be a different story. They say that the full moon opens a door to the pneumas that only they can see. It leads them to a world that only pneumas are allowed to enter."

"What is that world like?" I ask, intrigued now.

Brian messes with the fire, looking into it as if he is in deep thought. *"It is a world where all pneumas come from. It is our birth world."*

"Your birth world? You are not born on earth?" The pneumas' lives are still a mystery to me. Their relationships, children and what they think are all quite different from us. I still don't quite know how they came to be in the first place.

Brian takes a minute before he answers me. I wonder how much he will even tell me. He never seems to want to talk about the pneumas' lives. All pneumas seem to take this approach though, and it makes me wonder about them.

"I was not born on earth, but came into this world with your first thought. My life here is based around you like yours is based around mine," Brian thinks, turning to look at me.

"What was it like in the other world? What's the purpose of it?"

"There are more things you will come to know about the pneumas, but I will not tell you all about them now. Those are things you will learn in time, as we become closer as damned and pneuma. However, I will tell you this. I cannot be in this world without you, as I am your lifeline, and you are mine. The moment you died was the moment I became your life. Neither of us can be in this world without the other."

"What is the story with those wild spirits, then? The ones without the damned. Were they also born in your birth place?"

"Yes, all pneumas or pneuma like creatures are. Then there are also cases where they lost their damned to the seventh place in hell, where no one can escape from. I believe only one person has escaped. But enough of these stories now. It is time we turn in," Brian says, tuning into a fox and laying down at the foot of my bed.

"How come you seem to know so much about this?"

"In truth, I don't know that much, but unlike you who believed most of your life that the damned and the pneumas are stories and things of myths, I was one of them. I learned a lot in my eighteen years of being dormant to the world. Now, good night London. I will find a place where you can turn back into a human in the morning." Brian says, laying his head down but keeping his ears up.

I lay down my head and look back at the stars. I wish Brian would tell me more, but I know him and I know he won't. I fall into what I guess you would call sleep. Nothing seems the same being a skeleton. I think I only dream, without truly sleeping, about the damned and what the pneumas' world would be like.

CHAPTER 40

Prison cell

All the inmates try to find sleep in a cold, hard cell. Many lie there with thoughts in their head, wondering where they went wrong. Many of them are on death row, and the crack of dawn will be the last ray of light they will see.

The prison is a small one, with its long hall that goes down and rows of cells on both sides. Many small towns built their prisons this way. Normally, people didn't stay long in these prisons. Most of those sent here were only leaving through death.

One man at the end of the cells stares off into the distance, watching the door of the prison. The only light in the room is coming from the moon, which is coming in from high windows. The man looks old and tired. He seems to be a man who wants to welcome death with open arms, unlike many of the people in here who aren't ready for it yet. Although this man seems ready for death, something else seems to grab his attention on this cold night.

He stares at the door as if he expects someone or something to come. He holds onto the bars with both hands, with his eyes never drifting from the door. No one else here understands why he is doing this. They think he is just a little crazy. All of them probably are a bit crazy being here in the first place, one way or another.

The man isn't as old as some think, or then again, maybe he is older than many would have believed. He has dark long hair, with some white in it, and a scruffy face. He has wide shoulders and big hands. It is clear by the scars on his face and arms that he has seen his fair share of battles. What leads him to this moment now is a long story, but maybe it is time he paid for the sins he has committed.

This man knows that something is going to happen. He has felt the feeling a million times before. These prisoners are going to meet their fate sooner than they think.

"Are you going to stand like that all night?" asks a younger man, probably in his early twenties, as he looks up at the man. The younger fellow is sitting in his cell. He is dressed in a ragged outfit and isn't a very handsome man. He is in here for committing assault, amongst many other things. He is facing the block in the morning. He tried to fall asleep, but with the thoughts of tomorrow heavy on his mind, it is almost impossible.

The man does not look in his direction but speaks, "A darkness searches the lands tonight. It needs souls to consume to live. As black as the night it will be, and it will finish the job of death. It is hungry and those who have sinned are what it seeks. For most, they will lie in their beds and dream without fear, for they have not sinned. From this prison of Hell though, we can only wait for its appearance. I do not know how many it will take, but trusting your life in its hands is pretty much walking into the fire of hell yourself."

"What are you talking about?" the young man asks, looking confused, and only believing that the older guy is crazy.

Before anything else can be answered, they all feel a cold rush of air. Their blood runs cold as they feel death in the air. Too scared to talk, they all know it has come for them.

London

I walk down the prison slowly, as Brian moves first. I wear my black cloak with my hood up. When I am a skeleton, I can hear people's heartbeats. Brian tells me which one would be the best to take, and I take it. I don't like having to be the one to do this, but they are all on death row, pretty much for horrible crimes. Knowing this puts my mind a little more at rest.

I stop at a cell that Brian suggests. Brian stays as a mist. No one talks in here, but I feel their heartbeats are through the roof, all of them except for one. He is an older guy in the back, just watching us. There is something different about this guy. I will see what's up with him after I take the souls I need.

The man whom I stepped in front of has fear in his eyes as he looks at me. He knows that his life is about to end. I don't say anything as I reach my hand out to him, feeling his heartbeat. The man screams, either in pain or fright, but it is quickly cut short, as his soul is ripped from him and he collapses on to the floor.

I do this to two more men, with the last two begging for forgiveness as I approach them. I ignore their pleas, knowing there is nothing I can do about it. I must do what I must, and it is not like they have the right to live anymore, anyway. They killed, raped or stole from someone who didn't deserve it, and now they have lost their right to their life.

Now that I have the souls I need, I consume them. I fall to my hands and knees as I do, feeling that horrible burning pain as I start to gain my flesh again. Brian stays near me, but there is nothing he can do. I grind my teeth and close my eyes. The pain is intense for about two minutes then slowly fades away.

I take a deep breath and slowly rise to my feet, feeling weak and shaky. I look over to see the old man staring at us and he says, "I have had my fair share of how that feels."

Brian goes over to him as a mist. Brian moves a little back and forth just outside his cage, then thinks, *"I thought he was a damned. I want to know where his pneuma is though, and why he is here."*

I walk over to the cell, and the man and I both look at each other. He is a tall man, about two feet taller than me. He doesn't look like someone who would be caught in a place like this. Everything about him screams warrior and killer. So why is he here then? And where is his pneuma?

"Who are you?" I ask. "You don't look like someone who belongs here."

"I am here because I want to be. I have heard about the both of you. London and Brian, the first to have a black pneuma since Damon in about hundred years."

"Where is your pneuma? Did it leave you?" Brian asks. "Or is this something you just do?"

The man smiles, but it is creepy. He looks hard into my eyes as he replies, "He is with me."

Brian and I glance at each other and Brian telepaths, *"He seems to have lost his mind."*

I want to believe Brian, but I feel that cold feeling in my stomach, and have that voice in my head that is warning me about something not right. I think there is more to this damned than meets the eye.

"How could your pneuma be here?" I ask.

The man laughs as if I said something funny. Through teeth that I now see are missing or stained yellow and black, he answers, "You two don't know anything about Damon and Talon, do you?"

"What does this have to do with them?" I ask, liking this less and less.

He laughs again, only adding to his crazy look and says like this somehow humors him, "You two are the ones who are supposed to be defeating him? Well, I can see he doesn't have much to worry."

Brian, though still mostly a mist, reaches his hand into the cell and grabs the man by the throat, and says in a cold voice, "I wouldn't laugh if I were you. We are not a force to be missed around with."

The man only looks at Brian and says, "Then go ahead and break my neck. I am not in here because I am planning on living another day. But why would you do it? You know what I have to say could be worthwhile. Neither of you knows enough about Damon, and that is how he is going to win. He broke all the rules and did the most unspeakable things to get his way. Did you ever wonder why he stayed in power so long?"

"Let him go, Brian, we need to know if he has anything on Damon and Talon that could be worthwhile," I speak through thoughts to Brian.

I know Brian doesn't want to, but he withdraws his hold on the man and backs up. Even though he wants to get rid of this guy, Brian also knows that the man could know some valuable information.

"Tell me how your pneuma is here," I said, trying to sound a little more reasonable. I don't sound that friendly though. I don't like this guy, and I am going to treat him the way he treats us.

He looks at both of us, then looking into my eyes again, he says, "Damon wanted to make the strongest damned he could. So, he did just that. The strongest damned are formed when the damned and their pneuma truly become one. That is something that had been only talked about in myths, until Damon found his own way to make that happen. He made the most loyal damned eat their own souls. In doing so, they become the most powerful damned, but there is a cost. If the damned were to die, he remains dead."

"Is this what happened to you?" I ask, feeling a chill at the thought of a damned eating his own soul. It sounds sick, twisted and insane.

"Yes. I worked for Damon for many years. Now I hear that you and your pneuma Brian are going to take him out. I didn't think that the both of you were so young, nor did I know how little you know about him. I will give the both of you some advice; unless you understand Damon and what he has done, you will never be able to defeat him. You don't have anything to fight against him, other than your black pneuma. I have served Damon for enough years to know that you are not a match for him yet. I recommend that you visit him. Then you will see for yourself what I mean."

I don't want to believe that we are no match for Damon, but the way this man speaks, I don't think he is lying. Maybe Damon and Talon are worse than I thought they were. I knew it would be hard because of the experience Damon possesses. I am starting to feel that we are walking into a death trap. If we can't figure how to change or improve ourselves fast enough, we will fail.

"Thanks for the advice, I guess. Why are you in this prison cell then? Do you want to die tomorrow?" I say.

He looks at me, "I will decide when it comes. Now I think the both of you have done what you came for."

"We have. Good luck on whatever choice you make," I say, backing away from his cage.

Brian and I start to leave the prison. As we leave, the old man says, "Good luck to the both of you. You are going to need it."

Brain and I leave the prison with a lot on our minds. I know that the damned is right. I need to know more about Damon and Talon. Brian and I both do.

CHAPTER 41

Dream Land

M y mind rests uneasy with what the guy at the prison had to say. I realize how little I know about Damon and Talon, and I am really starting to wonder about the dangers we are about to face. I know this makes Brian uneasy too, even though he tries not to show it.

We are walking in a field. We walked some distance between us and the prison, and haven't talked since. We are both thinking about what was said back there. We are soon going to need to make camp. Over the next two days, we will have to travel fast if we plan to make it to that party. I feel tired, but I know my mind won't let me rest. Ever since I got into this mess, I have felt lost, and now it feels worse than ever.

Brain was a mist, but now shifts into a man. He soon falls into step with me. We don't say anything for a few minutes, then Brian thinks to me, *"That man in the prison, he does have a point. We do not know enough, London."*

I sigh, happy that I can breathe again. I look at Brian. *"Then what will we do about it?"*

"We will have to meet him."

I am surprised by Brian's response, but before I can reply he continues, *"There is a way we can see him, but it is dangerous. Remember that girl that visited you in your dream?"* Brain asks.

"Yes," I reply, thinking it is not a dream I would forget very easily.

"Well, you could visit Damon through dream land. It is the safest way to meet, although it still is not completely safe."

"What is the down side to it?" I ask, wondering how in the world I would be able to talk to someone in dream land.

"Those with weak minds can be corrupted by it. Damon will most likely be very good with his mind, but I think we both know that we need to figure this out for ourselves. The more knowledge we have, the better the chance we have to defeat him. Right now, we are fighting a blind battle."

I nod, knowing everything he is saying is true. Do I have a strong enough mind not to be corrupted? The whole thing makes me a little uneasy, but maybe we are overthinking this.

"Do you think I have a strong enough mind for it?" I ask.

"I would hope so. We wouldn't be able to continue if you don't. Either we are the sheep, or we are the ones to lead. I don't know what other way to see him. But I know we both want to truly know what we are up against."

"How will I do it though? I don't even know how to begin to enter someone else's dream."

"You will be able to, London. I am told it isn't that hard. It is all about mental control. The most important thing is for you to have enough mental power to not let anyone else use your mind."

I take a deep breath not sure about the whole thing. I look at Brian and ask, *"When will we do it then?"*

"In a couple of days, probably on the night of the party. There will be a lot of powerful people there, so if something goes wrong, we will have help."

"You think the chances of something going wrong are pretty high then?" I ask.

Brian doesn't look at me, but seems to be deep in thought. Finally, looking ahead of him, he replies, *"The chances of something going wrong are not as slim as I would like. It is either this, or we continue what we are doing. Since this is on your shoulders, London, I will leave it up to you. In the dream world there is nothing I can do to help you. It is the one place I will never be able to enter."*

I take a minute to think about this. This is a decision that I want to think on before jumping into it. I already know what I am going to choose though, even though I wish I can talk myself out of it.

"Then we should do it. We need to know once and for all who we are really up against," I try to say with confidence.

Brian seems happy with my choice. He turns into a mist and goes through the tall grass ahead of me. *"I think you have made the right choice. Now I think it is time we find a place to stay. You are going to need your rest."*

I agree with Brian, and we try to find a place to settle down for the night. It is probably about one in the morning now, and I need to sleep. I am exhausted after turning back into a man. It takes a lot out of you. Maybe I will sleep in a little tomorrow, and travel longer hours to make up for it.

We finally find a clearing amongst some woods. It is out of sight, so we will not be bothered. It isn't the best spot for a camp, but it will work for now. I don't plan to have a huge set-up or anything. I plan to just lay out some blankets on which to sleep and eat a cold meal. Part of it is me just being lazy about trying to make a nice place to stay, and the other part is too tired to do so.

After I lay some blankets out, I search through my bag for something to eat. Brian checks all around the camp, coming and going as different animals or as a mist. Finally, when he has decided the place is good enough, he comes and settles near me as a fox.

We both eat a little of what we have. Some dried fruit and beef are pretty much it. When I died, I lost the food I had, and this is what the others gave me just to keep us going until I show up at the party.

After eating, I lay back in my blankets trying to get comfortable. Since Brian and I took things into our own hands, there are often times now when it's just Brian and me. I have noticed that we work better when we don't have to worry about others. I like being with the rest though. It is hard to say what I think of Brian's company. It is not quite like that of someone else's. He feels too much like he is a part of me, so it's hard to look at him as someone else entirely. Even though I am not lonely when it is just him and me, in a way I do feel it. There are times when I would rather be by myself, but most of the time I prefer to be with people. I am not used to spending a great deal of time away from people. I am getting more used to it though, and I am sure soon enough, on most occasions, I would prefer it that way.

Brian turns into a panther and lies at the foot of my bed like he does every night. He doesn't seem to have any intention of sleeping though. His ears are perked up, and he doesn't close his eyes when his head is down. I get the feeling he doesn't like this place or maybe he still has our earlier conversation weighing too heavily on his mind. I know that is how it is for me.

I feel very tired though, so with it weighing heavily on my mind or not, I must sleep. I close my eyes, and soon I am in a dream, traveling on mountains and fighting other damned and their pneumas.

CHAPTER 42

Dining with Royalty

I fix my jacket to make it a little more comfortable. The last time I looked this nice was at my wedding. It's weird to think how much changed in this year. From getting married, my wife leaving, becoming a damned and my whole life being turned upset down, I feel like I was reborn and brought into a whole new world.

Brian walks to me. He is dressed nicely as well, but I don't think he likes it very much. Brian doesn't look like he is looking forward to this party. I, on the other hand, have mixed feelings about it. We will be completely in the spotlight, being the guests of honor. I don't think we deserve that spot and, in a way, I am a little annoyed by it. I think they are making such a big deal about it because they want me to continue to defy Damon and Talon, not because they really hold us to such a high standard. I just don't know what to think about any of this. I hate the thought that the kings and queens really could just think of us as their puppets.

We made it to the elf's palace at about one in the morning. I slept in this morning, so I am refreshed tonight. I feel a little nervous though, and I don't think I am getting rid of that. We are in our room that the elves gave us for our stay. The party has already started. The kings are all here, so the only thing left now is for me to enter.

Brian looks at me and thinks, *"I don't know why we ever agreed to this. We should be out there working, not putting on a show for some men in crowns."*

I look at Brian and reply, stepping away from the mirror, *"Just try to enjoy yourself, Brian. It is not every day that we get a break. Why won't you spend some time with Vixy, if you don't want to spend much time there? I am sure she will be happy to keep you company."*

Brian can't help but smile at the mention of her name. *"I would love to, but she will stay at the party. Besides, I don't need to make what has developed between us public. I don't trust this place; I would feel the same if we were in dangerous territory."*

"You think the elves are not to be trusted at all then?"

"Yes. I wouldn't trust them with anything. But for now, we will have to work with them." Brian steps away from me after saying this.

I wonder if Brian is just being extreme with the elves or are they not to be trusted at all. Sometimes it is hard to tell with Brian. He seems very prejudiced on some topics, and on others he is just very harsh.

I hear a knock on the door, so I call, "Come in." I assume it is someone I know or maybe someone with a question. Sully walks in with Danny. Danny and Brian go to talk to each other. I don't know about what they are talking, for they speak in low tones, but this is nothing new for they often do this when together. Sully comes to me with a smile. He is dressed nicely as well, in a brown jacket, brown pants and a white undershirt. He also wears a dark green cloak.

"Are you ready?" Sully asks.

"As ready as I will ever be, I suppose."

"Then let's go. It is better you get it over with. The kings are waiting and the party won't really start until you are there."

I start to follow Sully out with Brian and Danny, thinking I am not ready for this. Why can't I be like everyone else, so I can come and go as I please? But no, I have to be their guest of honor, and now the party won't start without me. Some people like this, some people want to be known by everyone, but I do not. I would rather live a life where I don't have to worry about what the rest of the world thinks of me. It doesn't look like it is going to play out that way.

"Smile, London, there are going to be a lot of people here tonight," Sully says looking at me, being his optimistic self.

I try to pull off a little smile. "It is a little hard to when everyone is waiting for you."

"Well, I have to say, kid, I am glad I am not in your shoes right now, but smile, anyway," Sully says, placing his hand on my shoulder.

"I wish I weren't either."

"Be a little more optimistic than that, London. It is better than them hating you, right?"

"I suppose so."

We come to the two doors that will lead us to the party. There are two guards on either side of them. They look at us and get ready to open the doors. Sully and I exchange looks and he says, "When I am in there, I will go find my seat. London, you will have to go to the kings. Good luck." He then squeezes my shoulder.

"Thanks, I might need it," I say, not sounding very thrilled with the whole thing.

The doors open and we walk through. Like Sully said, he doesn't accompany me down the hall as I make my way to where the kings are waiting. Brian comes to walk beside me, and I know he doesn't like this. He pulls off a smile though, as we come to a stop, facing the kings.

There are about 10 different countries represented here, with many of their rulers. There is the elves' queen and king, the king from my homeland, a few kings and queens from other lands, along with some diplomats standing in for some of their kings or queens. A couple of the rulers are men, then there are the elves, the dwarves, a couple of other species of man that I have not seen before and a diplomat for the fairies. There is no other damned though. I guess this is where Damon and Talon would be, if these kingdoms didn't want him dead.

The whole crowed is silent as they watch us. There are over a hundred people here from all cultures. Some people have wings or claws. There are some people who are over eight feet tall and as small as a child. Having them all watch Brian and me is uncomfortable to say the least.

"It is a pleasure to finally meet you and your pneuma, London. We have heard much about you," the queen of the elves says in a voice that sounds like that of an angel.

I don't show that I am nervous, so pulling off a charming smile, I reply, "The pleasure is all mine. Thank you for welcoming us into your halls. It is a nice change from our everyday travels."

I feel a little better once I start to talk. I am very charismatic and a good speaker once I get going. In times like these, it comes in handy. I don't really like how they only refer to Brian as my pneuma though. I feel in a way they are trying to degrade him.

"How is the progress going?" the dwarf king asks. He is shorter than me, with a big beard, and wears a crown that looks like it is made from horns.

Damon must be more of a problem than even I thought, seeing all these rulers here. Maybe they are here for other reasons than just that, but still I am their guest of honor. I am the one who is going to take down Damon and Talon. That's what they say, anyway.

"As good as it could go for now, I suppose," I reply. I am not sure what to say about their question. I have the feeling that Damon is worse than I can imagine. I no longer have any idea how close I am to battling him.

"Knowing you from our home kingdom, I have no doubt that things have been moving smoothly. You were popular for being one of the best-known sword fighters for your age," the king of my homeland, Sonara, says with pride.

I feel weird with him saying this, after what happened between his daughter and I. Sara and I didn't leave on the best of terms. I feel what he is saying is fake as well. I know he has a problem with me, after what happened between me and his daughter, but here he is trying to act like he is proud that I was born in his land. The thing I hate about politics the most is the lies and the bullshit. The truth would fit me the best.

I glance at Brian he watches all the rulers closely in the eyes, as if he is challenging them. His smile is friendly but the look in his eyes is dangerous. He doesn't like any of them, and I think he makes that clear. Brian doesn't care how high up you are; he cares about how you are as a person and nothing else. If you are a piece of trash, but are high up so no one will say anything to you about it, Brian is not afraid to call you out on it. He is always very straight to the point.

"It does help, but we still have a long way to go," I say, still with a charming smile.

"How is your magic with your pneuma?" the diplomat for the fairies asks.

"His name is Brian, if you didn't know, and it has been a work in progress," I say. I make it clear that they should start using his name. I don't know why they avoid using his name. Maybe they don't like him, so they try to avoid him. It is probably just because he is a pneuma, and people seem to look down on them. If your rulers are going to do it, I can see why so many people treat them this way. Maybe it wasn't the smartest move to come out like that, but I am not trying to make friends here.

"I am not trying to seem rude in any way, Brian, but normally when there is a damned and a pneuma, questions are usually directed to the damned," the fairy said as in apology.

Brian doesn't seem to care for his apology. He isn't trying to seek sympathy from anyone. Brian pulls a friendly smile anyway, and in his cool, calm voice he says, "There is no need to apologize. London is the better speaker. My opinions are often too strong and harsh for most."

There is silence for a few minutes, then a queen smiles and offers, "London and Brian, would you accompany us at the table? Being the guests of honor, you are welcome to join us here."

"I don't know about you, London, but I would feel more at home if I did not. I am not trying to humor them in any way. I want them to know that their supposedly kind gestures don't mean much to me. They are only kind because we are trying to get rid of Damon. They don't care much for the damned or us in the long run," Brian thinks to me. He doesn't look at me, so no one would get an idea that we are talking.

"I agree, besides if I am up there with them, this is anything but a party."

I look at the queen and reply to all of them, "I do appreciate the invitation, but I prefer to dine in the company of those I have been traveling with, if that is all right with all of you," I say very politely. I am trying not to insult any of them. It is probably one of the only times I will be getting an invitation like this, but I can live without it.

The rulers all look at each other, a little confused with my choice. The elf queen smiles politely though. "If that is what you want, then that is what you should do."

I bow my head to them and thank them again, then Brian and I find our way to the rest. The rest seem happy that Brian and I will be joining them. The group consists of Sully, Jennifer, Samuel and their pneumas. Breccan, Amass, and Livefen are higher up, and with their rulers or other higher people whom they serve.

I sit between Jennifer and Samuel, while Sully sits on the other side of Samuel. Brian sits near Vixy, and they are soon having their own conversation. Taylor and Danny are near Vixy and Brian, but they talk to each other, to let Brian and Vixy talk with each other. They both respect Brian and view him as their alpha. Unlike people, pneumas have a dominant one in charge, and they made Brian that way pretty much from the start, although I think Brian imposed that on them pretty much from the first day they met.

"I thought you would be tired of hanging out with us," Jennifer said with a smile, when we settled ourselves in at the table.

"Well, I am not tired of you guys yet," I smile.

"Well, we are tired of you," Sully said. "I was hoping you would stay with them." I see the smile Sully is masking as he says this.

"In that case then, I will make sure to always choose you guys." We all smile, happy to be together. Working together all the time, we are becoming very close friends.

We eat our dinner and when we finish, beautiful elven music starts to play. Sully looks at us and asks, "Any of you going to dance?"

"I have two left feet," Samuel quickly says.

I am getting to know Samuel well now. I know he is a pretty happy, relaxed person. He always wants to joke around and have a good time. He and Sully quickly became friends, and I am getting pretty close to him as well.

Sully gets up and going to Jennifer he asks, "Do you care to dance with me, my lady?"

Jennifer smiles, taking his hand, "I would love to."

They both walk to the dance floor, as I watch them. Jennifer is dressed beautifully tonight. She is dressed in a tan dress that comes to her knees and is wavy at the bottom. Her hair is half pulled up, while the other half is left to fall on her shoulders.

"I should have asked to dance with her," Samuel mumbles.

I smile, "You need to be quicker next time, then."

"Well, two left feet or not, I think I am going to dance. There are a lot of beautiful women here tonight. I would be dumb not to," Samuel says, getting up from his chair.

"Good luck then."

Samuel goes to the dance floor. I sit where I am, with a slight smile on my face as I watch everyone. The pneumas are off doing their own things, probably hanging out on the roof of the building. That seems to be the place they like going to hang out.

I scan the party with my eyes, watching people dance. My eyes lock with those of a young lady elf, who stands watching me. She is beautiful with long, very blonde hair that flows far past her shoulders. It was those deep blue eyes I would not forget. She is the elf that visited me in my dream. I don't know what to do. She watches me, so I must go and talk with her. I want to know who this woman is. She has captured my attention, and I feel she is someone who will be very important to know down the road.

I get up from my seat and casually make my way to her. She is dressed in a long white dress that perfectly fits with the outline of her body. She watches me closely as I do. I stop in front of her, with our eyes still locked on each other. A small smile crosses her features, and she says in that sweet, rich voice of hers, "It is nice to finally meet you face to face, London."

She holds her hand out for me to kiss, which I gently do. I smile politely in return. "I was wondering if I would see you again. Do you care to dance with me?" I am not sure what else to do. I want to talk with her, but I don't want to just come out asking her a bunch of questions.

"I would be more than happy to." She then takes my hand. I take her to the dance floor and we slowly start to dance with each other. I notice she likes to watch people in the eyes, for her gaze has never strayed far from mine.

After dancing for a few minutes, I say, "You never did tell me your name."

"My name is Hanna. It isn't really an elf name, but my mother called me by this name at birth, and the name stuck. Tell me, London, how have your travels been? Have you run into any overwhelming troubles yet?" she asks.

"No, I wouldn't call them overwhelming. And I think your name suits you."

She smiles slightly. "I am glad you like it."

She dances, getting up close to me. I get close to her, enjoying the dance. I don't know what it is, but there is something about this girl that I really like. Not only that, but elves are known to be some of the most beautiful people in the world, and with someone like her, I can see where they get that reputation. I want to be careful though. I think there is more here than meets the eye with her. I have a feeling she is someone to be reckoned with, and there could be a thin line between being allies and enemies with her.

"Tell me more about yourself, Hanna. How were you able to meet me in my dream?" I ask.

She leans closer to me and whispers in my ear, "There is a lot I want to tell you, London, but others should not hear."

I look at her questioningly. "Do you know of a place where we can speak then?"

"No place here is safe to speak, but I know a way."

She looks into my eyes, and I start to hear her thoughts in my head, like the way Brian and I talk. It is different though. When Brian and I talk through thoughts; it seems natural. With Hanna, it seems foreign and strange, like a voice that doesn't belong there.

"To answer a question you have asked before, yes I am a damned, but I am not dead yet," she thinks to me. Her voice sounds distant in my head, and not as clear as when Brian speaks.

"I thought the elves didn't like the damned."

"They do not like damned that have black pneumas. I, however, have a white pneuma. We are both pawns in a game, London. They want to use the both of us. I think that you and I have very different ideas for our ending though."

"Do you know what they plan for us?"

"They don't like the damned, and they don't like damned that have black pneumas. They need you, for you are the only one who stands a chance against Damon and Talon. They want me because of my pneuma. They believe because my pneuma is white I can do no harm. We are both being played, London, and I want to help you."

"How will you be able to help me?"

"I am more than just a damned. You can use another dominant pneuma. Brian and Cassandra used to see each other before Brian was with you."

"Brian knows about you?" I ask surprised.

"He has known about Cassandra, but he doesn't know much about me."

I take a deep breath, taking all of this in. I then hear Brian interrupt my thoughts. *"Who are you talking to, London? Why did you let her enter your thoughts? All the things you learned, has it taught you nothing?"*

I look up at the ceiling, feeling a cold shiver run down my spine. I see Brian up there on the rafters, looking down at me with red eyes. He is a black figure, but he looks like something that belongs in hell.

He looks hard into my eyes, and for the first time ever, I see Brian in a different light. Looking at him now, I can understand why people get the impression he is from hell. Could I really piss him off that bad for talking to Hanna through thoughts? Is Brian showing some of his true colors? No matter what, I don't like it.

"I am a lot of things, Brian, but I am not stupid. If you have something to say to me, why won't you come down and say it?" I snap.

I know this only makes Brian angrier. *"I will, but not here."* He then starts to move away and I watch him leave. I don't know what to expect when I see him again, but it's not going to be good.

CHAPTER 43

Into the Dream

I walk to my room in deep thought, feeling nervous. Last night when I was here, I tried to reach out to Damon and now I feel him calling. When I fall asleep tonight, I have no doubt I will be seeing Damon. I don't like how Brian and I stand right now. I don't want to go into this battle with Brian angry with me, for any reason. I am already worried about visiting someone in dream world. I don't need Brian as my enemy right now.

I have not seen Brian since that last comment he made. Hanna and I left each other after the dance, for I don't think she wanted to be seen with me any longer. I stayed at the party for a little longer, but had to leave, as the growing anxiety of meeting Damon became too much. I also can't relax when I know there is something I need to settle with Brian.

I can tell by the way Brian feels that something is up. I don't know where he has been, probably keeping to himself. I do not think he was hanging out with the other pneumas. I guess I will see him soon enough, so I will stop thinking about it.

I go into my room and shut the door behind me. I take off my nice jacket and hang it up. I sit on the bed, thinking about all that could happen. What would it be like to talk to Damon for the first time? I don't know what to expect and hope it doesn't turn into a disaster.

Brian comes into the room as his black spirit. I watch him as he circles the room a few times, then shifts into a man some feet from me. We both look each other in the eyes, then Brian finally starts, not letting the silence drag. "That girl you were talking to, why did you let her speak in your head?"

I set my jaw in a tight line, ready for a fight. "That was the only way she could tell me some things. You never told me you knew of another white pneuma, Brian."

"Cassandra is nothing to be worried about. She is not even an active pneuma yet. You need to be careful dealing with this elf woman though. She is a sorceress, and her mind is stronger than yours will probably ever be."

"I know what I am doing, Brian. She said she could help us. She doesn't trust the elves either."

Brian doesn't look convinced. He pauses then coldly replies, with a hint of annoyance, "Her pneuma is a dominant one, London. That means she will want control. Are you sure you really trust her? Is she just subduing you with her looks? It is obvious you two have an attraction to each other, and I think she is using it to get to you. Woman are poison to a man like you, London. Your attraction to her is a weakness and she has already found it."

"It is not a weakness, Brian," I said getting up. Brian and I face each other and I continue getting angrier. "You do not know everything. We will need all the help we can get. I know about women. I will not let one control me."

"There is so much you do not know yet, London. You know nothing of magic or mind control. We will never defeat Damon and Talon if that is how you think," Brian snaps, matching my anger.

Through anger, I throw a punch at Brian. I hit him and he staggers back, not expecting it. It is probably a bad idea to fight with Brian, but I think he deserves it.

Brian looks at me and I see the anger in his eyes. He comes at me, not saying anything. I try to get ready to fight, but Brian is a lot faster than I am. He throws me across the room, so I hit the wall.

I get up quickly, with my head dizzy and aching. It was a hard throw. Brian walks over to me, but I am going to be quicker this time. I lunge for Brian as we continue to fight. Brian and I are both equally strong when he is a man. In truth, even through the anger, I wonder why I am fighting with Brian. It is not a battle I can win. When I hurt him, I am basically hurting myself, but right now, neither of us seems to care about that fact.

I land a few good hits, but so does he. He once again throws me across the room, with a strength that no normal man possesses. I hit the wall again. This time, my arms have deep cuts in them from where he threw me. I don't rise as quickly this time. I could continue fighting, but what's the point? I started this out of rage, but it is a pointless battle and it is ridiculous to continue. I am going to have to face Damon in a dream tonight, I don't need this now.

Brian walks over to me and looks at me. He too looks like he is done fighting. I guess I was the one to start it in the first place. I don't know why I did any more. Usually, I don't go to fight that quickly.

Brian sticks out his hand and thinks, *"Let us not forget, London, that we are on the same side. We will live together and we will die together. When you fight with me, you are only fighting with yourself."*

I sigh and take Brian's hand. He helps me up. Both of my arms are covered in blood now. I don't know if Brian meant to do that, getting as angry as he did. I think at the time all he wanted to do was make sure I felt his wrath. He doesn't like being fought, and he makes that pretty clear.

"I didn't mean to deal the wounds on your arms, but it can be in easy fix," Brian thinks, sounding friendlier now.

I nod my head and walk past him. *"You are right, Brian. We are on the same side, but no more secrets. You say knowing about Cassandra is no big deal, but it would be nice to know what kind of pneumas are out there. A white pneuma could be another enemy to us or maybe an ally.*" I look at Brian when I speak the last part. We both know I am talking about Hanna.

Brian seems to think on this for a minute while I sit on my bed once again. Brian sits on the bed and starts to help my wounds. As he is helping me, he says, "She could be of help, London; I won't throw that thought out the window. I don't trust elves, sorceresses or someone quite like her though. As much help as she is willing to give, it will probably come in the same way as she is giving us problems. I can just see her doing this because of her own benefits."

"If you think about it, that is what everyone has in mind around us though. We are all here to stop Damon and Talon, and after that, we no longer share the same goal anymore."

"That still leaves us with the biggest question of all; what do we plan to do if we succeed?" Brian says, finishing up the bandages on my arm.

"I have more pressing things on my mind right now than thinking about that. I don't see how we are even going to take out Damon and Talon yet." Brian gets up and starts to pace. I take a deep breath and continue, "Damon is calling to me, Brian."

Brian doesn't answer. He looks to be deep in thought about this. Finally, he replies, "As we already know, I cannot go into the dream with you, but I will make sure to pull you out of sleep if trouble happens."

I nod. I don't know what rules there are in the dream world—maybe there are none. I am ready for it though; it is time I settle this. Not only will I get a better idea of Damon, but maybe I can see for myself what kind of person he really is.

Brian and I talk a little longer. After, I blow out the candle and lay down in my bed. I get into more comfortable clothes, but not too comfortable. Even though I am safe here, I want to be up and ready for a fight, just in case. I put my weapons on the table once I clean them up. I keep Wolfbane near me, for it is a smaller sword, and I can use it the fastest if needed.

I take a deep breath thinking about what lays ahead. I know that once I fall asleep, I will be meeting Damon.

Brian stays in the room, but he minds his own business. The window is left open, so Brian can come and go as he pleases. Brian is active tonight; I don't know what he is up to, but I am sure he has his reasons.

The room is a large one, with big windows letting the light of the moon in. The curtains are an ivory white. Like the rest of the castle, most of the colors in the room are gold and white. There is a fireplace in here, but it is not lit, for tonight is warm.

I turn in my bed, closing my eyes, and try to sleep. I jerk up as I hear the door open. I am surprised to see the slim, white figure of Hanna enter my room. She closes the door gently behind her and walks over to me.

I throw my legs over the side of the bed, ready to talk to her. She is dressed in a white robe, carrying a dim candle in her hand that is sheltered by a clear, beautifully designed glass cover. She is not wearing shoes. Her long, beautiful, blond hair is down and looks like gold in the moonlight. Her skin looks soft and perfect, as the fairest of elves and fairies look.

She sets the dim light down on the desk beside my bed and sits beside me. I watch her all this while. Her eyes met mine and she says in a quiet but pleasant voice, "I know you seek to see Damon, London."

"How do you know this?" I ask.

"I am a sorceress, London. I can help you. It is risky doing what you are doing, for your mind can be controlled, but I can protect your mind from anyone."

I don't know how much I fully trust her, especially after what Brian had to say. However, there is another part of me that feels some relief. If she can help me, then I know I don't have to worry.

Brian comes over to us as a man. I am not sure how he feels about Hanna being here, only by reading his face. He looks at her and doesn't seem too friendly. "Finally, I get to meet you in person, Hanna. You seem to have taken quite an interest in us."

Brian isn't rude, but neither is he polite. I think he is trying to make it clear to her that he doesn't trust her.

Hanna smiles. It is a small smile, but it is warm and polite. "We are both in very similar boats. I want to help, and I think you guys can use it. If not, I can leave, but if so, I can ensure your plan will go as planned. I will also not breathe a word to anyone. I have the feeling you guys want to keep this to yourselves."

Brian and I look at each other and he thinks to me, "*I will leave it up to you, London. I do not trust her, but she does have a powerful mind. We will have the upper hand with her on our side, for now.*"

"I understand your distrust for me, but I am loyal to my word, and my intentions are not to harm the either of you," Hanna adds. I think she notices the uncertainty we feel about her.

"We do not trust you fully, but for now we will trust you. I don't think you would try to screw us over, at least not yet," Brian says. I wonder if there ever is a time, he isn't going to be rude about how he feels about someone.

"Don't worry. I am nothing to be afraid of. You can stop flattering me now. You make me feel as if I am somehow a threat to you guys." Hanna says this, sounding so innocent, but with a twinkle in her eyes. She knows how to play innocent a little too well, I think.

Brian doesn't look convinced. "Don't worry, we do not fear you."

Brian walks away after saying this. He becomes a spirit once again and leaves the room, but I know he isn't far.

With Brian gone, I look back to Hanna. There is silence for a minute, then she says as she turns more towards me, "I will help you now. When you enter the other world, I will make sure to protect your mind, but I will not be there. I don't need to be."

"All right."

I lay back, thinking of the dream I had with her. It seems very familiar, and thinking about it, this room looks very similar to the one I was in with her in my dream. I wonder if she made that dream that way on purpose, taking a scene that she saw in the future.

She smiles and slowly runs her hand down my cheek. I know she is being a lot friendlier than she needs to be with me. In truth, I think of more than just help when I look at her. There is no denying that this girl has got my attention, and I can't help but think impure thoughts when we are together like this. Being a man, I can't really help if I start to wonder what is under the robe she is wearing. Thinking of that makes me wonder if she can read my thoughts. I hope she can't because my thoughts are personal and my own.

She leans over me, so our lips are very close. I smile slightly, looking at her and say quietly, "I like the way you are trying to help me." I say it not in any way trying to get rid of her. Besides wanting her physically close, I remember she also has her way of helping me.

"Is that supposed to be sarcastic?" she asks, getting even closer to me, speaking barely above a whisper.

"No, not even close." I run my fingers through her hair slowly and gently. We both go in for a kiss. Her kiss is warm and rougher than what it was like in the dream. Her lips are soft, and the kisses are very enjoyable.

Suddenly my head starts to spin, and my vision begins to change. Before I can really make out what I am starting to see, I pull away from her.

We both breathe hard and I ask, feeling a little out of breath, "What was that?" I know it is something she is doing.

"I was taking you to see Damon. You were starting to fall asleep," she replies. She isn't leaning over me anymore.

I take in a deep breath, "Sorry for ruining the kiss." I gently run my fingers down her cheek as I say it.

"Don't worry about it. It is time for you to sleep, anyway. We might make Brian mad."

I smile at her and we give each other a small kiss. We gently pull away from each other. I give her another small kiss then close my eyes. She gently runs her fingers through my hair.

I try to go to sleep. It is a little difficult to go to sleep while she is in my bed with me, but I need to manage. Not that I don't want her there, but my thoughts keep returning to her, probably even more so because I have no idea what to expect going into my dream with Damon. Part of me doesn't want to think about it.

CHAPTER 44

Throne Room

I am in a large hall, with torches lighting the way. It is dreamlike, but then again, it feels very real. I think I am in Damon's castle, but I am not sure. I believe I invaded his dream, instead of him invading mine. I like it better this way. I believe I am safer invading his world.

I feel Brian, but not near me. He is out of reach for me to talk with him. It feels like he is in a different world, like there is a wall between us that I cannot penetrate. I walk down the hall; I know that Damon will be waiting. I take a deep breath. At least he will not have his pneuma as well. It is not like we can hurt each other in the first place—at least not physically.

I come out of the hallway into a throne room. There is a large chair near the back wall that stands tall, and is built for a king. There are windows, paintings, torches lining all the walls, and a red and yellow carpet. It is hard to make out anything very well though. Everything besides the center of the room seems to be out of focus.

I step into the center of the room and look around. The throne is very tall, and anyone sitting in it would be looking down at the person before him.

"London, I have been hearing a lot about you. I am surprised that you would try to reach out to me. After all, you are doing all that you can to defy me."

The voice is cool, calm and smooth. It is obvious the voice belongs to a man who can talk his way out of anything, and is used to talking to all sorts of people.

I turn around to see the man who had spoken. He is a tall man, probably a little taller than me. He has short, dark hair that looks well kept. He is dressed in darker colors, along with a cloak. He wears light black, tall boots. He has wide shoulders and big hands. It is more than obvious he has seen his fair share of battles. On the first meeting, I could see why a lot of people would like this man. He has a good voice—one you feel you could trust. He is also fairly handsome. A lot of people seem to trust you more when you look nicer. I can see through first appearances though. I see the danger in those dark brown eyes of his. He is a murderer, a man who has slain more men than most warriors. I know from first meeting him, Damon is no one to mess with. He will do whatever it takes to protect his throne, and the only way to get rid of him is a fight to the death.

We stand facing each other for a minute, then I say, acting as smooth and calm as I possibly can, "I am not doing all that I could. I am surprised that you would let me visit. Obviously, I am doing enough damage that you would want to let me in your presence."

Damon smiles, with the smile never meeting his eyes. He walks closer to me and circles me. I watch him closely, but only move my eyes to follow him. Finally, he stops a few feet in front of me. "No, not quite. I let you visit me because you are the only other known damned with a black pneuma. Too bad that pneumas cannot visit dreams, for I would have liked to have seen Brian as well."

"He feels the same way."

"So, why did you wish to see me London? Have you given up? Or have you changed your mind on which side you want to be?" Damon asks. I am surprised he acts as friendly as he does to me, but hearing him say that, I know why. Brian said that it was very possible that Damon would want us to join him, and with Damon now saying this I feel that is very likely. I guess it is a good tactic. Before killing your biggest challenge, you should see if you will work together. It is risky, but if it pays off you can make some powerful allies.

"I wanted to see who you are for myself. I hear a lot about you, but I am someone who likes to see for myself what is really going on," I say. We are still standing facing each other.

Damon smiles at what I said. "I am glad to see that you are smart. There are many rumors about me. Some of them are true, but others are a myth, like the myth that pneumas come from hell."

"You have a lot of enemies, with some of those being other damned. I heard that you are known to fight for the damned, but what about the ones who don't follow you or the ones from whom you took their pneumas?"

He smiles as if he is humored about what I said. "You know little about the damned or their pneumas, London, and even less about the politics. This is not in insult, but the truth. If you want to get a better insight into things, then I recommend you join me for a while."

"You would want me to join you, even after the damage I have been causing?" I ask, as if I am surprised. In truth, I am not surprised. Brian already thought this would happen.

"You have done nothing that I cannot fix easily. Don't get ahead of yourself, London. You haven't done much yet to really change anything that I have been doing or done. The Sanctuary and all the kingdoms in it can flatter you and make you think you are doing something, but in reality, you have a long way to go before you damage me in any measurable way."

"I am a threat though or we wouldn't be here. I am more than just some-one with another black pneuma, and we both know that," I say, being sure about what I am saying. We are a threat, and no matter what he says it will not change the truth.

He doesn't answer right away, but I can tell he knows what I am saying to be true. He steps away from me and goes to a table to pour himself a drink. He comes over and hands me one as well. I don't think drinking or eating anything in a world like this would matter, but I go ahead and take it anyway.

"London, I want to meet you and Brian in person. I want you to consider our side and what you are doing now." He snaps his fingers and we appear on a very tall rock. It goes miles above the highest trees, with the top being a circle of rock. There is only one flat place to stand on, all the way up.

It is night and the moon is out, with thick clouds high in the sky. The moon is not normal, it looks like a full moon, but instead of silver it is black. Even though the moon is black, light still comes from it, like the light of a normal full moon would. I look at Damon after quickly looking around the place. He is watching me. "London, the day of the next full moon will be the day you and Brian come to this place if you wish to speak to Talon and me. There will only be us, as it will be only you and Brian. We will be able to meet in person, and you can decide what fate you wish to choose."

"How do I know it won't be an ambush when I show up?" I ask. I don't think Brian and I are ready to fight him yet, and leaving the rest of the group to meet Damon somewhere sounds very similar to suicide.

"I am a lot of things, but I always keep my word. If I wanted to kill you, London, I wouldn't ask you to go to the middle of nowhere to meet your fate. Where is the fun in that? If I wanted to finish you, I would come to wherever you are and take you out there. It is your choice, London. I will know if you are interested if you are there or not. If you do not come, then this will be the last time we meet on those terms. I don't make the same offer twice. Besides, you will have plenty of time to figure out what you want."

I don't reply right away, instead deciding to think on it. Damon does not wait for me to reply, for he says, "I will see you again, London."

Upon saying it, I fall out of the dream. I jerk up quickly to see I am back in my bed, at the elves' place with Hanna beside me.

CHAPTER 45

Deception

I wake with the light of the sun pouring into the room. They are early morning rays, but not too early. It is probably about nine in the morning, which is a fine time to wake up—better than when I normally do.

Hanna is no longer with me. She left some time earlier; she must have left when I fell back to sleep. When I woke up from my dream, only Hanna was there. I am not sure where Brian was. He was probably off doing something during the night hours, for I know he wasn't asleep or he would have been in my room.

Hanna stayed with me a while after my dream. I didn't tell her much about what happened, other than seeing Damon, although I think she has the feeling that I will be seeing Damon again soon. She is smart, and I am still not sure of all she can do with people's minds and thoughts.

I did not get much sleep after waking up from my visit with Damon. Hanna wanted to be there, for more than just helping me out and I didn't disappoint her. I don't really have a woman right now. There is Jennifer in my life, but she has made it clear she doesn't want any of that from me. We both feel something for each other, but nothing has moved. One time we did kiss and expressed how we felt, but neither of us has moved to the next step. We decided to stay as friends, at least for now. I don't know what kind of relationship Hanna and I are in, but we both enjoyed our time together, and that's good enough for now.

I look around the room. I see Brian come through the window as a mist, then turn into a man once he is inside. He looks at me as he enters the room. "It took you a while to wake up this morning."

"Where were you last night?" I ask, throwing my legs over the side of the bed.

"I was here, catching some of the creatures that roam the night, and I visited Vixy."

I get out of bed and put on my clothes, including my cloak. I turn back to Brian and ask, "Did you enjoy your time with her?"

"I would say otherwise if I hadn't. How about you and Hanna? I hope you know there are a few rumors out there about you," Brian says, turning into a cat and jumping onto the bed to lay down.

"What?" I said in surprise. I guess people know everything I do, even if I did do nothing. "What kind of rumors?"

"They talk about you and her spending a night together. It wouldn't be that big of a deal, but Hanna is seen as someone of great importance to the elves. They are the only ones who care about this. I don't think they want your hands anywhere near her. For they think she is a gift from God, and us demons from hell," Brian says this casually, laying his head down on the bed.

"I don't really care if they know or not. The thing that annoys me is how did they find out? For the record, she did help protect my mind like she said she would. No matter what happens between Hanna and me, I don't see how it is any of their business to know."

If Brian were a human, I know he would be smiling. He has never liked the elves, at least I have never seen him like one yet. I go over to the table in the middle of the room and grab a grape to eat. The table is all wood, with a round piece of glass placed in the middle. There is a bowl of fruit set on the table. There are many different kinds of fruits, some I recognize and others I don't.

"Out of curiosity, even though you don't like me asking questions, how was it with Hanna? I guess you got along with her rather well," he asks, turning back into a man and coming over to grab an apple.

"You are right. I don't like you asking those questions. If you need to know, all I will say is that it was one hell of a night," I answer with a smile.

"Well, I am glad," Brian says, then looking out one of the two windows of the room he asks. "I am surprised you haven't had that luck with Jennifer."

"Jennifer is a friend, a special friend. She is not just a woman I want to do," I say while eating another grape. I don't look at Brian. I like Hanna, but I know that is probably just the sexual attraction talking more than anything else. There is more when it comes to Jennifer. I care about Jennifer very deeply, on a friend and a lover level. She never let me close to her again after that one time, but I know that is what I want the most. She is a special woman. If we try again, she will be more than just a one-time deal. I want a relationship with her because I don't think I can ever get over her.

"True, I know you care deeply about her. I don't understand why you just don't make her yours. Enough talking about this though. It doesn't matter what you do with a woman or what kind of rumors the elves spread about you and Hanna. Last night, what did you hear from Damon?" Brian asks, being serious now. Earlier, he talked in a more relaxed voice, along with an easy-going manner. Now, he has a serious tone to his voice, and he seems a little less cherry than he did a couple of minutes ago.

I look at Brian and take a deep breath before I begin. "He wants to meet us. Like you said, he wants us to join him."

Brian smiles slightly. "I guess we are a bigger problem to him sooner than I thought we would be."

"He acted like we weren't."

"He only says that because he is trying to discourage you. They are afraid of us though; we are the first to challenge his throne like this in a very long time. I am glad to see he is willing to talk so soon."

"I assume we have no intention of telling the rest?" Brian and I haven't said anything yet, and I have the feeling that it is going to stay that way. There are many reasons to tell them, but there are also a lot of reasons why we shouldn't.

"No, it would be better if they didn't know. I trust Jennifer and Sully, but none of the rest. Samuel probably would be trustworthy too, but he is too new to put that much trust in him yet. The elves would probably make some kind of deal about it, and Amias and Breccan don't need to know," Brian replies.

I nod, then I ask the question to which I probably already know the answer. "So, we are going to see him, then?"

"I think we don't have much of a choice. It would be silly to go as far as we did and forget about actually meeting him. That will happen soon enough either way, but at least we can have an idea of him before we meet in battle."

Thinking about this, I wonder all about what Damon says, and what everyone else says. Who is the real evil in the battle? I have no doubt that Damon is a lot to blame, but is that the only place to assign blame? Are the people I work for any better? Will they help the damned or are they just using us?

Brian and I leave the room. We arrive at the place where all the leaders will be dining. It is one of the higher rooms. Brian and I dine with the kings and queens.

The room is long and round, with the inside walls painted a warm light brown. There are a lot of windows in the room lighting up the whole place, without the use of any candles or lanterns. It feels like we are on the treetops, for any window you look out from you can see the tops of the trees, with all their leaves and branches. I like this room. On the left side you have the wide forest, and on the right, you have rolling hills with dead grass, rocks and a view that goes on and on. This is where they often do their horse training, and anything else that requires space, as space is limited in the forest.

After we eat and talk to the kings, queens and other important figures for a while, Brian and I go off to find the rest. We find them in the training ground. The training ground is pretty quiet this morning. There are a few people out there, younger warriors probably learning the finer points to fighting while they have some extra time.

I smile as I see Jennifer fighting with Sully. They are both sword fighting, while he corrects her when she does something wrong. She is a hell of a sword fighter, but Sully is older and he has a great deal more experience than all of us damned.

Vixy and Danny train together. They are not training how most of the pneumas do though. They are practicing with the bow. They talk as they do so. I am surprised to see how good both of them are. I didn't know how well they could shoot. Every time we fought together; I never really had the chance to see how good they fought.

Samuel stays on the sidelines waiting for his turn to fight with Sully. Samuel is well trained, but he is best with magical tricks. Sully has been teaching him some other things about sword fighting that do not require magic. Taylor is doing his own things. Unlike his damned, he isn't as well behaved and polite. Even though he and Brian like each other and get along, he is always making problems as well. It's never anything too big. He can just be annoying one way or another, and seems to find a way to get on Brian's nerves. Brian doesn't take much before he snaps. In all the time I've known Brian, he doesn't seem to have much patience.

As we walk over to them, they stop practicing and welcome us with friendly smiles. I step beside Samuel as the rest come to greet me.

"Good morning, London and Brian. How are the both of you? I heard you dined with the rulers this morning," Samuel says.

"Unfortunately," Brian replies, not sounding very thrilled. He doesn't like being around the rulers. He thinks it is a waste of time to join in their talks, and getting engaged in their politics. He is probably right.

The rest stop walking as they are close to us now and Sully says, "It is supposed to be a privilege."

"Many unpleasant things are said to be a privilege," Brian replies. Brian's attitude is nothing new this morning. He will often behave in this way. They are all used to it by now.

"You are very cheery this morning," Jennifer smiles. She is not wearing her helmet today, which she usually has on. Her red hair looks wild and unkempt, compared to how she usually has it. I don't mind it though; I think her helmet hides her beauty more than when her hair is not perfect.

Brian smiles at her, "The peachiest out of the whole group."

We all know that is anything but the truth. Changing the subject, I say to all of them, "How was the party for you guys?"

"It was a little too formal for me," Sully says. That figures; he doesn't like being in a place where people will judge you on everything you do.

I notice that the pneumas don't talk as much as their damned, unless they are amongst each other. Usually, it seems the damned speak for them as well. I think I talk some for the both of us, but Brian will add his opinion if he thinks he needs to.

"Any party where you have to dress nicely is too formal to you," Jennifer says, giving Sully a devious look.

A ray of a smile touches Sully's lips. "I suppose that is true." Then, looking at the rest of us, he continues, "Jennifer, you should teach Samuel how to be a better swordfighter. I think you are more than good enough to be the teacher for now."

She smiles and replies, "I'm sure I am."

Samuel and Jennifer walk back to their training after exchanging a few more words with me. Taylor and Vixy leave as well. I watch them go, knowing they left because it is obvious Sully and Danny want to have a talk with us alone.

Once the others resumed training, Sully looks at me and says, "Do you want to go on a walk, London?"

"Sure."

We both leave the training ground and walk out into the field. The grass is brown. It has not been getting enough water, and the heat of the summer has further dried it out.

Danny and Brian walk as humans near us for the first part, then they shape-shift and go around in the field. With different pneumas, Brian will play around differently. Danny and Brian seem to talk more, and Danny is teaching Brian tricks. Brian only seems to listen to Danny about this. He learns from the others, but he doesn't like to think of it as them teaching him. Danny is old enough and experienced enough that Brian doesn't mind thinking of him as a teacher. Although you wouldn't think that because Brian still remains the dominant pneuma when he is with all the pneumas.

There is silence for a little while. I wonder about what Sully wants to talk about. It could be about Hanna. I have a feeling she is more important to the elves than I thought. I don't know what the rumors are all about, but why does it matter? The rumors are more than likely not true, and they won't know the true reason why she was there. I want to keep it to myself that she is helping me see Damon. I am sure that is how it will be. Unless people know about that, then that means she must have said something.

"What do you want to talk about? I know that you didn't want to go on a walk for no reason," I start, looking at Sully. Sully looked to be in deep thought before I spoke.

Sully smiles with good humor, "I can go on walks without something important to say, but I do want to talk to you about things. I don't care what you do with any woman, London, I have had plenty of my own. But this Hanna woman, I do not think she is good news. There are a lot of rumors going around, and I don't think the elves want you getting close to her. I think she is held very high amongst the elves."

I don't reply right away. Before I can reply Brian thinks, *"Sully has more sense than you, London. I am not the only one who has a bad feeling about her."*

"I never said you were wrong, either. But she helped me and you accepted that as well," I shot back at Brian. He doesn't reply, but I don't expect him to.

"I know that the elves praise Hanna, but I couldn't care less. As long as I don't hurt her, I don't see why it is any of their business. What are the rumors all about, anyway?" I ask.

"The rumors are pretty much what you would guess." There is a pause, then Sully continues, "You know she is very powerful, London. I believe she is a damned and something else."

"She is a damned, her pneuma Cassandra is a white one who is not activated yet, and she is a sorceress."

Sully looks a little taken aback at hearing this and says with some surprise in his voice, "She is more powerful than I thought."

"How come the elves never told me about her?" I ask, looking into Sully's eyes. I know he won't have the answer out loud, but I want to hear what he thinks. I need to talk to Livefen, he will know. I hope I talk to him soon. It makes me angry that none of the elves had mentioned her. Were they trying to hide her from me for some reason? The only thing I can think is that they plan to use her for themselves, maybe to even have her defeat me after I fight Damon. All I know is I will not be used, and the elves are going to learn that one way or another.

Sully shrugs his shoulders to my question. "I don't know, but the answer probably isn't good. I don't trust the elves, and if they know she is a damned with a white pneuma, I am more than certain they have some trick up their sleeve."

I nod my head. My thoughts exactly. I will get to the bottom of it one way or another. I wonder though, does she plan to go along with whatever the elves have planned or does she have her own plans, like she suggested at the party?

CHAPTER 46

Awakened by Death

Brian

Until recent years, the elves were a secret to the world. Now they seem to want to be known by everyone. However, many things still remain unknown about their culture to other people.

I have spent the day going through many rooms around the castle to see old manuscripts, weapons, art and other examples of a culture that is strange to the rest of the world. The elves are smart, I will give them that much, but in many areas they fall short. It is a shame, really, but they do it to themselves. One of those areas is believing they are chosen by God, and therefore the rest of mankind must look at them as holy beings. Having that view will destroy them, because in believing that, they believe they cannot do wrong.

London has been doing his own things. Right now, he is writing to his family. I know he wishes to see people back at home again, mainly his mother and John, but neither of us knows when that is going to happen. Sometimes I wonder about London's mother. She is a strange woman who knows sorcery, which is rare. I don't even think London knows his mother as well as he thinks he does. She is a mysterious woman, and I expect more than what meets the eyes with her.

I walk through the garden as a man. No one seems to be here right now. With the midday heat, I guess they are all inside. Many of the flowers are in full bloom with colors ranging from orange, pink, red, yellow, purple, blue, white—all of these are in different shades—and even blooms of bright shades of greens. You can hear water from within the flower garden from fountains and a small creek runs through the place, with a small waterfall that leads the water through the garden.

I stop as I feel the hairs on my neck start to rise. I sense a pneuma who is not activated yet and I know who it is. I feel her circle around me like the wind, and say sweetly in my ears, "Brian, I am glad that you have come to the elves' palace. I was wondering when you would show up."

"Hello, Cassandra," I reply in a friendly tone.

She goes into one of the beds of flowers and I feel her eyes on me. As with any pneuma that is not yet activated, I cannot really see her. If I wanted to, I could hurt them, although I wouldn't hurt her. She can't do much to me, not being as strong as I am. In that case, you risk visiting any other pneuma. Even though I can't see her, I can feel her. I know where she is. I can touch her or feel her when she brushes up against me, although she keeps her distance. I think even though we talked a lot before I was officially with London, she doesn't completely trust me now. If I were her, I wouldn't either. I have been known to change moods quickly. I am easily angered and snap when pushed very far.

"It is good to see you again, Brian. I am glad that you made it. You know it would be a different story if I didn't help," she says.

I stay some distance from her, letting her feel comfortable. I know she wants something from me. I am not one to give, but I will hear her out. If I don't like it, I won't do it, but because she helped me, I will see what I can do for her.

"You did help, but I wouldn't go as far as saying it could have been a different story if you did not help me," I say with a small smile towards her.

"Oh, but Brian, you don't know the whole story. If it weren't for me, you would have been found. I made sure those pneumas didn't find you."

Having an idea now that this might have been planned, I turn to a mist and approach her in the flower beds. I cannot hurt her when I am a mist, but I think it makes her uncomfortable. I know she is uncomfortable because she is hiding something from me.

"I owe you more than I thought I did then, although why were there two damned and their pneumas there in the first place? I think there is something you know that I do not," I say, being firmer this time, but still friendly. It is a warning. I know something is up and she better come clean about it. If not, things could go badly for her.

Her attitude changes, but not in a more frightful way. She comes up closer to me so I can feel her brush up against me and speaks softly. "Still as smart as when I first met you. I am not going to hide anything from you. It would be pointless to, anyway. I may have spoken a word about you coming for that castle. I did not do it to help out Damon and Talon. I did it to help you."

"You mean more like help yourself."

"It did help me, yes, at least I planned for it to. It helped you as well. It taught you and London to work better together, and you were able to take the reins from the rest after that. You know you wanted to for quite some time, and that gave you the perfect reason to do so."

Cassandra is smart and conniving like I knew she would be. I don't know if that really was her plan to help us, as much as it was to help herself. I want to get to the point now. What does she want from us?

"Okay, Cassandra, let's say you did do me and London a favor. Tell me what good might come from helping us?"

She moves away from the flower bed and up the creek to the small waterfall. I follow her, and she settles near the top of the waterfall. I move up close to her again like I was in the flower bed. I can feel her up against me and that is how she stays.

"Remember when I said I would want you to do a favor for me? Well, I would like you to do that favor for me now," she says in a low but soothing voice. Cassandra is a good talker and her gentle and calm voice is soothing to anyone. I have heard power in it as well though. She wants authority and she will fight for it. We are alike in many ways.

"What is this favor?" I ask, already having the idea of what it will be.

"I want for Hanna to die, Brian. I am tired of being an inactive pneuma. I don't know anyone else that can or will do it for me. If you do this for me, I promise to pay you back. You know in a way I might have helped you twice. The way London died wasn't a coincidence."

"You seem to be very interested in London and I, and making sure London died. I expected it was someone's doing, but I didn't expect you."

"There are a lot of things you don't expect from me." There is a pause, then she continues, "So will you help an old friend out?"

I think on it. Why not? I don't think she's thought everything through. I believe she is making a mistake on her part. She is normally not one to make mistakes, but she wants to be active badly. She is willing to make mistakes for it. If London or I kill Hanna, Hanna will more than likely develop a fear of us. It may be small, but it will still be there, and that is a wall I am happy to put up.

I let the silence drag a little. Once I know she can't take anymore, I reply as smooth as she was to me, "When do you want it done?"

— ◆ —

London

I am with Hanna and Brian, debating in my mind if killing Hanna is really the right thing or not. I am not really killing her, but I don't like the thought that I am doing it. I will be doing it in the nicest way possible. I am giving her some poison in a glass of water. It will be painless, like falling asleep. Brian lined it up this way, and says she will probably wake within an hour due to Cassandra. It is better than being killed by getting your head smashed by a hammer.

Hanna is sitting on her bed, as I get the drink ready. Brian is in the room doing his own things. He could have done this himself, but once he told me about it, I thought it best if I did it. I am closer to Hanna than he is. I think she would like it better if I am the one to be there for her as she slips away.

We are in Hanna's room. Her room is a lot bigger and even nicer than the one I was staying in. We are all leaving today. Brian said it would have been best to do this on the day of leaving. We will get some heat for this, and he thought it best if we weren't around for it.

If we need to be worried about Hanna and Cassandra, we are making that worry stronger now. With Cassandra around, there is a higher chance of her being a threat to us. I am not afraid, just wary. I think it is already hard enough with the ones I know are friend or foe.

I walk over to Hanna and sit down beside her with the poisoned water in my hand. Brian leans against the wall and crosses his arms, like he is just waiting for us to be done. He wants to get this over with quickly so we can go.

Hanna and I both look at each other and she says, "What is it like going to the other place?" She seems cool and not nervous about the whole thing, but I think she is just good at masking how she feels. Dying for the first time is a frightful experience. With me, it happened so fast, I didn't have time to think about it.

"It is cold and will be like nothing you have ever felt before. I got out of it quick thanks to Brian. Hopefully, Cassandra will do the same for you." It is hard to describe the feeling, but emptiness and the cold seem to come close to it.

She nods her head. I hand her the water and she takes it, gripping it tightly in her hand. I grab her other hand and hold on to it. She gives me a smile and says quietly to me, "Whatever the future may bring, London, know that I do admire you."

"The same here," I say, giving her a warm smile.

She takes the drink and puts it to her lips. She closes her eyes and drinks all the poison. She sets the drink down and lays back on the bed. She grips my hand tighter as she closes her eyes. The poison works fast, and in a couple of minutes she shall die.

I gently run my fingers through her hair, and kiss her on the forehead. She whispers quietly to me, "Don't leave until I am dead, London."

"I promise to stay until then," I reply softly. She doesn't reply, but I see the slightest of smiles touch her lips.

Her breathing becomes slower, as if she is sleeping. Finally, it becomes less and less until her breath stops. I let go of her hand, knowing that she is dead now. I get up from the bed and Brian thinks, *"It is time for us to go, London."*

I look at Brian, nodding my head. I take one last look at Hanna, then leave through the door with Brian. We slip through the halls without being detected, and make our way to the front of the castle where the others are making the last few adjustments to their gear before leaving.

I take a breath of relief seeing them. I know if we were caught giving Hanna poison, it would not look good for us. Now we are out of the danger zone. They won't know it was us now, unless for whatever reason Hanna tells, but I don't think she will.

Brian and I start to make our way to the rest of the group, but I stop short seeing Livefen approach us from the corner of my eye. I can tell by looking at him he has some words to say to us. Same here. I am pissed off that he never told us about Hanna. I know he didn't because the elves have something planned for her, and that more than likely includes me.

I walk towards Livefen and we meet in the middle. Brian changes into a mist and goes around us. He knows I am pissed off at Livefen, and Livefen is no happier with me. Brian, I think, enjoys this. For once, Livefen and I will butt heads, rather than him and Brian.

"London, I was hoping I could have a few words with you," Livefen says this, acting friendly, but I see the thoughts behind those eyes. Our talk will be anything but friendly.

"That's funny because I want to talk to you as well. Let's talk where it is only the three of us," I say, gesturing for Livefen to lead the way.

He doesn't need another invitation and leads the way as Brian and I follow him. Brian turns into a black hawk and rest on my shoulder.

"Do you plan to go to war with the elf?" Brian thinks.

"I don't plan to go to war, but I better get the answers I am looking for."

Livefen takes us into the woods and stops, turning to us as we have put some distance between us and the rest.

At first, neither of us says anything. Then Livefen starts, "I think before things go further, we should talk about Hanna."

"Yes, we need to talk about her. Why was I not informed that she was a damned?" I ask firmly.

He looks a little surprised at first, but I think that is just because he is a little shocked that I know. He shouldn't be though. A damned usually finds out pretty quickly when someone else is one.

"I don't see why that would be any of your concern, London. You don't have to know about every damned that is in the universe," Livefen says, like Hanna is none of my business.

"I think I should know about everyone that is gray, black or white. You guys have obviously known about her for a long time. What plans do you have for her?" I say this firmer than I was before. I am not going to take any excuses. I know something is up and he can't hide that from me.

Brian jumps off my shoulder, hitting the ground as a cat, then changes into a man. Brian stays near me, but he watches Livefen closely. I feel that he seems more like a cat who is hunting, waiting to pounce on his unexpected victim. I know Brian won't try anything, but he wants to make Livefen feel uncomfortable and to realize Brian is far from a friend to him.

"There are no plans, London, and if there were, there are none that concern you. You may be in charge of this little outfit now, but you are not in charge of the elves. The elves want you to keep your distance from her. The elves hold her highly, and it is elf business that no outsider has any part in."

Hearing this makes me snap. They don't want an outsider in their business? Then why the hell did the elves drag me into this? I never asked for this. I never asked to fight Damon and Talon. Many of the countries want this from Brian and me, but the elves push for it the hardest. Now he is telling me they don't want an outsider in their business. I don't know what in the hell Livefen is thinking about the world he is in, but he is making a war he doesn't want.

"How in the world can you say this is none of our business! The elves are the main ones to drag me into this. And I shall talk to Hanna whenever I damn well please. She is her own person, prized by the elves or not. Let's not pretend that she has no business with me. Everyone knows that elves and other people of that sort look down on the damned and their pneumas, especially those with black pneumas. She has a white pneuma and you guys know this. Tell me then why didn't you guys not have her do what I am doing instead? Are you afraid she can't? You are going to use Brian and I as puppets until we win, then throw us out and let Hanna in?" I said all of this with rage now. If this is how all the elves think, I think I am through. I will not stand being lied to.

"You act as if you know all about the elves and the damned. You didn't even know the damned existed until about a year ago. You have no idea at all about what is at play here. If I thought nothing of the damned or their pneumas regardless of their color, then I wouldn't be here in the first place," Livefen says with equal outrage.

"Are you sure you just don't need us?" I snap.

"Using the damned is not what I planned to do, London. I expected you would think a little more of me than that. Though being around Brian all the time I can see why you would think this."

Brian snorts in disgust, but does not say anything. I don't know what Livefen really thinks. Maybe I am accusing him of too much, but I don't trust the elves. Maybe Livefen does mean well, but do the rest of the elves? I don't know how much he knows or what his real intentions are.

"How can we trust you?" I ask, looking into his eyes to read them.

Livefen looks back into mine, and says in an honest voice, "I do not represent all the elves, London. I am also not in charge of Hanna and what they plan for her. I am here to take out Damon and Talon. We may have our disagreements, but I am not trying to screw either of you over, as much as I don't care for Brian." Brian seems to smile at those words. "The elves trust me. I promise I am here to help you, nothing more and nothing less. I am a soldier—one of the best at what I do—and my mission is to protect and train you to defeat Damon. Black pneuma or not, I have learned to trust and follow you, so respect that this elf is loyal to his duty, including obeying you in battle."

I wait to reply, thinking about this. I glance at Brian to see him deep in thought, but I can't read an expression there. I don't trust the elves, but the way Livefen says this, I believe he is telling the truth. I look at him and reply with a much calmer voice now, "I will trust you, Livefen, but know that what happens between Hanna and I will play out regardless of what the elves think."

Livefen shrugs his shoulders. "I think it is an unwise choice playing around with her, but it is the elves that will have their say in it, not I."

"She is her own person, and the elves can't change that."

There is an awkwardness that has developed. After a little bit, we make our way to the rest of the group. On the way back, Livefen and I exchange a few words to ease the awkwardness a little. When we make it back, we say a few last goodbyes to a few of the people at the castle, and then we are on our way.

CHAPTER 47

Brian and Cassandra

We are camped out, getting ready to fight tomorrow. There is another castle with a damned guarding it who Brian and I are going to fight. We are not far from the castle, so they know we are here. There is no sneaking around this time. This time, we also have a fairly large army. It is everyone who is usually with me, and then there are some soldiers that the sanctuary provided for us.

Brian and I were accused of Hanna's death. The charges were dropped because no one can prove it, but I think a lot still believe it was us. Hanna is accompanying us on this mission. I haven't talked alone with her or much at all since I gave her the poison. I don't really know how Cassandra is either. I am sure I will get my chance to talk with both of them soon enough. I am still very unsure about the both of them though.

I am glad Jennifer and I remain close. It has remained unchanged, and we are even becoming closer friends. It is the same for Sully and Samuel. All of us damned seem to be very close, except for Hanna, although I think she doesn't have any desire to know the rest. I can tell Jennifer thinks very little of her, but I believe the feeling is mutual.

I sit on the ground, facing Jennifer. We are near the fire playing a card game. All the plans have been made for tomorrow, and we have concluded our long talks about the war. All that is left to do is get a good night's sleep. At least that is what I was going to do, but then Jennifer asked if I wanted to play a card game with her, so I agreed. It will probably be better, anyway, to do something that is not war-related before I turn in. It will help me sleep.

There are many tents pitched up for the soldiers and several different fires. Only Jennifer and I are around this fire. This one is what we damned took, as the others seem to want to give us that space.

Brian and Vixy are nearby, talking to each other. They are far enough away from us that I cannot hear what they are talking about, and I am not interested enough to find out. They usually are very loving when it is just us, but they won't get very close with so many people around.

Jennifer is mostly lying down, propping herself up with her elbow as she plays the card game with me. She has her hair down and is wearing a comfortable outfit.

We casually talk to each other, not talking about anything that is very important. After a little bit, Vixy and Brian leave. When they leave, Jennifer looks at me and says in a quiet voice, "You know we won't be able to ignore that forever."

"What do you mean?" I ask.

"I mean Vixy and Brian behaving how they are to each other."

"They keep it to themselves; I don't see what is wrong with it."

Jennifer doesn't reply right away, but seems to be thinking. I put down the cards, thinking about it myself. "What are you most afraid of?"

She sighs. Sitting up straight, she replies, not meeting my eyes. "I am not afraid of anything. I am just a little concerned about it, although I guess it is nothing to worry about." She says the last bit while drinking the rest of her tea and getting up.

I get up as well, giving her a friendly smile. "I wouldn't worry about it, Jennifer."

"Don't worry, I won't. I was just thinking out loud. Well, I will be going to bed now. Good night, London."

"Good night, Jennifer."

We both give each other a smile, and in those eyes, I catch something as she walks away. I know she likes me, and she brings Brian and Vixy up because in many ways it affects us. I want Jennifer, but I know how this works. She wants to keep her distance from me, and until something changes, that distance will stay. I have decided that I am going to give those thoughts a break. There are too many things I need to worry about and concentrate on. There is Damon, more training in mind and magic, and all the governments, damned, people involved, and what they want in all of this, constantly going on in my mind. I need to start sorting it out.

I go to my tent and sit down, thinking. I need to turn in, but I don't feel very tired right now. There is too much on my mind, and with the battle tomorrow, it doesn't help.

I lay down and close my eyes. After a little while, I give up on the idea of sleep for now. I get up and go outside. I will walk around for a little bit, then turn in when I feel tired enough to sleep.

I leave the camp quietly. I don't want to be followed or caught. Sully or Jennifer are often seen up and around. I would rather be by myself to think.

The moon is out tonight, lighting up the forest. The grass is silver in the moonlight and it is peaceful out here. The light breeze rustles the trees and makes the grass sway.

I walk around in deep thought. Sometimes I look back and wonder, "Why am I even here?" Never in my wildest dreams would I have thought this, but yet again, here I am.

I stop in my tracks as I sense a pneuma around. It cannot be an enemy and has to be one I know, for I am too close to the camp for it to be a stranger. If it were, I know Brian would be here in a second. I know when another pneuma is coming because the hair on the back of my neck rises. It is not in a frightful way, but more of an uneasy feeling as if something is out of the ordinary.

I turn around to see Cassandra behind me. She is as a woman. She is crouched on a rock that I had walked past just a few seconds ago. She is beautiful like Hanna, but I see danger in her eyes. She doesn't show the same sweet kindness as Hanna. You know what Cassandra wants by looking at her.

Cassandra is dressed in a flowy outfit. She has very long hair that is practically white. She is tall and slender, almost cat-like in her behavior. Her voice is strong like Hanna's, but more firm and colder.

I slowly walk over to her and I see a light smile upon her lips as I approach. Her attention is fixed on me, and I wonder what she could want from me, or do I even want to know.

I stop some feet from her and say in a normal tone of voice, "I am surprised to see you away from Hanna."

"I am surprised to see you without Brian. It is because he is hanging out with that Vixy pneuma though, isn't it? I am surprised he likes someone of red, I didn't think it was his color."

I hear the venom in her words, and I know Brian's fondness for Vixy is what turns Cassandra's words sour. I know that there is some history between Cassandra and Brian. I do not know how far back they go, or how close they were, but I think Cassandra thought they were something. Now that she knows Vixy is in the picture, I think she has built up a lot of hate for Brian.

"Brian doesn't hate something or someone because of their color. Now I assume you are out here for a reason?" I ask this, wanting to get to the point.

Cassandra gets off the rock, landing lightly on her feet. She slowly starts circling me, looking into my eyes. I stand my ground and watch her just as closely. I feel tense though. I don't trust her and to have a pneuma I don't trust so close makes me uncomfortable. I know how fast they can change.

"People put a lot of faith into you, London. Although to me, you seem like any other man. You are capable of doing good and bad. You are not perfect, as some make you out to be."

"Well, the last thing I want is for people to think I am perfect. There is always going to be something good and bad about everyone, for we all have different ideas." I have no idea what to expect, but I am going to be ready for anything.

She smiles at me. "You are going to be a leader someday, London. I do not know if it will be for a long time or very short. There are so many paths you could take. It would take years to think of them all. I see the choices of many though, so what I know of you is little, but I know enough to see some of the bigger things that happen to you."

"So, you can see the future as well?" I ask. It doesn't come as a very big surprise, but I wasn't expecting it.

"A pneuma mirrors their damned. I see there is still much for you to learn about the damned and pneumas."

"I guess so," I admit.

There is an awkward silence for a few minutes, with only the stillness of the night around us.

Finally, Cassandra breaks the silence by saying, "London, I want to show you something if you will let me."

"Why would you want to do that?"

Cassandra makes another friendly smile, then says, "Because, like Hanna, I want to help you. We are on the same side, no matter what."

I think about this before I make any decisions. Thinking it over, I don't think there is anything bad that could come from it. Probably any choice I make will be the wrong one, according to Brian.

I look at Cassandra and make my choice. "If you have something to show me, then I will see it."

She smiles and steps even closer to me. "I am not going to show you how Hanna likes to do it. Your lips can stay with her."

She gently places her hand on my head and closes her eyes. Everything starts to spin, as I know my mind is going to another place. It feels like how it did that one night when Hanna helped me see Damon. I go to the ground, not being able to stand anymore and everything goes black.

❖

Brian

I walk with Vixy. She stays close to me as we talk. Normally, I don't give Vixy as much attention when there are so many others nearby, but I cannot say no to Vixy. She wants to be with me and I won't turn her down. Neither of us wants to make it known that we love the other, for I know if word got around, people will use one against the other. We keep it safe by letting no one know except for London and Jennifer. At least, that is what we try for. The people closest to us, I am sure, know.

I would love to continue to be with Vixy, but I feel I should go to London. For whatever the reason, it normally is a good decision to stay with him.

Vixy stops me by grabbing my hand. We turn to each other and she says, "I have been meaning to talk to you, Brian."

"What do you wish to talk about?" I ask. It could be about anything, but I think I have an idea.

"About Hanna and Cassandra. I don't trust them," she says this with her dislike for them obvious in her voice.

"I do not trust them either, but do not worry about it, Vixy. They are the least of our problems for now." I pull her closer to me as I say this and gently place my hand on her cheek.

Vixy leans into my hand with a small smile on her lips. She looks into my eyes. "I trust you, Brian, but how I feel about them won't change."

I kiss her lips, as she kisses me in return. As we kiss, I think about the real reason Vixy is probably worried about them. I think probably what bothers her most is London's liking for Hanna. I know that London and Hanna have something for each other, but it is a strange relationship. Vixy will find that it is pointless worrying about that. Besides that, I wonder what she even thinks of London. In part she would like it if London and Jennifer get together, but then again, she seems to have a dislike for him being very close to Jennifer. Maybe she can't make up her mind. She wouldn't be the first woman who can't.

I slowly pull away from the kiss, and she looks up at me as I do. "Do you have to go?"

"Yes, but do not worry. We will have more time to spend together, just not right now."

"I know. Good night, Brian."

"Goodnight, Vixy." I kiss her once again on the lips. The kiss is a long one, as we hold each other and continue to kiss. Finally, I let her go, knowing I need to leave. As we let each other go, she gives me one last small kiss on the cheek, then turns into a mist and leaves.

I watch her disappear into the night. Now that she is gone, I must go to London. I turn to a mist myself and go to where I know London is. I stop short from where he is, seeing Cassandra sitting near a rock, as London lays in the grass asleep.

Anger is the first thing I feel, but I restrain myself. London is not hurt, but I know what she is doing. I turn into a man and walk over to them. She looks up, catching my eyes. I cannot read hers, but I feel she is a little uneasy, although she will not show it. She knows I don't want her near London, showing him parts of the future of which I have no say.

I stop near her and look down at London. He looks to be in a peaceful sleep, although I know he really is in another world. I can wake him fairly easily I am sure, but I will wait to do so. I have to deal with Cassandra first.

"I am surprised you made it over here as late as you did, Brian." Cassandra said, looking up at me.

I look her in the eyes in return and reply, neither cold nor friendly, "I know that you wouldn't be stupid enough to do anything to London that would harm either of us, so what's the rush?"

"Is it the first thing you are going to think that I am hurting you or him? Brian, I thought you would think a little more outside the box." She says this, getting up and slowly circling me.

I watch her closely as she brushes up against me as she walks around. She believes, like Hanna, that she can subdue me with her looks, as Hanna can to London. I don't work the same way. Cassandra is beautiful, I cannot deny that, but I have more control of what I want. I know Cassandra is a poison, an enemy, and no matter how she tries to appear, her mask does not work to cancel herself from me.

"I am smart, Cassandra; it is better to be on the safe side. You haven't earned the spot of a trustworthy friend yet, and until then I will watch my back when around you," I say coolly, watching her, but keeping my place.

Cassandra puts her hand on my chest and moves closer to me. I watch her closely and she does the same to me. She knows that I can snap anytime, and it is smart on her part to be cautious.

She hangs her head a little and closes her eyes. I grab her wrist none too gently as she tries to move her hand to my head. She smiles slightly as she asks, "You don't have to handle me that way, do you, Brian?"

I do not loosen my grip on her hand and reply quietly, "I want you to get the message. Cassandra, getting too close is a bad idea on your part."

She giggles a little, pushing aside the threat. "Brian, you can trust me. You wouldn't have minded it before if I got this close. I thought I would be more appealing now that we can touch each other." She looks up slightly to meet my eyes.

I loosen my grip on her wrist, but do not let her go. "The only reason why a woman like you would give yourself to me is because you want something in return."

"I could just want you in return," she replies quietly. She presses herself up close to me and kisses my lips. She means to let me have her, but she will be disappointed.

I do not return the kiss and brush her to the side, walking past her. She stands where she is, I am sure confused that I will not take her offer. She is good, but not good enough. Besides, if I wanted a woman, I know Vixy would be happy to have me tonight, and I wouldn't have to worry about whether I should trust her or not the whole time.

I walk to where London is, looking down at him. I ask, "What are you showing him?"

She takes a minute, then turns to me and says, "I am showing him what he wanted to see. He can tell you if he wants what it is when he wakes up."

I sense the annoyance in her voice, although she tries to hide it. I ignore it as well. She can be annoyed, but it doesn't change anything.

She looks at me, looking more composed again. "You know that no one will trust you, Brian. I see how you are and I know how you feel. You have the same anger and wants as Talon. The elves and others will see this. They will feel as if being behind you isn't any different than being behind him."

I look at her and smile slightly. This could be her way to get back at me, comparing me with my enemy, but I let her. Let people think I am like Talon because they know London and I are the only ones they have against him and Damon. The same goes for her. She will not be able to defeat them, and she knows this.

"Then let people think that. I do not care of what the countries or the elves think of us. I am here to get rid of Talon and Damon and that is what we will do."

She stares at me. "Then I wish you good luck with that." There is silence for a few minutes, then she continues, "London will wake up soon. Now good night, Brian, and good luck for tomorrow. You never know when you are going to need it."

"The same for you, Cassandra." I watch as she leaves.

I turn into a fox and curl up next to London. I could wake him, but I will let him sleep through this dream, and let him wake up on his own time. Cassandra could have given him something important to see or could be filling his head with crazy what-ifs. I suppose I will find out soon enough.

In the middle of the night, London stirs beside me. He sits up and looks around a little bewildered.

I look at him and telepath, *"Can't remember where you are?"*

"I do now. How long have I been out?"

"For a while now." I get up and so does London. "We should go back to the camp now. The others won't like it if they do not find you in your tent when they wake up."

"You are probably right. Let us go then." With that being said, London and I make our way back to the rest.

As we are walking there, I ask while traveling as a mist, *"What did you see, London?"*

"Many things, but I don't know how useful they are or not. If it is true, I saw nothing I liked." Other than that reply, London doesn't bother to tell me anymore. Sensing this, I go ahead and let the matter drop. Normally I wouldn't, but for now I have an upcoming battle to worry about.

— 300 —

CHAPTER 48

Battle of the Two Brothers

London

I stand ready with Brian. Brian and I will not be the first ones to enter the battle; others will do that for us. Our main job is to take out the damned and his pneuma when he comes.

Brian and I are on a hill overlooking the battle field. Our men march to the enemies' castle, while the enemies get ready to defend themselves. Livefen stands with me, giving orders to his top men. Jennifer is also with me, while Hanna and Cassandra stay out of the battle. I think they are here to watch and nothing else.

Brian is beside me as a man for now. He watches as the battle begins to unfold. I don't like the waiting. I shift my weight from one foot to the other, anxious for our turn to fight.

I look at Brian, surprised to see how calm he is. He watches without any emotion, as if he is incapable of it. I know that is not true though, although at times people might think the only thing he is able to feel is anger.

Jennifer is on my right, while Brian is on the left. Jennifer is dressed in her reddish, light looking armor, with her helmet on. She has one of her hands resting on the hilt of her sword. Vixy is a red leopard with blackish spots in front of us, crouching like she is ready for a fight. Her tail moves back and forth in an impatient manner. Jennifer seems calm and cool though, unlike Vixy.

I can hear the voices of my weapons as they speak in my head, and to each other. They are quieter, for they don't have anything to really say to me, but knowing that war is near, they are restless. The voices seem to come from the back of my head, and I have to concentrate on one of them to hear what he is saying.

"You seem uneasy, London. Any reason why?" Brian asks me through thoughts.

I am glad when I speak through thoughts now. I don't use my mouth in order to do so. *"Just ready to fight."*

"You need to learn to hide it a little better. If becoming a leader is what you want most, then you can't show when you are uneasy. Jennifer is more composed then you are," Brian replies. I glance at her to see that she might be, but Vixy betrays that. Vixy is just as restless as I am. I decide not to point this out to Brian though. It won't do any good.

My attention is captured when I hear two loud trumpets blown. I look to see two mighty dragons flying up from the castle and into the air. They land onto the castle wall. They are both big dragons, but not huge. One of them is a dark reddish color, while the other has several colors. Its colors are black, green, purple and a few other shades, depending on what shade of light he is in. It looks like the color of some beetle's wings, metallic in a way.

Both dragons have riders. These are their damned. They are both dressed in dark black armor and helmets, with only a small slit in the helmet to show their eyes. I heard that there are two brothers who watch this castle. I am not afraid to take on two damned, although it will be a difficult battle.

Last night we went over our battle plan and they told me what they could about these two. They are known for being good fighters and are dragon trainers. They are half bothers from the same mom. They have been around for a while; I believe the older of the two is in his seventies. Being immortal, age doesn't do much, but says maybe how much experience you have had. However, this castle is a large trading place for Damon, and often where his troops pose to rest and get supplies. Taking this place out will be a blow to Damon.

Brian looks at me and says with a small smile, "It looks like they are ready to play."

"Then let us not disappoint them," I say, returning the smile.

Brian and Vixy turn into dragons, spreading out their wide wings ready to fly. I look at Jennifer and she says with a small smile, "You are not the only one who will be fighting the damned this time."

I smile in return. "I welcome the help."

We caught the attention of the two damned when Brian and Vixy turned into dragons. I climb onto the back of Brian, and crouch as he takes off in flight. Jennifer does the same with Vixy.

I pull out Raptor and nock an arrow to the bow. I feel a slight vibration in response from the bow, his way of thanking me for choosing him. Vixy and Jennifer fly near us. Jennifer stays with her sword.

The two brothers see us coming and take flight as well. This will be a battle where we will meet in the air. Brian normally isn't a dragon, so I wonder how he will manage, but I have no doubt he will.

Neither of us flies very high. All of us damned know that more than likely when the pneumas collide, it's going to be hard to stay on the dragons. The two brothers look accustomed to riding dragons, so I am sure they know what to expect from their pneumas.

Brian makes the first move. He goes after the bigger dragon and the fiercer looking rider, who is dark red. The pneuma Brian goes after is quick to respond. They immediately go at it with teeth and claws. It is a quick clash though, and they break away with Brian moving in a wide circle to come back.

I was able to stay on Brian during this little attack, but it was difficult. I don't know if I will be able to a second time. Brian comes for the attack again, and as both of them are about to collide, I fire the bow at his rider. The arrow buries deep into the damned's shoulder, making him yell with pain. I don't think he was expecting that.

Brian and the other pneuma are locked together once again in combat. With the attack, I can no longer hold on, so half jumping and half falling off, I come to the ground. I land on my feet, but it is far from a comfortable landing. I rise all the way up as the other dragon's damned lands on the ground to join me. His brother does the same, but not Jennifer. Glancing that way, I see that Vixy and Jennifer are taking on the other brother's pneuma, leaving me to face the two brothers.

The one who I was originally fighting, still with the arrow in his shoulder, carries a short sword in one hand and a round shield in the other. I glance at his brother who stands behind me. He is carrying a small sword that is carved, with his other hand carrying nothing. I know that could change quickly, though. I see a bunch of throwing knives at his hip, and I bet he knows how to use them well.

Raptor is put up now, and I have Wolfbane and Bone-Crusher in my hands. I stand so I am able to see both brothers. We are all waiting for the other to move. I am going to wait for them though. There are two of them, and I need to watch and see which one of them is going to make the first move.

The brother with the arrow in his shoulder makes the first move. He steps towards me, swinging his sword out to strike me. I step back quickly to avoid the hit, but then immediately have to block with Bone-Crusher to stop the other brother's strike.

Jennifer drops down near the brother with the one sword. Both of their swords collide as Jennifer tries to land a strike. I pay no more attention to them though, for this is my chance to take out the brother with the arrow through him.

He is a good fighter, and every time I try to land a hit, he blocks it and comes back with his own. I am one hell of a swordfighter though, and he is slowly losing to my skill. I notice as we fight that he becomes more tired and is making more mistakes. All I need him to do is make one very wrong move, and it will be over for him.

I quickly dodge as I hear the loud cry of an angry pneuma fly over my head. The pneuma lands some feet from us, with Vixy landing near Jennifer. I hear the commotion, but I can no longer pay attention, as the brother I am fighting comes forth throwing strikes at me and trying his best to land one.

I am thrown back from the force of him coming forward. Finally, I find an opening and smash Bone-Crusher into his already injured shoulder. He is thrown off-balance and yells with the pain as his shoulder is smashed and broken. He drops his sword in the process and drops to his knees. I am about to finish him off until I hear something being swung at me. I bring up Wolfbane to block the attack of the other brother.

Our weapons collide, making a loud ringing sound. He swings at me again as our weapons once again hit, but this time the power behind his strike is too strong and I drop Wolfbane, not expecting it.

In that split second, in my shock, he punches me in the face with his free arm. He has metal on his knuckles, so it hurts worse than a normal punch would. I half stumble with the hit, but quickly scramble to my feet. He tries to swing his sword at me, but I dodge just in time. I am back to my feet again and back up a little to give us some space.

My face hurts where I have been hit, and I need to get a grip on things again. He stands there now, holding his sword low, watching me. I can see his eyes through his helmet. Given this small chance, I glance to see how the others are doing.

The battle for the castle is pretty much at a standstill. These two damned are in charge and if they lose, we win the castle, and the other way around. Brian is now on the ground with Vixy as they both face off with the other two pneumas. Jennifer also stands with the pneumas. She is fast and quick, and she easily knows how to get away if needed. Normally, it is dangerous to try and get involved in a pneuma fight, for they move so fast, but I trust she knows what she is doing.

"You are strong, but I did expect a little more," the damned I am fighting says, looking at me. Looking at his weapon now, I know why that strike hurt so bad. His weapon is lit with a dark brownish purple color. It is obviously some kind of power to make his weapon stronger. My one big weakness is I do not know enough about magic yet.

His brother, still with an arrow through his shoulder, is standing once again, holding his sword in his good arm. I am surprised he is still pulling himself up to fight. They are definitely not quitters.

"Then let me not disappoint you," I say, putting Bone-Crusher up and pulling Misery out of his sheath.

"Damned is what I killed for a living at one point," Misery says with delight in my head.

Both the other damned and I go in for the kill this time. We once again hit weapons, but this time I hold my own, and even with his magic it only does so much to Misery.

We continue to fight. We are both running out of breath, and both landing hits—some here and there—but not enough to take either of us out of the ring. Finally, I stab the damned in the chest with Misery.

He yells in pain, but so do I as I feel pain in my chest, caused from Brian being in pain. I pull Misery back out of the other damned, but as soon as I do, the damned takes one of his throwing blades and drives it through my hip.

I yell and kick him away with my other leg. He falls onto his back and slowly makes an effort to sit up, but he is in more pain then I am. I back up and pull the small blade from my hip, grinding my teeth and making a sound of pain. Red, hot blood comes flowing out of the wound as I pull it out.

"Basil! Phoenix!" the brother with the broken shoulder yells.

Immediately, the two pneumas come to them, but Brian and Vixy come to me just as fast and ready. Jennifer steps beside me ready to fight.

All the pneumas breathe hard and have blood on them. Looking at Brian, I see he has a deep gash in his side, but he doesn't seem to notice it. He has his attention fixed on the other pneumas, who I guess are Basil and Phoenix.

These damned and their pneumas put up a good fight, but I know and they know, they don't have much more to give or much more they can take. One brother stays on the ground, holding his hand to his chest where I stabbed him, while the other with the broken shoulder is in no state to put up a good fight. Their pneumas don't look much better. They are panting for breath and are covered in blood. Unlike Brian and Vixy, I think the blood is mostly their own.

Before the battle can start again, the brother with the broken shoulder says, "We were entrusted to this Kingdom because we are known for being the strongest damned Damon has. Now I can see that doesn't mean much up against you."

Brian turns into a man, sensing that the brothers are going to try to talk their way out of this. Vixy also turns back into a woman. She stands with Brian, ready. The other two pneumas seeing them also change into men. I know that pneumas can change within a minute though. Just because they are turning into people doesn't mean the battle is over.

"Flattering, but saying I am great isn't going to save your lives," I say, still holding Misery tightly in my right hand. I am really starting to feel the pain in my hip now, despite the adrenaline, but I try to ignore the pain. I can fix the wound later.

The man smiles despite being in a lot of pain. He looks at us and continues, "I didn't think that would work, though that is what I am trying. However, if you spare our lives, we will serve you."

"You don't sound very trustworthy. After all, you are quick to turn on Damon," Brian says.

"Yes, true, but the only reason we serve Damon is because most damned don't have anywhere else to go. You are the first damned to challenge him like this in our lives. Either we try our luck with people who hate us or live a life where a damned could become more than someone who lives on the streets.

We are good warriors, and if you prove to be a great lord, we will serve you to the end." He says this, bowing his head in respect.

Thinking about Samuel, it could be definitely the same deal. We need more damned and the more powerful, the better—but can we trust them? Trusting Samuel turned out fine, but that doesn't mean it will be the same case every time.

"You two are aware that if you betray me, Hell would not do me justice for the both of you. You will beg for your, deaths," I say coldly, so they fully understand I am not just saying it. I mean my words.

Both brothers look at each other and the one who originally spoke says, "We swear to you that there will be no need for that."

"Then tell your men we won the battle, and get yourselves fixed up," Brian says.

The two brothers do what he asks and are soon on their way to the castle. Now that Jennifer and I are alone, she looks at me with concern, "Are you all right, London?"

I look down at my hip, which is a big bloody spot now. "I will be fine," I say with a small forced smile, assuring her she does not need to worry. Little did I know because of the wound, I am going to be in a world of pain.

CHAPTER 49

Death's Door Again

W̲e are now in the castle, and people are sorting things out and trying to settle down for the night. There is a lot to do though, so I think there will be little chance for sleep tonight.

I haven't talked much to the brothers since the fight. They are painfully getting themselves helped. I found that the one with the broken shoulder is the older brother and that his name is Cyrus and his pneuma is Phoenix. The younger brother, the one who stabbed me in the hip, is named Neo, while his pneuma is called Basil. Like I said, I did not have much time to talk to them, but Neo was nice enough to tell me that his dagger was poisoned so I will have to suffer a night of pain until I die. I will not come back as a skeleton and it will be like the first time I died, but I do not look forward to it just the same.

Jennifer spent some time with me trying to clean my wound and make a medicine to help ease the pain. Even with that, I will just have to suffer through it.

I was trying to help settle things, but with the pain coming on more now, I retire to my room and decide I will stay here until this is over. Sully and Danny came a little later to have a drink with us. I am happy that they did, as getting drunk is better than just sitting here and trying to face the pain.

I have my back up against my bed and am sitting on the ground. I have already had several drinks now and am feeling it, but I am also feeling the pain. Luckily, Jennifer's painkiller and the drink are making it a bit better. It makes me wonder if I really want to let those brothers live.

Sully sits on the ground near me. He has drunk just about as much as I have. Brian and Danny do not drink, but they talk to each other sitting at the table. Usually, it seems that they are the ones sitting in odd places, but this time it is the opposite. Brian will occasionally drink, but if I drink a lot, he won't. It is probably better this way. One of us should stay sober.

"How are you feeling?" Sully asks, drinking more from his glass.

"Well, if it weren't for the alcohol, I would be pretty miserable right now, so I will just leave it as that," I reply.

It is a burning pain that throbs. First it was just around the wound, but now it is moving up my body and the pain is starting to spread to every inch of my body. I just wish it would be quicker, so I can get it over with.

"Well, it could always be worse, right? Those brothers that are now hired, they are going to be having miserable times of their own. That one got a pretty bad wound from you breaking his shoulder like that."

I nod, thinking about it. At least I don't have that. Usually when I die from someone, I will develop a fear to that person. Technically Neo did kill me, but Brian says since it was through poison, I will probably develop no fear at all. Brian tells me the more I die, the more I become immune to fearing the one who killed me over time. Unless it is a very horrible way that I have died.

I pour my glass all the way to the top again. "So, do you think both brothers are worth taking in? or will it be a mistake in the end?"

"Only time will tell us that, but I have the feeling we will have quite a few damned that will do that. It will be same as with Samuel. They follow Damon because they have nowhere else to go."

"Do you think they will follow Brian and me because they have nowhere else to go? Not because they truly want to?" I ask. I don't want to be like Damon and I don't want people following me because they have nowhere else to go. I want them following me because we have the same goals.

"I don't think it is the same thing for you, London. You offer them more than Damon. You know I heard before Damon totally lost his mind, he was fighting for a better future for the damned."

"I wonder what made him change," I ask, taking another drink from my glass.

Sully shrugs his shoulders. "I have heard a lot of stories, but who knows which one is the truth. Maybe there is a little bit of truth and falseness in all of them. No matter what happened in the past, it is safe to say now he is far from a sane person."

"Aren't we all a little crazy though?" I ask. "For as long as I have been a damned, I haven't seen anyone who isn't."

"True, except for Jennifer. She seems saner than most."

I smile, thinking of Jennifer. It is true she seems the most well-balanced. Maybe that's why I like her so much, because at least I know that is one person that I can forever trust. She isn't going to betray me or anyone else I know and care about.

"She really is one of a kind," I say, continuing to think about her.

There is silence for a few minutes then Sully says, his manner changing a little more serious now, "London, are you planning something soon with Damon?"

I look at Sully as he meets my eyes. I sigh and think to myself, "Why keep it from him?" "How did you know?" I ask.

"I had the feeling you were doing something of the sort for a little while. I know that when you were at the elves' castle you visited him, didn't you? That was why you needed Hanna. Being a sorceress, she would be able to help you."

"I don't know how you would guess all of that, but yes, it is true."

"I am sure you have your reasons, London, but why did you want to see him?"

"I wanted to see for myself who he is. I will be seeing him again, Sully, but you have to trust what I am doing. I know that it will be dangerous, but I need to do it. If I am going to be fighting him someday, I want to know what I am up against, for myself."

"I understand, London, even if I do feel a little uneasy about it. Since you have been in charge, I think you have made the right decision, so I will trust you now."

I smile, "Thank you for understanding, Sully." I put my hand on his shoulder, feeling weaker and drunk now.

Sully helps me get up and lay down on my bed. He leaves after making sure I am as comfortable as I can be, knowing there is nothing else he can do.

As I lay there, Brian jumps on the bed as a black panther. He lays down beside me, resting his head on me. I put my hand on his head and try to breathe evenly.

I try to sleep through the pain, and soon I drift into what I believe is an uneasy sleep. The world quickly fades out into complete blackness, and all feelings, thoughts and breaths escape me.

CHAPTER 50

Just the Beginning

"*Am I finally back?*" I telepath, only seeing black.

"*I brought you back last night. You are just in a light sleep now,*" I hear Brian answer.

I stir a little. "*At least I feel better. What time is it?*"

"*Early morning.*"

I open my eyes to see some light coming through the small window in the room. I sit up in my bed, with my head hurting. Still, it is better than how I felt last night. I am just happy the night has passed and it is morning.

Brian jumps off the bed and lands on his feet. He is still a black panther, but now he changes into a man.

"*So, what do we do now?*" I ask, throwing my legs over the side of the bed.

"*We continue with our plans. It is becoming more and more clear, London, that we need more training, and more damned.*"

"*Well, we are slowly getting more damned. There are now six of us, including me.*"

"*I never heard of six being an army,*" Brian replies, turning to look at me.

"I know that. I am just saying at least we are getting some followers. There is Hanna too, but I don't know if we can include her."

"No, I do not think that would be wise. Besides, even if she is on our side, she will not be by our side like the rest of them. She will come and go as she pleases. I believe she has her own ideas, anyway. We are in some way part of her plans, but I do not know how yet. However, you can trust that we are."

"Where will we find an army then?" I ask. Last time I checked; I don't remember a bunch of damned waiting around to follow someone.

"Don't worry about that, London, we will find them. Right now, you should be more worried about your training. You will need to learn how to do more magic, and how to visit other damned in their dreams. It normally takes years to be good, but there are ways to learn it faster."

I nod my head, wondering to myself how in the hell am I supposed to get good at magic in such a short period of time. I have seen only a little of what some of the damned can do, for most of ones I have fought don't know a lot of magic either.

I get up and put on my weapons. Before I got drunk with Sully, I took off all my weapons and cleaned them. If I do not do this, they are not very happy when I see them again. I take good care of them, for there will be many times I will rely on them. I would rather not risk it, knowing that they can turn on you.

I stop, thinking about what Cassandra showed me the other night. She didn't show me much, but what she did, scared me a little. I know the future is never set, but she showed me a future where Brian was being tortured. It seems Brian and Talon will meet and not just fight at some point down the road. I don't know where, when, or why, but it looks like they will have to tolerate each other. Things didn't go well though, Cassandra showed Brian pushing Talon's buttons. Including killing one of Talon's sons, named Calloo, because of Brian's actions it takes him down a dark path of pain and suffering. The future she was showing me kind of got blurry towards the end, so either then having in idea,

I don't know nothing more than that. The whole thing has just left me feeling a little uneasy. I wonder if Brian notices it.

"Are you ready to go out?" Brian asks, watching me. He is leaning up against the wall and seems to be thinking. I see that the gash he got on his side is still there. I can't see how bad it is, but I know pneumas cannot heal very well on their own. That is when they rely on their damned to help them.

"Are you going to need help with that wound?" I ask.

"I will be fine. Vixy was more than happy to help me with it. It will heal slowly, but I do not need the help. Besides, it will probably be some time before we are in another battle."

"I would never be so sure," I reply.

"Normally neither am I, but I will take a risk this time. You can save your strength for another day."

I stop as I hear a light knock on the door. I look at Brian and he telepaths, *"It is just Jennifer and Vixy. She is probably coming to check up on you."*

I go to the door and open it. Sure enough, there are Jennifer and Vixy, who is a mist. I smile as I see Jennifer. "Good morning, Jennifer."

"Good morning, London. I thought I would come and check up on you. Sully told me last night that you were in a lot of pain."

"Well, I managed," I reply, opening the door more to let her in.

Jennifer walks in with a slight smile and turning around towards me again once she is in the room, says, "Sully also told me he got you drunk. Is that what you always do when you win a battle?"

I close the door once Vixy is inside and reply, "No, I only did last night because it was better than having none."

"That's usually why you drink. You weren't the only one with a rough night. The brothers had a pretty rough time as well. Trying to recover from a broken shoulder or being stabbed in the chest is no more fun than dying from poison."

"Well, if only they mentioned sooner that they didn't want to fight, maybe we could have all been spared from pain."

Jennifer smiles, "That is true."

Today she is wearing what she normally wears—her light bronze-colored armor with a reddish-looking colored outfit underneath. She is not wearing her helmet though, and is letting her long red hair free. I love it best when her hair is down. That usually means she is willing to play around more and is less about business.

Brian and Vixy are talking to each other. Now they stop and Brian says, looking at Jennifer and me, "I will be checking on the new damned and their pneumas. I would like to get to know them before we do much else."

"I will go with him," Vixy adds.

After saying this, both of them leave the room. I watch them leave, then look back at Jennifer. There is silence for a few minutes, then she says, "It is still early. Do you want to go for a walk?"

I smile. "I would love to."

We exit the room together and make our way out of the castle. We leave the castle grounds and take a walk through the terrain around the castle, where people do not live. Going through the castle and the castle grounds, I am glad to see not many are up yet, and the ones who are appear busy with their work. Most people are still pretty worn out from the battle yesterday, as well as staying up most of the night to settle things.

Jennifer and I walk mainly in silence. I am just happy to be walking with her, and I think she feels the same about me. It is not often nowadays that I can take a walk and not worry about everything.

We stop at the edge of a waterfall. It is about fifteen feet tall, and the water flows down into a clear pool of water below. It is not a very wide waterfall, but it is beautiful never the less. We watch the waterfall together. There are little flowers around it and green vines growing where they can get the water from the falls.

I stand close to her, watching the water fall. I take a deep breath and turning my eyes away from the water, I look at her and say, "Thank you for inviting me on a walk."

Jennifer meets my eyes with a ray of a smile, "Well, I enjoy your company."

I gently grab her hand, as she grabs mine in return. She steps a little closer to me and says quietly, "You will give the damned a better future than what they see now. I know you will."

"We will, not just me. If it weren't for you, Jennifer, I wouldn't be where I am now."

"I do not do that much, London."

"That is where you are wrong. Not only do you help me with your sword, but your company and friendship are more than I could ask. I need people like you, or this job I am expected to do would be impossible."

She looks up into my eyes and says, shaking her head a little, "I question how much of that is true, but never the less, I am just as glad I am here."

She gets a little closer to me and gently kisses my cheek. I smile at her and gently run my fingers through her hair. I kiss her on the cheek, just as gently as she kissed me.

She grabs my hand a little tighter and leans on me, placing her head on my chest. I put my arm around her, pulling her closer and lean my head on hers.

"No matter what happens, London, I am just glad that I get to be one of those who stands beside you," she whispers to me as she watches the waterfall.

"I am glad to have someone as loyal as you stand with me," I reply, watching the waterfall as well.

All I know is I am happy to be here right now, and no matter what must be done and what will come to pass, I will be ready for it, and I won't be alone.

ABOUT THE AUTHOR

Lily Johnson was born and raised in in the small town of Nevada City California. Lily has loved stories and books as far back as she can remember. Writing has been her passion and love, ever since she was little, and will continue to be forever.